T006029

SIROCCO

DANA HAYNES

SIROCCO

BLACK STONE PUBLISHING

Copyright © 2021 by Dana Haynes
Published in 2021 by Blackstone Publishing
Cover design by K. Jones
Book design by Blackstone Publishing

All rights reserved. This book or any portion
thereof may not be reproduced or used in any manner
whatsoever without the express written permission
of the publisher except for the use of brief quotations
in a book review.

The characters and events in this book are fictitious.
Any similarity to real persons, living or dead, is coincidental
and not intended by the author.

Printed in the United States of America

First edition: 2021
ISBN 978-1-09-409983-5
Fiction / Thrillers / Suspense

1 3 5 7 9 10 8 6 4 2

CIP data for this book is available
from the Library of Congress

Blackstone Publishing
31 Mistletoe Rd.
Ashland, OR 97520

www.BlackstonePublishing.com

To my literary agent, Janet Reid,
for fighting for me.

To Katy King:
  Some day, when I'm awfully low
  When the world is cold
  I will feel a glow just thinking of you
  And the way you look tonight
        —Dorothy Fields, Jerome Kern

C01

Pete Newsom entered the restaurant first, a full forty minutes before the principal of the Clarion Group was set to arrive.

The founder of the Clarion Group, Victor Wu, was still blocks away in a bulletproof vehicle. The dinner would be a fundraiser with some of the reigning bankers of southern Spain. Wu, an intensely charismatic speaker, would explain the good works his nongovernmental organization was doing in Saharan Africa, the roads they'd built, the wells they'd dug, the pollution sources they'd dammed up. The Americans, the Brits, and the French had signed onto the good works of Victor Wu's NGO almost a decade earlier. The Germans and the Dutch had come on board since. Spain came next and brought along deep pockets from the private sector. Greece and Italy had been slower to pitch in. Today's dinner was the third of . . . who could possibly know how many dinners, through which Victor Wu would, well, woo new investors into his fold.

The courtship began with drinks and a dinner, because this

was Spain and that's how they do it. They wouldn't even talk deals at this first gathering.

Newsom was there as security. The Clarion Group operated in some intensely violent portions of the planet, and the American military contractors Sooner, Slye, and Rydell LLC had the contract to keep Wu and company safe. Nobody was better at it. Sooner, Slye, and Rydell had contracts to keep half the US State Department and half the British Foreign Ministry secure while operating away from their home countries. The contractor had gained a reputation by hiring some of the finest people in all the land: Navy SEALS and Army Rangers from the States, SAS from England, elite units of the Israel Defense Forces, and more. And, of course, former spooks like Pete Newsom, who had spent his time in the CIA and had retired at the grand old age of forty-one as chief of operations for the Paris Station. He'd gone from risking his neck for a public servant's paycheck to a half-million-dollar signing bonus, profit sharing, fully paid health and life insurance, and a salary that matched some Big Ten coaches.

All to keep NGOs like the Clarion Group safe, while they made the world itself safer.

Good gig, Newsom thought, as he checked the details for the fourth time.

Wu's staff had picked a restaurant just off Las Ramblas in Barcelona, in the old Byzantine El Raval neighborhood. The place looked a tad seedy from the outside but had been a favorite of the Partido Socialista Obrero Español for decades. Sucking up to party hacks was as good a way as any to get a deal green-lit by the banks. The restaurant was nestled back in a dark, twisty side street, far from the tourists. Wu had paid to have the place to themselves; it only featured eight tables, so that wasn't hard.

Newsom had selected a menu of Spanish dishes and good local wine. He arranged for a string trio from the Academy of St.

Martin in the Fields to play softly in the background, pieces by Spanish composer Isaac Albéniz, whom Newsom had never heard of, but whatever. He appreciated that the primary—the guy he protected, Wu—sweated the details.

The restaurant had been the wine cellar of a great house in the sixteenth century. The walls were brick and rounded like a cave. The floors were rough slate slabs the size of baseball plates.

Newsom watched the street and saw two motorcycles pass by the darkened windows of the candy shop across the narrow labyrinth-like street. His guys: the outriders, sprinting two blocks ahead of Victor Wu's armored SUV, scanning for trouble.

Newsom nodded to the restaurant owner and head chef, who scuttled to the back of the house to get everything ready. He nodded to the string trio, who took their stools.

His smartphone chimed.

The screen read *Blocked.*

"Newsom," he answered.

"Pete? Hi."

He recognized the voice. More accurately, he almost recognized the voice. He checked his watch. "Ah. Hi. This isn't a good time. Can I call you—"

"You don't recognize me, do you?"

It had to be someone at Sooner, Slye, and Rydell, or someone from the US Departments of State or Defense. Maybe CIA. Who else would have this number? Newsom watched as Wu's bulky SUV cruised down the alley, the passage as tight as a cannonball in a cannon, and turned left into the well-hidden lot behind an ancient Catholic cloister. The motorcycle outriders would have gone ahead to block the oncoming traffic. One of Newsom's guys would be waiting in the lot for the SUV. Everyone had earjacks and sidearms.

"You there, Pete?"

He switched the phone to the other ear. "Hey. Geez, I'm

sorry. This really isn't a good time and . . . it's a bad connection. Can I—"

"Your favorite Hitchcock movie is *Notorious*. Mine too. Jog your memory?"

The caller was right. It was his favorite Hitchcock movie. But anyone could know that. He tried to think back and remember who . . .

Two of his men in somber suits walked around the corner onto the narrow street. Right between them was Victor Wu, small in stature, dressed to the nines. They seemed to be laughing, and Newsom appreciated that Wu chatted up his security detail. Some primaries treat their detail like butlers. Not Wu.

"Do you remember Hitchcock's definition of suspense, Pete? Do you remember what he said about shock versus suspense?"

It came to him in a rush. The voice. Talking about Hitchcock.

His blood pressure sank, turning his face a putty gray under the offset track lighting of the restaurant.

He blinked stupidly. He stood, frozen, feeling sweat prickle the back of his neck. This call could not be happening. It was perfectly impossible. Not *improbable*. Not *unlikely*.

Impossible.

Wu and the security detail approached the restaurant. Thanks to the glare in the window, Newsom could see them but they couldn't yet see him.

"Hitchcock said: Two guys sit at a table and—*ka-boom!* That's a shock. But two guys sit at a table, and the audience can see *under* the table . . ."

Newsom glanced around the restaurant. It couldn't be. It absolutely could not be.

He felt his knee bend before he was even aware of it.

He knelt like a penitent man and glanced under one of two tables in front of the windows. The table to his right.

Nothing there.

"Remember? Pete? What Hitchcock said?"

He looked to the table to his left.

He felt his stomach lurch.

"Hey? Pete? Smile."

He glanced up.

Outside the restaurant, an aide opened the door for Victor Wu. The entourage smiling, then noticing the American spook down on one knee.

Pete Newsom looked past his men, past his primary, across the street, to the familiar figure in the darkened stoop of the candy shop.

Pete dropped the phone.

"*B—!*"

C02

The cleric was younger than people might have assumed. It was difficult to tell beneath his deeply tanned leathery skin and full beard, but he appeared to be in his thirties.

He wore the simplest robe, a cheap thing, thin and colorless. He wore a checkered kaffiyeh, one end thrown over his right shoulder. He spoke Arabic with the accent of a college-educated Cairene.

The room behind him had been scrubbed of any discernible clues regarding his location. This tape—like previous tapes—had been delivered by a street urchin to the headquarters of Al Jazeera television in Qatar.

His deep-set eyes, under prominent brows, seemed to sparkle like dark opals.

"My friends. By now you have heard that another enemy of the people, another enemy of freedom, another sworn foe of the Prophet—peace be upon him—has been killed."

His voice was not guttural, was not deep. He sounded academic.

"The Khamsin Sayef has reached out to the heart of the Spanish crusaders, and has snuffed out the life of a man who has secretly provided funding to the war criminals who have stolen the government of Alsharq from the people. The forces of the Khamsin Sayef can strike anywhere in the Western world. Those who oppress the beloved believers of Islam cannot hide from us.

"Victor Wu was an agent of the CIA. His so-called Clarion Group is a CIA front. He thought himself safe behind the lies of the West. We proved him wrong.

"We are the Sword of the Storm. We are the just and righteous bringers of death.

"All praise to the Prophet. Peace be upon him."

C03

Katalin Fiero Dahar, wearing a very short skirt and a black tank and sneakers with no laces, sat at a round iron table on the promenade on the marina front in Kyrenia. She hunkered low, legs outstretched, crossed at the ankles. She wore her hair scraped back in a ponytail, revealing pointed, almost elfin ears. Her classic Ray Bans obscured her almond-shaped eyes and she hadn't moved in more than a dozen minutes.

Several men could attest to this. They'd been covertly staring at her.

The tourists of Kyrenia, in the Turkish north of Cyprus, tended to be English or Russian. Which is to say, fair-skinned people unused to the August sun of the Eastern Mediterranean. The flesh on display that sleepy Monday ranged from alabaster white to the raw red of fresh sunburns. Which explained why so many tourists and townies were covetously glancing at the exceptionally long and exceptionally tanned legs of the Spanish/Algerian woman lounging, or perhaps sleeping, in the chair.

Michael Finnigan stepped out of the restaurant behind her and took the other chair at the table. He deftly laid out two small glasses, a bottle of vodka, and a high hat of crushed ice. He nodded amiably to a couple of guys strolling the promenade, who quickly averted their gaze.

Finnigan—Irish American, and himself fair of skin—had become accustomed to the Mediterranean island and the sun. He wore sunscreen and a Yankees cap to shade his eyes, plus a pair of wraparound snow-skier glasses, currently hanging by a rubberized lanyard and bouncing against his chest as he poured the vodka.

Fiero stirred for the first time in ages, reached for her glass, and drained it in a shot. Finnigan poured again.

"Tourists are staring at your legs."

"Yes, they are."

"You really do got great legs."

"Yes, I do."

They sat and sipped and enjoyed the moment. The town, on the northern coast, not far from the Turkish mainland, formed around an ancient caldera, with a small lagoon and marina in the center, the promenade circling it, and the commercial core of Kyrenia built up on the cliffs above the promenade. The town itself started flat near the coast but rose quickly, built up on the wall of craggy mountains, the Pentadactyl, or "Five-Finger" Range. A hulking Venetian and Ottoman fortress loomed to the south of the town, behind which sat another, more commercial lagoon. Sailboats maneuvered into and out of the marina, and a small fleet of fishing boats bobbed in the Med, just past the rocky breakwater.

A waitress stepped out of the restaurant with a tray, delivering plates of fresh salads and tissue-thin strips of carpaccio stewing in lemon juice with capers, horseradish, and a sprinkling of herbs. She chatted up the partners, whose offices took up three stories over the restaurant. They spoke English, which was their common tongue. She also brought a paper cup with more ice and poured it around the vodka bottle, cocked at an angle in the high hat.

A Scottish tourist couple happened by with a map and a perplexed scowl. They glanced meaningfully at Finnigan, who jumped up, studied their map and guidebooks, and began putting together an itinerary for them.

Fiero suppressed a smile. It wasn't just that the Boy Scout insisted on helping every stray that crossed his path. There was something about his three-days growth of beard and messy, tousled hair, and his easy smile and laugh lines. People instantly trusted Michael Patrick Finnigan and, more to the point, people instantly liked him.

That had never been the case with the laconic Spaniard. Taller than her classmates, more athletic, and lacking that mutant super-power of small talk, she'd attended the finest boarding school in the south of Europe. She'd learned the haute école of classical dressage but not the art of gossiping or sharing a joint or *shooting the shit* (a Michaelism).

But Fiero could chat to Finnigan. Could, and did. The list of people she could chat with ended there.

Finnigan used the Scots couple's phone to take a snapshot of them with the rainbow of boat sails in the background. They strode off as he sat and refilled their glasses. Fiero said, "I might have found us a job."

He glanced up quickly. "For real?"

She shrugged. "It would pay extremely well."

"I like the sound of that." He dug into the carpaccio. "My God. What's in this?"

"*Ras el hanout,*" she said.

"What's that?"

"A Moroccan spice mix. My mother's favorite."

"This is insane," he said, spearing more of the meat. Finnigan couldn't remember ever having a bad meal on Cyprus, and they'd been there for three years. "A job. We haven't had one of those since Serbia."

Fiero nodded and shifted in her seat to reach for her fork and knife. Sitting unmoving, she appeared to be thin, even skinny, all angles and no curves. But when she moved, the density of the knotted muscles beneath her tanned skin made themselves evident.

"The judge hasn't been able to throw any work our way in months," Finnigan said around a mouthful of local tomatoes dressed in green olive oil and the juice of lemons that probably grew within a mile of the restaurant.

"Hard for her to do. Bounty hunters tend to be personae non gratae at the International Criminal Court."

"True. Me, I think we're public servants."

"People get the wrong impression about us," she added. "Like we're uncivilized or something."

"Crazy." He shook his head.

Hélene Betancourt, senior-most justice at the World Criminal Court, had sustained the partners for three years. There were certain people around the world whom Judge Betancourt wanted brought to trial but who had eluded law enforcement. So she had turned, through an intermediary, to St. Nicholas Salvage & Wrecking, a supposed marine salvage company that, in fact, served as a front for Finnigan, the ex-cop, and Fiero, the ex-spy.

The marine salvage work explained how they made money. It worked as a pretty good cover, although not, they discovered, with their families. Finnigan's whole clan had been cops or married to cops. His grandfather and uncles. His dad and little sister. All were New York's Finest. Finnigan had worn the badge, too. Back in the day. He wasn't prepared to tell any of them that he now made his living illegally smuggling kidnapped criminals across national borders.

Fiero's father was a well-heeled Spanish businessman and aristocrat. Her mother, a famed academic, Islamic activist, and ardent feminist. There was no way Fiero wanted them to know she made a living holding a gun.

Neither of the partners could tell their families they were in the marine salvage business. Who'd believe that, knowing them as only family can? The pretend job might also require anecdotes over holiday visits. What anecdotes could they share?

So, as far as the Finnigan and Fiero clans were concerned, Michael and Katalin were low-level, paper-pushing bureaucrats for the European Union, stationed in Cyprus. The work they invented was dull enough that nobody asked too many questions.

It was perfect.

Of late, they'd taken a couple of small cases in other countries—Greece, Austria—but had mostly stayed off everyone's radar.

"We're not broke," Finnigan said, pouring more vodka. "Bridget goes over our finances with me every Tuesday. We're doing okay. But that won't last forever."

Fiero nodded and stabbed at her raw steak.

"Who's the client?"

"Someone who wants our help finding the leaders of the Khamsin Sayef."

Finnigan looked up from his food. "Is that what I think it is?"

"Terrorist cell blowing up people in Europe; yes."

"You're kidding!"

She shook her head.

"Who?"

"I'd tell you, but you'll tell me to go fuck myself."

He blinked, mouth open. "What the—I would never. Why would you think that? We're partners. All decisions, even Steven. Fifty-fifty."

Fiero smiled from behind her glasses.

"I'm right in saying this Kham Whatever are the assholes who blew up that NGO guy in Barcelona last week?"

"You are."

"And the other two bombings this year?"

"Yes."

"Am I right in saying every law enforcement and intelligence agency on the continent is looking for them?"

"Goes without saying."

"But someone wants *us* to get involved?"

"Yes."

"Who?"

"Someone who can pay," Fiero said. "And pay well."

Finnigan removed his cap and wiped sweat off his forehead. "Wow. Who is it?"

"Someone who can get us access to the police investigations to date. All of it. Whole case files."

He sipped vodka. "Wow. Who is it?"

"Someone who can keep us off the radar of the various intelligence agencies looking for the bombers."

"Wow. Who is it?"

She told him. Then waited a bit. "So. Go fuck myself?"

"Goes without saying."

C04

They argued half the night. But the next day, Finnigan took the Land Rover and headed out to rendezvous with their would-be clients.

The first of the two flew in from Tel Aviv, arriving at the island's only real airport just after ten. Finnigan had a photo of her and knew her real name, not the name she would be flying under.

Fiero waited forty minutes then followed. Dressed in leathers and a helmet, she rode her Ducati south from Kyrenia, winding up the rough-faced Pentadactyl Mountains until she hit the high plateau that made up the centermost geography on the island of Cyprus.

She'd been shot in the right arm earlier that year, and riding the cycle hurt—but not badly. It was almost a good ache, like that of a tattoo needle. Fiero smiled wolfishly from behind the smoked face shield and laced her way between slower-moving cars, roaring south. On Cyprus, cars and steering wheels are oriented in the British style, not the American style. She bypassed the capital, Nicosia, and entered the Greek-held territory at one of the United

Nations checkpoints. She had a Cypriot driving permit, so the border guard waved her through quickly.

She made it to the airport at Larnaca with time to spare. She pulled off the helmet revealing her hair worn in a low chignon, parted in the middle, in the Spanish style. She tapped in a six-digit code to unlock the storage space under the Ducati's seat, revealing a leather folder with euros—coin of the realm for the two thirds of the island with a Greek government—and Turkish lira for the other third. Larnaca was on the Greek side. The storage space also held her SIG-Sauer P226 Tactical Operations autopistol with its front cocking serrations and short reset trigger. She kept it with a fast-draw belt holster and two additional .9 mm clips. Many female soldiers opted for a smaller gun, but Fiero had spent her youth riding horses and crewing speed yachts. She had a pianist's fingers and a sculptor's strong wrists.

She swapped out the lira in her wallet for euros but left the gun where it was. From beneath it, she withdrew a butterfly knife, folded in on itself, the blade hidden and patient. She slid it into her right ankle boot and relocked the seat's cover.

She was leaning against a tourism bureau kiosk and drinking a takeaway coffee when Hugo Llorente emerged with a cluster of other travelers. They did not greet each other, nor did they even appear to make eye contact. But a few seconds after Fiero started walking away, Llorente fell in, thirty paces behind her.

She hailed a cab out front of the terminal. She stood outside the driver's window and paid cash for the short ride into town— you can see the boardwalk of Larnaca from one end of the main runway. She told the driver where to go, described Llorente, then turned and walked back to her motorbike.

Hugo Llorente didn't emerge from the terminal until Fiero was gone.

FINNIGAN HAD MET ANNIE PRYOR at the same airport, but twenty minutes earlier. He parked behind the Budget rent-a-car booth in a vast parking lot of rentals. By dragging her wheeled carry-on all the way to that lot, anyone following her would have been stuck a mile from their own vehicle and unprepared for a driver to pick her up. But as it was, neither Finnigan nor Pryor noticed any tails.

Annie Pryor was fifty, he guessed, blond with a short, efficient bob. He had no idea what name she'd traveled under and didn't care. The island was warm but not hot, and not humid; a trick of the Eastern Med, Cyprus often missed the humidity and blistering heat of the lands around it. Pryor wore casual clothes but with the élan of a rich person. Finnigan, in jeans and a T-shirt and boots, looked like her hired driver. Finnigan imagined a backstory for her that included Princeton and Yale, the State Department, and eventually the CIA. Where—and this part he didn't have to make up—she'd become a senior station director for Europe. Her current *shop*, to use a term of intelligence circles, was Madrid.

He drove from the airport to Larnaca and quickly got the Land Rover into the narrow, Byzantine old town. They spoke not a word to each other. It would have been impossible to follow them unless the enemy had a drone, and Finnigan relaxed a little as they doubled back on their own trail for the fourth time.

He parked behind a ninth-century church and postage-stamp-sized cemetery, a block from the waterfront esplanade. The neighborhood was overrun by stray cats and old men playing backgammon. He climbed out. Pryor did too, taking her carry-on. He pointed to a cheap hotel and crossed the street.

She spoke for the first time. "You're good at this, Mr. Finnigan."

He held the door for her.

"You're not happy I'm here."

Finnigan said, "No shit," and let her enter first.

Hugo Llorente's taxi let him out in front of the same ninth-century church. He went in, lit a candle, prayed, dropped a euro in the donation box, and exited through the tiny graveyard, where Fiero pried herself from the shadows and led him to a small seafood restaurant.

Llorente was five five, in his late sixties; a thin, birdlike man with bony shoulders. He wore the pencil mustache of a cinema villain. His suits never fit properly. Shrapnel scars pocked his jaw line on the right side, a gift from a mortar attack in the Golan Heights many decades ago.

The entire block was one large building, constructed in the seventeenth century and remodeled a dozen times. There were six entrances on five streets—no such thing as right angles in the map of Larnaca's old town—with six different addresses. If one knew their way around the building, you could get from one entrance to all the others. If you didn't, you probably couldn't. St. Nicholas Salvage & Wrecking paid the building owner a monthly fee for the right to meet clients here.

Fiero led the older man through the ill-lit corridors, eventually into the hotel part of the building and up to the third floor. She rapped on a door and Finnigan opened it.

The room was grungy but clean. Fiero spied the antisurveillance equipment that normally stayed tucked under the bed and knew her partner had swept for bugs.

Llorente nodded to the American woman. "Annie."

"Hugo."

She'd flown in from Tel Aviv. He'd flown in from Ankara. They had not, nor would they ever, be spotted together on Cypriot soil. St. Nicholas knew what it was doing, and the two older spook-masters let them handle the details of the meeting.

Finnigan ran downstairs and picked up the preordered lunch: lamb and flatbread, assorted fresh vegetables, plus a brass pot of good Greek coffee. On Cyprus, coffee was almost always served with low, plastic cups of water sealed with plastic lids. He paid and took the tray up himself.

Fiero had taken her favorite position in any room, standing back to the wall, one boot sole up on the wallpaper, arms crossed under her boyish chest. "Michael, this is Hugo Llorente. Centro Nacional de Inteligencia. He was my handler for years."

Finnigan wiped his palms on his jeans and extended one hand. After a beat, Llorente took it.

"Howdy. You're the guy turned Katalin into an assassin. I've wanted to kick your teeth in for some time. Welcome to Cyprus."

The smaller man smiled. He wore his skin the way a boxer wears tape around his wrists—taut, stretched thin, showing the strain.

"I appreciate honesty, but I'd appreciate a cup of that coffee more, please."

He accepted a cup and doctored it with milk, while Pryor accepted a sealed cup of water. Finnigan made himself a gyro as Fiero stood in the darkened corner, watching.

"This is Annie Pryor of the CIA," Llorente said, fiddling with his coffee. "She is the station chief for Madrid. She is here without the knowledge or consent of her government. She came at my request."

"We don't want to work for either of you guys," Finnigan said.

"Do you speak for your partner?" Pryor asked. She picked at the seal of her water cup. "Look, we don't think that highly of bounty hunters, who tend to be profiteering cowboys. But here we are."

Finnigan couldn't help but smile. "You got a sales pitch? This oughta be good."

"Yes," Llorente said, "but first I want to talk about Thomas Shannon Greyson."

The partners let their poker faces slip, if only a little.

"Greyson is the aide-de-camp of Judge Hélene Betancourt," the Spanish spymaster said, sitting on the squeaky bed. "He was tortured—maimed, really—by a splinter cell of Kosovo soldiers earlier this year."

This was not common knowledge, and Finnigan was none too happy to hear the tale being told by the spy crowd.

"I was prepared to sneer at this company of yours, this St. Nicholas Salvage & Wrecking, as an amateur operation. I was prepared to try to get Katalin to return to our service. To our country."

Finnigan said, "As a killer."

Hugo Llorente dismissed the word as if it carried the same moral weight as *dentist*. He turned to Pryor. "Katalin is truly gifted. Among the best we had."

Pryor said, "I know."

Fiero said, "Among?"

Finnigan flashed her a grin, then turned to the older man. "What's this crap gotta do with Shan?"

"You and Katalin rescued Mr. Greyson," Llorente said. "And I know you've been using your own resources to pay for his rehabilitation and surgery. For round-the-clock care in a private home, here on this island. For charter flights to surgeons throughout Europe."

The partners didn't deny any of it.

Pryor set her bottle down. "That tipped it for me. Hugo, too, I think. Our agencies are not as scrupulous as you about taking care of our assets. I wish that weren't true, but it is. You did right by Greyson. You give bounty hunters a good name."

Finnigan chewed his food and turned to Fiero. "Ain't we something?"

"Noble," she agreed, standing statue-like, away from the others.

Pryor sighed. "Okay, so what do you know about the Khamsin Sayef?"

"Arabic," Fiero said. "Sword of the Storm."

"Bullshit Islamist psychos," Finnigan added, "who went

from blowing up bankers and engineering companies to a nongovernmental organization trying to feed Africa."

"A bizarre escalation," Llorente agreed. "Victor Wu and the Clarion Group had raised millions for agrarian projects in the Maghreb."

He raised a short, calloused finger and read off the country names, west to east. "Western Sahara, Mauritania, Morocco, Algeria, Libya, Alsharq, Egypt."

Fiero cut in. "Sword of the Storm started in Alsharq." She turned to Finnigan. "It was a tool of the ousted government, which lost power three years ago. Now it fights against the new government."

Finnegan nodded and turned back to their guests. "This *cleric* dude? It's his group?"

Pryor nodded. "The cleric is the figurehead anyway. No one knows who the hell he is or which faction he was trained with. He's the one who appears in the YouTube videos, extolling the death toll from each bombing. We *think* he's the shot caller for the Khamsin Sayef. He could just be a pretty boy. We don't know."

Finnegan ate some lamb. "What do you need us for?"

"Killing Victor Wu was an escalation," Pryor said. "But for us—for Hugo and me, for the CNI and CIA—the bigger problem is that the bomb also killed a man named Pete Newsom and two of his operatives."

Fiero said, "I know that name. He's CIA."

"Was," Pryor said. "He took early retirement and joined a military/intelligence contractor called Sooner, Slye, and Rydell. Do you know about them?"

Again, the partners shot each other a look. Fiero muttered, "Bloody hell."

Finnegan snorted. "*Suicide Ride.* Yeah, we ran into them with that thing involving the Kosovars and Shan. Big-time military contractors. Multi-million-dollar worldwide operations. The Walmart of war."

"Yes," Pryor said, and the word sounded bitter on her tongue. "They started out as mercenaries in the Afghanistan and Iraq wars. They had a famous, Wild West gunslinger name. When the American Congress and—more importantly—the *Washington Post* found out about their wartime atrocities, the contractors bought the rights to the name of a small, Oklahoma law firm, Sooner, Slye, and Rydell, and traded in their Kevlar for pinstripes. Same violent war dogs, new respectable branding."

Llorente huffed irritably into his coffee cup.

"The real problem with these bastards is, they're good at what they do," Pryor said. "Good and profitable. They pay incredible salaries to get high-ranking military and intelligence assets to come on board. I served with Pete Newsom when he was an assistant station chief, an operations director. He was good but not excellent. He left the agency for a half-million-dollar signing bonus."

Llorente sighed and drained his coffee. "Half of Spanish Intelligence wants to work for them. Same for the CIA. Annie and I have discovered that our investigation into the Barcelona bombing is being leaked in real time to Sooner, Slye, and Rydell. We want to bring Sword of the Storm to justice. These mercenary bastards want them dead. Not out of any sense of justice, but because of *branding*."

Finnigan said, "I'm sorry: Branding?"

Pryor nodded. "They've put on a full-court press on this. Literally hundreds of operatives assigned to getting the bombers. We had some possible suspects and tried to put them under surveillance; Sooner, Slye, and Rydell—Suicide Ride, as you put it—swept in, guns blazing, and killed everyone."

"The same thing happened with us," Llorente said.

Finnigan spoke around about a third of his sandwich. "Lemme guess: The Spanish prime minister wants Spain to bring in this nameless cleric and the Storm of the Whatever. He wants a trial."

He paused to swallow. "Suicide Ride needs to bag him, or they lose face before their clients. So now it's a race."

"It's not just the Spanish prime minister," Pryor said. "Do you have any idea how much money Congress throws at Sooner, Slye, and Rydell to handle security at State Department facilities overseas? There are forces in Congress that would love to privatize the Intelligence Community. And believe me, every one of those congressmen is looking forward to a position on the Sooner, Slye, and Rydell board of directors as soon as they tire of *public service*."

She all but spat the last words.

"Your investigations leak like a colander," Finnigan said. "You want the Khamsin Sayef brought to trial. You want this cleric schmuck in prison. And you can't let Suicide Ride make you look like chumps. So that's where we come in."

Llorente set down his cup on the lacquered tray. "You have garnered a reputation, Mr. Finnigan. You and Katalin. You have proven adept at finding people and bringing them to justice. Even well-armed people. Anything Annie or I do, the mercenaries know instantly. You have the luxury of working without our bureaucracy, and also without the tentacles of Sooner, Slye, and Rydell."

"If you find the bombers," Pryor cut in, "we can get them in a court of law. Do this thing properly. Show the world that terrorism on the European continent won't be tolerated."

"We don't trust you," Finnigan said. "Either of you."

Pryor said, "Don't blame you."

"No offense or anything, but CNI turned Katalin into an assassin, trading on her soul. And I was a New York City cop before I was a US Marshal. In both roles, I never met anyone from the CIA who wasn't a huge dick."

Pryor spoke without a smile. "Neither have I."

"So why should we believe you?"

"Because of this." Pryor reached into her carry-on and produced a folded square of heavy-stock notepaper. She held it out.

Finnigan stood, wiped his fingers on a napkin, and reached for it. He unfolded it and read the dollar figure. "Sweet mother of God."

"And we'll put it in your Cypriot bank account today," Pryor said. "You get the money, results irrespective."

Finnigan read the number again. It was more than they had made in the three years they had worked together.

He turned to Fiero, handed her the note.

Fiero read it, handed it back, poker face in place. She turned to Annie Pryor. "Do you want us to find the cleric and the Khamsin Sayef because of the three bombings? Is that the only reason?"

Pryor bought time by peeling the cover off her water cup. She took a sip.

Llorente pretended to straighten the crease in his trousers.

"No," the American said. "The cleric and his people killed my best friend. Three years ago. This is personal."

Fiero used her shoulders and boot sole to push herself away from the wall. She reached for the door.

"We're in. You have planes to catch."

She exited.

The other three blinked at each other.

Llorente said, "Ah . . . to be clear . . . you're in?"

Finnigan wiped his lips with a napkin. "Sure sounded like it."

C05

They got Llorente and Pryor back to the airport, forty minutes apart, threw the Ducati in the back of the Land Rover, and drove north to Kyrenia, going through the flat and arid center of the island—lush forested mountains to their left, rich farmland to their right—around the capital and through the UN checkpoint between the Greek and Turkish sides of the island.

Finnigan drove because he'd finally gotten accustomed to being on the left side of the road, right side of the car, British style. It had freaked out his American sensibilities for their first couple of months together.

"What was that last bit about?" Finnigan asked. "Annie Pryor had a best friend killed by the Storm of the Douchebags? Did you know that before you asked?"

Fiero sat low, cycle boots up on the dash, as was her habit. "Pryor said she'd served with the dead man, Pete Newsom, when he'd been an assistant station chief and an operations director for the CIA."

"Yeah?"

"I knew this story from before. Newsom had been chief of operations for the Paris Station. Three years ago. Just when you and I stopped shooting at each other and became beasties."

He grinned, liking it when she tried for Americanisms. "*Bes*ties. This was three years ago?"

She nodded.

The penny dropped. "Holy shit. The Paris bombing that killed that CIA chief?"

Fiero scrunched lower in her seat, knees higher than her nose. "Hmm. A bomber blew up a restaurant in Paris, killing the CIA station chief, her husband, and her daughter. The child was two or three, I think."

"I remember that. Ah . . . Marine . . . ?"

"Dinah Mariner. I met her once, just in passing. We were both at the same debriefing. It wasn't enough to plant a bomb and kill her, but her daughter and husband?" Fiero glowered behind her shades. "Evil."

"That was linked to Sword of the Storm?"

"It was, and it brought down the old government of Alsharq," she said. "A pro-Western faction in the capital, Baharos, staged a revolt after the bombing. Europe got behind them. Before the hard-line Islamist government could react, the people were on the side of the revolutionaries. The Islamists fled to Tripoli."

Finnigan sneered. "It hasn't gone that peachy for the new government, right? I mean, the quote-moderates-unquote. They're bombing their own capital now."

"True. Less than three years in, and the moderates seem to lack moderation."

Finnigan blew past a farm truck. "I've had girlfriends last longer than that government."

Fiero laughed, and Finnigan secretly rejoiced. It wasn't easy to make Katalin Fiero Dahar laugh, and he always counted it as a victory. "You do tend to go through girlfriends."

"It's because I'm complex."

"By all means," she said, "let's go with that answer."

In fact, the *pro-Western* government hadn't proved all that pro-Western, or even pro–its own people. The first street protests in Baharos had been met with heavy-handed military reaction, which had led to more dissent, which led to an even harsher crackdown. Three years later, the country of Alsharq now had open warfare in the city of Baharos and a refugee crisis that, proportionally, rivaled that of the much larger Syria.

The Khamsin Sayef, or Sword of the Storm, had been a terrorism cell linked to the old hard-liner government. Now that trouble had again invaded that war-torn country, the terrorist cell was back and had racked up three bombings in less than a year.

"Three years ago," Fiero said, "Dinah Mariner was CIA station chief in Paris. Pete Newsom was her chief of operations. That means Annie Pryor must have been her chief of intelligence. She's the last living member of the old Paris Station command staff, and if she'd have lied to me and said she didn't have any emotion in this manhunt, I'd have told them to go fuck themselves."

Finnigan smiled. The daughter of a Muslim mother and a popular and well-connected Spanish diplomat, Fiero would dress conservatively and speak eloquently when visiting her parents. When it was just the two of them, she dressed in pure goth mode and swore like a carnival hand.

"Would you have told Llorente to go fuck himself? Really?"

A few kilometers hissed under their wheels as she sat quietly.

"Even Hugo, yes."

"When you were nineteen or twenty, that asshole screwed with your head," Finnigan said, and he felt his partner tense up in the left-hand seat. "You should have been comparing grades and shrieking at Eurovision stars and blowing undergrads. Instead, that bastard turned you into a fucking ninja."

Fiero faked a smile—Finnigan could tell the difference—and nudged him again. "Well, I was doing one of those three."

"You were a Eurovision groupie?"

"Ha!" It was a real laugh this time, and Finnigan mentally called it a draw. He let the topic lapse as the Pentadactyl Range rose into view.

C06

They let their friends know they might be back in business after a "dry spell." *It's always good to know who's available at the start of a gig*, Finnigan thought. Just in case.

Their friends were an unusual assortment of ne'er-do-wells, as his grandmother would have said. They included a corrupt banker who was to money laundering what Jascha Heifetz was to the fiddle, a Scottish mercenary who could put together an army on a moment's notice, and a crew of subcontracting thieves and con men known as the Black Harts.

Finnigan—son of a cop, grandson of a cop, and at his soul, a cop through and through—wasn't all that comfortable with the *friends* they'd established.

Fiero—a soldier at heart—believed that all jobs fell into one of two categories: wins or losses. Whatever rules you had to bend to stay out of the second category were fine by her.

If it sometimes made for uncomfortable feelings between the partners, well, no business model is perfect.

As for the Khamsin Sayef, the Great God Google provided all the answers, as it tended to during the first hours of any investigation.

The partners got home and Fiero went for a run, which would end at her dojo and a strenuous workout. Finnigan hit the books.

After making a name for itself in the Paris bombing three years earlier, the Khamsin Sayef lay low for a while. But this year, they'd come back with a vengeance, launching three strikes in eight months. The first was a bank in Geneva, taking out two of the bank's midlevel officials and six others in an adjacent office.

Next, in May, the Khamsin Sayef hit a café in the lake town of Annecy, France. Again, they showed no mercy for family, killing an engineer who'd designed a dam for the newly emerged government of Alsharq. Rick Caldwell, and his wife, Joan, had died. Plus three innocent passersby.

Then the terrorists hit Victor Wu in Barcelona, killing three operatives of the American military/intelligence contractor Sooner, Slye, and Rydell, and thus hamstringing any investigation by either the Spanish or American spy agencies, and leading Hugo Llorente and Annie Pryor to reach out to St. Nicholas Salvage & Wrecking.

Finnigan was simultaneously pleased and worried that the CNI and CIA knew about their business. He and Fiero thought their cover, as a marine salvage broker, had kept them off the radar of most government agencies. It seems that assessment had been wildly optimistic.

A messenger delivered a flash drive to their Kyrenian office over the Turkish restaurant that afternoon. Finnigan opened the package to find a flash drive but no note, no letter, no instructions. He fit the drive into an extra laptop they stored in a closet—in case the drive was infected—and found the entire case file of the Khamsin Sayef, courtesy of the Spanish Centro Nacional de Inteligencia.

In Spanish, of course. He'd been attempting to learn Spanish, if for no other reason than his friendship with Fiero's parents. But he wasn't by any means fluent. He'd have to put Fiero on reading it.

As the day wore on, Finnigan studied everything he could understand on the flash drive and found on the internet about the terrorist cell and the bombings.

Fiero hated inactivity and was prohibitively bad at research. She'd been that overly smart and underserved student in school, bored and troublesome, with an irksome quality of memorizing all lessons instantaneously, then disrupting the classroom for everyone else. When Finnigan was in research mode, Fiero knew to clear out—to her dojo, to go running in the craggy mountain range behind the village, or to take up a new sport like scuba diving or hang gliding.

Finnigan was much the opposite: Not a naturally good student, but bad grades meant disappointing his mom, and who needed that? He'd fit in homework around pickup games of basketball at the J on Victory Boulevard on Staten Island. Irish kids versus Jewish kids. They'd literally had T-shirts made up with crosses and Stars of David for tournaments, team names like *Cabbages* and *Challahs*, being fourteen and not giving a crap about stereotypes and clichés.

He never had to worry about career counseling; his grandfather and father and uncles had all been cops. His path was laid out for him.

Or so he'd thought.

While Fiero went running, Finnigan remained cooped up and enjoyed it. He'd read for an hour then go clean something, make their beds or fold the laundry or scour out the coffee maker. That was his version of research/tai chi: read, putter, and ponder, repeat.

Their offices were largish for their needs and they'd been lucky to find it. Although the luck was a residue of a clever tactic. One of the very first cases they had ever taken on was the recovery of a con man in Lisbon who'd stolen nearly a million euros from a pension fund set up for the Central Intelligence Service of the Cyprus Police. They'd returned the money, no questions asked. Inspector Rafael Triadis, Nicosia Division, had called upon them to give them thanks, and to assure them he knew what St. Nicholas Salvage & Wrecking was really about. His two-edged greeting had included an introduction to his cousin, the landlord of their new office, and a warning to keep their extra-legal activities off the island of Cyprus.

They'd agreed. Triadis had remained a friend.

Their building was narrow and vertical: a bar facing the harbor on one ground floor; a Turkish restaurant facing the mountain range on the second ground floor—the streets of Kyrenia switch-backed madly—and three floors of offices, only three rooms wide, for St. Nicholas. In the mornings, the office smelled of the sea; in the evenings, of jasmine rice and kofta and lamb.

They had space for themselves and their office manager, Bridget Sumner; a living room, a kitchen, bedrooms; and storage space for things like Fiero's bicycle, Finnigan's Game Boy, and their many, many guns.

After a full day of Finnigan's research, Fiero brought home a curry takeaway for dinner. Her parents may have been Cordon Bleu trained, but Katalin's culinary expertise began and ended at Top Ramen.

As part of his research, Finnigan watched tapes of the Khamsin Sayef front man, the nameless cleric. After each bombing, the man appeared in a video on Al Jazeera. He had Fiero watch the YouTube videos too. She took notes and translated the speeches into English. She came to the same conclusion.

"There's a professionalism about him. Not a passion," she said. "He's almost addressing *voters*, instead of true believers. He insults nonbelievers and the West and Israel and capitalism, but he doesn't rant. And he doesn't equivocate. The bombings are good things. The deaths have political value."

"He's a fucking nut-bar."

She nodded. "Still . . ."

FINNIGAN HOLED HIMSELF UP the next two days. Fiero exercised and puttered and read. She helped translate Hugo Llorente's flash drive, when necessary. Their two employees, pilot Lachlan Sumner and officer manager Bridget Sumner, were on vacation in New Zealand. The quiet of the office drove Fiero a little crazy, and she spent time learning to wind sail off the island's eastern coast, in the Turkish-controlled city the Greeks call Famagusta and the Turks call Gazimagusa. Cyprus is so small that most every city is a fairly quick drive away.

That evening, over Chinese takeaway, Finnigan waved his chopsticks in the air and said, "Start at the very beginning. It's a very good place to start."

Fiero speared a shrimp from one of the boxes. "Who said that?"

"Maria."

"Maria who?"

"Never mind. I want to go to Geneva. I want to walk through the first new crime scene."

She said, "Not Paris?"

"Three years apart, between that first bomb and these three. I'd like to take the current cluster as a separate case."

She nodded. He was the investigator. "What do you expect to find in Geneva?"

He drank some Belmonte beer. "Dunno. Sometimes you find things by walking the scene and sometimes you don't. Can't tell until you try."

"Then we should go."

"Not we. Me."

"You don't think I'd be helpful walking the crime scene?"

"I think you'd get bored and find someone to punch."

"You think my every interaction ends with me punching someone?"

"Oddsmakers are standing by." He dug out a spoonful of spicy salt-and-pepper noodles. "But you've got another job."

"What's that?"

"What do we know about the Swiss banking industry?"

"Nothing," Fiero said and chewed a mushroom. "For that, we usually—wait . . ."

He grinned. "Yup."

"No!"

"Absolutely."

"Michael!" She stamped her bare foot. "I can't! He's in love with me!"

"Half the people I know are in love with you."

"But Ways and Means . . ."

". . . Is the most crooked banker we've ever met. He knows everything there is to know about Swiss banking, probably knew the banker who got killed in January. Plus, you know, there's the whole he's-in-love-with-you thing."

"I won't do it," she announced.

"Okay, I'll go."

They ate for a while. Fiero scowled at him and munched through her dinner.

"Really?"

"Sure. I'll go to Varenna and talk to Ways and Means. You go to Geneva and walk the crime scene and absorb information. Conduct interviews. Analyze data. Detect."

"Oh, please," she glowered. "I try to do that, I'll end up punching someone."

C07

For a guy widely recognized as one of the powerhouses of the Afghanistan and Iraqi wars, Colonel Cole Sanger, US Marine Corps, retired, was smaller than people expected. He stood maybe five eight, but he ran and lifted weights almost daily, and it showed. He was in his midforties, with close-cropped hair of so fine a shade that it might have been dark blond or light brown or sandy red. He'd retired as a full bird colonel and accepted a position at Sooner, Slye, and Rydell—and was the most decorated war hero to ever accept the company's offer. For the American military contractor, it had been like being a pretty good playoff team bidding for LeBron James in the off-season—and getting him.

The company put Cole Sanger in charge of the Khamsin Sayef investigation within hours of the death of Pete Newsom and his two men. Sanger immediately set up shop in Barcelona and put together his team. He had carte blanche: anyone on the payroll could be diverted to Spain in a heartbeat.

That Tuesday, Sanger met with police investigators in

Barcelona but learned nothing new. The investigators came away with their wallets considerably enlarged, promising that all information on the bombing would be forthcoming. Sanger returned to the Sooner, Slye, and Rydell offices on avenue Carrer d'Arago and waited while a dour woman named Frau Gunsen from Zurich conducted a sweep with two men in overalls and blue plastic booties over their shoes. Gunsen stood and watched, shoulders hunched together, mousy brown hair in a tight bun. A lattice of scar tissue climbed out of her ill-fitting jumper, mottling her throat, cheek, and temple along her left side. She must have broken her nose as a child because it hooked left. She wore oversized glasses, Sanger suspected, to draw attention away from her nose and the scars.

She eventually nodded, and her men began packing. They hadn't been sweeping for bugs; Sooner, Slye, and Rydell did that daily.

They'd been sweeping for bombs. It had become necessary in high-end offices throughout Europe.

When the office was clear, Sanger sat and accessed the company's secure server—they leased time on a string of communications satellites—and rang up the firm's signal-intelligence unit, housed out of a decommissioned NASA engineering facility in Galveston, Texas. A team of brainiacs there had been tasked with hacking information from Centro Nacional de Inteligencia and the Central Intelligence Agency regarding the nameless cleric, the public face of the Khamsin Sayef.

A young supervisor from San Francisco, Chen Yiu, had been waiting for the video call, facing the screen and impassive. Chen's cubicle in Galveston was spotless and barren, with no mementos or tchotchkes. Sanger had visited the SigInt office once and noticed the mathematician sprayed down his cubicle with a heavy industrial cleaner in a spritz bottle before every shift.

"I have something maybe interesting," Chen said.

Sanger appreciated that the twentysomething PhD never overpromised. "Go ahead."

"Hugo Llorente, head of CNI's special projects team. We have his personal banking records."

Sanger knew the name. Llorente ran a kill shop for Spanish Intelligence. He was a well-respected, low-profile professional who'd never expressed the least interest in being hired away by a multinational contractor like Sooner, Slye, and Rydell. He was considered a spook's spook.

"Yesterday afternoon, Llorente hired a licensed and bonded courier service, using his own money, not CNI money, to have a package delivered. My team thought it could be interesting, so we hacked into the courier service. The package was a portable hard drive. It was delivered to the office of a marine salvage company on Cyprus."

Sanger listened while he thumbed his way through a stack of emails on his smartphone, throwing most away unanswered. "Go on."

"We tried to hack the salvage company but can't."

Sanger looked up. "What?"

"Their security protocols are top notch," Chen said. "They're similar to the protocols I would have established, had it been my company. They're superb."

Sanger waited. He knew the younger man to be highly competitive and wouldn't have called in with a simple *we can't*.

"This morning, my people tried going the long away around, through business contacts with the salvage company. It's, ah . . ." Chen peered at his handwritten notes. "A St. Nicholas Salvage & Wrecking."

"Okay." The name rang no bells.

Chen looked up at the pinhole camera over his monitor.

"Cyprus is the problem. The more corrupt a banking and government system, the harder to hack. The Russian petro-lords hide their money on Cyprus. I am *not* riling up those guys for a fishing expedition."

Sanger began to issue a countervailing order but stopped himself. The way one gives orders to a Marine Corps intelligence unit wouldn't work with these civilian PhD types. He was considering how to proceed when Chen beat him to it.

"Instead, I had my guys try to prove the bona fides of this company. We checked every bonded marine salvage operation in the Mediterranean and the Atlantic Coast of Europe over the past three years. We did find evidence that St. Nicholas Salvage & Wrecking exists and issues invoices, but we found no employees, no flight plans, no hotel reservations, no rental cars, no reimbursements, no liability claims, no insurance coverage for employees on scene. In short, none of the footprints you'd find from a real contractor doing the dangerous work of marine salvage."

Sanger said, "This St. Nicholas thing, it's a front?"

Chen shrugged. "So it would seem."

C08

As Fiero packed for her half of their research trip, Finnigan called an attorney in New York City. Gerry Trevalian called him back in five minutes and said, "Who is this again?"

"Michael Finnigan."

"How do I know it's really you?"

"Because we played hoops in high school and you couldn't go to your left for shit. We once beat the crap out of some frat guys from Vermont after a pickup game at the J, up from where your folks had that video store."

Trevalian said, "How's it going, Mikey?"

Finnigan checked to make sure he had their third-floor office to himself. "Is my old man in trouble?"

"I figured that's why you were calling. You know I can't talk about my client to anyone without Paddy's permission. Anyone."

"I tell my old man I'm asking if he's under indictment, we'll go twelve rounds of the Guilt Trip Olympics. You know how he is."

"Jesus . . ." the lawyer whined and lapsed into silence.

Finnigan watched the foot traffic on the promenade three stories below him, and the boats slipping into and out of the small marina.

"Yeah, he's in it pretty deep, Mikey."

"Ah, for . . ." Finnigan groaned. "The man's housebound! He's wearing a goddamn ankle bracelet! How much shit could he get into—"

"Patrick Finnigan?" The lawyer laughed without mirth. "Captain Paddy Finnigan, New York's Finest? So how come you got naive all of a sudden?"

Growing up, Finnigan had been raised by cops with a clear understanding that he, too, would be a cop. And he'd fulfilled that destiny, rising quickly—even mysteriously, at least to himself—in the New York Police Department, getting cushy assignment after cushy assignment.

He hadn't realized the much-honored Captain Patrick Finnigan had been bent until he'd been on the force for a year. His response had been quick and unequivocal—Michael quit the department and took a job with the US Marshals Service.

Paddy Finnigan and two of Michael's uncles were indicted a year later. Captain Finnigan did time and was still on monitored parole, hence the tracking bracelet on his ankle.

"Is this city trouble?" Finnigan asked.

Trevalian hesitated. "State's attorney. Albany."

"Big-time?"

"Yeah, Mikey. Big-time."

"Ah, for Christ's sake . . ."

Finnigan never thought to ask: *Whatever it is, is dad guilty?* He already knew the answer.

"If you were thinking of helping, Mikey, the next couple of weeks would be the time."

"Helping?"

"Character witness, information we could use for the defense. Whatever."

"Gerry, I . . . dude, I gotta think about it."

"What's to think? Your dad's in hot water. I'm not liking our case. If you *can* help . . ."

"That's the thing. Could be I can help. But probably the prosecution."

Trevalian said, "Oh."

"Yeah."

"Hey, you know I'm obligated to tell Paddy we talked."

"I understand."

"He's . . . ah, your dad's not gonna be over the moon about this, man."

Finnigan said, "Welcome to my fucking world."

C09

The company pilot, Lachlan Sumner, returned from vacation and tuned up the de Havilland DHC-6-300 Twin Otter seaplane. Bridget Sumner once again took charge of the Kyrenia office and squealed when she saw the dramatic, upward spike in the balance in one of their pristinely bent Cypriot banks. The partners explained the windfall.

When the de Havilland was ready, Lachlan flew the partners north.

LACHLAN LANDED THE PONTOON CRAFT in the blue waters of Italy's Lago de Como, near the resort town of Como. Fiero remained unhappy about debriefing their friendly neighborhood criminal banker, Gunther Kessler, but conceded the need.

Lachlan and Finnigan left her there and flew to Lac Léman and Geneva, at the lake's westernmost point.

Finnigan had called in a favor from a friend of a friend and found someone in the Swiss Federal Intelligence Service who agreed to meet with him. René Vonlathen was a messy-looking, haggard investigator with bad skin, an unstructured jacket, and a too-wide knit tie that had to have been a gift from one of his kids. He looked less Swiss than anyone Finnigan had ever met.

They gathered on a street of banks, east of the Pont du Mont-Blanc and beneath the shadow of the hilly old city. It was a neighborhood of serious old money, Finnigan thought, in a city weirdly isolated from the rest of Switzerland, surrounded to the north, west, and south by France and on the east by the gorgeous Lake Geneva.

One cop in another cop's town can hope to rely on reciprocal agreements of cooperation, but Finnigan wasn't a working cop. He had to hope for the best. He took a gamble and said, "Before we start, can I stand you a beer?"

The hangdog investigator shrugged. "I wouldn't say no."

They found a tavern beneath the Cathedral of St. Pierre and talked through the first round about anything and everything except the January bombing. They hit it off as two cops will, despite very different backgrounds. It didn't matter what part of the world you were from: dumb bureaucrats, crappy stakeout food, and funny accidents during chases were the same the world around. The beer was crazy expensive, but good.

They eventually headed into the sparkling clear air of the August day. Vonlathen pointed out the dramatic Geneva Water Fountain, which launched a jet stream remarkably high over the lake, and a few other tourist attractions. Eventually they made it to the front of a bank near the shopping district of Rue du Rhône.

"The bombers targeted the rear of the bank," Vonlathen said, his English good and his accent swinging from French to German and back again. "Initially, I thought they were stupid. They'd have killed far more if they hit the front. They could have killed two, three dozen people on the street and in the bank. Blowing up their van in an alley in the back only killed eight employees total. Two outside, six in the bank when the first floor collapsed."

Finnigan scratched his head. "These terrorist types always want to maximize the body count."

"Yes," the investigator shrugged. "But look."

Vonlathen stopped midblock and began pointing out the CCTV cameras that hung off every building. He spotted seven quickly and, after a pause, found two more, then two more.

"Geneva is like London," Vonlathen said. "Cameras everywhere. I'm police, and they even make me nervous."

"Park outside the bank, in front, and you'll get spotted from every angle," Finnigan said. "That includes walking away from the van, getting into another vehicle, or whatever."

"Exactly. Multiple angles, which means disguises generally don't stand up well. But . . ."

Vonlathen led him to the entry of the alley around the corner from the bank and noted two more cameras. They walked the length of the alley, a full city block, both men carrying their jackets over their shoulders as the temperatures topped eighty degrees. At the other end of the alley, he pointed around the perpendicular street.

"No cameras. Drive into the alley from this direction, walk out the same way, and you're scot-free." He paused. "That is a thing in English? Scot-free?"

"Yup. It's a thing."

They walked back to the middle of the alley.

Finnigan could tell at a glance that the windows behind the bank were new, very clean, and explosive-resistant. The brickwork was new too, and not in the least sun-faded. They found a metal door to the bank and a single riser, a truck-sized parking space, and a very new surveillance camera. The alley was wider in parts, thanks to the differentiated depths of the buildings facing the street. From the air, the alley would look like an old-fashioned skeleton key. Plenty of room to park without impeding traffic, even room to turn around.

"It happened here," Finnigan observed.

"Yes. At twelve-fifteen p.m. on that Tuesday, two bank officials stepped outside for a smoke. This camera," he pointed up, "is new, but there was one here then as well. It was destroyed, of course."

"Two guys stepped out for a smoke, got blown away. Four people inside died?"

"This wall caved in." Vonlathen touched the new brick with his palm. "The floor above them caved in as well. It killed people in an office that specialized in international monetary trades or some such. I don't know much about banking."

"You're Swiss," Finnigan said with a smile.

"My mother remains disappointed." He consulted a spiral-bound notepad. "Adrian Chassot was director of the bank's office of third-world project lending. He'd arranged for loans to Egypt and Alsharq."

"Where this Khamsin Sayef group comes from."

"Yes."

"The other guy who needed a smoke?"

"Cedric Brecher. From Human Resources. And before you ask, one or the other of them walked to the other one's office almost every morning to suggest they step out for a smoke. It was perfectly predictable. Not the exact time, but within fifteen minutes either way."

"But Chassot was the target."

"Yes. That nameless cleric of the Khamsin Sayef bragged about it on a video."

Finnigan muttered, "Motherfucker."

"Indeed. One of the clerks who died inside was two months pregnant. Another had just auditioned for a singing role in a

professional theater company here in the city and got it. Motherfucker, for certain."

They talked some more, Finnigan's questions seeming random
as he learned all he could about the scene. He asked about the
video from the camera mounted over the door and Vonlathen had
it on his smartphone, ready to share.

It was eerie, but not the first time Finnigan had stood in a spot
as he watched a video of that exact same place in the course of a
criminal investigation. The video was black and white, high quality, with no audio. Vonlathen had cued it up from the time the
van arrived. It was a white or off-white Opel Combo. Mid-1990s,
Finnigan thought. It drove into camera range then ducked into
one of the carve-outs from the adjacent building. There, the driver
conducted a series of short back-and-forth maneuvers to turn the
van around. Facing the opposite direction, he pulled into a spot
striped on the sidewalk with a sign, mostly off-camera, which
probably said *no parking, except for bank business*, or some such.

"The explosive was packed into the right-side wall of the
Opal," Vonlathen said. "They wanted that side of the van nearest the bank."

"Crappy driver," Finnigan said. "I could've made that turn in
two tries. Took the guy, like, six."

"Vin Diesel," Vonlathen said. "You Americans and your driving prowess."

"I'm a Steve McQueen guy myself."

On the video, only one person emerged from the van, the
driver. The person appeared to be male, bearded, wearing a white
coverall suit under a coat with a gray, fake-fur collar, scuffed work
boots, and a thick stocking hat. It had been January, and Finnigan
saw patches of snow on the cement.

"Can't tell if that beard's real or not."

"Neither can we," Vonlathen conceded.

The driver walked away the same way he'd come, the direction of no video cameras, and stepped out of visual range in only a few steps.

"They'd done their homework."

Vonlathen said, "The bank camera, yes. He never looks up. He cheats to avoid the lens. This was well planned. Do you want to see the . . . ?"

Finnigan nodded.

This was not the original video but edited snippets of it. The investigator let it run forward a bit, to an obvious edit, and the scene resumed. "Eighteen minutes later," he said.

The security door opened and two men in stylish pinstripe suits stepped out. Both carried overcoats but hadn't put them on. Both were in their late fifties or early sixties. Both had white shirts and striped club ties, very conservative. Both had some sort of round lapel pin, a sigil of the bank, no doubt.

"The van doesn't surprise them," Finnigan said, speaking mostly to himself. "It's not parked illegally. Some kind of bank logo? A well-known delivery company?"

"That's good. I thought the same thing. We didn't recover enough of the Opal side panel to tell."

The two men talked. The smaller of the two was one of those people who talked with their hands, fingers splayed, elbows out, as if miming a story. The taller one laughed, and it seemed genuine.

You could tell just by looking they were old friends.

A white flare obscured the scene, followed by static.

"I can get you still frames, but the overpressure of the explosion was significant," Vonlathen said. "The last frame doesn't show much more than this. Chassot—that's him, the taller fellow—and Brecher were almost vaporized. We would have had trouble identifying them had it not been for the video and for their shoes."

That wasn't unusual. A lot of bombing victims were blown

out of their shoes, Finnigan knew, because the blast wave of an explosion tends to surf a few inches above the street surface.

"The cleric made a YouTube video. Did he say why this guy was targeted?"

"Adrian Chassot had arranged for loans to Egypt and Alsharq. The loans were to go toward an irrigation canal but the cleric claimed they were for American oil interests."

Finnigan shrugged. "There *are* American oil interests in that part of the Mediterranean. I wonder if he was telling the truth."

The investigator shrugged. "I'm a dumb cop, Michael. What do I know from petro-politics?"

"My partner is talking to an international investment banker right now. I'll make sure she asks him."

"Give me your email, I'll send you this video. Also my case files." Vonlathen tucked away his phone. "When the bombings continued, my colleagues and I begged to go to France and Spain. Form a task force. But the bosses handed the investigation over to the intelligence agencies. A bunch of flatfoots would just get in the way."

He sounded bored, but Finnigan recognized that as a thin veneer over anger.

"I hope this has been helpful," Vonlathen said. "And you notice how I haven't once asked exactly what your role is in all this? Your bona fides were good. My own boss said I should speak to you. But . . . ?"

"My partner and I got a contract to bring in this cleric guy."

Vonlathen nodded. The words *bounty hunter* never came up. "Ah. Can you?"

"I don't know. We're good. We might not be this good."

Vonlathen scratched his neck. "If the Geneva Police Department cannot bring in this cleric and the Khamsin Sayef, I honestly don't care who does. Besides which . . ."

His voice faltered. Finnigan waited.

"It is absolutely none of my business what shape the cleric is in when he's captured. Healthy, wounded, dead, disintegrated. Deliver him in cuffs or in a box; I'll sleep like a baby."

Finnigan nodded, getting the message.

"Do you know Geneva?"

"First time. And I'm on a budget."

"Eating in Geneva is only expensive for tourists. Come, I'll show you."

C10

Chen Yiu, head of the signal intelligence unit for Sooner, Slye, and Rydell, cleaned his desk with ammonia wipes. He also cleaned the handset on his phone, plus the cradle upon which the handset rested. He cleaned his keyboard then Purelled his hands.

Then he initiated a video call with Colonel Cole Sanger.

Sanger was seated in his office in Madrid. Chen recognized the framed medieval map of the world on the wall behind the colonel. He didn't like Sanger; he didn't like most of the military types with whom he worked. Sanger, like the rest, was cold and calculating, and were used to giving orders and being obeyed. Chen Yiu had a PhD in applied mathematics. He didn't much appreciate taking orders from those whose math skills consisted of counting the chevrons or stars on another man's uniform.

Sanger took the video call but continued to go through notes on a legal pad, turning pages that momentarily bloomed into view like yellow algae at the bottom of the video image. "Any good news?"

"We might have a little more information on that maritime group, St. Nicholas Salvage & Wrecking."

Sanger nodded, scratched notes on his pad.

"It's the name. St. Nicholas. It came up in internal discussions at the CIA."

Sanger glanced up, the light catching his close-cut hair, which might or might not have been blond. "I'm not following."

"We have access to the CIA's email and telecommunications systems. We—"

"Chen," the colonel said, and stopped writing. He looked into his pinhole camera. His eyes were crystal blue. "That's not necessarily something I need to know, is it?"

Chen blinked. He wasn't sure how to respond. In what set of circumstances could someone at Sooner, Slye, and Rydell think *not knowing* something was advantageous to *knowing* something?

"Whatever." He shrugged. "Anyway, the station chief in Madrid—ah, her name is Pryor, comma, Margaret Anne—she mentioned St. Nicholas in a text to her personal assistant."

Sanger set down his pen. Whatever he'd been writing, his attention locked on the video screen now. "Annie. She goes by Annie Pryor. When?"

"Yesterday. We added *St. Nicholas* and *Cyprus* to our usual key word searches. The algorithm spat this out. This Pryor woman sent a text to her assistant. It read . . ."

He brought up the image on his widescreen monitor so he could see it and still see Sanger. "Ah, *thanks for covering at budget meeting. St. Nicholas meeting fruitful. See you in 30.*"

"You have access to text messages inside the CIA station?"

Chen smiled. "Can you imagine us *not* having that?"

"I . . ." Sanger shut his mouth and smiled, shaking his head ruefully. "Never mind. Thank you, well done. This is the highest priority, okay?"

"Might be a wild goose chase."

Sanger said, "No. There can't be two topics right now that are top-of-mind for the CIA Madrid Station and for the CNI. This is connected to the unnamed cleric and his group."

Chen said. "I'll call when we get more."

"I'm going to ask the partners for additional resources. I want a full-court press on this St. Nicholas company. Everything. I want to call in the corporate division too, for their articles of incorporation. And I want to get boots on the ground on Cyprus."

"That'll mean more data streaming my way," Chen said, but not as a complaint, just an observation.

"You can handle it."

"Yes," Chen Yiu said. "We can."

C11

Fiero had deplaned in Como, a gorgeous and bustling community snuggled between blue-green peaks that straddled the Italian–Swiss border and overlooked the lake that shared its name. The place was jammed with tourists this time of year, but then it almost always was.

They'd brought the Ducati, wheeling it down the long wooden dock from the pontoon plane into town. From there, she threw on her helmet and snaked up the mountain via a tourist-clogged switchback road to Bellagio. The going was torturously slow, and she spent as much time balanced with one motorcycle boot down on the pavement as she did actually moving.

But she did arrive and queued up to get a ticket on one of the ferries that ply the route between the communes of Bellagio, Menaggio, and Varenna. Lago de Como looked a bit like a stick figure running man or an upside-down Y, with the three stunning villages located across from each other where the three finger lakes come together.

She wouldn't necessarily need the bike on this mission, but jobs tend to change quickly, and she'd appreciate the flexibility if the need arose for a Plan B.

Gunther Kessler, known as Ways and Means, met her at the Varenna dock, wearing a yellow suit and a bow tie. He was an egg-shaped man with an egg-shaped head, bald, with thick glasses. He all but bounced on the balls of his feet as Fiero came into view, wheeling the bike off the ferry.

Behind him, the town hugged the blue-blue coast and tourists strolled languidly around mustard and terracotta-red buildings, like something out of a nineteenth-century impressionist painting.

"Katalin! My god, you're a vision!"

Fiero spoke a wide variety of languages but German wasn't one of them, so they stuck to English. "Gunther. Thank you for—"

"You must let me buy you dinner! You must!" He seemed to flutter a few inches off the ground.

"I ate on the plane. We need—"

"Good, smart. Avoiding Italian food. Don't blame you. A drink?"

"That would be . . ." Her voice petered out. "You don't like Italian food?"

"God, who does?" he sighed in despair.

She thought for a few seconds. "Every other living soul on earth?"

"The bank sent me to hide here, so hide I do. Do they care that this place is barely habitable? Don't be silly."

She never, ever understood Ways and Means. She knew he'd managed to steal millions upon millions for the bank where he was a senior executive. So embarrassed were they—and so grateful—that they hid Gunther Kessler away in Varenna, far from the eyes of prying international bank investigators. Here he continued to play the role of a monetary Geppetto, moving money around the globe and raking in absurd piles of secret cash for his bank and their clients. And for his friends.

Among which St. Nicholas Salvage & Wrecking was counted. Again, Fiero didn't quite know why.

"Come, come! A drink!"

She had hoped for a shot of whiskey or a vodka, but the portly German led her to an adorable little restaurant decked out in alpine wood with stenciled flower tendrils on all the beams. He'd reserved a table overlooking the lake, with a sturdy brass ice bucket and a bottle of German Sekt.

A server brought frosted flutes and opened the wine. The girl was blond and wore an extremely short calico uniform based on a *Heidi* theme. Fiero glanced around to see if the girl had a shepherd's staff. Or a stripper pole.

"This comes from a little winery I've been using to launder money," Kessler boasted. "It's perfect. Made in the *méthode traditionnelle*, of course. Much superior to French Champagne. A toast!"

She sipped. The wine was heavy and sweet, a sparkling cough syrup. She winced and tried to make it look like a smile.

"We're looking into a terrorist organization," she said.

"Ah." Kessler's face fell. So much for romance. "The Khamsin Sayef, Michael said."

She nodded. "Their first bomb was three years ago in Paris but this year, three more. They started with a banker in Geneva. Michael's there now. I'm hoping you can tell us a little about why the group targeted this man."

Kessler gulped his wine. Fiero thought hers would make a pretty good solvent for cleaning her guns, but she kept that to herself.

"Six people died. I remember," he said, cleaning the lenses of his thick glasses with a corner of the tablecloth. "Adrian Chassot was the target. I knew him, of course. Had known him for years.

Decent, lovely man. Terribly upright and honest, but I can over-look such shortcomings."

"Not everyone has your flair for criminality," she said.

He blushed. "That's too kind. Accurate, but kind. My dear Adrian never stole a bean. Very Swiss. A ticktock man; you know the term?"

She nodded. "The other banker who died? He wasn't directly targeted?"

"Cedric Brecher. He and I had worked together in Paris. Not really a banker so much as, ah, an efficiency expert. No soul what-soever. A dull and officious man."

"One shouldn't speak ill of the dead."

Kessler poured himself more of the sparkling wine. "Really? Speaking ill of the living can get you slapped. The dead rarely take umbrage."

"Fair enough. The official voice of the Khamsin Sayef is a nameless cleric. He made a video, taking credit for the bombing. He said Adrian Chassot had been investing in Egypt and Alsharq on behalf of American oil interests."

"He was not," Kessler said. "I can attest to that. I, myself, have invested heavily in American oil and natural gas interests in that region of the world. I'd know if Adrian had been in that game."

"Chassot said he'd brokered a deal to finance an agricultural project in the Middle East. Do you know if that's true?"

The German shrugged. "It sounds aboveboard, honest, humanitarian, and noble. I wouldn't touch it with a ten-meter pole, myself. But yes, I can check to see if Adrian's bank dealings in Alsharq were going where he said they were going."

"Might not be easy," she said. "The capital of Alsharq is having another of its regularly scheduled revolutions. The current government is bombarding portions of the city. It's block-to-block fighting, I hear."

He frowned. "Why do you and Michael want to find this Khamsin Sayef group?"

She smiled. "We're being paid an obscene amount of money."

"Ah." He brightened up. "Now that I understand. Yes, I'll look into it. Into Adrian Chassot's whole unit at the bank. His office might have been involved in something else. I'm happy to help. Adrian Chassot was a nice man. He had a lovely family. His wife is Danish, you know. Widow, I should say. Yes, I'll look into this for you."

"Thank you. I should rendezvous with Michael." She patted her lips, dropped her napkin on the table next to the still-full flute.

"Can you stay for dinner?"

"Thank you, no."

"Another drink?"

"Alas . . ."

"Have you considered being a kept woman?"

"Gunther, we value your assistance so much. My shooting you would be a waste of resources."

"You see?" he said. "You're so practical. Just like me. We're very, very alike, my dear Katalin. We're practically soul mates."

Fiero rose. "I haven't a soul."

Gunther gulped his wine. "That's what I just said."

C12

The world first heard of the group the Khamsin Sayef three years earlier, in the bombing death of CIA Station Chief Dinah Mariner and her family. After a long slumber, the extremist group started up again in January with the death of banker Adrian Chassot in Geneva.

The next bomb, in May of that year, killed engineer Rick Caldwell in the Alpine town of Annecy, France.

The investigation would move there next.

Finnigan wasn't done in Geneva, however. He had more witnesses to track down, case files to read, unedited video to watch. He wanted to know more about the van. He wanted to see the forensic analysis of the bomb components. Chassot and the other fellow, Brecher, hadn't been outside long before the bomb went off. Had the crime-scene techs found evidence of a remote detonator? Another camera to monitor when the target was in place?

Finnigan needed to learn more about banking, and about Adrian Chassot. He hoped that Fiero was getting much of that from Ways and Means.

She called him that evening and reported in on her meeting. Despite the seriousness of the conversation, Finnigan found himself lying on his back on the double bed in his room, laughing his ass off.

"Are you heading to France?" she asked.

"Gimme a day. I've got a lot more to absorb here."

After a pause over the line, Fiero said, "Something bothering you?"

"Yeah. Something I saw or heard today. Just not sure what. It'll come to me. Are you riding your bike to Annecy?"

"God, no," she said. "The ride from Italy to France has horrible long tunnels through the Alps. I hate riding that route. I've called Lachlan."

"Good. I'll see you in France."

They hung up.

LACHLAN SUMNER PICKED FIERO UP in one gorgeous lake surrounded by imposing peaks, crossed the Alps in style, and set her down in another, Lac d'Annecy, north of the looming Massif des Bauges and the famed Mont Blanc.

The ancient downtown core looked as Alpine as it did French, the old town bisected by a quirky little river filled with gargantuan swans and lined by cafés and restaurants whose offerings were, again, as much Swiss as they were French.

Fiero had been a soldier, a spy, and an assassin. She had no skill whatsoever as an investigator. Nor the patience to learn.

Where to start?

Or, more properly: What would Michael do? He'd magically conjure up people who *wanted* to talk to him. No matter where they went or the nature of the case, Finnigan found people who simply opened up to him.

That was weird, she thought, but weirder still, it had happened to her as well. She'd never found it easy to make friends. She lacked the ability to chat. When she and Finnigan had agreed to partner up—a spook and a detective, they possessed complementary skill-sets—she assumed they'd be successful. She never dreamed he'd become a friend.

Now on strange turf, and on her own, Fiero went with her *what would Michael do* scenario. A quick Google search resolved the question of a starting point. Engineer Rick Caldwell had been dining with his wife at an outdoor café within sight of the twelfth-century island prison, Le Palais de l'Île. He'd come to town for some sort of engineering project involving the city's canals.

Fiero headed for the restaurant.

She stood across the street from the restaurant, in her matchstick jeans and T-back tank and motorcycle boots, and saw . . . nothing. Nothing of importance, at any rate. The bombing had been in May; this was August. The café was fully restored, as were the adjacent businesses. All the smashed mortar had been repaired; the entire block of shattered windows replaced. The outside tables, under a deep-red awning advertising *crêpes* and *glaces*, were filled with American and Asian tourists, enjoying the sun, eating and drinking, taking selfies.

Fiero thought: If I stand here for ten minutes, I'll see something important. Something Michael would appreciate.

The canal was lined with wooden boxes, each stuffed to overflowing with pink and white flowers. Bikes were chained between them. Fiero found an empty slot and leaned against the black iron railing.

She made it three minutes before boredom set in. "*Joder,*" she muttered. *Fuck it.*

The crime scene had refused to give her even an inkling of a notion.

CI3

Sooner, Slye, and Rydell had all the pertinent data on the de Havilland Otter owned by the mysterious maritime salvage company that had to be a front for someone that was on the radar of the American and Spanish intelligence services.

The American military contractor had offices throughout Europe, as well as in Asia, South America, and Africa. Every time the de Havilland filed a flight plan and sought permission to land on a body of water, Suicide Ride would be there.

The Otter pilot sought and received permission to land at Lac Léman, near the western point of the lake and the city of Geneva. It took off again and flew to Lac d'Annecy, just a bit south of the first body of water, in France. While the plane was still in Turkish airspace, Suicide Ride had sent three-person teams to both Geneva and Annecy, to figure out who these St. Nicholas chumps were.

It wasn't difficult to create two teams in a little under an hour. Sooner, Slye, and Rydell had seventeen offices throughout Europe with roughly three hundred operatives available. Most of those were on one job or another; the military/intelligence contractor worked for most of the State and Foreign Service offices of the NATO alliance, and also hired itself out to the upper echelons of the Fortune 500. Still, Colonel Cole Sanger had been given the highest priority, and he could take resources from any of the seventeen offices, no questions asked.

The Annecy team consisted of two Americans and a Frenchman; the preferred protocol was to have one native resident in each field team. The Americans were a former Navy SEAL with the basic build and demeanor of a great white shark, a woman who'd served as a military police investigator in the army, and an ex-cop, formerly of the French *Police nationale,* who'd been raised in Lyon, not far from Annecy.

Surveillance on the woman who emerged from the de Havilland wasn't all that hard: she was five ten and stunning. The SEAL and the French cop agreed that this gig would be better than most; the ex-MP just rolled her eyes.

It was the MP who got close enough to the dark woman to get several good photos from various angles. The photos were forwarded—highest priority—to the Sooner, Slye, and Rydell intelligence office in Galveston.

It took the facial recognition experts in Texas less than sixty minutes to come up with the name Katalin Fiero Dahar, a (supposedly) retired agent of la Centro Nacional de Inteligencia.

The field team reported to Cole Sanger in Madrid, confirmation that the wild goose chase had paid off, and that this St. Nicholas thing was a cover for a CNI op.

MEANWHILE, IN GENEVA, a second three-man team reported that the other person to step off the de Havilland was a man, about five eight, with three-days' beard and wavy hair. This guy met with a Swiss criminal investigator, shared a beer, toured the crime scene of Bomb Number 2—the banker—then grabbed dinner with his host.

That Suicide Ride team never got close enough to get a decent photo of the target; the Swiss cop gave them the dead eye every time they got near.

The target retired to a hotel room after dinner, ordered up a room-service beer, and asked the front desk not to be disturbed.

THE NEXT MORNING IN ANNECY, Fiero walked around for two hours, jumping in and out of offices and stores, stopping passersby to ask directions, making detailed notes in a pad she'd just purchased. She ranged from the train station, through the shabby business sector, into the touristy area around the main canal, and returned to the station. Then she started the rotation all over again.

In two hours, Fiero got a pretty good feel for Annecy. The canal made a natural division in the old town, with footbridges every so often. It all became a bit of a maze, especially when the tourists were out in force. It was easy enough to get turned around.

It also made surveillance a foot race: you could drive near the train station or the working-class side of town, but no privately owned cars were allowed in the old town.

The three-person surveillance team stayed just slightly outside her peripheral vision. They used a Vespa scooter, plus two on foot, switching every forty minutes or so. They all had backpacks and changed clothes every so often: hats, scarves, light sweaters, sunglasses.

Fiero called Lachlan Sumner, who'd stayed in the same hotel that night, and asked him to dig out one of the company's fake ID sets and to rent a particular type of vehicle. St. Nicholas had several sets of IDs, thanks to the good and predictable corruption of the Cypriot banks.

It took him a little while—it was a weird request—but he found just the thing she needed.

At one point, Fiero passed Lachlan Sumner, who didn't make eye contact. He leaned against an old and ill-painted gelato vendor's bike. The handlebars, seat, and rear wheel of the bike were welded like a chimera onto a boxy freezer on four small wheels. Fiero moved past him without stopping and, maybe a minute later, he folded his map and moved off in the opposite direction.

FIERO'S PERAMBULATIONS WERE DRIVING the three followers nuts. She didn't seem to be going anywhere, just rotating around the same central core of streets over and over again. At first, they assumed she was trying to ditch her tail, but she was simply moving too slowly to do that, stopping every so often to jot down some notes or to peer in a store window. Had she made them? Maybe, but as counterintuitive as it sounded, she was moving as if to *avoid* losing them, rather than the opposite.

Right around two in the afternoon, she checked her smartphone, then moved slowly along the Quai de l'Île, threading gingerly through the knots of outdoor tables and tourists. Her left hip brushed against the iron barrier between the diners and Le Thiou, the canal. They were on the northern side of the canal. She cut quickly across the little footbridge at Passage de l'Île, winding through the narrow alley into the market square on the south side of the canal.

The big American was on the Vespa at this point, and he hung back near the square of Église St-François de Sales simply because there wasn't enough room for him to get much closer in the tight confines of the canal-side avenues.

The threesome had communications arrays that looked like

the earbuds of an iPhone. The American woman tapped her earbud and said, "I'll cut around on Rue Perrière; cut her off."

Why not? She'd made this same passage three times.

That left the ex-cop from Lyon to follow Fiero on foot, nudging past the diners on Quai de l'Île, taking the same hard left onto the tight, humpbacked little bridge at Passage de l'Île, onto the south side of the canal, in the darkened shadow of the twelfth-century prison.

As he emerged onto the south side, Michael Finnigan stepped out of a little card shop, grabbed him by the collar, and plowed a fist into his gut. The man from Lyon folded in two.

Fiero appeared from out of another small passage and whisked away the man's communications piece, as well as his wallet.

Before he knew who'd attacked him, Finnigan hauled the man around and flipped him over his hip, into the open top of the wheeled freezer box of the gelato bike that their pilot had bought used that morning.

The ex-cop from Lyon crumpled into the empty freezer, landing on his neck and shoulders, his feet in the air.

Finnigan reached into his jacket, pulled forth a Taser, and zapped the ex-cop. Then he folded his legs down and closed the top.

Fiero turned quickly and kept walking around the Quai des Vieilles, south of the canal, screwing the stolen earbuds into place. She immediately heard the chatter of the other two watchers.

"Got her," the American woman said from the larger footbridge at Rue Perrière. "Looks like she's making the rounds again."

The American man on the Vespa said, "Well, shit. This got real boring real fast. At least she's easy on the eyes."

Fiero repressed a smile.

Neither American noticed that the ex-cop from Lyon didn't chime in. They assumed he was on Fiero's six, hanging back out of sight.

FINNIGAN WHEELED THE MAKESHIFT BIKE / gelato freezer—with the innards removed the box up front was the same temperature as the air around them—west to Rue Sainte-Claire, dodging around slow-moving clusters of tourists, past French restaurants with names like Tête de Cochon and L'Alpin, and snack joints with Americanized names like Yogolicious Yogurt. He turned the little wheeled cart right onto Rue de la République, walked it back over the canal into the commercial core of the city, where their pilot, Lachlan, awaited with a rented van. The two of them loaded the gelato bike, and the unconscious ex-cop, into the van.

ALL MORNING AND THROUGHOUT THE NOON HOUR, Fiero had been working hard not to lose the threesome until Finnigan could get down from Geneva to join her. She had spotted the surveillance team the day before, as soon as she'd left their seaplane. She'd immediately called Finnigan, who faked a night in at his hotel in Geneva then secretly grabbed a fast bus due south to Annecy.

She'd made it easy for the threesome to tail her as she walked in circles, writing down the words *I'm pretending to write* over and over and over again in various languages.

When the rolling gelato cart and Michael were in place, and when they'd made their grab, Fiero had finally been freed up to lose the other two followers. Listening to their covert conversation on her own comms unit, she made her move.

She lost them in under three minutes.

She reconnected with the boys at the train station, hopping into the van.

"So who's your dance partner?" Finnigan asked, pulling back into traffic on Avenue de Brogny.

She showed him the wallet she'd stolen. "Sooner, Slye, and Rydell."

Finnigan rolled his eyes. "Are you fucking kidding me?"

She shook her head.

"Sons a' bitches!"

"It took them fifteen minutes to confirm they lost me and another fifteen to realize they lost their friend." She rolled down the window and threw out the comms unit and its earbuds. "They changed frequencies. The other two are Americans, by the way."

Lachlan Sumner dragged the ex-cop out of the ice-cream box, set him on the floor of the van, and tased him again. Fiero edged back into the rear of the van and used the man's own handcuffs, linking his wrists behind his back. She searched him for trackers.

Finnigan drove out of the village, curving along the lake, toward the commercial dock that catered to pontoon planes like theirs.

Lachlan revved up the de Havilland as Finnigan and Fiero dragged the semiconscious ex-cop into a shed that was used to store garbage and recycling cans. Finnigan picked the Yale lock, and they dumped the man inside.

They raced back to the plane.

C14

Within five minutes of climbing aboard, Lachlan had the plane lined up for a takeoff along the long axis of Lac d'Annecy.

Because of the nature of their work, the de Havilland served as a home away from home. The rear third of the fuselage had been turned into a storage room with all the equipment—from weapons to toilet paper to extra toner for the printer—they might need. The central portion of the fuselage was taken up by a low table, bolted to the floor, and four club chairs. The chairs could be swung to face each other and had hinged backs and pop-out leg supports, transforming into passable but uncomfortable beds. In the event of turbulence, two airliner-style seats sat beside each other along one wall, with headrests and three-point restraints.

As the pontoon plane rose out of the lake, Fiero popped the cork on a bottle of a tart tempranillo from a winery in the Rioja region of Spain—her father, Alexandro Fiero, co-owned the winery—and poured it into the plastic glasses they used in flight.

She leaned forward over the low table, letting Finnigan pace and rant. Her beat-up messenger bag rested against a leg of the table.

"Suicide Ride? What the fuck, man!"

"So what?"

He slapped his forehead. "They're huge. They have operations on every continent. Their clients include the US State Department! And we just made one of their teams look like the Three Stooges. Plus we kidnapped their guy and stole his gear."

"Which was helpful," she responded. She handed Finnigan a glass. "They started it."

"Yeah, but we declared war. No way these guys are gonna take it lying down."

Fiero had retrieved a can of lemon-flavored seltzer water and took it forward to Lachlan. She returned and opened a bag of toast rounds and a jar of tapenade. She coiled her long frame into the club chair, one boot heel up on the seat, her knee pointing straight up, and rested her chin on her knee. "You're scared of them?"

"Fuck, yeah."

"Options?"

"We contact them. Reach out. Olive branch."

"You think?"

Finnigan shrugged and glugged his wine. He had absolutely no palate whatsoever; the man had never had a beer or a wine or even a cup of coffee he hadn't liked.

Fiero nibbled on a toast round. "Tell me about them."

"Military," Finnigan said. "Espionage. Law enforcement. They started out small, like McTavish."

Their friend Brodie McTavish had been fighting other people's wars for pay for more than twenty-five years. His clients had included St. Nicholas Salvage & Wrecking more than once.

"Difference being," Finnigan said, "Suicide Ride got huge. They had a couple thousand solders fighting in Afghanistan and

Iraq under some really cool name. Black Flag, or something. Mostly they were known for providing security for State Department officials and other noncombatants in Iraq's Green Zone. In actuality, they were working with warlords and heroin cartels in Afghanistan. Word got out. There were congressional hearings, exposés in the *Washington Post* and on CNN, and some low-level guys did time in Leavenworth. The contractors pulled out of the war zones. But the whole thing was way too profitable to just go away. The company changed its name to Sooner, Slye, and Rydell. Went corporate."

"Annie Pryor told us some of this."

They both reached for the glasses and the bottle as Lachlan changed altitude and direction. Finnigan sank into one of the chairs. "The rest I know because they tried to recruit me once."

"When?"

"When I was a deputy US Marshal. Couple of months before we met. They were paying crazy-good salaries to get the best people."

"Then why recruit you?"

Finnigan threw a disc of toast at her. Most people would have laughed and ducked. Fiero smiled and caught it. After three years together, her eye-hand coordination and her reflexes—which had landed her on the Spanish Olympic biathlon team—still surprised him.

"Why did you say no?"

Finnigan drained his glass. "I was working for a big bureaucracy in the public sector. I didn't want to work for a big bureaucracy in the private sector. But I'll tell you the truth: when you and I met, and you talked about doing something different, I had Suicide Ride in the back of my mind."

"Hmmm . . ." She spread the olive paste on a round and handed it across the table. "If my memory serves, you shot me that day."

"You stabbed me."

"You had it coming."

"That's fair." He ate. The de Havilland changed course again.

"I say we call up the Big Bad and offer them a peace treaty. Soon as we land. We patch this up."

"D'you think they will accept?"

He shrugged. "We didn't know the guy we bagged was their man, right? They were staking us out. We're looking for this Sword of the Storm group; it coulda been them."

"True."

They sat and sipped wine and thought about it. Neither of them registered the steady rumbling of the twin Pratt & Whitney engines; they'd grown accustomed to it.

Fiero said, "Think they'll buy it?"

"Why not?"

"We left their man handcuffed in a garbage bin."

"Precaution," Finnigan countered. "He wasn't in danger. Someone was gonna find him."

"We destroyed one of their communications units."

"They probably buy those things wholesale."

"We embarrassed their team."

"Their team embarrassed themselves. Didn't need our help."

Fiero reached down into her messenger bag and withdrew a roll of euros. "I stole his money."

Finnigan pondered that one, then snapped his fingers. "Expenses. We had to buy that gelato bike."

She nodded. "You have an explanation for everything."

"That's because I'm a businessman. I speak their language."

She reached into the messenger bag again and tossed something over the table. Finnigan caught it against his chest.

"I stole his watch."

"Why?"

She sipped her wine. "My father's birthday is coming up."

Finnigan eyed the watch. Then his partner. Then the watch. Then his partner.

She cocked an eyebrow at him.

"Gimme a second on this one . . ."

C15

René Vonlathen of the Swiss Federal Intelligence Service had called his counterpart in Annecy and arranged for more surveillance footage and case files to be mailed to Finnigan. The de Havilland was rigged for Wi-Fi, and as they crossed into Greek airspace on the route home, Finnigan loaded the new videos onto his tablet.

In May, an unidentified person stopped at an outdoor café in Annecy and selected a two-top. The person wore a floppy hat and a largish scarf, and it might have been a small man or an average-sized woman.

A woman, Finnigan thought, through he wasn't sure.

She sat with her back to the nearest and best CC camera, which was on one of the squares near the main canal, with its white iron tables and their peppermint-colored parasols.

She set a backpack on the ground by her table then adjusted the chair, lifting it and setting it down a foot from where it had been. The backpack nestled squarely between the four legs of the chair.

Finnigan played the video for a few seconds, stopped it, ran it backward, played it again. He shook his head.

Fiero had been using a whetstone to sharpen a combat knife. "What?"

"Suspect's backpack. It's the exact same color as the chairs at the café. I mean, *exact*. Wow, that's smart."

On the video, the suspect sat and the backpack became all but invisible unless you were looking for it, one more off-white thing amid a garden of off-white table and chair legs.

The woman sat with her back to a couple. They looked like Americans, in their forties. The man had a sandy beard and longish hair, looking more like a few missed haircuts than an actual hairstyle decision. The woman grinned broadly and took phone photos of seemingly everything.

"Rick Caldwell," Finnigan said, glancing at the case file notes balanced on the arm of his chair. "And his wife, Joan. He was an engineer. Worked on a project in Egypt and Alsharq. She ran some kinda tourism website based out of Paris."

Fiero hadn't been looking at the video but nodded. She knew Finnigan often spoke to himself when he was thinking.

The suspect ordered an espresso, nursed it, left coins in the plastic tray the size and shape of a deck of cards. Finnigan realized the suspect wore gloves. No fingerprints.

He or she left the backpack. It nestled between the legs of the now-empty chair, and the back of the chair was inches from the back of Rick Caldwell's chair.

The suspect walked out of the frame without ever looking up. As she walked, Finnigan became more convinced it was a woman.

The weather was slightly overcast that day and the tables were three-quarters empty. A cold wind had been blowing off Lac d'Annecy. With few customers outside, the waitstaff didn't bust a gut clearing that table. Why should they?

Rick and Joan Caldwell chatted and smiled. She shot images of passersby, of a small vase of alpenroses on their table, the blossoms lipstick pink. Rick Caldwell leaned back, front legs of his chair an inch of the ground, as guys sometimes do. They drank white wine and chatted. Joan Caldwell adjusted her own scarf several times, probably chilly but not wanting the moment to end by saying anything.

The bomb obliterated the Caldwells and six sets of tables and chairs, shattered the café's windows, set the tables' pink-and-red parasols shooting away like javelins.

Finnigan didn't flinch away. He ran the scene again on one-quarter speed.

He knew the couple died without feeling anything. The bomb disintegrated them. He knew from the report that nothing of them remained intact. No way they suffered.

"Fuckin' . . ." he muttered, taking notes on a legal pad. He always made notes irrespective of the lines on the paper, sometimes writing with the lines, sometimes at right angles, sometimes cockeyed between earlier notes. He circled thoughts, and a page of Finnigan's notes often looked like a jigsaw puzzle, words upside down to each other, or perpendicular, or curved weirdly because he'd misjudged how much space he'd need for his latest thought. If anything ever happened to him, there would be no possible way for Fiero to translate the notes. Better to just burn them.

He loaded another video onto the tablet and watched it. Lachlan Sumner called back on the PA system to tell them they were an hour out from the Mediterranean.

René Vonlathen had labeled the next video, *Giveaway vehicle* in English. Finnigan figured he'd meant *getaway*.

This video was grainy and black and white, where the last one had been in color and high-def. The camera for this one had been three stories off the ground and showed an alley behind whitewashed commercial buildings. The setting was in a less touristy area of the town.

A van sat nose-first against a dumpster. The van might have been white, but it was caked in road dirt. The plates were semiobscured with speckles of clay or mud.

The suspect in the hat walked into the alley, into the camera frame, hands jammed into the pockets of her coat. She did not look up. She knew where the CC camera was, just as she'd known back at the café.

If it was a *her*.

She climbed into the passenger side of the van. The taillights blinked on.

The van tried to turn around. The driver tucked it twenty degrees to the right, rolled backward, turned the wheel twenty more degrees, rolled forward, did it all over again a couple of times, the van inching around, counterclockwise.

Finnigan said, "Fucker drives like my grandma."

"Didn't your grandmother spend time in jail for car theft?"

"I meant my mom's mom."

"Ah."

"Here. Watch this." He leaned over the low table and showed her the tablet. Fiero watched the whole video, up to and including the dance of the van in the narrow confines of the alley.

"Notice anything?"

"The man who walked into the alley is a woman."

"Yeah, but I mean anything about the driver?"

She squinted at the screen, watched it again.

"He's turning to his left," she said. "He should have turned to his right. He'd have made it out of there in two, possibly three tries, rather than going backward and forward six or seven times."

"Right. You're a crappy driver, and even you saw that."

Fiero said, "I'm an excellent driver."

"Acknowledging limitations is no vice. You can fight, you can dance, you can swim. So you can't drive. It's not the end of the world. You can't sing, either."

"I have a lovely singing voice."

Finnigan shook his head. "That is just so sad."

He took the tablet back, consulted his weird mishmash of illegible notes. "So the Khamsin Sayef uses a woman to plant bombs. And their driver sucks, big time."

"Are those things important?"

"Yesterday, we didn't know that stuff. Today we do."

"Yes," Fiero persisted, "but is any of it important?"

Finnigan shrugged. "I don't know."

C16

Annie Pryor's team wanted her to wear a light ballistic vest and to pack the heavier SIG MK25 handgun. She declined, explaining that they wouldn't be necessary for a meeting in the fucking Renaissance.

Pryor had agreed to take a meeting with her counterparts in Spanish Intelligence, and with Spanish Foreign Minister José Ramón de Cordoba. The meeting would take place at the ancestral castle of the Cordoba clan, a massive pile of rock in the Aragon region sometimes referred to as the Fontainebleau of Spain.

The great castle, a stone megalith the color of wheat, hunkered over a river in an otherwise arid part of the country. It had been the seat of government in the fifteenth or sixteen century— Pryor was terrible at remembering things like that—and featured something like a hundred and forty rooms, long halls of ornate paintings, gilded frames and frescoed ceilings, tapestries so faded as to look like depictions of fog, and the baroque Chapel of Saint Vincent Ferrer, a golden oval built on two levels and overlooking the dammed-up river.

It was policy for all CIA personnel on foreign soil to make their whereabouts known, 24-7. This, despite the fact that senior personnel were lowjacked, with transponders built into their clothes, their wallets, their purses, even their holsters. It was a policy of redundancy, and Pryor was okay with that. She'd served under Dinah Mariner, the Paris station chief, who'd been blown to bits three years earlier along with her husband and daughter. Pryor took security seriously.

The parade grounds outside the Alcázar Real de Aragon looked, from the air, like part of an enormous chessboard, with oyster-shell squares separated by squares of emerald-green lawn. The bureaucratic offices of the old Aragon government flanked the parade grounds on two sides, two stories tall with row after row of terracotta chimneys. The two arms stuck straight out from the main castle and reminded Pryor of two concourses of an airport. Each held close to fifty offices on each floor, but almost all of the two administrative wings were closed these days, structurally unsafe, with floors rotting through.

As her helicopter approached, the great Alcázar seemed like an apt metaphor for much of Europe. Glorious, when seen from a distance, but with infrastructure ready to crumble into dust at any given second.

Her helicopter landed in the parade grounds next to three others. One belonged to the director of the Centro Nacional de Inteligencia. Another, she assumed, had delivered the foreign minister himself. His own family had ruled parts of modern-day Spain out of this great castle for a couple of centuries. He lived in Madrid, as had his father and grandfather, but this was still the ancestral home.

Pryor didn't know who owned the third helo on the ground, but she recognized it as a high-end civilian affair.

The foreign minister had called the meeting, asking for Pryor to meet a prominent Spanish leader to discuss the situation with the

Khamsin Sayef. The bombing in Barcelona, the death of an international activist like Victor Wu, had left certain elements of the Spanish community in an uproar. Spain's government and a large section of the Spanish business community had partnered with Victor Wu of the Clarion Group. They had financial skin in the game, even if they weren't personally terrified for their own lives.

Back in the day, CIA station chiefs hadn't been asked to hold businessmen's hands or to calm their fears. The job had become much more political over the decades. On occasion, Annie Pryor was more diplomat than spook. Nobody tells you that when you join the agency.

Pryor gathered her shoulder bag with its small satellite phone and SIG pistol, but no extra clips, and began walking between the massive shell and grass checkerboards toward the main hulk of the castle. She was glad she'd picked flat boots to go with her skirt and jacket, rather than heels. Twin stairs shaped like the letter *omega* wound around ground-level stable doors, up to an ornate entrance on the second floor. She found a cluster of important-looking people waiting there.

An aide met her halfway from the helipad. "Ms. Pryor?"

The aide was an android, she thought, one of the ubiquitous models found in most high-end European business and government circles: slim, young, beautiful, wearing heels, carrying advanced degrees in law or economics. Pryor had met a dozen of them in her time at the Paris and Madrid field offices. All completely identical.

"We are gathering outside while the Chancellery de Trastámara is being swept." The aide spoke flawless English. "Do you mind waiting two minutes?"

Pryor shifted her tote to her other shoulder. "Swept?"

The aide reddened. "For explosives, ma'am."

This was happening more and more throughout Europe. Even

before the Khamsin Sayef bombings, every few months some lone wolf went crazy and drove into a crowd, or set off a bomb, or hacked innocent bystanders. And neither the police nor the military/intelligence agencies seemed capable of doing anything about it. So the rich had begun hiring their own sweepers to look for explosives in their offices. They'd done this for listening devices for decades, since well into the waning days of the Cold War. Now the sweeps differed.

It galled. It was an admission of failure on the part of the CIA and the domestic intel agencies, Pryor thought. She understood why the aide blushed.

She and about seven other people stood atop the omega stairs and introduced themselves. Each important person had an aide, except for Pryor. She hadn't wanted to waste any personnel on a feel-good meeting.

The main double doors bloomed open—the doors dated back to the time of dinosaurs, or some such, she remembered, and had been designed by some famous so-and-so in honor of some great feat of such-and-such—and José Ramón de Cordoba lurched out amid his usual entourage of security and staff. Pryor had met him on several occasions, and they'd hit it off. De Cordoba was a quiet and efficient bureaucrat. He'd been an academic and an economist before turning to politics. He was tall, nearly six eight, and painfully thin, with horrible posture, a widow's peak of swept-back hair, and enormous ears. He bought expensive handmade suits that never fit right, and high-end Italian shoes that looked clownish on his huge feet. He greeted the others first, Pryor last.

"Annie." He leaned down and they air-kissed both cheeks.

"The chancellery of whoever is being swept?" she asked.

De Cordoba had a bit of the stage clown in him. He put one hand to the side of his mouth in the style of a vaudevillian, throwing a reveal out to the audience. "We tell the toffs that we're sweeping for explosives. Fact is, the castle has rats."

The aide look shocked. Pryor snorted a most unladylike laugh. "You know, some castles have cats."

"Do I look like I can afford cats?" He had joined the government twenty years earlier but could never shake his smart-aleck sense of humor, one that got him into trouble occasionally.

The aide received a text on a smartphone that likely was surgically adhered to her palm. She turned to them. "The chancellery is ready, Minister."

They entered the great hall, which stretched the depth of the castle, with vast, curved staircases off to either side and enormous portraits of kings and saints dominating the stone walls.

The aide made directly for the double doors, about thirty feet down the ornate corridor. The floor featured a complex wooden parquetry pattern under Pryor's boots. De Cordoba made introductions to everyone as the aide emerged, moments later, with a crew of three in blue-gray overalls, each carrying heavy boxes or backpacks of electronic equipment. Pryor knew who they were: the sweepers. A woman led the way and as soon as they stepped into the grand hall, she went to one knee and set down her thick-handled plastic box. Her movements were quick and precise as she reached into the box.

Pryor reached into her tote, her fingertips brushing the pebbled leather of her holster, even before she realized it.

But the sweeper pulled a monitor out of the bag, twisted open the butt end, and slid two D batteries into her palm. The device had a long, thick antenna like a walkie-talkie. Pryor knew it scanned for trace elements of the byproducts of explosives.

I'm more on edge than I thought, she realized, releasing her grip on the automatic.

The foreign minister, his entourage, Annie Pryor, and the aide all scrummed into the Chancellery de Trastámara, an ornate room with a chandelier the size of Pryor's apartment in Madrid and stained-glass windows that threw colored parallelograms around the room like shards of a shattered rainbow. It reminded her of the mother ship from *Close Encounters*. The walls were, again, ringed with portraits of gloomy men, several of whom shared the outsized ears and turkey necks of their host, de Cordoba. She liked the man enough that she tended to forget he was actual royalty.

Pryor kept her eyes on the backs of the three sweepers in the grand hall, as they packed away their tech. De Cordoba noticed. "An annoying truth of our time." He spoke without his usual broad humor. She nodded.

Since they had a little room away from the others, Pryor kept her voice low. "If this is about the bombing, there's not much I'm going to be able to tell your friends."

"It is about bombing," he replied, sotto voce. "And we're awaiting one last guest. He is, as you say, my friend. He's also a reasonable fellow. But the important things to know are these: He has the ear of the prime minister. He's a distant cousin of the king of Spain. And he's highly respected in the business and philanthropic communities. If he's assured the CIA is working with the CNI, that there is a plan to address the civil war in Alsharq and this Khamsin Sayef group, it will be an act of pouring oil on troubled waters."

"And you'll owe me a favor," Pryor added.

"And I'll owe you a favor." He flashed her his death's-head smile.

From the grand hall, a final guest arrived with his own coterie of aides. He was a tall, regal-looking man in a splendid suit, black hair going silver around his ears, his A. Lange & Söhne watch glinting on his wrist, a chunk of silvery metal that cost as much as Pryor's car.

"Ah!" De Cordoba beamed, and offered the newcomer the traditional Iberian air kiss. They gripped each other's shoulders like old comrades.

The newcomer turned to Pryor. His English carried an Eton/ Oxford lilt. "Ms. Pryor. Your time is most precious, and I cannot thank you enough for coming all this way to address our group."

The foreign minister said, "Annie, may I introduce my oldest friend, Alexandro Fiero."

C17

The partners arrived home, the de Havilland splashing down and coming easily to a stop at the lesser bay to the east of the hulking Venetian fortress, obscured from the downtown of the lovely seaside Cypriot town.

Bridget Sumner, their office manager, called via the cockpit satphone to report that strange men had been hanging about. One had made a delivery intended for the address down the block but knocking on their door instead, while two others dined at the Turkish restaurant on the ground floor and asked the waitstaff probing questions about their upstairs neighbors.

"I'm in Nicosia," Bridget said. In the left-hand seat of the cockpit, her husband visibly relaxed. "I just checked with Rafael. He recommended I head to the capital."

Inspector Rafael Triadis, their friend in the Cyprus Police, had obviously stepped in to help.

"Rafael said one of his officers received a largish bribe to answer questions about us," Bridget told them via the satellite link.

Finnigan said, "Okay. Lay low. Lachlan's on his way to you."

They disconnected.

Finnigan had wedged himself into the cockpit to take the call, seated in the right-hand copilot's chair. Fiero stood in the doorway with one forearm thrown over the top of the hatch and leaning in to listen. The mobile in the pocket of her skinny jeans vibrated. She cocked a hip to dig it out.

"Hugo Llorente," she said. She set the phone on speaker mode and listened to the telltale clicks of antieavesdropping technology filtering the call.

She said, "Hallo. Michael's here too." She chose English, so Llorente followed suit.

"You had a run-in with Sooner, Slye, and Rydell?" the intelligence commander asked.

Fiero smiled. "You heard."

"Yes, and if I were you, I'd be thinking about calling them up and asking for a truce. Please don't."

Finnigan twisted in the copilot's chair. "How come?"

"Because Sooner, Slye, and Rydell believes you to be a Spanish Intelligence operation," the older man replied. "A senior partner called me from their headquarters in Dallas, Texas. He was quite angry that two of my operatives had kidnapped and beat up one of his people."

"We didn't beat him up," Finnigan said. "Like, hardly at all."

"Well, they've positively identified Katalin. Not you, Mr. Finnigan. Not yet."

The partners exchanged looks. Fiero leaned her forehead against her forearm, resting against the top of the hatchway. "They are here in Kyrenia," she said. "Our office is under surveillance. They'll figure out who we are quickly enough."

"Agreed. Once they do, then suggesting a nice, convivial peace treaty might, just *might*, work," Llorente said. "They would never allow you to keep investigating the Khamsin Sayef, of course. Your investigation would end then and there."

Lachlan had retrieved powerful field glasses from a kit in the cockpit and was scanning the few access points to the lesser bay, looking for surveillance. No tourists ever used the lesser bay, with its commercial dock, oily waters, and high rocky shoals. They favored the colorful marina around which the downtown was built. It appeared as if the surveillance team had yet to figure out where the de Havilland docked.

"I should tell you," Llorente added, "they likely would try to buy you out. That's their modus operandi. And the money would be considerable."

Finnigan winked up at Fiero. "How considerable?"

"Considerably."

Finnigan said, "Can you get us in touch with a criminal investigator? Someone with Interpol maybe? Someone who can access law enforcement databases?"

"Why?"

"For years now," Finnigan said, "people have been asking you, *why?* And you're all enigmatic-like and going, *don't ask.* Yeah?"

Llorente didn't respond.

"'Sides, you owe us."

"And why is that?"

"Because the Suicide Ride goons were onto us from the time our plane landed in Geneva and Annecy. Long before we asked our first question. They were on us so fast they had to know we were coming. And that means . . ."

". . . The leak was in our shop. Ours, or that of Annie Pryor." They heard the old man sigh. "I warned you our operations were compromised."

"You misunderstand, sir," Fiero said, and her voice grew sharp. "We're not saying Centro Nacional de Inteligencia is compromised. We're saying *you* are. You came to us. Personally."

They waited, listening. The rangy New Zealander, Lachlan, kept his eyes on the docks.

Hugo Llorente waited a few beats. "Mr. Finnigan? You'll receive a text, today, from a criminal investigator not connected in any way to Spain or the Spanish government. You'll get all the help you need."

Fiero disconnected without saying a word. She reached out and touched Lachlan on the shoulder. He lowered the field glasses.

"Bridget's safe."

He nodded.

"Do you have enough petrol to get us to Larnaca?"

"'Course."

Finnigan turned to her. "You thinking of flying commercial back to Europe?"

She nodded.

"Me too. I wanna see the next crime scene. We could fly Tel Aviv to Barcelona, keep the de Havilland here in Cyprus so they can't track us. How's our stash?"

The partners kept money and false passports onboard the seaplane at all times. "Sufficient," Fiero said.

The partners left the flight deck as Lachlan buckled himself back into his seat. They picked two of the four club chairs and adjusted their own seat belts.

"Why do you need a criminal investigator?" Fiero asked. "The Khamsin Sayef isn't a criminal organization. They're terrorists."

He shrugged. "Just an idea I had."

They felt and heard the Pratt and Whitney engines rev to life.

C18

Cole Sanger called the meeting for 10:45 a.m. Spanish time, and everyone made sure they were present by 10:35 at the latest. Such was his reputation as a perfectionist. Some of those in the meeting were in Madrid; others attended via a proprietary bit of video software that made conference calls untraceable and unhackable.

The Khamsin Sayef team included four signal intelligence experts, seven on-the-ground surveillance experts, two real estate / banking experts to chase the money, and three fugitive-recovery team leaders who'd served in American special forces branches.

The only stranger in the room was a compact, pale-skinned man with badly cut hair. He could have been forty, maybe thirty-five, maybe forty-five. He had shock-blue eyes and a contained demeanor that might have been the result of excellent self-control but might also have been jet lag. He brought neither a notepad nor a laptop, just a cup of coffee.

Sanger sat at the head of the table. He wore a starched white shirt, sleeves buttoned, a blue-and-black striped tie knotted firmly under his chin. His trousers were creased, his shoes shined. None of his clothes were expensive, but all were fastidiously cared for. He opened a leather portfolio and took out a legal pad and a cheap pen, and squared them before himself. "Before we get started, this is Syarhey Valazko. He'll be joining us."

The very pale man nodded, his eyes on his coffee cup.

Two of the ex–army officers glanced toward each other. One of them said, "May I ask: What's Valazko's job here?"

Sanger said, "No. What do we know about the CNI team in Annecy?"

One of the investigators swiped his laptop to life. He touched some keys, and a four-year-old picture of Fiero popped up on one of the monitors, visible to those in the room and those watching via satellite. Everyone leaned around to study the photo, except Valazko, who'd found a price sticker on the bottom of his coffee cup and seemed inexplicably intent on peeling it off.

"Ah, the woman is definitely Katalin Fiero Dahar. For sure. She was an Olympic biathlon champion for Spain before joining the army, then the CNI. She crewed racing yachts in the Med. Just an all-around jock. We were under the impression she'd retired. We obviously were mistaken."

One of the Americans laughed. "Jesus, what a smoke-show! Can I be the one gets to bring her in?"

Sanger made notes on his legal pad. "We need to stay ahead of this St. Nicholas unit of Spanish Intelligence. If you have comments that lead to making that happen, don't hesitate to speak up. If your comments are just sexism, keep it to yourself. What do we know about the man she works with?"

"Don't know, sir," someone piped in via the video call. "We're scanning Spanish Intelligence files. Nothing so far."

Cole Sanger wrote that down. "Figure it out."

"Yessir."

Across the table, Syarhey Valazko sipped his coffee, his eyelids drooping.

"About Fiero Dahar," one of the computer experts chimed in. "We think she's an assassin. Part of Hugo Llorente's kill shop."

That drew the attention of the very pale man, who cocked his head, slightly, the way a dog will when he hears prey. He stopped fiddling with his coffee cup and studied the image on the screen.

He grew very still.

Sanger said, "Really?"

"Yessir. We're not for sure, but we think she's one of Llorente's shooters. These guys are supposed to have an impressive kill rate."

Sanger glanced at Valazko, who nodded a little.

"That makes no sense," Sanger said, pen hovering over his legal pad. "We know Spanish Intelligence is trying to capture the cleric and his operation. They want a show trial. There's no evidence they've tried to kill these people."

One of the criminal investigators shrugged. "Could be they've given up on that idea, sir. Could be they woke up to the real threat here. What's a trial gonna do? Piss off another raghead splinter cell?"

"Assassinations create martyrs," someone else chimed in. "No, the colonel's right. We've hacked all the CNI communications. Spain is looking to arrest these guys. Standing orders, all the way down from the prime minister."

They debated the issue a bit more. Sanger asked to hear from the team on Cyprus, which had tracked the tall, dark beauty and her mysterious partner that far. To everyone's surprise, it appeared as if they were stationed in Cyprus. Why Spain had a station there was anyone's guess. The island, situated between Turkey to the north, Syria to the east and Egypt to the south, had drawn international attention from the English (for their airbases), the Russians (for their corrupt banking system), and the Americans (for their offshore oil). But the Spanish?

The mysterious duo had fled Annecy, France, after capturing a Sooner, Slye, and Rydell operative. They'd filed a flight plan to Cyprus. But so far: nothing.

"Keep on them," Sanger said. "I don't know what their role is in all this, but they feel wrong. Anything else?"

They heard reports on the team tracking the funding for Sword of the Storm. They heard about center-left politicians in France and Spain who'd supported the Egyptian opposition, which leaned toward the West and away from radical Islam. One group of Spanish businessmen, the Galician Trust, had been particularly helpful for the Egyptian activists. Right up until they'd set off their first bomb in Paris.

"Listen up. I've heard from the partners in Houston. They want the murderers of Pete Newsom brought to justice. They want us to do it. If anyone else does it, we'll look weak. Looking weak will cut into the public image of Sooner, Slye, and Rydell. This is *the* priority of the entire company. Are we clear?"

Everyone nodded.

With nothing more to report, Sanger called the meeting closed. Those in the room packed up their belongings and left in groups of two or three. The video connection snapped off, the flat screens going charcoal gray, then black.

The very pale man finished his coffee.

Sanger returned his legal pad and his cheap pen to the fake-leather portfolio. "Assassin?"

Syarhey Valazko said, "Yes. I didn't know her name before this."

"But you know her?"

He shrugged. "Yes. We had competing interests. Once."

Sanger said, "Who won?"

Valazko blinked and smiled. Sanger decided not to press the point. "You're from Belarus. Belarus and Spain don't have that many common enemies. Do they?"

Valazko stood and moved to a cabinet with a sink in the corner of the room. He washed out his cup, wiped both the insides and outside with a square of paper towel, then set the towel on the cabinet and the cup upside down atop it to drain.

"Should we try to hire her away from the Spanish?" Sanger asked, also standing.

"Sure," Valazko said. "She's good."

"If need be, should we kill her?"

"Always an option."

"Could you do it?"

Syarhey Valazko chuckled a little bit. He washed his hands and wiped them with a paper towel and wadded the towel up, tossing it in the lined garbage can.

He didn't bother responding to the question.

C19

The partners spent the next day doing things they rarely did and worked hard to avoid.

They waited in queues at airports. They paced terminals. They ate junk food and drank bad beer—or at least Finnigan did—while keeping one ear cocked for flight announcements.

They crowded into a commercial 747 and flew economy.

That meant traveling without weapons.

Their first big purchase, three years earlier, had been the de Havilland Otter. Their proudest find had been Lachlan Sumner, the kick-ass pilot who could land on a steno pad. The Otter served as a de facto office, with most of the supplies they might need for a week or two of bounty hunting. It gave them flexibility and speed. And an arsenal, should the need arise.

Which it often did.

Flying commercial under false passports was an agony of inefficiency. But since Sooner, Slye, and Rydell had tagged the Otter, they had little choice in the matter.

They flew Lufthansa from Larnaca to Frankfurt, which took four hours. They had a three-hour delay on the ground before their flight to Barcelona, with nothing to do but feel anxious that the case was slipping away from them.

Sky News played on TV monitors throughout the airport. Reporters were covering the carnage in Baharos, the capital of Alsharq, where forces loyal to the new, so-called moderate government had laid siege to the eastern half of the city. Three years earlier, Western allies, including the United States and the European Union, had supported the new government. As the atrocities rose, support from the West wavered.

The Americans and the Europeans hadn't pulled their support yet. And, ironically, the Alsharqi government probably had one of its own enemies, the Khamsin Sayef, to thank for that. Fear of the antigovernment terrorists bolstered the government. At least a little.

Meanwhile, the Alsharqi government continued to drop barrel bombs from helicopters and to roll tanks through residential neighborhoods. Entire blocks of the ancient capital had been smashed, buildings pancaked, roads demolished. A steady stream of refugees poured out of the city, east into Egypt or west into Libya. Or, more often, on rickety watercraft across the Mediterranean to Europe.

St. Nicholas Salvage & Wrecking wasn't immune to these terrible scenes. But they had violence much closer to home to worry about.

The Khamsin Sayef had killed a CIA station chief three years earlier then apparently had gone dormant. But since the beginning of the year, they'd hit Geneva, Annecy, and Barcelona.

"They're escalating," Finnigan said, sitting in a thermoformed and dreadfully uncomfortable seat at the frenetic Frankfurt airport, a bag of chips and a Diet Coke at his feet. "They're escalating and we're growing roots."

"There's a game on the television in that bar," Fiero said, nodding to their left. She wore skinny black jeans, a beat-up leather jacket—despite the season—and motorcycle boots, along with her sunglasses. She caught almost everyone's covert attention. "You should go entertain yourself and stop complaining."

"There's no sports on that TV."

She turned toward the bar in the concourse. "Of course there is. I can see it from here."

"That's not sports. That's cricket."

"Snob."

"Fucking A."

Fiero's phone vibrated. She dug it out of her hip pocket. It was an international number, one they didn't recognize.

An Englishman, or at least someone with a fine London accent, introduced himself without introducing himself. "I am told that I should be assisting you," the voice said, "though I've no idea who you are or why this should be."

"Hang on." Finnigan turned to his partner and mouthed a name: *Llorente.* They got up and moved to a row of broken seats, as far from the other passengers as they could get. Fiero put the phone on speaker but turned down the volume.

"We're looking for someone," Finnigan said, leaning with his forearms on his knees. Fiero scanned the causeway, looking for trouble. "We're trying to identify a guy, and our mutual friend figured you could help."

"I don't know who the *mutual friend* is. Who are you seeking to find?"

"The guys blowing up people in Paris and Geneva and Barcelona and some Podunk town in France."

Fiero kept her eyes on the crowd. "Annecy."

The voice said, "Yes, I understand who it is you're seeking. What do you require?"

"Driver," Finnigan said. "Wheelman. A guy with an injury to his neck or back that means he can't turn his head to the right."

They waited, listening to the hiss of the open line. The people hurrying through the Frankfurt airport fit all of the clichés: business-people with efficient and tightly bound rolling luggage; moms with crying or giddy children; grinning tourists; frightened refugee-seekers; flight crews; custodians stopping to tidy up the rows of seats.

The austere English voice dripped with derision. "Not sure I'm following you, sir."

Fiero said, "Almost no one does."

Finnigan ignored her. "The getaway driver in Geneva and in whatever-the-town-in-France, there are videos of the guy trying to back up like he's the crappiest driver in the world. Thing is, I don't think he's a crappy driver. I think he can't turn his head to the right. Like that kink you get when you sleep wrong, or when you pinch a nerve. You know? I think—"

"Sir," the Englishman cut in then paused. For several seconds. "Sir? I have been asked to terminate this call."

"Wait, we—"

The line went dead.

The partners sat for a few seconds, elbows on knees, huddled toward each other, staring at the inert phone in Fiero's palms.

Finnigan said, "The hell?"

"That was odd."

"No shit. This is the guy Llorente said was going to help us?"

She shrugged. "I believe so."

They both leaned back in their chairs. "Huh."

THE PA ANNOUNCEMENT CALLED FOR THE START of boarding for the flight from Frankfurt to Barcelona.

Fiero's phone vibrated. The same number.

They had been queued-up, but stepped back away from everyone else.

The accent they heard was still English but a different English. It was rougher, with the guttural edge of a lifelong smoker. The first voice sounded like Notting Hill; this one slogged through Manchester.

"This the cop looking for the bombers?"

Finnigan smiled. "Never said I was a cop."

"Oh, you're a cop all right. Name's *Charlie*. For today."

"Hi Charlie. I'm Joe."

"Joe, I had five cops, myself included, watch those fecking videos. Each of us laughed at the driver, but none of us made the connection that he had a bad neck. Now that we hear you say it, o' course, it's obvious."

Finnigan winked at his partner but spoke into the phone. "Fresh eyes, man."

"Color me impressed. But before I wade any more into this pig's breakfast, answer me this: Why're we sticking with *Charlie* and *Joe*, and why're we using secure phone lines?"

"Ever hear of Suicide Ride?"

"'Course. Cowboys, the lot of 'em. What're they to this?"

"My friend and I were hired to find the bombers. The guys who hired us are so infiltrated by Suicide Ride, they can't take a piss without it being in a memo. Their communications are compromised right up to the very top."

"Shite." Charlie practically spat the word. "Explains that, then."

"We want to stay a step ahead of these schmucks."

"'Course. Just before I called back, we ran a search through Interpol. We found a crew doing bank jobs in Germany and Austria. Also hit an art gallery, jewelers in Belgium. Cases going back seven years. They're based out of Paris. Driver is a German name of Julian Ritter. Hit a jeweler a year and a half ago. Guard had a shotgun. The driver took shot to his neck and shoulder. Got himself arrested. Serious nerve damage."

"Where's he being held?"

"He got sprung," Charlie said. "From hospital. This was near fourteen months gone."

"So he's driving getaway cars again."

They listened to the pause. "We don't know that, Joe. Not for sure. But . . ."

"But you like my hunch."

"I do, and that's a fact. Dunno where our man Julian Ritter is these days. Fell off the feckin' map."

"But he drove for a crew. Took banks, jewelers, art galleries."

"That's right."

Finnigan looked up and grinned. Fiero gave him her *what?* face.

"So if he's still driving, Charlie, he's driving for people who are loyal to him."

"That's what I'm thinking, Joe. He's driving for people he's got history with. Friends and family, as it were."

"And that doesn't sound like Sword of the Whatever."

"No, it does not."

Fiero said, "I don't understand."

"Then you're in fine company, ma'am," Charlie assured her.

Finnigan said, "Charlie? I might need to back-channel with you. Can I text you at this number if I need help?"

"Do it. One cop to another."

"Our only goal here is to catch these fuckers."

"You do, you'll never buy your own beer 'round here. That's a promise."

The line went dead.

Fiero said, "I still don't understand."

"Same for me. Same for *Charlie*." He made air quotes around the name. They noted people queuing up at their gate. They grabbed their carry-ons and threaded through the seats. Fiero deactivated her phone.

She spoke sotto voce. "The man who drove those vans for the Khamsin Sayef is part of a gang of thieves?"

"Maybe. No proof yet, but . . . yeah. Maybe."

"Why would an Islamist terrorist group hire a nonbeliever to drive for them? And why would a common criminal want to drive for terrorists who aren't in it for profit?"

Finnigan whispered, "They wouldn't. Not unless they felt bad that he got hurt, or they felt guilty and they're throwing him jobs even though he isn't the driver he once was."

"As if . . . he drove for them before?"

"During the heist where he got shot, yeah."

"This Julian Ritter was hurt during a jewelry store robbery."

"Yeah," Finnigan said.

She looked more than a little doubtful. "You're saying the Khamsin Sayef, the Sword of the Storm, is *knocking over* banks and jewelers?" He liked it when she tried American aphorisms.

"Hell, no. That wouldn't make much sense. They're financed by the freedom fighters of Alsharq, by Saudi princes, by the Muslim Brotherhood. They got ninety-nine problems, but a bank ain't one."

She smiled. "I actually got that reference."

"I'll mark it in the calendar."

"You believe the Khamsin Sayef is a bunch of bank robbers and jewel thieves? This may be your dumbest idea to date."

"And that's saying something." He turned and peered at a bank of flat-screen monitors, his eyes scanning for departures. He shouldered his canvas bag. "C'mon. There's a flight in forty minutes to Paris. Let's grab it."

"You want to find this Ritter on a hunch?"

"You got anything better to do?"

She hoisted her carry-on and started scanning the departures board.

C20

Sooner, Slye, and Rydell boasted an impressive network of "associates" ruled by clockwork bribes. The detective chief inspector in Manchester, going by the name "Charlie," had been off the call less than ten minutes when one of his subordinates called a friend of a friend at the private military contractor and dropped a dime.

THE NEWS REACHED COLE SANGER in Madrid within forty-five minutes. Sanger's assistant brought him the news. "A guy we own in the police department in Manchester says one of the people on the call was a woman with a Spanish accent."

Sanger's interest rose. "The Spanish assassin? The one working out of Cyprus?"

"Could be, sir. The other person on the call? Our guy says he was an American."

Sanger rarely showed surprise to underlings—or to anyone, really—but that caught him off guard. They'd been searching for this Katalin Fiero Dahar and her mysterious male partner, who nobody in their Spanish branches could identify. If the man was American, that might explain it.

Sanger and his team had been assuming that Fiero and the man were part of the covert kill shop of Centro Nacional de Inteligencia.

Could be they were something else altogether.

Sanger had memorized the number for the burner phone he'd assigned to the Belarus shooter, Syarhey Valazko. He sent a text, ordering Valazko to rendezvous with the Paris office and begin pursuit of this so-called St. Nicholas group.

C21

One of the very first cases for St. Nicholas Salvage & Wrecking, way back when, was a contract to track down a Polish Army general who was selling military-grade weapons to terrorist organizations. Their brief had been twofold: find the evidence, but also find the general. They were bounty hunters, after all.

They prevailed, and the general had appeared before Judge Heléne Betancourt at the International Criminal Court in The Hague.

In the process of rounding up the general, Finnigan and Fiero came upon a crime cartel in Paris that acted as a go-between for the illegal sale of the weapons. It was said at the time that nobody moved military-grade ordnance in Northwestern Europe without going through this particular arms broker, who went by the pseudonym *Para Pacem*. The guy even had a tattoo sprawled across his chest in gothic script that read *si vis bellum, para pacem*. Which, Fiero explained, translated as, *if you wish for war, prepare for peace*.

At the time, Finnigan had observed, "That makes jack-shit sense."

"Nor does a criminal adopting a pseudonym to avoid detection, then having it inked across his chest like a billboard."

Finnigan had nodded sagely. "If it weren't for stupid criminals, this gig might actually be tough."

Now, THREE YEARS LATER, the partners arrived at Charles de Gaulle Airport with plans to track down their favorite arms broker, Para Pacem. Who, in turn, might lead them to the German driver with an injured neck named Julian Ritter. Who, in turn, might know something about an Islamist organization blowing up cities in Europe.

It might not have been a great plan, but it had the benefit of being their only plan.

TROUBLE WAS, PARA PACEM HAD DIED of complications of Hepatitis C, just two months previously. "Tattoo came back to bite him in the ass after all," Finnigan observed glumly, as the partners sat in a coffee shop on rue de l'Arbalète.

Fiero sipped her espresso and nibbled a *pain au chocolat.* "You call Ways and Means; it's your turn. Ask him if he knows any gunrunners or arms brokers in Paris."

"Okay. You call Shan. He knows pretty much every lowlife in Europe."

"We need a classier level of friends."

"You're telling me."

They made their calls. Finnigan drained his cappuccino, nodded approvingly at the 1920s travel posters of Nice, Monte Carlo, and Cannes on the bustling, narrow street around them. "Nice. How'd you find this joint?"

Fiero pointed to the nearest street sign. "I like the street name."

He looked around. "Rue de l'Arbalète?"

"It means Street of the Crossbows."

"Yeah." He grinned and paid. "That would be your style."

THEIR FAVORITE AMORAL BANKER made some calls and two days later led the partners to the den of an arms broker working out of a botanical garden center in Bobigny, France. It took them another day to track the guy down and to get him alone long enough for Fiero to ask him some questions.

She asked the questions because, a) she spoke French and b) she did so after breaking the man's left wrist and threatening to start on his right. In general, Finnigan thought up better questions to ask suspects, but he appreciated that her approach had its advantages.

The Bobigny broker, though, knew nothing of the crew knocking over bankers and jewelers. He specialized in selling guns in Southeast Asia.

THEY CALLED THEIR OTHER FRIEND, Thomas Shannon Greyson, in a hospital in Vienna, undergoing a series of operations on his spine. Shan—groggy, in excruciating pain and doped to the gill—still managed to remember the name and contact number for a former SAS soldier and expat, indulging his love of heroin and living (if you could call it living) in the French coastal town of Luc-sur-Mer.

The next morning, the partners headed to the coast, traveling past fields of shockingly yellow rapeseed under the shadow of gargantuan wind turbines.

The former soldier in Luc-sur-Mer roused himself out of his heroin funk long enough to tell the partners that the Parisian most likely to have contacts with the crew of thieves worked out of a horrible little tavern in the Nineteenth Arrondissement, the Archer and Boar.

Finnigan and Fiero thanked him and climbed back into their rental for the return trip to Paris.

They'd burned five days on the ground. The Sword of the Storm hadn't blown up anyone in the meantime, but they both sensed they were working against a bad clock.

C22

The Archer and Boar had been kitted up, likely in the 1950s, to look like a quaint English tavern. It might have seen better days. But in point of fact, none of its days had been good. It was situated not far from the Colonel Fabien Metro stop, north of Hôpital Saint-Louis. The area was known for low-income, low-rise apartments, graffiti, and homeless encampments in pup tents along the Canal Saint-Martin.

Finnigan went into the tavern with a used Rick Steves tourist book and a map. He started with a too-loud "Hi there!" then ordered a Miller Light and sat at a table in the corner, with a view of all the other patrons. Nobody gave the loutish American a second glance.

He nursed his beer for two hours, noting everyone's movements.

The British cop going by Charlie had provided a photo of Julian Ritter, the guy who might, or might not, be driving for the Khamsin Sayef. It was about the only potential lead the partners had.

Meanwhile, Fiero found them a cheap and not-overly clean

third-floor hotel room a block away, with a view of the Archer and Boar. She observed the comings and goings throughout the afternoon, then well into the night. The bar featured two doors on the same street. One was signed and lit from within by a string of white lights. The other had neither sign nor lights. Most patrons used the lit-and-signed door. A few men—and only men—used the other door. They looked pretty much like the Central Casting version of lifelong criminals.

Finnigan joined her in the hotel room around nine. The partners ordered a takeaway curry and ate it seated at the window of their crappy little bedsitter. Fiero had never found good Indian food in Paris, and this was no exception.

"That other door leads to a semiprivate room with only three tables, nine chairs," Finnigan told her between bites. "I checked it out when I took a whiz."

"You detectives and your clever ways."

They ate and watched. The clock struck eleven in the evening.

"These guys are crooks."

"I think so, too," Fiero said. "Should I go in and observe?"

"If I've counted right, there are twenty-two men in the bar right now. If you go in there, approximately twenty-two of them are gonna throw pickup lines at you like a pitching machine at a batter's cage."

She grinned at him. She knew it was true and never fooled herself about that.

It had taken a team of local detectives the better part of four days to track down the tall Spanish woman and her unknown partner and to set up surveillance on them. What they discovered was that the Spaniard and her partner were involved in their own surveillance, of a down-on-its-luck tavern in the Nineteenth Arrondissement.

Local cops on the Sooner, Slye, and Rydell payroll confirmed that the bar was the usual hangout for an array of criminals. Now they knew, generally, what Fiero and her partner were doing, if not specifically whom they sought.

Valazko and a crew from the Paris office of Sooner, Slye, and Rydell found a hotel room with a view of the Archer and Boar, and also a view of an equally crappy hotel two blocks away.

This time they used the best watchers in the city, a rotating cast of fifteen people, three shifts, some on foot, some on wheels. The mysterious couple had had no problem spotting—and thwarting—their surveillance in Annecy and Geneva. The contractors were taking no chances in Paris.

Once Fiero had booked a room down the block, the surveillance team got its own matching room and set up a tripod in the window, with a mount that would work for a camera and long-distance lens, but which could be swapped out quickly to fit a rifle should it come to that. They'd gotten photos of the statuesque Spaniard in the window, but because of the angle and sheer bad luck—she sat to the right of her window, he sat to the left—they had yet to get a good image of the suspected American.

Valazko sat on the room's single bed with a yogurt cup and a plastic spoon. He gingerly peeled off the metallic wrap-lid, set it upside down on the bed stand. He dipped only a quarter of the spoon into the smooth yogurt, and tasted it.

"Why this place?" he asked.

The Sooner, Slye, and Rydell team captain, an ex-soldier from Avignon, turned from the window. "The Archer and Boar? It's a toilet of a bar. But a man named Clément Lacombe calls it his office. We know of Lacombe. He's a fence. He also brokers thefts. Big ones. We think that's who the Spaniard is targeting."

The team spoke English with the sleepy Belarusian, their only common tongue.

"I put a man inside the Archer and Boar. He said Target Two was in there for a couple of hours. He's definitely American."

Valazko scooped out another third-of-a-spoon of the creamy yogurt with blueberries. He tasted it slowly, licked the spoon. "Did he interrogate everyone?"

"The American? He didn't say fuck-all. He sat in a corner and read a tourism book."

Valazko smiled.

"What?"

He ignored the question, eyes on his yogurt.

"If the Spanish bitch and the American are after Lacombe, do we want to grab him first? Find out why he's important to them? Or grab them first?"

Valazko took another slow bite. From the look on his face, each spoonful might have had a different flavor. He closed his eyes and meditated over it.

"Hello?" the team captain tried again. "What's our target?"

"Sooner, Slye, and Rydell will want this man Lacombe." The Belarusian spoke softly. "He might lead them to the Khamsin Sayef."

"How?"

"I don't know."

The team leader watched their guest for a moment, rolling a toothpick in the corner of his mouth. Valazko didn't appear to notice.

"How will we find out?"

"Sooner, Slye, and Rydell will interrogate this man."

"Why do you do that?"

"Do what?"

"Refer to Sooner, Slye, and Rydell in the third person. We're all with the company."

Valazko slowly scooped out more yogurt. The question went unanswered.

C23

Clément Lacombe ate his supper and yelled with his wife and watched football highlights until around eleven, when his wife went to sleep. He slipped into his shapeless jacket and grabbed his ever-present porkpie hat—he'd bought it, blind drunk in New Orleans, almost three decades ago. He checked his pocket for his wallet and keys and switchblade knife, and left his crumbling apartment building on rue Alexandre Parodi, heading to the Archer and Boar.

He'd received word of a classic collection of Triumph Spitfires, all circa 1970, for sale. All were in good enough shape to net something like twenty thousand euros. Each. The six cars sat in a warehouse in Brussels, awaiting an auto show.

Lacombe also had six buyers in Saudi Arabia.

The problem?

He had only three drivers with half a brain among them. He needed drivers he trusted who could hot-wire the Spitfires and to drive them—carefully!—to a waiting fleet of lorries, which would transport them up the E19 to a cargo ship waiting in Antwerp.

Easy money.

Lacombe slumped through the streets of the Nineteenth Arrondissement, contemplating this problem, his black pork-pie with its upturned brim catching his cigarette smoke, briefly, before releasing it into the city.

FIERO SPOTTED THE MAN in the short-rimmed hat when he was still two blocks from the tavern. "Got him."

She threw on her leather jacket—far too hot for most people that time of year, but the Spaniard/Algerian seemed immune to heat. The partners grabbed their gear—no guns—and danced down the three flights of stairs at nearly half the speed that gravity would have taken them in free fall.

They had rented two cars and parked them—when spots became available—to the east and to the west of the Archer and Boar. They'd asked the rental clerk for two keys each, so no matter who was closer to which car, they were ready. Clément Lacombe could come from either direction, and they wanted the snatch to happen quickly and cleanly either way.

They hit the street-level door of their hotel and started walking toward Lacombe. One of their rentals sat on the curb, in the perfect position for a quick exit. They couldn't see Lacombe's face under the hat because that stretch of the street was ill-lit, the shadows long and oblong. They closed the distance between themselves and their target.

What they hadn't anticipated was the opposition picking that moment to show up.

They didn't look like run-of-the-mill thugs, like patrons of the backroom of the Archer and Boar. They looked like pros.

They counted five, two behind Lacombe, two across the street on the opposite sidewalk, one parking a Vespa.

Fiero whispered, "Bravos."

Finnigan nodded. "Ghost."

"Are you . . . ?"

"Yeah."

Finnigan was expecting it. He'd called the play. But even he was surprised by how quickly Fiero ghosted into the night. She turned ninety degrees, stepped behind a parked Hyundai, zipped up her black jacket to her chin and . . .

. . . was gone.

Finnigan kept walking forward, toward Clément Lacombe and, behind him, the human blockade.

He hadn't been able to bring guns on a commercial flight, but he did have a lead-filled leather sap that his father had given him when he graduated from the New York Police Academy. He got it through airport X-ray machines thanks to a recess built into the brace for the wheels of his bag.

He figured the guys in the blockade had to be Sooner, Slye, and Rydell. Who else? They might have been tracking Lacombe, hoping he could lead to the getaway driver who, in turn, might know about Sword of the Storm. But then again, they might have been tracking St. Nicholas Salvage & Wrecking. That seemed more likely.

He counted off: Guy 1 and Guy 2 on his own sidewalk behind Lacombe. Guy 3 was perched on the Vespa. Guys 4 and 5 on the opposite sidewalk.

Lacombe walked with his head down, smoking, shoulders slumped, unaware of the drama around him.

When he was fifteen feet away from his target, Finnigan grinned and shouted, "Clément!"

Lacombe stumbled, coming to a quick halt. His left hand reached into the pocket of his baggy coat. His eyes blinked owlishly under his hat.

The Suicide Ride goons kept approaching, but they stutter-stepped a bit, surprised by Finnigan's convivial approach.

Finnigan jacked up the grin. "How's it hanging, bro?"

Lacombe, like many Parisians, spoke passable English. "Do I know you?"

Finnigan eyed that left hand. Gun? Unlikely. Knife, more likely, based on the way Lacombe spread his feet, shoulder-width apart for balance. You don't need much balance for a gunfight; you do for a knife fight.

Guy 1 and Guy 2, behind Lacombe, exchanged perplexed looks, wondering what Finnigan was up to. Also, likely it had just dawned on them that someone was missing. Had they spotted Fiero before she did her smoke-and-mirror thing? Probably, but not clearly, not on this darkened street.

Lacombe turned now and spotted his pursuers.

Finnigan wanted all eyes on him. He kept narrowing the distance to Lacombe, grinning like the village idiot. "Who're your buddies, buddy?"

He caught a glimmer of movement at the corner of his right eye. Without turning his head, he saw Guy 5, across the street, fold up and fall. Silently.

He'd been watching for it. So far, he appeared to be the only one who'd noticed.

Guy 4 would twig to it, for sure, so Finnigan waved his free arm and boomed, "Fellas!" He'd reached the side of Clément Lacombe now. He pulled his left fist out of his pocket, the lead-filled sap falling free. He did a short handball-style windup and let the leather pouch connect with Lacombe's thigh.

The Frenchman's eyes bulged and his cheeks bulged and his shoulders shot up and outward. He stumbled back into the sooty brick wall of a locksmith shop, falling to his ass, drawing every eye in the drama. A shot to the meaty part of the thigh incapacitates but doesn't do too much real damage, as opposed to, say, hitting the kneecap. Lacombe was down but not out.

Across the street, Guy 4 crumbled silently, hands at his gut, going to his knees then his back. Without a sound.

Finnigan walked another two paces, now about eight paces from Guys 1 and 2.

"Suicide Ride?" he said, smiling.

This was, obviously, not going as the assault team had planned.

Guy 1 said, "Ah . . . a car is coming. We know who you are. Get into it."

Against the wall, Lacombe muttered in guttural misery, hands wrapped around his thigh.

Finnigan said, "What kind of car?"

The guys stopped walking. "Sorry?"

"The car. The car you got coming, or you say you got coming. Which, I don't know, maybe you do, maybe you don't. I have trust issues. What kinda car?"

To Finnigan's surprise, Guy 2 actually answered. "Ah. Renault van?"

Guy 1 shot his partner a glare. He turned back. "You are one. Yes? We are five. Pick up this turd, Lacombe. Get him in the van. Tell us where the girl is."

"I am one. Yes." Finnigan said, and closed the gap. Now they were six paces apart. "I am one with the universe. You say you're five?"

The pursuer was about to answer but the Vespa clattered to the pavement. He and Guy 2 glanced that way and realized their three friends were on the ground.

Fiero stood over the fallen bike, holding a Smith and Wesson revolver in a two-hand grip, not smiling, not frowning. Just standing. She'd borrowed it from one of the men she'd downed.

Guy 1 drew his own weapon, right-handed. Finnigan let the

sap fly again and caught him in the right elbow. From the sound, it likely broke a bone. Thanks to momentum, the man let go of the gun and it flew into the side panel of a parked Volkswagen, spinning into the gutter.

Finnigan made a fist and punched Guy 1 in the throat. His head snapped back.

Guy 2 found himself the last man standing. He looked around, eyes never straying far from Fiero's S&W, centered on his body mass.

Finnigan casually took the man's own pistol from his shoulder holster. "Do me a favor?"

Guy 2 gulped. "Oui?"

"Call the van."

C24

Finnigan frisked the uninjured guy and came up with a gun and a high-tech Bluetooth comms unit clipped to his belt. Fiero took the guns and comms units from the three on her side of the street.

Finnigan squatted and took Clément Lacomb's switchblade too.

The fence sat on the sidewalk, back against the grimy wall, both hands holding his thigh. He looked angry but the anger was overlaid by confusion. "Who the fuck are you?"

"The good guys." Finnigan nodded to the others. "They're the bad guys. You're better off with us, friend."

He helped the Frenchman up onto his feet and even rescued the man's porkpie hat.

He turned back, grinning, and saw a newcomer appear across the street to Fiero's left.

"Bravo!"

Fiero reacted quickly, catching a glimmer of movement at her peripheral vision and dance-skipping back three paces, out of the new guy's reach.

The man appeared to be very pale, but otherwise was remarkably unremarkable: Average in height, weight, hair color, clothing. He might have been forty, or ten years younger, or maybe ten years older. He likely hadn't grown up poor, or grown up rich, but you couldn't tell by looking why you even thought that. He looked relaxed and completely at ease on a darkened street with two armed strangers and four men littering the sidewalks.

Fiero aimed her borrowed revolver at him.

The newcomer cut the distance between them in the blink of an eye, grabbed her wrist and twisted. The gun spiraled away.

He stabbed at her shoulder, fingers stiffened into a sword point.

Fiero dodged the blow and used his mass as a counterweight, pivoting a swivel kick that came in high, aimed at his right ear.

The very pale man ducked back. The kick missed.

He kicked at her brace leg and Fiero shuffled back.

The man kicked her in the gut.

Fiero landed on her ass.

Across the street, Guy 2 started grinning. Finnigan kneed him in the balls and drew one of the revolvers.

"Hey!"

Fiero turned her fall into a backward somersault, rolling to her feet, crouched and ready, a dozen feet between her and the bravo.

The very pale man cut the distance between them. They pivoted clockwise, and now Fiero was far too close to Finnigan's line of fire.

The very pale man kept his eyes on Fiero but raised his voice for Finnigan, across the street. "Do you think you can hit me with that gun?"

He spoke English with a thick Eastern European accent.

Finnigan didn't like how fast this guy moved. He turned the gun from the brawl across the street to Guy 2 at his left. "Pretty sure I can hit this asshole!"

"And you think I care?"

The pale man grinned. He and Fiero danced in a circle around each other. Fiero feinted, and the guy backpedaled.

Two of the Sooner, Slye, and Rydell goons were climbing to their feet. The tide had turned.

Fiero moved. She came at the man like a summer storm on the plains: fast, violent, and without warning.

She opted for a combination low-kick, high-kick, knuckle-blow to his sternum.

The man faded back; her blows all missed.

He fired a bullet-fast rabbit punch to her chest, dead center.

Fiero stumbled back and avoided falling over. But barely.

The man kept dancing, kept Fiero between himself and Finnigan's gun. He called out mockingly. "You want to shoot, American? Americans always want to shoot."

Finnigan said, "A little, yeah."

He turned and fired one shot into the window of the Archer and Boar.

It hit in the far upper corner, the bullet likely traveling up into the ceiling of the darkened back room. The entire window shattered, turning granular in a fraction of a blink.

Finnigan let the gun spin in his hand, gave it to Lacombe, handle-first. The fence paused, then took it.

"Remember," Finnigan said, "we came for you empty-handed. These shit-sticks came for you with guns."

Six rough-hewn men stormed out of the tavern. Each was armed, with everything ranging from pool cues to knives.

Lacombe looked at the gun in his hand, looked at Finnigan, at the injured soldiers now rising, at the duel happening across the street.

A human rhino with a full-sleeve tattoo and a cricket bat stormed up and grabbed Finnigan by the sleeve.

"Not him," Clément Lacombe said. "Them."

C25

The street melee was impressive.

Clément Lacombe's compatriots went full-body piñata on the Sooner, Slye, and Rydell operatives. The soldiers, not quite understanding the dynamics of a street fight, scrambled for their guns on the sidewalk. That was a mistake, as the bar patrons hit them like a sneaker wave.

The *wee-wah* of French police sirens joined the chaos, growing louder and closer.

The Suicide Ride soldiers, in a fair fight, likely would have won hands down, but they'd already run into St. Nicholas Salvage & Wrecking and were worse for the wear.

A van screeched to a halt, the driver speaking into the same kind of high-end comms unit the others used. His eyes were on Finnigan and Lacombe as the driver's-side door burst open and Fiero yanked him out and onto the pavement.

Finnigan squeezed Lacombe's upper arm, his lips near the

fence's ear. "These guys are military contractors! Cops are coming! We can get you out, but we gotta move now!"

Lacombe seemed to agree. He limped forward, favoring his left leg. Finnigan kept a grip on his arm, and they wove through the battle toward the van.

Finnigan threw open the side door and all but fell into the uncarpeted, unlined back of the van, Lacombe at his side.

Fiero burned rubber.

Police lights began strobing the scene from about a block behind them.

"Who the fuck are you?" Lacombe growled, lying on his side on the cold metal floor of the van. His eyes had taken in the collection of handcuffs, leg irons, and weapons that Sooner, Slye, and Rydell had brought for his rendition.

Finnigan sat up but stayed in the back. A solo woman driving the van at night might draw less suspicion than the two of them. He also poked through the supplies of violence they'd discovered. "This isn't ours. We stole their van, remember?"

That seemed to calm the Frenchman down. He'd stolen plenty of vehicles in his life; it was an action he understood.

"We're bounty hunters, man."

"Then you're scum, you son of a whore."

"You leave my mama out of it. Those Fascist fuckheads back there are mercenaries. American military contractors. And this"—he used a knuckle to tap a car battery attached to two cables and alligator clips—"is how they were gonna get you talking. We didn't bring guns. You saw that."

Lacombe held his bruised leg with both hands. "What do they want with me?"

Fiero took corners too fast, hitting boulevard de Magenta, putting as much distance as she could between them and the others.

"We're all looking for a German wheelman, Julian Ritter. We think he's working with Muslim terrorists blowing the shit out of Europe."

Lacombe's eyebrows rose. "Ritter?"

As if he knew the man.

"'Fraid so."

"Impossible!"

"You know about his shotgun wound?"

Lacombe said, "To his neck?"

Bingo, Finnigan thought. "I'm not judging, man. You're a driver, you get hurt, hey, guy's gotta make a living. We get that."

Up front, Fiero shook her head, awed as always by her partner's ability to spew horseshit. And to have it believed.

"Jesus, God," Lacombe muttered.

"Maybe it's hospital expenses. Maybe the damn ragheads have got something on him."

Fiero made eye contact through the rearview mirror but he ignored her. He'd apologize later.

Lacombe shook his head as they made another fast turn onto another darkened street. "Fucking German."

Finnigan shook his head the same way and held onto one of the exposed rib braces of the van. "Well, you know how they are."

"Why should I help you? Ritter is nothing to me."

"Because those guys back there, they think *you're* working with the terrorists."

Clément Lacombe, fence, thief, and overall felon, looked hurt. "Me?"

"They're no judge of character, guys like that."

Lacombe lapsed into silence. Fiero took a few more turns, although driving at a more sedate speed now. Neither man knew where in Paris they were.

"My partner and me, we just want these terrorists. Your

business is your businesses. I tell you this: We find Julian Ritter, and those bastards back there, they start leaving you alone. Why wouldn't they? You're a means to an end. We get Ritter, and everyone forgets about you."

Lacombe scowled. "I have your word?"

Fiero managed not to laugh.

"Hand to God."

The fence looked vaguely ill. "I am not, as you say, the grass."

Finnigan thought, *grass?* But kept it to himself. "Naturally."

"But these fucking bombers . . ." Lacombe shook his head.

"I hear you, brother."

"Muslims . . ."

"Hey, I'm Catholic."

"Me too."

Finnigan nodded as well. They might have been sharing a beer at any racist bar. He dared to glance up at the rearview mirror, just in time to see Fiero roll her eyes dramatically.

C26

A protest rally was scheduled for noon on the picturesque Las Ramblas walk, in honor of Victor Wu, founder of the Clarion Group, who'd been murdered by Islamic extremists three weeks before.

The organizers represented the kind of left-leaning, progressive organizations that had supported Wu's NGO and its humanitarian efforts in Northern Africa. Truth be told, many of those same groups had supported the "reformers" who'd sought independence from the hardliners in the government of Alsharq. But that was before the "reformers" bombed Paris.

Among the organizers of the Barcelona march was a noted academic and leftist spokeswoman who appeared on European television and in newspapers often as a standard-bearer for the left. Khadija Dahar wore her usual blend of feminism and Islam in sharply pressed white trousers and blazers, plus a headscarf. She was among five people to speak from the dais before the march. She also gave interviews to Sky News and Al Jazeera.

She wondered, briefly, if her daughter, Katalin, would see the interviews. Khadija often wished her daughter had inherited her political gene and would get more involved in the world. She was fine with Katalin not wearing the hijab; Khadija was Muslim and her husband, Alexandro, was Catholic. They'd raised their daughter to make her own decisions. It was simply too bad that her decision ended up leaning toward indifference and nonparticipation.

Khadija had expected more from her daughter.

And it wouldn't kill Khadija to see her daughter in a hijab—or in a mosque—at least occasionally.

She was thinking just that as news began to spread that far-right counterprotesters were lining up near the bay, at the southern end of Las Ramblas, to protest Islam in general.

By the time Khadija Dahar got to the front of the march, fights had broken out, police in heavy armor poured out of militarized personnel carriers, and the protest had turned into a bloody riot.

Fool, she fumed to herself. *There are worse things to worry about than Katalin not wearing a hijab!*

C27

Katalin Fiero Dahar sat in front of Finnigan, not wearing a hijab, or a shirt, or a bra, her right arm held high over her head, eyes squinting in pain.

Fiero sat on the toilet while Finnigan sat on the edge of the bathtub, applying antiseptic to a long cut that raked her torso from under her right breast to a few inches from her navel. Finnigan had already used half a bag of cotton swabs to daub away the tendrils of dried blood that stretched like a fever chart from the wound to her beltline. The blood had dried as they were driving around the Nineteenth Arrondissement, avoiding police and listening to Clément Lacombe. By the time they got to a hotel, Finnigan had had to cut off her tank top and gingerly peel the cotton away from her torso, which started the long cut bleeding again.

The antiseptic hurt like hell. Before finding an isolated and cheap hotel out near Charles de Gaulle Airport, Finnigan had stopped at a *pharmacie* for the swabs, the ointment, aspirin, and a stretch bandage. He touched her flank, just under the long cut, and Fiero winced.

"Ribs broken?"

She spoke without separating her teeth. "Don't think so."

"Man, you got your ass kicked."

Her eyes narrowed. "Thank you for that observation."

An airliner passed overhead, shaking the walls.

Finnigan began wrapping the stretchy roll around her midsection. It was pungent with the smell of plastic things that have sat in their packaging for too long. He had to reach around her flank both directions, which wasn't difficult.

"No, really. That guy kicked the hell out of you."

She gritted her teeth. "It was a fairly even fight."

"No, it wasn't. Man, you got shellacked."

"Michael . . ."

"Here," he reached for the phone in his pocket. "I already posted it on YouTube."

Fiero smacked him with her good right hand.

"Ow!"

Her anger boiled over but just for a split second. Then she coughed out a laugh, winced at the pain, and hit him again. "You're such a bastard!"

Finnigan took the blows and inwardly relaxed. He'd known her for three years and had never seen her bested in combat. He wasn't at all sure how she'd react. But he was pretty sure that patronizing her or showing sympathy would have driven her inside her own head.

With his hands on her torso, Finnigan could feel a little of the tension ease out of Fiero's muscles. She'd been as taut as a guitar string. He finished stretching the tape and applied butterfly clips to hold it in place. He'd draped one of her tank tops over the edge of the tub, and handed it back to her. "Who was that punk-ass bitch?"

"I recognized him. He's a Belarusian agent." She gingerly slid into the top, rolling it down over the tape, and freed her hair.

"Belasco, or something like that. We danced around each other a few times when I worked for Llorente."

"He's an assassin."

She nodded, gingerly tugging down the black tank. Finnigan took the plastic wrap off a glass, filled it with tepid tap water, and used his thumbnail to break the seal on the aspirin bottle. "What did Spain and Belarus have to spar over? Your countries had nothing in common."

"He's *from* Belarus but he worked as an independent contractor. He'll do whatever, for whoever's signing the checks. He's very good."

"I could see."

She gulped four tablets and sipped the water. "Thank you."

"He got away?"

"I think so. I never saw him take on any of Lacombe's men from the bar. As soon as the police sirens started, the man disappeared."

The same way you do, Finnigan thought, but didn't need to say it out loud. "He works for Suicide Ride."

"Yes, but not as one of them. He cared nothing for the men we hit. He let me take out three of them before he picked the fight. If he'd have hit me while I was working my way through the others . . ."

"So this jackass made it personal. He knows you."

She stood, her face a stoic mask. "Likely. He was hired to kill a Ukrainian journalist in Oslo one time. I got there first, got the man out. Killed two of his men. I assume Belasco took it personally."

Out in the shabby main bedroom, Finnigan pulled a bottle of whiskey out of a brown paper bag, cracked the seal, and handed it to her. "So we got ourselves a new enemy."

She took a slug.

C28

The next morning, the partners drove past the place Lacombe said the German driver could be found.

Finnigan groaned. "Tough."

Fiero nodded. "Smart."

Julian Ritter and his crew, they'd been told, had been laying low at a farmhouse forty kilometers east of Paris, on an arid and dodgy-looking bit of farmland well off the beaten path. Neither of the partners knew anything about agriculture, but the land didn't look particularly well tended. The old house, sun-faded to the color of old fish, sat on a steep incline with a view of the ill-paved country road leading between two small villages. Any car passing would be visible for well over a kilometer.

The partners slow-rolled past the house without stopping. Finnigan lowered the sun visor on the subcompact rental, obscuring most of their faces, in case they were being watched through field glasses.

"Wanna bet the villagers have been paid off not to answer

questions? Or worse yet, to answer them, then call up Ritter and his buddies in the farmhouse?"

Fiero stared through her sunglasses, trying to memorize the one-story wooden house. "If he's there at all."

They drove in silence. The sun glinted off all the south-facing windows of the old house, making it impossible to glance in, even if they'd had binoculars.

Fiero said, "We are wasting time."

"I know."

They kept driving. The road was dusty and pitted, and the subcompact jolted badly through gravel-rimmed potholes.

Finnigan said. "Three bombs so far this year. Before that, a three-year quiet time. Before that, they blew up that CIA station chief—"

Fiero said, "Dinah Mariner."

"—and her little girl and her husband."

Fiero glanced his way and waited, let him think out loud.

"Sword of the Storm got her and her three-year-old and her husband. Then went quiet. Then killed a banker, an engineer, and a guy who runs a nonprofit."

"Odd pattern," Fiero said.

"Yeah. Odd targets. Odd timing. One successful bomb, three-year time-out, then three more bombs . . . CIA station chief and family, then a banker, engineer, philanthropist."

She let him stew.

"Butcher, baker, candlestick maker . . ."

Fiero's phone vibrated. Before she could reach for it, Finnigan's phone did the same.

Finnigan removed his one-handed and checked the display, keeping the other hand on the wheel. Fiero checked hers.

"McTavish," he said.

"My father," she said.

A HANDFUL OF TIMES OVER THE PAST FEW YEARS, the work of St. Nicholas Salvage & Wrecking had required a small army.

That meant hiring Brodie McTavish, a Scottish mercenary with more than a quarter century of experience fighting in all of the earth's political hot spots.

Like a newly married couple who bring their friends into the marriage, McTavish had been Fiero's associate long before she met Finnigan. Hugo Llorente's dark-arts unit had hired him on a couple of occasions to provide culpable deniability for military actions on foreign soil. The Scotsman and Fiero had hit it off. When she went independent and joined Finnigan, she insisted they hire McTavish for those occasions when shock-and-awe was a better answer than sleuth-and-stealth.

Earlier that same year, McTavish had joined the partners on a raid of a military base in Kosovo, where they'd managed to rescue two dozen immigrant children from a corrupt major who was selling them.

Finnigan couldn't remember a time when McTavish had called them.

He waited until they were out of sight of the hilltop farmhouse, parked, and answered the call.

"Michael?"

Finnigan felt his blood pressure tank. The effusive Scotsman generally greeted him with an exuberant *Michael!* Today he sounded like a schoolboy called to the principal's office.

"What's up, big guy?"

"I'm using a scrambler," McTavish said. "We've maybe thirty seconds."

So at least their conversation was safe. In theory, at least. "What's wrong?"

"Just accepted a contract."

"Target?"

"You."

Finnigan said, "Ah, Jesus, man . . ."

"Big, American outfit. Military contractors. They know who you are, Michael, an' they know who Katalin is, and they're gunnin' for you."

"Suicide Ride."

"That's them."

He glanced at the passenger seat. Fiero held a finger to one ear, blocking out Finnigan's voice, while talking to her father. She looked worried.

She never looked worried.

"What's the score?" Finnigan tried to fake a smile, knowing it would affect his voice. "You coming after us? We need to strap on the pads?"

"Don't talk daft. The fuckers would've paid a premium for me and mine to come after you, Michael. Instead, I took a third as much *not* to take your call. We'll be sitting this one out. Not coming for you, but not coming to help, either."

Finnigan relaxed. But only a little.

"This call's a mitzvah, brother. Appreciate the heads-up."

"What'd you do to—"

The line went dead.

Either McTavish's scrambler had reached its limit or they'd been cut off.

Finnigan tossed his phone onto the dashboard and rubbed his eyes.

If Sooner, Slye, and Rydell knew enough about them to know they'd hired McTavish in the past, then they no longer were under the illusion that Finnigan and Fiero worked for Spanish Intelligence. The military contractor had dug up the real nature of St. Nicholas Salvage & Wrecking.

It had to happen eventually.

Fiero hung up. She, too, tossed her phone onto the dashboard, where it spun and slid into Finnigan's.

"My mother was in a riot."

"What the hell?"

She turned to him, and for the first time since they'd met, Finnigan thought he saw tears in her eyes. "She was leading a march in Barcelona. Protesting the killing of Victor Wu. An anti-terrorism march. But a right-wing anti-Islam group staged a counterprotest, and a fight broke out."

"Is she okay?"

"She might have a concussion. She's in hospital. My father just flew in from Madrid, but he's in traffic, hasn't made it to her yet."

Finnigan checked his watch. "We're maybe ninety minutes from de Gaulle. There's a jillion flights daily, Paris to Barcelona."

She said, "Julian Ritter, the driver, we—"

Finnigan hit the engine. He did a quick U-turn and punched the gas. Getting to the airport meant driving past the old, rambling farmhouse again, which wasn't ideal tradecraft.

"Michael . . ."

"Fuck it," he said, and redlined the tachometer.

An American held a pair of Leupold 8×25 field glasses up to his eyes, holding them two-handed for stability. He stood in the living room of the old farmhouse and watched as a dusty, nondescript subcompact barreled down the rural road in the valley. He was black, built powerfully, the kind of physique usually found only in prisons and Hollywood movies. He watched the little car swerve to avoid potholes.

"Seen this car before," DeMarcus Washington said. "About five minutes ago, going the other direction."

Two men sat at an antique, wooden dining room table behind him. One, Ron Perry, cleaned a disassembled rifle. The other had been trying to watch a soccer match on an iPad but hadn't been able to concentrate. He got up now, wincing painfully, and moved to Washington's shoulder to peer out the window.

A fourth person remained seated at the table, poring over a laptop and making copious notes in her fine, precise, spidery handwriting.

Julian Ritter stood by DeMarcus Washington and squinted out at the little car, moving far too quickly on the rutted road. The German was spare and wiry, where Washington was absurdly muscled. Ritter fidgeted; Washington rarely moved unless he needed to.

The old agricultural road was designed for heavy working-class cars and slow-rolling farm vehicles. The subcompact dodged potholes like a running back.

"Well," the German said, "whoever that is, he can drive."

Ron Perry wore a vintage Oak Ridge Boys concert T-shirt and khakis, a thick, downturned mustache and dirty blond hair that brushed his collar. He shook his head, his eyes rolling. He snorted a laugh.

"I remember when you could too."

The woman at the laptop glanced his way.

Ritter bristled but didn't turn to the table.

Washington said, "Car passed, heading east, five minutes ago. Musta turned around, heading west. Moving fast."

It was fine for DeMarcus Washington and Julian Ritter to stand at the big picture window together. The crew had adhered sheets of one-way reflective film over the south-facing windows, so nobody could look in if they wanted to.

The woman went back to her meticulous notes.

Ritter's hands shook. He moved with the stiffness of a man with a neck injury, which he was. "I don't like this."

"Lotsa shit you don't like," Perry said. "You ever try yoga? You're gonna get . . . what do you call it? Hypertension."

"Shut the fuck up," Ritter snapped.

The woman kept writing. "Don't worry about it," she said to the room at large.

Ritter turned and limped into the kitchen. "I know drivers. That's no farmer out there. I don't like it."

When he was gone, Perry and Washington exchanged smiles and headshakes.

"Guy's a liability," Washington intoned under his breath.

The woman spoke softly. She'd broken her nose as a child and it never healed correctly, and some days she had difficulty inhaling.

Frau Gunsen, the owner of the company that swept businesses for bombs, said, "Don't worry about it."

C29

The temperatures spiked in Barcelona as the commercial Bombardier prop-jet touched down at El Prat. A hot, dry wind was blowing in from Africa and the sky was the color of bleached bone. The air tasted chalky on their tongues as Finnigan and Fiero stepped out of the terminal and joined the queue for taxis.

The Hospital Sant Agustín de Déu was upscale and gleaming. Even in countries with a national health system, the health care of the rich wasn't like the health care of the rest.

They checked in at reception and were told how to find Fiero's mother. It wasn't until they were in front of the elevator that the penny dropped. "Hold on!" Finnigan barked, and sprinted for the gift shop. "Wait for me!"

He returned five minutes later, taking an oversized pearl-pink sweatshirt out of a shopping bag.

"Are you insane? You went shopping? My mother—"

"You look like a thug, dummy. Here."

Fiero looked at her reflection in the strip of brass between the elevators. Sure enough, the matchstick jeans, motorcycle boots and T-back tank were *her*, just not the *her* she ever presented to her parents. She sported yellowing bruises on her upper arm and shoulder from her fight, and a bit of the stretch bandage revealed itself beneath the crop top.

She slipped into the women's restroom and pulled on the bulky sweatshirt, with its *I heart Barcelona* logo. She quickly did her hair in a low chignon. She emerged and kissed Finnigan on the cheek.

"Thank you."

FINNIGAN HAD NEVER SEEN FIERO'S MOTHER without her head-scarf. Or without makeup, one-of-a-kind jewelry, and a designer suit. She looked much closer to her actual fifty-five than usual. Her eyes were sunken, surrounded by puffy, purple skin, and she sported an enormous rectangular bandage over her right eyebrow. Her hair was brushed back, limp and tangled.

Fiero hugged her mother and started crying. That set Khadija off as well, and they hugged and rattled off their Gatling-gun blend of Spanish and Algerian Arabic.

Finnigan stood back, hands jammed in his jeans pockets.

Khadija was rattled. The woman was made of marble, near as he had ever been able to tell. Today she looked petite and petrified, a porcelain thing.

She finally noticed Finnigan and blanched. She knew how she must have looked and all of a sudden turned self-conscious.

Finnigan frowned. "We'd heard you got hurt. Were we wrong?"

Fiero glowered at him. Khadija's hands fluttered to her hair, growing aware of being bareheaded in the presence of a man not in her family.

"How many stitches you get?" Finnigan asked. "What, three? Four?"

Khadija said, "Four. They—"

Finnigan pulled up a chair and sat backward in it. He pushed his naturally wavy hair away from his left ear and revealed the long, squiggly scar that almost no one ever saw.

"See this? My brother did that. When I was nine. Eighteen stitches. You got four? Damn, we would have driven here if we'd known. Saved ourselves the airfare."

He scowled at the women. He saw Fiero, on the far side of the hospital bed, relax; she got it.

Khadija looked mortified. "I . . . that's terrible. How did your brother . . . ?"

"Baseball bat. Kapow."

"Ah . . . why?"

Finnigan shrugged. "He said he saw a horsefly."

The barest wisp of a smile escaped the lips of Khadija Dahar. "Did he?"

"Are you calling my brother a liar?"

Khadija laid a hand on Finnigan's knee. "Of course not, Michael. It must have been a truly terrible horsefly indeed." She laughed, and laughing hurt, but she did it anyway.

Finnigan felt a hand on his shoulder and looked up to see Alexandro Fiero, tall and noble, impeccably dressed and groomed. The Hidalgo smiled down on him and nodded.

The women returned to their staccato patois, and the men excused themselves to get coffees.

C30

Finnigan picked a lock, and Fiero followed him up onto the roof of Sant Agustín de Déu. The air was thick with African grit, the temperature well over ninety and dry. The Mediterranean's Balearic current was bringing heat but no moisture. But Finnigan never could stand the smell of hospitals. Better to breathe in half of the fucking Sahara, he thought, than the reek of formaldehyde, age, and death.

He'd scored a fifth of cheap blended whiskey while Fiero spoke to her parents. Now up on the roof, Fiero doffed the pink sweatshirt and shook out her hair. Finnigan found a couple of old-style, wood-slat crates, inverted them to create chairs, and set them up near the edge of the roof.

"My mother said my jeans were a bit scandalous."

"You show her the knife in your boot?"

He handed her the whiskey, and she snapped the cap with a single twist. The wind caught her hair.

Finnigan felt sweat begin to form on his neck.

She reached out and ruffled his hair. "You're a good partner to have." She handed him the bottle and he lifted it a few inches in her direction then took a sip.

"Jesus. I can taste the sand in my teeth."

"It's a sirocco," she said. "It blows out of Africa this time of year."

Finnigan slipped on sunglasses to shade his eyes from the grit more than the glare.

"You know what this city needs?" he said. "A kick-ass burrito truck."

"I'm sorry?"

"I'm serious. A burrito truck. That's what Spain needs. Good Mexican food."

She studied him a while. He sipped from the bottle. "That's either culturally insensitive or brilliant."

He shrugged. "It's a fine line."

The wind picked up the faintest echo of chanting, below them and blocks away. Finnigan said, "While you were talking to your mom, I got a message from Ways and Means."

She glanced his way.

"Sooner, Slye, and Rydell has been poking into his business. Which would be bad for investments. Which means . . ."

"Which means Gunther won't be taking our calls for a while," she said. She'd never liked the crooked banker all that much, but he was almost always useful.

"That leaves the Black Harts," Finnigan said. "They'll be next."

She nodded. The team of thieves, con artists, and hackers were every bit as corrupt as the banker. They weren't fighters by nature. If Sooner, Slye, and Rydell started looking into their activities, the Harts would evaporate like dew.

The partners sat on the roof, breathed in the hot, dusty air from Africa, and thought.

Finnigan took another sip. The wind carried chanting for a moment, then it faded.

"Hear that?"

She nodded.

"Right-wing anti-immigrant crowds protesting the government's response to the Khamsin Sayef bombing." He handed her the bottle.

"One of those people hurled something and hit my mother on the head."

"Yeah." They sat and drank and thought. "If we can dredge up video, maybe news feeds, we might figure out who. Then we track him down, and you beat the shit out of him."

"You believe that will make me feel better?"

"I do."

She nodded. "Me too."

Finnigan said, "A whole hell of a lot here doesn't add up." He squinted out at where the Mediterranean should have been. "Why would an Islamist cell use a German driver with a history of bank robberies? Why would that driver work for them?"

The bottle exchanged hands. "Why hide near Paris?" she asked. "I know half a dozen neighborhoods in Algiers alone that would be safer for the Khamsin Sayef. To say nothing of Egypt or Libya."

They sat and pondered.

Fiero said, "Ways and Means told me something else. The . . . banker fellow. In Switzerland. He's clean." She used her open-splayed fingers, palm down, to rifle her hair. "God, I'm so worried about my mother I'm forgetting who all the players are in this thing? The banker . . . ?"

"Adrian Chassot, yeah. The January bombing in Geneva."

"Thank you. Anyway, he apparently wasn't working on oil deals in Africa, as the cleric claimed. Ways and Means said he and the other one were both scrupulously clean." She sipped the whiskey.

"Yeah, so that leaves us with . . ."

Finnigan's voice faded away. He squinted toward the invisible horizon. The sounds of the protest came and faded, like an over-the-horizon AM radio station at night.

Fiero knew that a stray thought had fluttered through his mind, and he was trying to catch up to it like an errant kite string. She sat, long legs out, crossed at the ankles, leaning back against an HVAC vent. And waited.

"Ways and Means told you he knew the other banker, right? Guy named Brecher?"

"Yes."

"Ways and Means had known him in Paris?"

She nodded and held out the bottle. It wasn't much diminished; they were sipping.

"So says our most corrupt friend."

"That was the January bombing. In May, the Khamsin Sayef hit Rick Caldwell, the American engineer."

"Yes."

"And his wife, Joan Caldwell. Who had a gig running some kind of tourism website. Based out of Paris."

The wind brought another spate of chanting, then faded it back.

Fiero took over the puzzle. "Hold on. The first bombing was three years ago. Paris. Dinah Mariner of the CIA and her husband and daughter. Bombing Number Two was Geneva. And the nameless cleric sent a tape to Al Jazeera claiming the target was Adrian Chassot. But the other banker who died had worked in Paris."

"Right. Which takes us to Bombing Number Three. The American engineer in Annecy, France. Again, the cleric went on the air, saying the man was the target. But his wife died. And she worked in Paris. Hit me."

She passed him the bottle. "That takes us right back here,

Michael. Barcelona, and Bombing Number Four. Victor Wu, the philanthropist."

"Sure," Finnigan said. "But also . . ."

Her eyes popped wide. "Pete Newsom, formerly the CIA Director of Ops for Paris Station."

"Boom like that."

"The cleric has been sending tapes to Al Jazeera saying the Sword of the Storm killed a CIA chief and a banker and an engineer and a philanthropist . . ."

"But maybe, just maybe, the real targets were the CIA chief and the Chief of Ops at the Paris Station and a banker working in Paris and a woman running a website in Paris."

"And the others were misdirection?" Fiero handed the bottle back.

He shrugged. "Maybe."

She sipped. "Do we tell Hugo?"

He shrugged. "Maybe."

THEY DID CALL HUGO LLORENTE, but first they needed to get out of the gritty wind buffeting the hospital roof. Alexandro Fiero had insisted they come stay with him in an ancestral mansion, owned by a friend of a friend, overlooking the city. The partners declined—Katalin had to decline at least four times, to her father's growing consternation. They needed the ability to move around the city, and her parents still thought she and Finnigan were some sort of deskbound analysts for the European Union.

They found a cheap hotel near Plaça de Catalunya that catered to young Russians, a major component of Barcelona's tourism trade. A surprising number of them were bodybuilders, Finnigan noted. There might have been a convention of them in town, or maybe they just liked sun and sand to show off their comically disproportionate physiques.

The hotel was aged and falling apart, with an elevator the size of an old-style phone booth, no water pressure, and an unparalleled view of an airshaft and pigeon droppings from the only window. They showered, and Finnigan helped re-clean the wound on Fiero's flank.

"Heard from the Black Harts," he said.

She nodded.

They called the number Hugo Llorente had given them, then hung up. The room was stifling, even with the window open to the bricked-in airshaft. They sat on either side of the dusty double bed, Finnigan in his boxers, Fiero in a jogging bra and panties. Finnigan had that lean and muscled look of a man who got into a lot of fights and could get himself out of them, not the overdefined build of a Hollywood star. Fiero could count his old scars, and he could count hers. And they had.

Llorente called back in twenty minutes.

"There is a farmhouse," Fiero said, speaking toward the phone they'd tossed into the middle of the bed. She rattled off an address and the names of two adjacent villages. "It's east of Paris. There's a driver, a German, Julian Ritter. He may be hiding there, and he may be driving for the Khamsin Sayef."

They explained how they got to this conclusion.

Llorente didn't bother saying that Spanish Intelligence couldn't operate on foreign soil. His kill shop almost always operated on foreign soil. And for several years, Fiero had been his agent of choice for such illegal operations.

"What is your confidence level in all this?"

"I'll get to that in a sec," Finnigan said. "First: We ran into Suicide Ride again. And a guy we think's named Belasco, who might or might not be Belarusian."

After a short pause, Llorente said, "Syarhey Valazko. Remember, Katalin? He—"

"I remember." She fingered her bruised rib. "And he remembers."

"Ah. Valazko is . . . problematic. He's quite good. He is in your league, my dear."

"Guy's got a hard-on for Katalin. Anything you can do to take this bastard off the table would be appreciated."

"I concur. I will look into it."

"As for Ritter? It could be a wild goose chase, but we don't think so. The farmhouse is in full view of all incoming traffic, both directions. Tough to get to with stealth. Best to just bluster your way in and hope for the best."

"Mr. Finnigan." The temperature in Llorente's voice dropped a few degrees. "Stealth is all my people do."

"If the only tool in your toolbox is a silencer, then every problem starts looking like an assassination."

"You have a . . . colorful way with words, Mr. Finnigan."

"You get used to it," Fiero said. "I haven't, but I'm told that you do."

"Will you meet us there?" Llorente asked.

Finnigan said, "Nope."

"Why not? We hired bounty hunters."

"We haven't put all our chips on that number. We're looking into something else."

Fiero mouthed, *What?*

Llorente said, "What?"

"See you, buddy. Kick some ass. Bye."

Finnigan reached out and disconnected. He tossed the phone in a high, looping arc and Fiero caught it one-handed, eyes on him. He reached for his jeans.

"We're not telling him that the supposed targets might be misdirection?"

"Not yet. I wanna see if Llorente can put together an operation without Suicide Ride crawling up his ass. If he can, we got an ally. If he can't . . ." Finnigan shrugged. He buttoned his jeans, looked around for a T-shirt.

"Now what?"

"Two potential situations here. The first, the Khamsin Sayef blew up the CIA's Dinah Mariner and her family, plus a banker, an engineer and a philanthropist, all with ties to the country of Alsharq. The second, the Khamsin Sayef blew up Mariner, her former chief of ops, a banker doing business in Paris, and a website designer in Paris."

"We need to see if the banker and the website woman, Joan Caldwell, have connections to the CIA."

"Right. And you know who might know?"

She thought about it. "Annie Pryor."

"The former chief of intelligence for the Paris station, right."

Fiero rolled onto her back on the bed, legs straight up in the air, and inched her jeans up her thighs. Finnigan said, "My pants are a lot easier to put on."

"Yes, but I make these look good. Pryor is here in Barcelona, looking into Victor Wu's assassination. According to my father."

"Wait, he knows her?"

"The business community is up in arms over the killing of Victor Wu. The government has asked my father to pour oil on troubled waters. He knows everyone. He's connected to everyone. What is that thing, circles overlapping and not . . ."

Finnigan said, "Venn diagram."

"Yes. My father is at the epicenter of any Venn diagram of politics and business and social activism in Spain. That's why my parents were in Barcelona this week. That's why my mother was speaking at that march."

"Looks like tensions are really rising out there."

Fiero held her flank gingerly as she leaned over to slide on her short motorcycle boots. "There's another protest march planned for tomorrow. The authorities feel certain it will turn into a riot. They say anti-Muslim activists from all over Europe are heading here."

"We might be able to use that distraction." He whisked up two black T-shirts, tossed one of them to Fiero. She held it up at arms length, bunched it up, and tossed it back. Finnigan looked at the one in his hand and did the same. They shrugged into them.

"We use the riot as a distraction?" Fiero said. "Grab Annie Pryor?"

"I guess."

He sounded distracted. Fiero freed her hair. "What?"

"Just wondering who else might use the riot as a distraction."

C31

A five-man team from Hugo Llorente's kill shop staged up at a closed Elf petrol station less than two kilometers from the farmhouse on the hill.

The advance man had come first; he'd been on Paris on other business. He'd crept on foot close enough to observe the farm through field glasses. He'd spotted no activity. Back at the gas station, he sat up all night logging traffic, waiting for his mates to join him.

"No sign of Capstone," he informed the others, as they double-checked their weaponry. *Capstone* was the random-generated code name for the Khamsin Sayef.

"We go in at dawn," the team leader said. "There's a gate eleven meters off the road to the north. Beyond is a rutted driveway. How long?"

"One hundred and ten meters," one of his men piped up. They'd checked the numbers over and over again.

"And what's the grade?"

"Six percent grade."

"Correct. We'll approach from the west, hit the gate, drive straight—"

"Trucks," their advance man intoned from the window. "More than one."

"Farm trucks?"

But before he could answer, three armor-reinforced Humvees with military-grade shocks and axles, using run-flat tires, screamed past the unlit Elf—Le Pris Bas sign.

Sooner, Slye, and Rydell was on the scene.

THE HUMVEE CONVOY BLASTED DOWN the rutted road at seventy, leaving a half-mile rooster tail of dust in its wake. In the lead car, a rangy ex-SEAL from Florida had the wheel and the guy could flat-out drive. The team leader sat behind the driver. Syarhey Valazko sat next to him, smiling blandly as if enjoying the ride. The team leader didn't trust the quiet guy. He'd heard how Valazko stayed out of the fight in Paris with the bounty hunters until *after* the other guys were down, only then engaging the Spanish bitch. Had Valazko been more of a team player, that whole shit might have gone down differently.

The lead car drew abreast of the gate and the ex-SEAL swerved sharply. The battle-hardened chassis featured a carbon-fiber cowcatcher in front of the grille, which sliced through the wooden gate like a shark fin through calm water. The other two cars swerved as well, and all three raced up the six-percent grade toward the dilapidated house.

Two of them screeched to a halt in front of the house, to the left and right of the door. The third truck threw up clods of dirt and weedy grass as it ripped through the old garden, circling around to the back.

Four guys poured out of the first truck, four guys out of the second. Each in full battle-rattle: helmets, vests, fingerless gauntlets, pads for their knees, shins, elbows, and balls. They carried British L85s with standard NATO 5.56 × 45mm ammunition.

All except Valazko. He'd refused the armor and the machine gun. He wore a fucking windbreaker, for God's sake.

The team leader pointed to him. "Spanish Intel is holed up at that gas station. You stay back. If those pricks follow us, you stop 'em."

Valazko smiled and shrugged and sauntered back toward the gate, in no hurry.

The leader made a gesture and his six guys converged, stepping up onto the covered, wooden veranda that stretched along the front of the house, flanking the door. Two men covered the living room window, two took the master bedroom window. A former Cal State Fullerton defensive end dragged up the two-handled battering ram. He swung back and slammed it into the doorknob.

Twenty paces away, Valazko head the *whoosh* of air and turned in time to see the explosion. The pressure wave knocked him on his ass.

The C4 wasn't behind the door; that would have killed two or three of the men, tops. No, Ron Perry had squirreled it away under the warped floorboards of the veranda, beneath the combat boots of the invaders. All the vests and helmets and pads in the world wouldn't save a guy from bleeding out if everything from the hips down was vaporized.

Everyone always sends a team around to cover the back door. It's SOP. So Perry also rigged sympathetic charges back there. As the row of explosives ripped upward into guys in front of the house, frangible ballistic debris erupted from beneath the cheap siding to the left and right of the back door, becoming thousands of supersonic, microscopic bullets that bounced off

Kevlar but buried itself deep in any meat it found: faces and necks, mostly.

Twelve mercenaries hit the farmhouse. Seven took the front, four took the back, and Valazko watched from a distance.

Eleven of the twelve died simultaneously.

C32

THE PYRENEES

At that moment, Frau Gunsen and her team of "bomb sweepers" crossed the border from France into Spain in the back of an office supply delivery truck tricked out with a false panel to hide their weaponry. Julian Ritter drove with Ron Perry riding shotgun, both figuratively and literally.

Thanks to the Schengen agreement, freight vehicles from all European Union countries could pass through borders without being stopped and searched. But Gunsen took nothing for granted, hence the false panel and the hidden area in the trailer. She and DeMarcus Washington rode in back.

Sitting behind the steering wheel was excruciating for Ritter, but driving was all Ritter knew or loved in this universe. He'd been injured in one of Gunsen's jobs, knocking over a jewelry wholesaler to pay for their missions. She owed him. She knew he was popping Vikes for the pain and Dexies to stay awake. She knew he was a burnout, weeks, not months, away from being physically unable to do this anymore.

That was okay. The mission wasn't going to last months, or even weeks. They were within days of the end.

As the truck hit the highest elevation over the Pyrenees, DeMarcus Washington woke up and blinked and looked around. Like many soldiers, he could sleep in any conditions. In this case, that meant lying on his back on the floor of the trailer, his head cushioned by a far-from-soft rucksack of C4.

He took in his surroundings and nodded to Gunsen, who sat beside him, leaning back against another rucksack.

Washington said, "Spain?"

"I think so. We stopped climbing."

He settled back down, fingers laced, hands over his chest as if practicing for the casket. "We locked down the target?"

"We have."

"Hmm."

They rode in silence. The truck began to tilt downhill.

Washington spoke without opening his eyes. "Target know we coming?"

Frau Gunsen removed her reading glasses and rubbed her red-rimmed eyes with the pads of her thumb and forefinger.

"Pryor knows. Or at least she suspects."

C33

Members of the business and civic communities gathered the next morning in the ground-floor lobby of a glass-and-steel corporate office, across the bustling Passeig de Gràcia from the Plaça de Catalunya. Alexandro Fiero's Galician Trust owned offices on the eighth and ninth floors, but lacked a large conference room. The lobby was the only meeting space large enough for the fifty or so community leaders who had gathered. They had come, in part, to hear assurances from a community outreach coordinator from Centro Nacional de Inteligencia. The official, a smiling, avuncular, and slightly elfin fellow, had come to tell them that the threat of the Khamsin Sayef, the Sword of the Storm, was greatly exaggerated. They had nothing to fear.

Annie Pryor was expected to wrap herself in the American flag, the navy's Mediterranean-based Sixth Fleet perched on her shoulder, and back him up 100 percent.

Which she did, despite her belief that the CNI community outreach coordinator was shoveling shit as fast as his short arms would let him.

Neither intelligence agency knew where the Khamsin Sayef was at the moment. Or what the group was planning. Or how large or how well funded it was or its logistics support or its popular support in Egypt or Alsharq or whether it had support from the oil barons of Saudi Arabia or the holy men of Iran or if it favored Hamas over Hezbollah.

In fact, all they knew for sure was that the Khamsin Sayef had blown the crap out of Paris and Geneva and Annecy and Barcelona. And that the group's charismatic young cleric—so far unidentified—had managed to make Western law enforcement and intelligence agencies look like morons.

Nothing to worry about? Pryor wanted to say to the elites of Spain. *Bullshit. Worry.*

But Annie Pryor was a good soldier. Langley had taken on an overtly political role, post-9/11. It was her job to placate the backers of the current Spanish government, who in turn had backed the United States in a series of domestic overtures.

The entire north-facing wall of the lobby of the Galician Trust building was glass. Glass doors recessed into twenty-five-feet-tall glass windows, all overlooking the fountains and pools of Plaça de Catalynya.

And the protesters.

The group outside the building had grown in size and anger, morphing from hopeful activism to shouting, and it wasn't yet 10 a.m., Pryor thought grimly. Her smartphone told her the temperature would hit ninety-five today. As the temperature rose, so would the violence. She was sure of it.

Inside the lobby, the CNI bureaucrat crooned reassurances. Señor Fiero nodded sagely, his wavy black hair catching the light, his Vandyke meticulously groomed, his suit resplendent. The foreign minister tried to nod sagely as well, but Pryor thought he looked like one of those bobblehead dolls they hand out at

Fenway, his neck too long, his pants a full two inches too short.

Pryor also nodded. Nodded and smiled. Even though her decent Spanish only caught about a third of what the bureaucrat was saying.

AND THE PROTEST OUTSIDE GREW.

Members of a half-dozen anti-immigration, white-pride, and nationalist factions from as far away as Poland and Slovakia had converged on Barcelona. They didn't outnumber the pro-immigration protesters. Nor did they outnumber the locals who favored stricter immigration reform. But as the temperature climbed, the nationalists proved enough of a spark to turn the protest into a melee.

Add to that a small minority of anarchists who just wanted to smash windows.

Add, too, the small number of criminals who figured if there's glass on the streets, there's loot to be grabbed.

It all came together in a bubbling cauldron, the perfect ingredients for a proper riot.

FINNIGAN AND FIERO WATCHED IT ALL come together from a window on the second floor of El Triangle mall. They stood just outside a bookstore, at tall windows with a direct view of the plaza's fountains and pools.

From that elevation, they could see the protest come together quickly: people arriving on foot, by car along Carrer de Pelai and Rambla de Catalunya, and pouring out of buses. Beyond the plaza, they could see directly into the Galician Trust building, where several dozen men and women in business suits had gathered in the lobby.

Fiero had brought along a light pair of binoculars that fit into her palm. "My father is in there," she muttered.

"Lemme see."

Alexandro stood by a tall and gangly man with enormous ears. To his left stood Annie Pryor, CIA chief of station for Madrid.

"That's just peachy."

"My father doesn't know what I do."

"Sweetie, *our* fathers don't know what *we* do. I get the problem."

When the partners had arrived, most of the crowd in the plaza stood listening to the speakers, who used light, portable PA systems on shoulder straps. But as more people poured in, fewer and fewer seemed to be listening to the speeches. They just looked agitated.

"Mob like that can go south quick. I saw enough of that when I was a cop."

Fiero's phone vibrated. She pried it out of the back pocket of her jeans and glanced at it.

"*Me cago en la leche*," she muttered.

"What?"

She showed it to him.

The phone displayed a text from a false-front number they knew to represent Hugo Llorente. It read: *France. SSR got there first. Trap. 11 dead.*

Sooner, Slye, and Rydell had hit the farmhouse before Llorente's Spanish agents, proving that no communications within CNI were safe from the military contractor's hacking.

And if eleven Suicide Ride mercs were dead, it proved that the farm had, indeed, been a safe house for the Khamsin Sayef. The partners had been right.

"I feel like we're making progress but not getting one goddamn inch closer," Finnigan said. "We made the call on the farmhouse. Fat lotta good it did us. We sent our client's team into a trap."

"At least Suicide Ride got there first," she said.

"Yeah but . . . hang on. *Me cago en la leche?* I'm sorry, did you just say, *I shit in the milk?*"

"It's an expression."

He made a face. "It's a fucked-up one!"

"Could we concentrate on this problem for now? Do we grab Pryor or wait until she's away from my father?"

"How?" he asked. "She's CIA. If she stays in Barcelona tonight, it'll be in a top-of-the-line hotel, which the agency will have had checked out for security purposes. If she heads back to Milan, it'll be to her home or to the station. Both will be tough grabs."

"Not as tough as grabbing her in front of my father."

"You know, she hired us. We could maybe get her attention, then she'll come to us."

"No. We agreed that all communication would go through Hugo. She'd be suspicious if we just showed up." Fiero stared at the building across the way. "I suppose we could call in a fire alarm, evacuate the people."

Finnigan shrugged. "Might work."

"Or we could call the CIA, report some sort of espionage thing. Get them to call her back to the Barcelona field office. It's the reason we got the bike."

Upon leaving her mother's hospital room, Fiero had gone online to find a used motorcycle for sale. They also secured a bike helmet and leather gloves. They paid cash and then chained the Honda up outside their cheap-ass hotel, not far away. If Annie Pryor took off from this meeting in a cab or an Uber, Fiero likely could follow her, and the crowds would play to their favor. A car would have difficulty getting out of the neighborhood very quickly, which would allow Fiero time to get to the bike.

They would have bought two bikes, but Finnigan couldn't ride worth a damn and didn't pretend any different.

"I'm gonna hit the crowd," he said. "Try to get closer to that building. Your dad isn't likely to notice me. You stay here and observe."

"There's another complication. My mother is being released from the hospital today. If she calls, I have to go to her. She knows where my father is, what he's doing today. I keep expecting her to call at any second."

"I thought of that. 'Course you do," he said. "Look, however it plays, it plays. We just roll with it."

She watched through the binoculars for moment, then lowered them and leaned his way and kissed him on the cheek.

"You're a good partner, Michael."

He shuddered. "*Me cago en la leche* is just wrong."

C34

The Powers That Be in Houston demanded answers.

Colonel Cole Sanger wasn't yet in a position to give any, but he'd grown up in the military chain of command. It never dawned on him to dodge the call.

He had eleven dead soldiers on his hands. He had French national police and the media all over the crime scene. And worse yet, the names Sooner, Slye, and Rydell were on the lips of every European news presenter.

Sanger took the call in his Suburban. "Where are you?" boomed a voice with a smoker's growl. He recognized the voice: Robert Slye, chairman of the military contractor. His father had owned the Oklahoma law firm whose name the military contractor had usurped.

"Heading to an airfield. I'm taking this investigation to Barcelona."

"Well, what the hell happened in France?"

"Ambush. Intended for Spanish Intelligence. My mission brief was to beat those desk jockeys to every potential lead, and we did."

"And got your whole field team killed!"

"Yessir. They were exceedingly well paid to be in harm's way. Their next of kin will be taken care of in perpetuity. The men knew the stakes."

He could hear the shock in the partner's voice. "Pretty damn cold, son."

"Sir." Sanger opted to take it as a compliment.

"And this media shitshow?"

"That's the work of a Spanish Intelligence officer, Hugo Llorente, sir. We know for a fact that Llorente had underlings contact every news outlet on the continent and inform them that the men on the scene belonged to Sooner, Slye, and Rydell. Bastard didn't even try to hide his play. He used a desk phone he knew we'd had bugged."

"He declaring war on us, this Llorente guy?"

We declared war on him, Sanger thought.

"For the time being, you remain in charge of this clusterfuck, Colonel." If that phrasing was intended to make Sanger fearful for his job, it failed. "What's your next move?"

"Two freelance bounty hunters. One American, one Spanish. I underestimated them. They've been on top of this thing from the start. They were the ones who tracked down that farmhouse, not Hugo Llorente and his bureaucracy. We believe they're in Barcelona. I'm putting a team on them. Goal One: See if they lead us to the Khamsin Sayef. And if we can't accomplish that, at least get them off the playing field."

"How?"

Sanger said, "By whatever means are necessary."

"Do it, Colonel. Get us that smarmy bastard, this cleric. I want his turban stuffed up his ass and his head on a pike."

"Sir."

Sanger disconnected the line.

His car sped out into the suburbs, toward an airfield and a compact jet the firm had put at his disposal.

Eleven dead.

The Khamsin Sayef would answer for that, as would St. Nicholas Salvage & Wrecking. He had no interest in playing nice with a couple of lowlife bounty hunters who'd cost him eleven men and made him lose face.

He was glad that he'd brought in Syarhey Valazko. The time had come to kill these amateur idiots before they caused any more damage.

C35

Finnigan flash-browsed the mall and found a *Real Madrid* cap that looked pretty much like thirty others he'd seen in the plaza. He wore a cotton shirt unbuttoned and with sleeves rolled up over a T-shirt. It was too hot for the overshirt or the hat, but the shirt would allow him to change up his image in a flash, if he needed to. He slid on his aviators, satisfied with his camouflage.

Getting out of El Triangle proved tougher than he anticipated. Protesters had started seeping into the ground floor of the mall the way floodwater creeps into a basement. Finnigan finally nudged his way outside amid a sea of protest signs ranging from professionally designed and illustrated to felt markers on flattened cardboard boxes. Messages included everything: pro-immigration rights, anti-immigration rights, religious tolerance, Islamic slurs, law-and-order pleas, Black Lives Matter banners—written in Spanish, naturally—fans of the Spanish monarchy, fans of abolishing the Spanish monarchy, and, improbably, one Ku Klux Klan sign. His Spanish was limited, but he deciphered signs blaming

America, the EU and, of course, the Jews for, well, everything.

He started trying to make his way through the crowd, vectoring around the speakers and the fountains toward the Galician Trust building.

Finnigan was half-convinced that if he could make eye contact with Annie Pryor, she might step out and meet him. She had hired St. Nicholas, after all. And if she sussed a trap and bolted, well, that's why they had the used Honda chained up outside their hotel. In an urban chase in a city with such notoriously bad traffic as Barcelona, advantage motorcycle, every time.

The center of Plaça de Catalunya was getting too crowded, and the mood was tanking, fast. He changed tack and headed back out onto the street. Out by the parked cars, he began making much better headway, drawing closer to the glass monolith building.

He spotted something ahead and stopped dead in his tracks.

A cluster of young protesters collided with him. "Sorry," he muttered. "*Lo Siento.*"

Finnigan righted himself and eyed a parking meter. He moved toward it, head down, palm up as if counting invisible coins. He looked out over the tops of his sunglasses and beneath the rim of his cap, at an SUV parked along the road.

A man leaned against the passenger door. He was blond, squat, with navy tattoos on his forearms. And his right hand was up, rubbing his neck as if trying to untangle a knot under his skin.

Julian Ritter. The German driver.

Finnigan pretended to read the instructions on the parking meter as he dug out his phone and hit speed dial number one.

ON THE SECOND FLOOR OF EL TRIANGLE, Fiero's phone vibrated in her pocket as a hand descended onto her upper arm.

She lowered the field glasses and turned.

A leering man stood behind her. She could tell from a glance that he spent a significant portion of every day with free weights, and a significant portion of every paycheck on anabolic steroids. He had a neck like an on-ramp girder, a barrel chest, narrow hips, and biceps so comically out of proportion that his free arm hung slightly akimbo away from his torso.

"My God, you are so facking beautiful!" He spoke English, but she clocked his accent as Russian. He was not the first extreme bodybuilder from Russia she'd spotted in Barcelona.

Fiero's phone vibrated again.

She glanced down at her arm and his hand, then up into his face. His skin was flushed and lined with acne, his pupils dilated. She'd seen the telltale evidence of steroid abuse on soldiers when she'd served in the army.

"Pardon me," she said in Spanish and attempted to pull away. He didn't let go.

"These jeans are looking so good on your ass, yes? And you have the long legs. You are the model? Victoria is Secret, yes?"

Her phone vibrated again.

He stayed with English, so she switched. "I'm waiting for my husband. Excuse me."

"He leaves you in mall? Come, I make it up to you. I buy you drink."

"No."

Vibrate.

His eyes did the slow-slide up and down her torso and legs. "Come! I buy you the champagne. You like the champagne!"

"Go away."

Vibrate.

He grinned. "I am the nice guy!"

She raised one leg and reached into her boot.

The butterfly knife starts as a long, thin bit of complicated metal, but with a flick of the wrist, the five-inch blade bares itself and the housing fans out then folds into a handle. Fiero knew how to make a butterfly knife dance; she used the same wrist snap that a tango dancer uses for her fan. Done professionally, it's too fast to see, but it's also something a person can't take their eyes off of when it's happening a meter from their face.

She said, "Get a very long way away from me. Do it now."

The man backpedaled quickly. He raised his hands, palms out. He rattled off something in Russian that sounded like panic.

Fiero drew her phone with her free hand and glanced from the Russian ox to the screen.

She saw Finnigan's name. Then the screen went blank.

She glanced back up and spotted two more hulking steroid abusers step out of a music store and join their friend.

C36

Finnigan turned and glared up at the second story window of the mall. The weak light of the off-white sky created too much glare to see his partner.

Sweat trickled down his spine.

Fiero hadn't answered his call. Had her mom phoned her? No, Fiero would have alerted Finnigan first.

If Julian Ritter was here, then the Khamsin Sayef was targeting someone in the big glass building across the way. The foreign minister? Maybe, but Finnigan had started to believe his own theory that the whole series of bombings was tied up with something that happened in the city of Paris three years earlier. And that pointed to Annie Pryor as the target.

As if it mattered: José Ramón de Cordoba and Pryor were standing three feet apart.

Bomb one, get one free.

And Alexandro Fiero, Finnigan's friend and father of his partner, stood with them.

Finnigan checked his phone.

Nothing.

He made up his mind and turned again, wending between protesters, walking toward Julian Ritter and the SUV.

FIERO STOOD WITH HER KNIFE, facing nine hundred pounds of steroid-infused Russian beef.

This time she didn't wonder: What would Finnigan do? Finnigan would talk his way out of it. He and the body builders would end up as fast friends.

When last she'd looked, Finnigan seemed to have stopped moving. He looked like he was trying to feed a parking meter on the street, although that made no sense.

Fiero couldn't look again. Not without turning her back on the Russians.

The first guy's face had turned citrus-pink with rage. His two friends picked up on it as soon as they'd spotted the butterfly knife.

"What the fack is this bitch, she threatens me with knife!" the first guy bellowed. Other shoppers veered sharply away from the cul-de-sac of corridor nearest the window, not wanting to get involved in the drama.

Fiero didn't like playing the helpless-female card, but she needed this to end quickly. "Get away from me!" she shouted in Spanish.

The three hulking Russians didn't look intimidated.

"The bitch! I am being nice to her! I compliment her, how she is looking, and she is with knife!"

One of the others stepped a little closer. With their twenty-five-inch shoulders, they created a wall of testosterone and sheen. "You need lesson in manners."

The third man stepped closer too. Fiero's back was to the windows.

She waited until the first man did the same—took a menacing step forward, weight on his rear foot. Her free hand snapped out, grabbed his already-straining polo shirt by the collar, and yanked him forward while he was off-balance. He stumbled into her.

She shoved the knife against his crotch.

She hissed under her breath, keeping her voice even and unemotional, "You move and I cut it off. Tell them."

His eyes popped. His mouth fished.

"I have a collection of Russian balls at home, you bloated pile of pig shit." She'd learned the art of insulting Russians when she'd been a spook. She knew which buttons to push. She kept her voice low, maintained eye contact but noting his two mates with her peripheral vision. She and the first man stood as close as slow-dance partners. "This is Spain. I'm Spanish. You'll be dick-less, and you'll go to prison for rape. But not here. Oh, no. I work in the office of the king of Spain, and when they convict you, they'll send you back to a Russian prison, with no dick but plenty of new friends, you unsophisticated peasant."

The third man jostled forward.

Fiero jammed the knife harder into the first man's crotch.

"*Stop! Stop! Stop!*" he yelped in Russian. Which was the same as English. "Don't! Stay back!"

The others froze.

Fiero added a few ounces-per-square-inch of pressure.

And gave him a low, slow, wicked smile.

"Go!" the Russian squeaked.

That was enough for his cohorts. They banged into each other, attempting to turn and flee.

Over the big man's shoulder, Fiero noted two men in the deep blue shirts of mall security moving their way.

Fear and rage battled behind the first man's eyes. Fiero ratcheted up her smile and kept the sharp pressure on his crotch.

"Now that your friends are gone, perhaps we could . . . play?"

That was all it took. The Russian broke her grip and backpedaled.

Fiero flicked her wrist and the butterfly knife spun elegantly, becoming a long, hollow handle. She stood on one foot and slid it into her boot, tucking down her cuff.

The Russian, his face florid and sweat-slick, had some space now and began growling about bitches and blades, and how to treat frigid Spanish women. The mall security had picked sides in this fight before they arrived, and he was doing nothing to dissuade them. More blue shirts began running down the corridor toward them.

Fiero turned and tried to spot Finnigan.

He was nowhere to be seen.

C37

The crowd in the plaza was large and grim, and nobody was expecting anything good to come of it.

Finnigan heard a scuffle break out a little deeper in toward the fountains. A lot of eyes turned that direction.

He walked directly up to Julian Ritter, pretended to stumble into him, and drove his fist into the German's gut.

Ritter folded like a pocketknife.

Finnigan knew the man suffered from severe damage to his neck. He grabbed the man's shoulder and squeezed.

He spoke overly loud. "You okay, buddy?"

Ritter groaned, knees buckling.

"Whoa. C'mon. Too much paella, man."

Finnigan held the man up, boxing him up against the van's side panel with his body, and reached for the sliding side door. Like all getaway drivers, Ritter kept his doors unlocked. The door swished open, and nobody waited for them inside.

Finnigan found two bucket seats in front, a row of three seats in the middle and a row of three seats in back. He pushed Ritter in, all the way to the back, and the man fell sideways across the last row.

Finnigan hopped in and slid the door closed in his wake. The van's windows were deeply tinted. Nobody could see in.

Bending low, he stepped around the center row of seats and gripped the man's wounded neck.

Ritter tried fighting back, growled something in German.

Finnigan drew his lead-filled sap from his pocket. There was no room to wind up in the van, but he knew how to use the little weapon. It was all in the wrist. He let it land hard on the man's right kneecap.

Ritter leaned over and barfed onto the floor of the van.

Finnigan frisked him and took away a short-barreled .9 millimeter Glock G26. A nice gun, he thought. He wedged it into his belt at the small of his back. A gamble, carrying a gun in Spain, but Ritter had comrades, and Finnigan assumed they were nearby.

"Your buddies blowing up somebody today, Julian? Hmm?"

"Who . . . the fuck . . . are you?" Ritter wiped vomit off his chin with the back of his hand.

"Where's the cleric?" Finnigan squeezed the man's shoulder.

"Fuck . . . you!" Ritter pinched his eyes tight, tears flowing down his cheeks.

"Who're you targeting, asshole?"

Ritter cried but kept his mouth shut.

"Huh? Where's the cleric? Who's your target? How many guys you got with you? Hmm?"

"Fuck . . . you . . ."

Finnigan's phone vibrated.

He set down the sap and drew his phone. "What, did you go shopping?"

Fiero said, "I just stabbed a half ton of Russian beef in the cock."

"Hand to God, I did not see that answer coming." Finnigan peered out the windows, looking for trouble. "I found Ritter."

"Wait . . . the driver?" Fiero sounded like she was moving quickly in a crowded space but still indoors.

"He's here. Yeah."

"My God. My father."

"Yeah. The Khamsin Sayef is here. That meeting's gotta be the target. We have to get them outta there."

"I'm calling Hugo."

The line disconnected.

Finnigan tucked away his phone and kept pressure on the man's shoulder. "How many guys? Huh? Julian, c'mon, man. Your team is blown. Give it up."

Ritter tried swinging his elbow at Finnigan's nose. Finnigan brushed it aside and applied a little more pressure to the man's neck.

Ritter keened, eyelids screwed tight.

Finnigan checked the approaches again. The melee in the plaza was growing more intense. He saw fists flying. It was stifling in the SUV, and sweat stung his eyes.

Not seeing the rest of the Khamsin Sayef—whoever they might be—was a blessing. The mad bombers' playbook was pretty simple: Set the bomb, escape, then blow it up. You don't blow it up before you scram.

Not seeing the gang meant the bomb hadn't detonated.

Yet.

Alexandro, Annie Pryor, and the foreign minister were safe for now.

FIERO STOPPED ON THE GROUND floor of the mall and dialed the number they'd been given for Hugo Llorente. Unfortunately, it was a cut-out number; she was sending a message to one phone, which would send a message through a series of other phones to Llorente, telling him to call back as soon as he could. There was no voicemail option.

Last time, at the crummy hotel on La Rambla, it had taken twenty minutes to get a return call.

If the Khamsin Sayef had planted a bomb in her father's building, waiting for Llorente and Spanish Intelligence wasn't an option.

She dashed from the building, out into the crowded plaza. As she slipped her phone into her trouser pocket, someone caught her by the shoulder and spun her around.

She didn't have time to duck as one of the Russians backhanded her in the cheek.

Fiero went flying into the crowd.

C38

The German driver wasn't going to talk, and Finnigan had neither the time nor the temperament to torture him. He searched the man's pockets and found an amber vial, the label peeled off, holding three pills. *Vicodin*, Finnigan thought.

He found no cell phone.

Ritter tried scrambling up again, tried fighting. Finnigan held him down and used the sap, clocking him at the base of his skull. He felt the German's muscles unclench under his hands, and the man slumped down, unmoving.

Finnigan checked the windows again and scrambled forward to the driver's seat.

Ritter's cell phone sat in a dashboard holder. Finnigan touched the screen. A GPS app popped to life.

The SUV showed as a glowing blue dot on the grid of Barcelona's streets.

The Galician Trust building glowed as a red dot.

He touched the home button twice. Other screens came

into view: Ritter's email, his call history, a solitaire program, an English-to-German translator app.

Finnigan exhaled with relief: Ritter had disabled the sleep mode so his phone wouldn't go dormant while he was driving.

THE GATHERING OF BUSINESS and civic leaders had devolved from a pep talk to a frightened scrum, watching the fighting break out beyond the floor-to-ceiling windows of the Galician Trust.

Annie Pryor touched Alexandro Fiero's forearm. "Señor. Perhaps it would be a good idea to move these people upstairs? I understand you don't have any conference rooms large enough, but . . ."

"My God. Of course." The Spaniard gripped her hand for a second, then strode to one of his young aides. He spoke sotto voce. The girl nodded and drew her mobile.

"Ladies and gentlemen!" Alexandro could boom like an opera-trained tenor. Every head in the room turned his way. "We think it would be a good idea to move upstairs. Just for the duration of . . . this."

His onyx cuff links glinted when he gestured toward the troubles in the plaza.

"There is plenty of room on the eighth and ninth floors. As soon as . . . ?"

His aide nodded, then moved to the back of the lobby, toward the bank of elevators.

Pryor held her phone in landscape mode and used two thumbs to tap out a text to her staff: *Riot in Plaza de Catalunya*. She grumbled as the autocorrect changed it to *Riot in please a de catalyst*.

The Galician Trust aides began herding the four-dozen people away from the plaza-facing windows and toward the elevators. Pryor and Minister de Cordoba with his staff of five followed along. In fact, someone on his staff tried to elbow their way through first, and José Ramón de Cordoba grabbed his assistant by the elbow and shook his too-large head atop his too-long neck.

Pryor got to the elevator banks and noted that all six cars were on their way down, the nearest passing the third floor. She checked her phone—the text hadn't been delivered yet. She had no reception.

Cursing under her breath, she waded against the tide, back out toward the wall of windows, holding the phone in front of her and watching for the connectivity bars to light up.

Behind her, she heard the first elevator ping.

As Pryor moved away, the doors swished open and three people in coveralls, carrying tool kits and heavy canvas bags, stepped out.

Alexandro Fiero moved to the front of the crowd. He paid good money to have his building swept for explosives, and on this of all days, he had no intention of letting his guard down.

"Frau Gunsen. All clear up there?"

She nodded. "All clear, sir."

KATALIN FIERO DAHAR LOOKED UP at the forest of legs that stretched over her. For a moment, she wondered why a couple dozen people were looking down at her.

It came back to her quickly. She tasted the acidic bite of blood on her lip.

One of the huge Russians stepped into her vision. Lying on her back, on the ground of the plaza, the man looked like a redwood tree, towering toward the edge of space.

"What staring!" He bellowed in English at the crowd, which backed up several feet.

The Russian grinned down at Fiero, whose arms and legs were spread akimbo. She brought her arms in toward her torso: nothing seemed broken, but the rib she'd injured fighting Syarhey Valazko in Paris clearly was unhappy.

"You are bitch!" the big man said, and worked his way down onto one knee by her side. Given his muscle-bound mass, it wasn't an easy trip. Like his friend, the edge of his jaw and his neck were peppered with acne.

"You like knives, eh? This makes you tough bitch girl, yes? You—"

Fiero made a sword of the middle knuckle of her first two fingers and drove them into the man's Adam's apple.

The Russian's eyes bulged. His left hand went to his throat, his right arm out to balance himself on one knee.

Fiero bicycled her long legs, used the pendulum energy to rise in a blink. She knelt like he did, one boot and one knee on the ground, her right leg beside him, braced like a sturdy table. Her rib shrieked, but she ignored it.

Fiero gripped the Russian's tree-trunk arm. She shoved him in the chest. He toppled backward.

His thick torso slammed into the pavement.

His right arm didn't.

Outstretched over Fiero's braced leg, the man's arm caught on the stable shelf of her knee and stopped falling.

She heard his shoulder muscles rip, felt the shimmer as the ball of his humerus bone wrenched free of the socket of his scapula.

It was a maiming injury, a remnant of her training in Llorente's kill shop. At best, the Russian was in for a long set of surgeries and even-longer physical therapy to rebuild the rotator cuff she'd demolished. More likely, he'd lose the arm entirely. If he didn't die from internal bleeding first.

Fiero was on her feet and moving through the crowd like a broken-field runner before the Russian screamed.

C39

The pulsing red dot on Julian Ritter's phone wasn't coming from inside the Galician Trust building anymore. As Finnigan watched, it moved outside the outline of the building.

Then the one red dot became two.

He pushed through the crowd, moving as fast as he could, keeping one eye on the growing crowd and the other on the stolen phone. Ritter's Glock nestled against his spine beneath his unbuttoned overshirt.

He skirted around a shoving match. The tall glass building loomed over him. From thirty feet away, he saw three people, two men, white and black, and a white woman, step out of the building. They wore gray coveralls and carried large, red tool kits and shoulder-strapped duffel bags. Finnigan's undisciplined mind went straight to *Ghostbusters*.

Could they be the red dot represented on Ritter's phone? Finnigan glanced down.

The two dots had become three.

He looked up in time to see a Goth punk guy with black lipstick take a swing at him.

Finnigan ducked the blow and rabbit-punched the kid right over the kidney. The kid's raven-black hair flopped into his eyes as he doubled over and fell.

Another youth came at Finnigan, plus two more with the same black lipstick and eyeliner.

Finnigan stepped close to the nearest kid and drew the gun, showing him. "Wanna go?"

They might not have spoken English but they definitely spoke Glock. They evaporated back into the melee.

Finnigan hid the gun again and turned back to the Galician Trust building.

The trio in gray coveralls was gone.

He checked Ritter's phone. The three red dots were moving away from him. Away from Ritter, too. Plus Ritter's SUV that Finnigan had disabled by breaking off the key in the ignition.

"Michael!"

He glanced up. A man in a swastika T-shirt went flying, and Fiero appeared as if she'd beamed down from a starship. She was bleeding from her lower lip, her hair unpinned and hanging straight to the middle of her back.

Finnigan stood close and raised his voice to be heard. "Ritter's here. Three people in coveralls with tool kits just left your dad's building, heading that way."

She said, "The Cleric?"

"No. White, white, black. Male, male, female."

"My father is still—?"

"Think so. C'mon."

They raced to the building.

"Do you have a key card?"

"No."

"I do." He drew the Glock and fired at the magnetically lock-ing door. The glass shattered.

His goal was twofold: to get into the building, and to draw every cop in Barcelona their way. With a riot underway, he wasn't too sanguine about the latter. But alarms began screaming.

The doorframe and some of the glass remained. Fiero kicked it with the sole of her boot and the entire frame toppled in, clat-tering to the black-and-white parquet floor and spraying out a fanfare of glass.

She winced and held her side.

A uniformed but unarmed security guard came running from deeper inside the building. The man's boots skidded on glass when Finnigan pointed the Glock at him.

Finnigan roared, "Bomb! Upstairs! We need to get everyone out! Now!"

The guard shook his head and replied in English. "The build-ing's clean! We just had it swept seconds ago!"

Fiero and Finnigan glanced at each other. "The people in the coveralls," she said. "Bomb-sweepers!"

"Jesus, that's brilliant!"

Fiero relieved the guard of his walkie-talkie. She toggled it. "Anyone in the building: Evacuate! Evacuate now! There is a bomb in the building! Evacuate!"

They grabbed the guard and gave him the bum's rush back to his station. Finnigan knelt and spotted the red panic button in the kneehole of the desk. He punched it. More sirens sounded and recessed red lights in the wall flashed.

The walkie-talkie in Fiero's hand squawked. "Who is this?"

It was the voice of Alexandro Fiero.

Finnigan grabbed it and jammed it into the guard's face. Also the gun.

"Full evac, buddy. Now."

The guard relayed the news, his voice rising with every syllable.

Fiero said, "How many in the building?"

"I don't know! Eighty?"

Finnigan turned and eyed the glass-shard-carpeted lobby. "They're gonna logjam getting out that door."

Fiero took the gun from him and moved to a weapons locker behind the guard's station. She shot off the lock, and the aluminum door sprang open.

She grabbed a shotgun and a box of shells.

"No, they won't."

C40

Frau Gunsen led Ron Perry and DeMarcus Washington out of the Galician Trust building and walked around it, bypassing the worst of the rioting, circling back to Julian Ritter and their SUV.

Gunsen's biggest fear at this point was finding that the pain-killers and wideawakes had finally caught up with the German. It was going to happen at some point. Both of her American soldiers, Perry and Washington, could drive, so even the worst-case scenario wasn't that bad. Still, it gnawed at her. Ritter had been wounded on one of Gunsen's missions, a heist she'd organized to fund the real jobs. His injuries were on her.

They got to the car but didn't see Ritter, who always waited outside. With his nerve damage, sitting was excruciating.

They found the SUV unlocked. Perry wrenched open the side door, and the stench of vomit wafted out. He glanced in and saw Ritter's legs and feet in the far back seats. "Aw, Jesus H. Christ," he muttered.

Washington pinched his nose. "He drunk?"

Perry climbed in, folded at an angle, to get to the far back row, and turned over the German driver.

"Fuck." He climbed back out. "He's been beat."

Gunsen stood a little taller, began scanning the hostile crowd in the plaza. "You're sure?"

"Sure as shit." Perry hawked a gob of chewing tobacco into the gutter.

Gunsen climbed into the van and moved into the back. Shorter than the others, she had room to maneuver. Ritter was badly bruised and unconscious, but his breathing was even. She patted him down. No gun.

She crabbed sideways, moved forward, and checked the driver's seat. Then backed out.

"His gun's gone. Phone too. The ignition's been jimmied. This car isn't going anywhere."

Perry said, "We walking out?"

Washington glowered down at him. "Carrying Ritter? And all our gear?"

"I could steal us another van but the traffic . . ." Perry shook his head. The rioting had pushed out into the street. Just getting this van out would have been a challenge, even with a professional driver, which now they didn't have. Getting to another car, hot-wiring it, and getting back here would take forever.

Perry, with his thick blond mustache and slicked-back hair, could look more forlorn than any man Gunsen had ever met. "This here's fucked *up*."

"Could've been a mugging," Washington said.

"Wasn't," Gunsen said, eyeing the crowd with growing malevolence. "Why monkey-wrench the car?"

"Okay, but what—"

They heard the not-too-distant boom of a shotgun.

Nearly every protester in sight flinched or screamed or hit the ground.

Washington nudged Gunsen and pointed back toward the Galician Trust building.

They couldn't see the door or the sidewalk from their angle—protesters in the way—but they watched as one of the twenty-five-foot-high windows disintegrated, and granular bits of glass began falling straight down.

As they watched, they heard a second boom and a second window turned into glittering shards of glass.

Gunsen watched and said, "Blow it."

"What? We gotta get out before—"

"Now! Do it now!"

A HELICOPTER FROM BETEVÉ NEWS caught the images of the ground floor windows of the Galician Trust building being blown out by someone with a shotgun. The assailant had stepped out of the building and was firing back inside.

The mob on the plaza attempted to scatter, screaming. Those who fled found themselves hemmed in by those who hadn't heard the shots or didn't realize where they'd come from.

From the vantage of the BTV News chopper, the shooter appeared to be a woman with long, dark, straight hair. She fired into three of the windows.

Within seconds, she was swallowed up by a flow of people erupting from within the building, all running out into the street.

INSIDE THE GALICIAN TRUST BUILDING, the stairwell doors burst open and people began streaming out into the lobby.

Fiero pulled her tank top away from her torso and wiped

down the shotgun, tossing it into a corner behind a large potted fern. Three of the six tall windows were gone. Glass covered the parquet floor like sand at the beach.

The people poured out of the building through the breached windows. Finnigan and Fiero joined them.

A protester in the plaza recognized Fiero as the woman who'd been firing the shotgun. He pointed and shouted. Finnigan clocked the guy, who fell like an anchor.

Fiero grabbed Finnigan's collar and leaned in close to be heard. "Go for the bombers? Or go for Pryor?"

Finnigan checked the stolen phone. The red dots no longer glowed. He suspected the bombers had found Ritter and the damaged SUV, and had shut down their own phones.

"Pryor."

Fiero stared into his eyes a beat, then nodded.

He understood. Staying to catch the CIA station chief increased the likelihood that Fiero would be spotted by her father.

José Ramón de Cordoba had only one actual security guard in his entourage. The other four were bureaucratic underlings. All six raced down the stairs toward the lobby.

"I'm getting you out of here!" the security man shouted.

The foreign minister said, "You're getting all of us out of here."

They reached the lobby to see two of the elevators open, disgorging more people than could legally ride in them.

Everyone was shocked to see the high windows shattered, the frame of the main door lying on the floor. People fled the building, pouring out into the clogged street and the violent protest beyond.

ALEXANDRO FIERO RUSHED DOWN the stairs, scuffing his well-polished shoes, ushering the entire staff of his eighth-floor office ahead of him. He'd been the last to leave the floor. He'd insisted.

Annie Pryor had been on nine. She was a half floor above him, racing down too. She'd drawn her service revolver from her tote bag and was holding it, finger indexed.

They'd almost reached the lobby when the building shook. Plaster rained down on them. They felt the explosion before they heard it. It was rumbling, guttural. The roar of a dragon.

It came from behind them. From above them.

A few people fell. Some stepped over them. Some helped them up. Down near the lobby door, she spotted Alexandro Fiero helping someone to rise, pushing them through the door.

OUT IN THE PLAZA, Finnigan and Fiero looked up to see the eighth-floor windows explode.

Harsh white light filled the space, followed by fat, rolling clouds of oily smoke.

People under the windows covered their heads, screamed, and turned away, or fell to their knees. The glass pattered down into the crowd.

Fiero watched the survivors stream out of the building. Her face showed no emotion, her dark eyes hard as flint, straw-straight hair fluttered before her face.

They waited. Waited some more.

Alexandro Fiero strode from the lobby, directing his staff and keeping them moving.

Fiero's hand shot out and gripped Finnigan's arm so hard it hurt.

Finnigan hugged her, then made the sign of the cross and lipped a silent *thank you* to the sky.

Annie Pryor emerged a moment later.

The staff of the Galician Trust had moved off to their left into the pedestrian-clogged street. Pryor studied them a moment, stuffing her hand into her tote bag. Then she pulled out a cell phone and began marching in the opposite direction.

FROM A BLOCK AND A HALF AWAY, Frau Gunsen and her men watched the smoke roil out of the eighth-floor windows. Even from street level, they could tell that a river of survivors flowed out of the lobby.

Too many. The building had been evacuated.

DeMarcus Washington said, "Gotta go."

Ron Perry used his knuckles to flatten his mustache. "Yeah, but how?"

Gunsen grabbed her shoulder bag and turned to make eye contact with him, held it.

She turned to Washington, did the same.

She climbed into the SUV, bent in half like an upside-down L, shuffled to the back. She sat on the outer seat, by Julian Ritter's legs. She set her bag on the floor by her boots, withdrew a Glock LE and a sound suppressor. She fitted the tube, clicked it in place on a bayonet mount. She placed the barrel against Ritter's ear and fired one into his skull.

The bullet exited and embedded itself under the seat.

She retrieved the shell and threw it in her bag. She disassembled the weapon and climbed back out.

She repeated what she'd done earlier: made eye contact with Perry; held it. Made eye contact with Washington; held it. She reached down and hefted one of the tool kits. She used the sleeve of her left arm to wipe tears off her cheek.

She said, "We walk."

PRYOR RANG UP HER BARCELONA STAFF—the CIA had only two agents in the city—and the call connected just as a woman's hand snapped out and snagged her phone away.

Someone else pressed up against her right side and displayed—briefly—a .9 millimeter auto.

She blinked up at the people crowding her from both sides.

The bounty hunters from Cyprus.

The tall Spaniard dropped Pryor's phone and smashed it with the heel of her motorcycle boot.

"What are you—?"

The sandy-haired American said, "Keep walking, Jane Bond. We gotta talk."

"Are you insane? I'm—"

Fiero stripped the tote bag off Pryor's shoulder and spun it, letting go and sending it straight into a dumpster in an adjacent alley.

Finnigan clicked his tongue. "Nothing but net."

Fiero spoke softly, one steely hand on Pryor's left elbow. "My father nearly died in that explosion. If I find out you lied to us, you'll wish you'd been up there when it detonated."

They hustled her faster, away from the building and the plaza and the protesters, the police sirens and the media helicopters and the panicky survivors. Finnigan pressed the muzzle of his gun against her flank, his hand obscured by his unbuttoned shirt.

"It's the Khamsin Sayef. They—"

Finnigan said, "It's Paris, bitch. It's always been Paris. Right from the start."

Annie Pryor thought about protesting but stopped. She realized in a blink.

They knew.

C41

"My friends. By now you have heard that yet another enemy of all good people has been destroyed. A leader of the devils who beset the Prophet—peace be upon him."

As always, the tape from the cleric contained no clues as to its origin; the room behind him was a whitewashed cube, void of details. His robe and kaffiyeh could have been purchased in any market, in any decade. His voice suggested he'd been raised in Cairo, but so had tens of millions of others. He'd been educated, but where? The world had no shortage of well-educated murderers. Between his first bombing and now, the man had lost weight and his skin appeared sickly; television analysts had spewed a thousand theories about that.

"José Ramón de Cordoba led Spain's Holy War against Islam. He was an architect of our suffering, our bloodshed. He supported the monstrous government of Alsharq as it defies Sharia Law. José Ramón de Cordoba was an enemy of the

Prophet, may peace be upon him. José Ramón de Cordoba has paid for his evil ways.

"As will all who oppose our people."

The tape ended.

SIX MINUTES AFTER IT ARRIVED at the Al Jazeera office in Qatar, a doctor in Barcelona, Spain, checked the pulse of José Ramón de Cordoba and declared him to be in good health.

Like every other occupant of the Galician Trust building, the foreign minister had survived the bombing.

C42

Chaos today in Barcelona, Spain, as sparring protests for and against immigration policy devolved into a riot. A bomb was detonated in a building overlooking the Plaza Catalonia, the site of the largest of the riots. No one was killed in the explosion because authorities had evacuated the building only seconds before.

Within thirty minutes of the bombing, a spokesman for the Khamsin Sayef, an Alsharqi terrorist organization, took credit for the bombing, saying it was in response to Spanish colonialism in Africa. Fierce fighting between government forces and rebels in Alsharq have all but destroyed the capital of Baharos. Spain was an early supporter of the Alsharqi government.

In a video sent to a television station in Qatar, the so-far unidentified spokesman for the militants said Spanish foreign minister José Ramón de Cordoba was the intended target.

A spokesman for the Spanish National Intelligence Center confirmed that de Cordoba had been present in the building but escaped before the detonation.

A riot outside the building broke up shortly after the explosion. Police say anarchist and criminal groups quickly departed the scene as police and firefighters descended on the area.

Police say two people died and twenty-seven were injured in the plaza, including a Russian tourist taken by helicopter to a local hospital after his arm was nearly separated from his body. Police suspect he was attacked by anti-immigration activists because of his nationality.

Spanish police, Catalan police, and national intelligence agencies have begun pointing fingers at each other.

Meanwhile, the dead included a protester who suffered a heart attack, possibly caused by the excessive heat of the day. And a man's body was found in a car adjacent to the protest. He'd been beaten and shot in the head. Catalan police suspect it was a case of robbery, unrelated to the protest or the bombing.

Tensions remain high in the city, and police and the military authorities warn that further protests are planned tomorrow in Barcelona, Madrid, Valencia, and Zaragoza . . .

IN THE BARCELONA SUBOFFICE of Sooner, Slye, and Rydell, a former South African security officer had been left in charge. He sat at his desk, watching the news report, as someone knocked on his door. "Come!"

A blond woman with enormous eyeglasses stepped in.

"What?"

"Rumpus. Cyber security. Chen Yiu sent me from Galveston."

The South African blinked at her. "Wait. Your name is *Rumpus?*"

She looked indignant. "It's German."

He hadn't the time for the cybernerds. "Whatever it is, send me a memo."

The blond woman—she sounded American—shook her

head. "You wish. We've been running the traps. We're absolutely sure Spanish Intel is on your phones, your computers, the works."

The former cop started to realize he couldn't blow her off. "You're sure?"

Rumpus snorted a derisive laugh. "You guys are leaking like a bad diaper. Here, look."

She all but shoved him aside, bending at the waist and hijacking his keyboard. Within a few keystrokes, he began to see the green-on-black writing of the behind-the-wall coding of the Sooner, Slye, and Rydell security system. "You see that?" She pointed a chewed fingernail at the screen. "Hacks."

"Damn it."

"We don't get paid by the hour. If we say there's a threat, there's a threat. Here." She brought up the command protocols for the Barcelona station.

"Can we get around them?" the station chief asked.

"Negative. Galveston says we keep them where they are but we establish an end run. Spanish Intel is going to keep their eyes and ears on this office. We'll move everything important off-site. Let them listen. They'll hear what we want them to hear."

She pulled back and the station chief tapped in his security override password.

Rumpus grinned. "Got 'em by the balls now."

C43

Colonel Cole Sanger streaked south in the company's Embraer Phenom, heading toward Barcelona. He arranged for his primary team to stay in place—he currently had units in Madrid, Paris, and Geneva—and the midrange jet was decked out with a good videoconferencing system.

He'd taken only a beefy, beet-faced ex–chief petty officer named Swensen, with whom he'd worked for years. Plus Syarhey Valazko, who lounged low in his rotating seat, legs up on the seat behind him, arms folded, chin on his chest.

Once the video hookups were established and encrypted, Sanger got to the point. "Spanish police and military are watching all roads, all railroads, all aircraft, all boats," he told the twenty top lieutenants in three offices. "The Khamsin Sayef is in Barcelona. It's unlikely they can get out undetected. I'm on my way there now."

Sanger leaned forward in his seat, the safety harness dragging on his tie.

"Every agency in the country has one priority, and only one.

Capture these bastards. But we will get them first. They killed a senior official of Sooner, Slye, and Rydell and his team. They lured eleven of our men into an ambush in France. This cannot stand. If you have police contacts, open your wallet. If you have military or intelligence contacts, you have permission to park a bank truck. If you have contacts in the criminal underground, then crack heads. No questions will be asked, now or later. Am I clear?"

Through the crystal clear video feed, he watched the groups nod.

"Our rules of engagement are shoot-to-kill. If you have to break a few laws to find these vermin, you'll have the full weight of Sooner, Slye, and Rydell's legal resources at your disposal. To say nothing of the US State Department."

His own screen was split between the three images. He pointed to the Madrid office.

"My office gets reports from each of your units, every thirty minutes, from now until boom."

He saw people glancing around. In this large an operation, reporting up the corporate ladder every half hour would be a logistical nightmare.

"Sounds like a lot of paperwork, doesn't it?" Sanger said, eyes scanning the feeds. "Let me put it another way: The team that success- fully tracks down the Khamsin Sayef will share a five-million-dollar bonus, to be split as the team sees fit. The teams that don't, your contracts with Sooner, Slye, and Rydell will be reevaluated."

That got everyone's attention.

"Report every thirty minutes. Sanger out."

He disconnected, slammed closed the lid of the laptop, which rested in the spun-around seat before him. He reached for the bottle of mineral water in the armrest holder.

He turned to the ruddy-faced former chief petty officer. Swensen was built like the professional boxer he used to be.

Sanger had personally seen the navy man put down much bigger opponents with a single blow.

"Chief, there are two bounty hunters in Barcelona. An American, ex–US Marshal, and a Spanish woman who served in the army and intelligence, and, we think, probably worked as an assassin."

The big man listened and nodded. His hair was cut in a perfect flattop and his fire-hydrant neck threatened the integrity of his polo shirt.

"I put together a team. Same three guys you worked with that time in Venezuela. They should be in Barcelona by now. You'll work with Valazko here. Everyone else is focused on the Khamsin Sayef. Your target is the bounty hunters. Clear?"

Swensen glanced at the possibly sleeping man, two rows down in the jetliner. "My team answers to me, and I answer to you, Colonel. Don't know this guy."

Sanger almost smiled. He'd personally recruited Swensen, and not because of the man's tact. "Swensen, Valazko. Valazko, Swensen. There, you've met. Valazko, I've known the chief for years. I trust him. Follow his lead. But you're partners, understand? Keep each other in the loop."

Valazko shrugged. "Sure, okay."

"The company HQ in Dallas does not need to know about this. This operation is between the three of us. It is organic unto itself."

Organic unto itself: a black box. No communications, no coordination with anyone not on this flight, save for Swensen and his team.

The decision to kill these bounty hunters was Sanger's, and Sanger's alone.

Swensen nodded. "Sir."

Sanger turned to the third man on the flight.

The very pale man sipped his coffee and shrugged and smiled sleepily. "Sure, okay."

44

BARCELONA, SPAIN

Fiero took Annie Pryor to their crappy little hotel, knowing from experience that the front desk clerk wouldn't look up from his televised soccer game as they entered. He didn't disappoint.

She marched the CIA station chief into the tiny, humid bathroom and, at gunpoint, made her strip. Pryor was livid, but the look on Fiero's face suggested that protesting would do little good. She removed all of her clothing, self-conscious to do so in front of a stranger.

Finnigan arrived a few minutes later. He'd stopped in a store and brought a cheap tracksuit and flip-flops. He also brought aluminum foil. He wrapped Pryor's clothes in roll after roll of foil and chucked them out the hotel room window into the airshaft. They didn't know how thoroughly she'd been lo-jacked but took no chances.

They sat Pryor on the room's double bed.

"You're both finished," she said. "You're blackballed. I'll see to it you never receive another contract from any country doing business with the US."

Finnigan said, "Got that out of your system? Feel better now?"

He took the room's only chair and sat backward, arms folded over the back. Fiero stood against the wall, weight on one boot, sole of the other against the wall, arms folded.

"Paris," Finnigan said. "Three years ago. The Khamsin Sayef emerges as a new player in the terrorism world, killing your old station chief, Dinah Mariner, and her kid and her husband. The group goes dormant for three years. Then reemerges this year to kill a banker in Geneva, an engineer in Annecy and a do-gooder in Barcelona. And today, they tried to kill the foreign minister."

"What do you want?" Pryor spat.

Finnigan ignored her. "But here's the B Side cover: Three years ago, the Khamsin Sayef kills the Mariner family in Paris. This year, they return. They kill a quiet little banker who was working in Paris three years ago. They kill the wife of an engineer, a woman who ran a website in Paris three years ago. They kill your buddy Pete Newsom, now of Suicide Ride, but who formerly worked with you and Mariner in Paris three years ago. And today, they tried to kill you."

Pryor opened her mouth to respond. But nothing came out. So she squinted at Finnigan and said, "Fuck you."

She turned to Fiero, who did her impression of the Sphinx. "And you."

Finnigan said, "What happened in Paris three years ago?"

Pryor glowered. The sweats were a sickly light green and too large on her. Finnigan should have been standing, like Fiero, so that both towered over her. That was the classic interrogation position. But he chose to sit, to be physically on the same level with her. He'd handled many interrogations over the years, and he knew that a false sense of equality could be as big a leverage as a true sense of inferiority. Especially with a smart, educated person.

"What's the Khamsin Sayef really after?"

She glowered. "I paid you to find them. Remember?"

"Who are they, for real?"

"Islamists. Fundamentalists. Terrorists. Jesus Christ, turn on a goddamn TV, you amateurs! Their front man sent video!"

Finnigan said, "Bullshit." But that was all.

He waited. Pryor glanced his direction. "How can you say that?"

"Because their driver is a German. Julian Ritter. He's not an Islamist. He's a career criminal. I grabbed his phone this morning. Know what he was running? GPS, email, solitaire, and a German-to-English translation app."

He let that sink in.

As he suspected, Pryor was smart and quick. He could see it behind her eyes.

Fiero stood like a statue, arms crossed, only her shoulders and boot sole touching the wall. She looked strung as tight as a guitar string.

"Not German-to-Arabic. German-to-English. Wanna see something?" Finnigan fished out the stolen telephone. Ritter had disabled sleep mode, so it would stay alive while he drove cross-country. He showed it to Pryor, but out of her reach.

"German-to-English. See that little box, upper right-hand corner? It's set to *American standard*. Ritter was driving for Americans."

"That's insane."

"I saw them. Outside the building, this morning. Male, male, female. White, black, white. No beards, no olive skin. They moved like Americans."

She didn't need to ask what that meant. Annie Pryor, like Finnigan, had sat through enough stakeouts to know that many Americans walk and move with a confident stride that Europeans usually can't or don't match. To Europeans, the walk appears to be arrogance. And maybe it is.

"Al Qaeda recruits from Western countries," she said. "Daesh. The Taliban. They—"

Finnigan twisted in his chair and plugged the stolen phone into his own charger. They'd lucked out and hadn't needed to stop to get a new charger.

"Wait." Pryor licked her lips. "That's the driver's cell phone?"

Finnigan fiddled with the charger.

"You're sure? I mean, about the driver?"

Finnigan nodded.

"My God! We need that. Now! His email contacts, his call record . . ."

He shrugged, set the phone down on the cheap particleboard side table.

"I mean it! The CIA, we can—"

"Yeah, but you're not CIA right here, are you? You're the woman who came to our place of business and hired us, and lied about what you knew. You're the one who withheld information that could have helped grabbed the Sword of the Storm by now."

"I didn't! Finnigan, Jesus Christ! I . . . listen, all right? If I knew how to find these bastards, I would have! I don't know where they are! I don't have some secret stash of information!"

"But you knew the announced targets weren't the real targets. You knew about Paris."

She shut her mouth so hard her teeth clacked. She stared at Finnigan, who sat and waited.

Her eyes darted to the phone. The phone that—if the bounty hunters were right—was the first solid lead anyone had ever obtained on a member of the Khamsin Sayef.

She glanced at Fiero: an iron statue. She glanced back at Finnigan, who stared at her, but not with anger or dominance. With patience.

"Yes! Okay? I suspected—I *suspected*—that there was another thing going on here! That the targets they identified might not be the targets. I . . . I had a hunch . . ."

"So you knew the other banker, not the stated target, but Cedric Brecher, had been in Paris three years ago. And you knew Joan Caldwell had been running a tourism website there three years ago."

Pryor didn't deny it. She looked close to panicking.

"Which means you knew them then too. You knew them three years ago in Paris."

"I can't talk about that."

Finnigan belched a laugh. "Who the fuck are you kidding, sweet pea? Can you hear yourself right now? Can't talk about it! Lady, your *not* talking about it damn near got Katalin's dad killed! Damn near got the foreign minister killed." He laughed again. "Damn near got you killed, though I'm kind of okay with that one."

"It's . . ." She turned to Fiero, looked up into the impassive, dark eyes. "I'm sorry they targeted your father. But *they* targeted your father, not me."

"They targeted you," Finnigan grabbed her attention again. "Alexandro just had the bad luck to be standing near you. As were, like, forty other people. Bitch? Please."

Finnigan dismissed her argument with a wave.

"I want them!" Pryor spat, her hands curling into fists. "Fuck both of you! I want them dead! They killed Dinah. They killed Pete Newsom. They tried to kill me. Of course I want them fucking dead! I will move heaven and earth to do that! But I cannot talk to you about Paris three years ago! Now give me the goddamn phone, get me the hell out of here, and let the CIA do its job!"

Fiero's phone vibrated. She broke her stance, drew it from her back pocket.

She stared at the screen for a moment.

"Gun."

Without asking for clarity, Finnigan reached for the small of his back and let the Glock rotate on the axis of his finger and the trigger guard. Fiero took it by the grip and pointed it at Pryor's forehead.

"Be quiet."

She put her phone on speaker. "Hugo?"

The smoker's voice of Hugo Llorente came back over the line. "You called. I've tried getting back to you for the past half hour. You weren't picking up."

Fiero stepped closer, the barrel of the Glock an inch from Pryor's eyebrows. The station chief froze.

"We have someone who knows the truth behind the Khamsin Sayef. She knows their origin. She knows their goal."

Llorente said, "By the grace of God . . ."

"She won't talk. She requires some time in one of your black sites."

Pryor's eyes snapped open. She started shaking her head.

Fiero shook hers too and stepped even closer.

Pryor scuttled back on the bed.

Llorente's voice was a studied neutral, as gray as his eyes. "That can be arranged."

"It will not please the Americans."

"I have done many things in my career. Pleasing the Americans has rarely been one of them."

"When you extract the information, our informant will have to disappear. Permanently. Or there will be repercussions."

Pryor snapped. "Jesus God! Are you insane? I'm in the CI-fucking-A! You can't!"

Fiero said nothing. Her eyes never left Annie Pryor's.

Hugo Llorente didn't have to ask about the voice he'd just heard. He recognized it.

Finnigan didn't interfere.

Annie Pryor came close to hyperventilating.

Llorente said, "I can have a van to you in thirty minutes."

"Hugo! It's Annie! They're insane! They have a phone! They have contact lists for Khamsin Sayef! We need to—"

"Katalin?" Llorente interjected. "Thirty minutes."

He disconnected.

C45

The military contractor's Embraer Phenom touched down at a corporate airfield a couple miles outside of town. Two people waited for them. One was a black woman dressed all in black with black driving gloves, standing next to a black Escalade and looking a bit like part of the machine. The other woman stood at proper parade rest, wearing a military-style tunic, trousers, and riding boots.

The woman in the lead offered a hand and a quick, firm shake. "Colonel. Deirdre Kinney, Barcelona office. Some of the streets have been blocked by rioters. We've a roundabout route mapped out."

They climbed into the massive matte-black SUV, the two women up front, Sanger and Swensen in the middle. Syarhey Valazko got in back, propped up against the side, his legs stretched out on the three seats.

Sanger adjusted his safety belt. "Welsh?"

Kinney, the woman in the tunic, offered a brief smile. "Aye, sir. First Battalion, Twelfth Armored Infantry Brigade. Part an' parcel of the Prince of Wales Division, sir."

He nodded, satisfied.

"We heard from the boffins in Galveston, sir. Spanish Intelligence has tapped our phone lines. I've taken the liberty of moving us to a beta site."

Sanger nodded. He'd anticipated that Hugo Llorente wouldn't take any of this lying down.

Kinney didn't seem worried. "Spanish mutts straining at their leashes, biting back. Here." She handed him a tablet computer. "We can tie your command protocols, all Sooner, Slye, and Rydell comms, through to the new office without routing a thing through the old ones. If the Spanish have ears, they'll hear naught."

He input his passwords, handed the tablet back. "Acceptable . . . Major?"

"Captain, sir."

"Captain," he said.

She faced forward and smiled with pride.

CAPTAIN KINNEY HAD MOVED the Sooner, Slye, and Rydell contingent to an office park outside the main turbulence of the protests. Sanger noted that the route there was circuitous and that the buildings surrounding them were sterile, dull, and indistinguishable from each other: a perfect 1980s corporate park. He could move a cavalry division in and out of this area, and nobody would notice.

Kinney rode the last quarter of the way with her mobile phone to her ear, jotting notes. When they arrived, she hung up.

"That was Galveston," she said. "These bounty hunters you asked about? They used a false ID and credit card to hire an Uber in Barcelona. Here."

She handed back a slip of paper with the details of the hired car. "The tech people have the car's anti-theft transponder. It's on the move, through the Gothic Quarter. That's not two kilometers from the Catalonian Plaza, where the Khamsin Sayef set off their bomb."

Sanger handed the note to CPO Swensen.

"Go get them."

IT TOOK SWENSEN AND VALAZKO forty-five minutes to get to the Plaça de Catalunya. The riot had broken up, and the adjacent streets were cheek by jowl with police and fire trucks and ambulances. Discarded placards lay strewn about, a few leaning into the fountains and becoming waterlogged. Media was all over the scene. Across the plaza, black-on-yellow police tape, with warnings in Spanish and English, cordoned off the Galician Trust building with its blown-out windows and door. The window frames on the eighth floor were blackened with soot and vertical smoke particulate, looking like the rotted teeth of a grinning cadaver.

Swensen's phone vibrated. He checked the incoming text.

"They found that Uber, hired by these sons a' bitches."

Beside him, the very pale man smiled pleasantly.

Swensen called his team. They'd rendezvoused with his three guys, who were staged in a stolen and repainted laundry truck. Swensen brought up a map app on his phone. A blue dot pulsed.

"Let's go."

He and the very pale man started walking through the crowds of tourists along the famed boulevard, heading toward the hulking la Boqueria market and the Gran Teatre del Liceu.

Valazko kept his head on a swivel. Swensen glanced up from his phone. "The car's still nine blocks that way."

Valazko said, "Sure," and kept his eyes on everything.

He'd done a lot of research on Katalin Fiero Dahar. He'd

talked to soldiers and spooks, to mercs and crooks. He'd used Sooner, Slye, and Rydell bribe money, where that would work, and his own fists where it wouldn't.

He didn't know everything about her. But he knew she liked to use small and tough street bikes when staging in an urban center. She'd done so in Oslo, the first time they'd met.

She also would pick a lowbrow, low-profile dump of a hotel, near the heart of the action, and use it to stage her operation.

Valazko spotted both: a used motorbike chained up outside a bottom-of-the-barrel Ibis. "I need cigarettes. You go on ahead."

Swensen glowered down at him. "Are you shitting me?"

The very pale man smiled blandly. "Afraid not, no."

"We spot these fuckers, we ain't waiting on your sorry ass."

Valazko said, "Okay, sure," and began wending his way through tourists, heading at a right angle away from Swensen.

TWO HUNDRED YARDS AWAY and three stories up, Annie Pryor stood, fists shaking at her side, her face livid with rage.

"These bastards just tried to kill me! These shits killed Dinah and Teddy and Bess in Paris! *Bess was three!*"

Fiero, ignoring her, turned to Finnigan. "The Uber?"

"It's about six blocks south." He turned to Pryor. "We won't be going with you when Llorente's guys get here. I'm a sensitive soul. Can't stand violence."

"You're fucking mercenaries!" she spat.

"I'm an aggrieved and loyal daughter, and your lying just imperiled my father." Fiero bobbed her head toward Finnigan. "He's a fucking mercenary."

Finnigan stuck a pugnacious finger at her. "Yeah! What she said!"

"The weight of the US Intelligence Community is about to

come down on your both! The rest of your lives will be spent at a nameless prison in Turkey. Do you understand me?"

Finnigan turned to his partner. "This would be the same US Intelligence Community that missed the hacking of an American election, 9/11, and the fall of the Berlin Wall."

"This is some kind of joke to you?"

"Nope," Finnigan said. "You lied to us about a bunch of bombers. That's no joke at all, honey."

Fiero's phone vibrated. "Hugo's here."

"No Spanish intelligence operation would do what you're suggesting. Not in a million fucking years! You're bluffing."

Fiero shrugged. No one shrugs with as much nuance as the Spanish.

She received more texts and sent some, and they got ready to decamp.

Pryor was quickly making the transition from outrage to terror. As Finnigan reached for the door, she said, "I'll scream! I'll bring out the entire hotel."

Fiero said, "I'll knock you unconscious. I might anyway."

Someone rapped thrice on the door. Finnigan moved into an oblique cover position, gun in a two-hand grip, and Fiero opened the door.

Three men stood and nodded. They were small, dark-skinned, and nondescript.

The leader nodded to Fiero.

Pryor's knees buckled.

C46

CPO Swensen and his guys—on foot and in the laundry van—headed south toward the Uber.

Syarhey Valazko loitered in a tobacconist, pretending to study magazines written in a language he couldn't read.

Three stories up, Hugo Llorente's three men barged into the small hotel room, crowding Finnigan and Fiero, and Annie Pryor. Fiero recognized the leader, a sparse, mustached man with skin like an old wallet. One of his men took Pryor by her upper arm.

"Stop this immediately! Do you know—ow!"

She looked down at her arm. The tiny narco needle had been embedded in the palm of the guy holding her.

"Borgia ring," Finnigan nodded. "Old school. Nice."

The drug didn't knock Pryor out, but she felt it hit her blood stream with an onrush of lethargy. It felt like becoming physically lighter. Her peripheral vision warped a little, and she tasted anise on her tongue.

The Spanish team led the way into the ill-lit corridor, Finnigan and Fiero riding drag.

The elevator was rickety and coffin-like. The team leader nudged Pryor into the cage and crowded in after her. They jostled shut the squeaky accordion door, and the cage jerked to life.

The other two Spanish agents and the partners took the helical stairs, their shoulders scraping the aging and faded wallpaper. They reached the lobby first and found it empty; the old hotel shared its lobby with a pawnbroker, who wasn't doing much business. The day clerk of the hotel stayed behind the check-in counter, his back to them, watching the football match on a portable TV. He didn't even glance back. It might not have been his first abduction.

When the cage finally groaned to a halt, they extracted Pryor and walked her through the lobby with its faded tile floor and old radiator.

The sirocco continued to blow in from Africa. The sky outside was white, the sun a painfully brighter clump of white than the rest but otherwise indistinguishable. Finnigan tasted dust. He checked his phone. "The Uber's moving."

The team leader spoke to Fiero, who stood a good five inches taller than he. "We're around the back," he said, as Syarhey Valazko stepped out of the crowd.

He slammed the sole of his boot into the leader's knee. The man fell as tendons shredded.

He'd been guiding Annie Pryor by the arm, so she stumbled into Fiero.

Finnigan drew his stolen Glock.

Valazko blocked the draw and hit Finnigan in the nerve cluster inside of his elbow. The gun clattered to the pavement.

Valazko caught the second Spanish agent with a chop to his neck and, as the man gasped and fell back, Fiero came out of a crouch with her butterfly knife. It fluttered and floated in midair, almost alive. She swiped, and a splash of Valazko's blood spread in a perfect horizontal arc.

The Belorussian darted away, out of reach. He had a gun with a long chrome sound suppressor, and he raised his good arm and fired twice.

The third Spanish agent and Annie Pryor spun and fell. Pryor stumbled into the used motorbike, chained to a standpipe.

Tourists began reacting, but with surprise, not fear. Some went for their cell phones' cameras.

The arc of Valazko's blood hit the littered pavement and splashed.

He pointed the silenced gun at Fiero and smiled.

Finnigan swung a fist at him. He dodged, but too late to see the lead-filled sap obscured by Finnigan's arm. The leather pouch caught him in the ear and he stumbled back, grunting.

Fiero pirouetted, a sweep-kick connecting with the silenced gun, which spiraled into the distance.

Tourists began to see the fallen, the blood, the weapons, and curiosity turned to terror. Someone screamed. Someone else tripped over a baby pram, a father cursing. Another tourist shrieked.

Valazko backpedaled into the street. A cab screeched to a halt, rocking on its shock absorbers. The driver began cursing in Arabic.

Finnigan and Fiero spread out, at ten o'clock and two o'clock, their backs to the hotel. Valazko stood in the one-way street, his back to the wide, pedestrian walkway of Las Ramblas, with its tents for food and touristy trinkets.

He grinned and *didn't* put a hand to the cut on his left arm, not wanting to get blood on his right palm.

Two police officers pounded through the crowd, one blowing into a whistle, strong-arming civilians out of the way. They wore the easy-to-spot lime-green sleeves and black-and-white checkered baseball caps of the Barcelona street police.

Behind Finnigan and Fiero, the leader of the Spanish team lay on his back, cradling his ruined knee and keening in pain. One of his men held his throat, his lips and fingernails turning blue. The other bled out.

Finnigan spotted the incoming cops and said, "Friendlies," ditching his sap and showing the cops his palms.

Fiero kept her knife out, a panther baring its fangs.

Another guy showed up, flattop, thick neck, red face, often-broken nose, looking like he knew Valazko.

The cops stepped between the combatants. The newcomer shoved the first cop, making her stumble.

Valazko swung an elbow into the woman's neck and reached for her gun. Spanish cops on the beat often kept their side arms tethered to their belts on springy cords, so one can't easily separate an officer from the weapon.

The male cop reacted in shock as Valazko threw a blood-drenched arm around the first cop's neck and spun her about, aiming her tethered gun at her partner's stomach. He fired and the male cop crumpled.

Fiero kicked the Belorussian in the kidney.

The hitter grunted and stumbled forward, taking the female cop with him, and both of them fell on the second, wounded cop.

The taxi driver stepped out of his car and continued to curse in Arabic, fear of missing a fare somehow obscuring his own danger.

The leader of Llorente's snatch-team crawled to his partner and began applying pressure to his gunshot wound.

A gun fired—whose?—three times. Glass shattered in the pawn-shop window and brick dust mushroomed from the hotel facade.

Finnigan grabbed Fiero and dragged her to the ground.

Sirens sounded.

More cops pushed through the tourists, whistles shrill. They came from both directions.

From beneath Finnigan's protective torso, Fiero brushed hair away from her eyes and scanned the scrum in front of her, seeing dead and wounded, agents and cops, and Annie Pryor.

But no Valazko.

Finnigan rose off her, eyes on the incoming friendliest. "Ghost."

She didn't argue, spidering sideways into the street and rolling under the cab.

Finnigan rose to his knees, palms up, shouting, "Good guy, good guy! Amigo, Amigo, Amigo!"

Cops pushed through the ring of tourists like tackles coming through the line of scrimmage.

Fiero rose on the right side of the cab, quietly opened the back door without getting in, and she, too, started yelling in Arabic. The driver turned and seemed pleased to have picked up a fare, despite the carnage. When a cop waved a gun his way, he and his new passenger both hopped into the cab.

Half a block away, CPO Swensen pushed through crowds, Syarhey Valazko at his six, moving away from the action. Valazko stole a scarf from a spinner rack en passant and tied it around his arm as he ducked into a steamy row of squid merchants in la Boqueria.

C47

Finnigan remained on his knees and laced his fingers behind his head. A cop in full riot gear kicked him in the back, landed atop him, and roughly pulled his hands back, binding his wrist with white plastic tie-strips. He felt the asphalt scrape his cheek.

He'd been a New York City police officer. Today, a cop had been roughed up and another had been shot. Finnigan thought the guy on his back was using just about the right amount of excessive force.

No hard feelings. He'd have done the same.

Finnigan couldn't rely on Hugo Llorente's surviving guy getting him out of this jam. The spooks came from a covert intelligence unit. They were as likely to carry badges as they were to have gills.

That's why he'd called an audible, getting Fiero off the field of play before she got arrested too. He had no way of knowing how long he'd be held, and they couldn't afford for both of them to get caught up in this for hours or days or even weeks.

And *weeks* wasn't an exaggeration. A cop had been shot. People take that stuff seriously.

He was taken to the Spanish equivalent of a paddy wagon, parked behind an ancient church. The massive van was airless and stifling even with the rear double doors open, and Finnigan's shirt clung to his torso.

Ambulances staged nearby. Finnigan bided his time, watching the wounded being treated, both the identified and unidentified: two Barcelonian cops—one shot in the gut and one with a strained neck and side—and a male with no ID and a torn ACL. The third was a woman in an ugly green polyester tracksuit without ID, shot in the stomach but alive, taken to a nearby hospital under police guard.

How long before Hugo Llorente realized what had happened and got his guy out? There was no way of knowing, and no way of knowing if Llorente's reach would extend to Finnigan.

How long before the CIA tracked down its missing Madrid station chief? Would they get to Annie Pryor first?

And if either the CIA or the CNI could get to her—or to Finnigan—could Sooner, Slye, and Rydell?

Of course.

Finnigan hunched over and used his very damp shirt over his shoulder to try to wipe sweat off his forehead. He'd meant to call his mom that week and hadn't. He'd meant to go to Mass and hadn't. He'd meant to beat the holy shit out of that pigment-challenged Belorussian bastard and hadn't. Yet.

Several men approached the paddy wagon. Most were uniformed cops. One wore street clothes but was clearly a cop, too. One wore a nice summer-weight suit, no tie and a pocket square. He produced a badge folder with ID in Spanish, which Finnigan couldn't read. He faked it and nodded anyway.

"You are American?" the bureaucrat asked.

"Yup."

"You are, ah, Finnigan, Michael Patrick?"

Finnigan had been carrying ID. He nodded.

"First, may I ask, have you been treated properly by the police?"

"Oh, hell yes."

That seemed to catch everyone by surprise.

"Can you tell me what happened here?"

Finnigan said, "Nope." He smiled.

"Ah . . ." Apparently, the bureaucrat had expected either a straight answer or an elaborate fabrication. "We require an answer, Mr. Finnigan."

"Sorry, dude." He shrugged and kept smiling.

The bureaucrat looked peeved. Everyone backed off and they talked among themselves a moment.

Finnigan sat and sweated.

The bureaucrat stormed away.

A squat man with a fierce mustache approached. Finnigan knew for a fact the guy was a cop. Any other cop would have known it too.

The squat man spoke halting English. "You wish a cigarette?"

"No, I'm good."

"Is . . . ?" The man motioned toward his own cheek, meaning the fresh scrape on Finnigan's cheek from when he'd been shoved to the pavement.

"Nothing. No worries."

"What happened?"

It was the same question as before, but Finnigan gambled that this guy wasn't from Sooner, Slye, and Rydell. "Belorussian fucker called Valazko. The dead guys are CNI. So's the guy with the busted-up knee. The blond chick with the GSW is American. CIA. If she survives, she's got information your guys are going to need regarding the bombers."

The squat man studied Finnigan for a while, not responding. He pulled a cigarette, lit and smoked half of it.

"You are a cop," the man stated simply.

Finnigan nodded.

The man tossed down the cigarette and ground it under his scuffed shoe. "*Joder.*"

Finnigan smiled. "My partner says that."

The cop used the fingers of his left hand to circle his right wrist, indicating Finnigan's plastic cuff. "I cannot . . ."

"I know."

"This . . . Valazko? The officers who were injured, they spoke of a man who attacked them and fled. Pale, brown hair, average height."

"That's him."

"We will find him."

Finnigan said, "He shot a cop. Kick his ass for me."

The cop nodded and pointed toward a brick wall that made up the rear of a fifteenth-century church. "Is cooler, yes?"

Finnigan stood as best he could, and the cop helped him step out of the van.

As they walked toward the shade, he spotted Fiero behind an ambulance, amid a crowd of twenty or so lookie-loos.

He jutted his chin at her to wave her off.

C48

The bureaucrat returned with more bureaucrats, all of whom had good suits and badges. More people asked Finnigan questions. He didn't provide answers.

Almost eighty minutes later, new people arrived in nicer suits. Everyone argued. One guy, a wiry, redheaded man in a black suit and black tie, seemed to have the high-trump card. He took custody of Finnigan, moving him to a black Escalade driven by a woman in a similar suit.

Before putting Finnigan in the back seat, the redheaded man plowed a fist into his gut. Finnigan folded over. The man pushed him into the car.

A half hour later, the Escalade pulled into a generic corporate park on the outskirts of Barcelona. Every government building Finnigan had seen since moving to Europe had been stately, grandiose, and ancient. Well, except for Brussels, where acres and acres and acres of European Union buildings resembled the world's largest junior college. Whatever this office building was, it certainly wasn't government.

The redheaded man in the suit guided Finnigan by his upper arm, leading him into the foyer of the building and into an elevator, up four floors. The elevator played an easy-listening version of "Girl from Ipanema." The man led Finnigan down a corridor and into an office, where he was greeted by a woman in a tunic suit and two men. One guy was ruddy-faced, with a flattop cut and badly broken nose. He wore a shoulder rig with an enormous automatic weapon. Finnigan had seen him before. In the fight on Las Ramblas.

The other had been a marine. Finnigan didn't need to see the tattoo to know that; anyone could tell. He stood five eight and was economically built. Middle to late forties, with hair that was light of color, though Finnigan couldn't tell what to call it. Not quite blond, not quite brown. His trousers were okay and his sports coat was okay and Finnigan suspected the guy thought of them as a suit.

He said, "How you guys doing?"

The marine nodded. The redhead in the suit undid Finnigan's cuffs. He and the woman in the tunic excused themselves.

"Mr. Finnigan," the guy in charge said. "Formerly Officer Finnigan. And Deputy US Marshal Finnigan. Now St. Nicholas."

Finnigan studied the room. The furnishings were generic, the shades drawn. The ceiling was low popcorn. The desk and chairs were IKEA. He noted the laptop on the desk and the green desk blotter, a phone that had been fancy and modernish ten years ago and a heavy, green glass ashtray, the size of an Olympic discus, that might never have been used. Finnigan said, "Are you Sooner, Slye, or Rydell?"

The man smiled, but the smile was a quick reflexive jerk of the muscles of his cheek and reflected no actual mirth. Like an alien who'd seen humans do it and knew it reflected something or other.

"My name is Colonel Cole Sanger. I work for the company, yes. Thank you for coming."

"Glad to do it." Finnigan turned to the big blond man, who he'd come to think of as the boxer. "Is that a Ruger 1911? Dude, that is, seriously, a nice gun."

The big man stared at him, unblinking.

"Can I hold it?"

"You can have one of the bullets."

Finnigan grinned and turned to Sanger. "Very good handgun. Ten millimeter. You park on a hill, you could chock your tire with that thing."

Sanger thrust his hands in his trouser pockets. "I know a little bit about guns, Mr. Finnigan. Why don't we sit?"

"You got anything to drink? Whiskey? A beer?"

Sanger again gave it the slightest pause, again damping down a reaction. "I don't drink."

"Water would be good." He turned to the boxer. "Get yourself one too while you're out there."

That got a reaction. The man's hands curled into fists that were only marginally smaller than Finnigan's skull. Getting hit by those would be like getting hit by a wrecking ball.

"I saw you," Finnigan said. "At the fight. When those guys got shot. You were in the crowd."

Sanger said, "Sit."

Finnigan stood and smiled at the boxer, ignoring Sanger. He measured every facial tic. Just like taking suspects into the interrogation tank. Everybody has facades. Everybody. The goal was to see what lay behind them before you start asking the real questions.

Sanger said, "You and your partner, Katalin Fiero Dahar, have been paid good money to investigate the Khamsin Sayef. And these bombings. When you leave here, you're going to gather your partner and you're going to return to Cyprus. Keep the money

Llorente paid you. Give it back, give it to charity. We don't care. One of my people is going to give you a cashier's check before you leave here. It will more than compensate you for your troubles. How does that sound?"

"A hundred thousand," Finnigan said. "Dollars, in case you were wondering. Then we walk away. You never hear from us again."

Sanger seemed to think about it. "It's a lot of money."

"You guys got money."

"That's true. And it's your final offer?"

"Yeah."

Sanger moved the green glass ashtray out of the way and sat on the corner of his desk. "Deal. You're going to tell us everything you've found out over the past couple of weeks regarding the Khamsin Sayef. You'll make your statement. You'll attest to its accuracy and wholeness. And we'll cut you that check."

"That's it? That's all you need from me?"

"Well, we need you to make a call to your partner and bring her in, too. She also is going to make a statement."

Finnigan said, "Can I ask a question first?"

Sanger shrugged. "Go ahead."

But Finnigan turned to the boxer. "What's your name?"

The boxer paused. "Swensen."

"Swensen. The Belorussian hitter, Valazko. You work for him?"

Swensen offered a grim smile. "Other way around, asshole."

Finnigan turned to Sanger. "You know Valazko shot a cop today."

Sanger shook his head. "Sooner, Slye, and Rydell has no knowledge of any criminal actions taken today by anyone in Spain. Sooner, Slye, and Rydell has no connection to any individual going by the name Valazko."

"Yeah, but the dude shot a *cop*." Finnigan shook his head. "A lotta lines are porous, you know what I mean. Bend a little here, break a rule there. But shooting a cop . . ."

He kept shaking his head.

Sanger nodded to Swensen, who dug a generic flip-phone out of his pocket.

"Call your partner."

The big man stepped forward, the phone in his hand.

Finnigan reached for it. But took Swensen's hand instead.

He kept moving forward, spinning, dragging Swensen's right hand with him.

Sanger began to react, moving off the desk, as Finnigan hip-checked the boxer, using a judo throw Fiero had taught him.

The big man spun over Finnigan's back and landed on the carpet.

Colonel Sanger stagger-stepped out of the way.

Finnigan knelt, swiping the green glass ashtray, and bought it down on Swensen's already-broken nose.

"*Your guy shot a goddamn cop!*" Finnigan bellowed.

He reared back and got in one more shot, blood flying, cartilage snapping, two broken teeth spiraling away, before Sanger tackled him. The ex-marine knew how to handle himself, and he got Finnigan pinned to the floor, his arm twisted high against his back.

"*Get in here!*" Sanger bellowed. "*Now!*"

The door burst open. Swensen's guys, who'd been staking out the Uber they never found, burst in. The woman in the tunic and the redheaded man in the suit raced to the door.

The mercenaries got Finnigan standing, arms pinioned behind him, in a choke hold.

Sanger adjusted his suit, straightened his tie. He looked down at Swensen, who moaned, unconscious, his nose a pulpy thing like a hollowed-out peach, his upper lip missing, teeth scattered.

"Shot . . . a fucking . . . cop!" Finnigan hissed, a forearm across his throat.

Someone decked him, and he slumped to the floor.

C49

Fiero wasn't worried about Finnigan. He could take care of himself.

As soon as she cleared the site of the street battle—she paid off the Algerian taxi driver just three blocks later—she circled back on foot to the scene. Having an ex-cop as a best friend had paid off in unpredictable ways. For instance, Finnigan had taught her to predict where cops, firefighters, and ambulances would stage: close enough to the action but not so close that they got caught in the traffic pileups or near the *lookie-loos*, to use one of his goofy expressions.

She found police cars and an ambulance behind a nearby church. She watched as paramedics loaded Annie Pryor into the back, barefoot, her tracksuit stained with blood. The CIA officer looked badly injured but alive.

She got close enough to spot the ambulance driver's ID badge. Hospital Sant Agustín de Déu. The same hospital her mother had been in.

She saw a stocky man lead a handcuffed Finnigan away from

a prison wagon. She made eye contact. Finnigan waved her off with a jut of his jaw.

Her phone vibrated. Hugo Llorente.

She answered, said, "Església de Sant Felip Neri," and hung up.

THE CHURCH OF SAINT FELIP NERI was a bit isolated, down a narrow, winding street in the Barri Gotic sector of the city, not far from the restaurant where Victor Wu and his security detail had died in the bomb blast almost five weeks earlier.

Hugo Llorente came alone, on foot. He stood in the shadows of the courtyard behind the Baroque church and waited until Fiero emerged from the shadows.

The old man wasted no time. "What happened?"

"Ambushed. Valazko and at least one other. Your men are dead or wounded. Pryor was shot in the stomach. She's en route to Sant Agustín. We stripped her of all ID and tracker tags. You might still be able to get to her before the CIA does."

Llorente took the time to find a cigarette pack, to light a cigarette, and to take his first drag. Fiero waited.

"What is it that you think she knows?"

"None of the targets of the Khamsin Sayef are who we thought they were. Except for the first one: Dinah Mariner, chief of station, Paris Shop. After that, it was Cedric Brecher, the *other* banker, who'd been in Paris when Mariner died. Then it was the wife of the American engineer, who'd been in Paris working on a website when Mariner died. Then Pete Newsom, Mariner's chief of operations. Then Pryor, today, Mariner's chief of intelligence."

Llorente worked the cigarette down, then peeled apart the filter with stubby, nicotine-stained fingers and spread the content around the courtyard. An old sniper's trick. "My God."

"Also, the Khamsin Sayef itself is a front. Their driver was

German. We believe others were Americans." She didn't elaborate about seeing the bomb-sweeping squad leaving her father's building. Not yet.

"Pryor knows what's going on. She knows why the Khamsin Sayef is targeting the remnants of the CIA's Paris shop and hiding behind the propaganda of the other victims."

"I'll have to move fast, get her out of there before her people canvas the hospitals."

"They might have already."

He grunted, nodding.

"Did you know?" she asked, and raked an open palm through her hair.

"I did not." He replied without umbrage. "I swear to God, although I am a very good liar; indeed, a professional, so I expect you to take that for what it's worth."

She studied him. Llorente withstood it.

"The CIA may get to Pryor before you, but remember: Suicide Ride will want her too. And the Khamsin Sayef. They failed to kill her today, and likely will try again."

The muscles in Llorente's cheek bunched as he stood and thought it through. "We are assuming now that Cedric Brecher and Joan Caldwell were CIA assets in Paris?"

"We are."

"Then Annie might well be the final target. After she's dead, if you and Mr. Finnigan are correct, the bombings could stop."

Fiero had not, in fact, gotten there herself. "If they're not who we think they are—terrorists opposed to the government of Alsharq—they may kill Pryor and disappear forever?"

"Yes. If it's been a confidence game all along." He lit another cigarette. He took a very long drag and squinted at her through the smoke. "Mr. Finnigan?"

"He's all right."

"You're sure?"

She shrugged. "Sooner, Slye, and Rydell has him."

Llorente's eyebrows rose, corrugating his forehead.

Fiero began walking away, but backward, still facing him. "Keep an eye on the Khamsin Sayef. Suicide Ride won't be a threat for much longer."

"But they have your partner."

She kept walking backward and smiled a particularly predatory smile as the shadows of the Church of Saint Felip Neri began to envelope her.

"Have they?"

C50

Colonel Sanger's men threw Finnigan into an empty office in the suite, his wrists bound again, one man staying to keep an eye on him, even though he was unconscious.

In the main office, Colonel Sanger stood with his hands on his hips, looking down at the shattered face of Chief Petty Officer Swensen and the pool of blood forming under his neck and shoulder. The Welsh woman, Captain Kinney, stood at parade rest, awaiting orders.

"That driver of yours. You trust her?"

"Yessir."

"Can she steal a car?"

"Yessir."

"Steal a car. Get him to a hospital." He nudged Swensen's thigh with the toe of his wingtip.

"Sir." She turned smartly and walked out, closing the door behind her.

Captain Kinney carried a leather portfolio and felt it vibrate.

She waited until she was outside the generic office building and several paces from the door before opening the portfolio. It contained two phones, one with a small K scratched into the surface, for Captain Deirdre Kinney.

The other with a small R, for Rumpus.

That one vibrated. She answered with an American accent. "Rumpus."

All traces of Welsh captain evaporated.

On the line, the head of the Madrid station sounded like he was about to soil his shorts. "What the hell! Still no sign of Sanger?"

She checked to make sure she was alone. "Negative. His phone, his computer . . . nothing."

She looked up as Fiero pulled her motorbike into the parking lot. The woman nodded.

The redheaded man in the suit stepped out. He walked directly to Fiero and, as she doffed her helmet, embraced her in a warm hug.

The man on the phone said, "Well, should we lock out his accounts?"

"Absolutely not!" she snapped. "We have to trust the colonel! What if he's got a plan to capture these goddamn bombers? We cut his account now, and he's screwed!"

They argued some more, and she hung up.

As Fiero walked up, the woman placed both hands on either side of Fiero's skull and kissed her on the forehead, parting with an immature "Mmmmmm-wah!" Then tousled her hair. "Hi, sugar plum."

Fiero was *not demonstrative* in the same way that Sheetrock is *not food*. But she tolerated it in the brassy American. "Sally. Mercer. Is Michael . . . ?"

Mercer, the redheaded man who'd pretended to punch Finnigan earlier, winced. "Our boy took a beating but indicated he didn't want us to interfere."

"Suicide Ride?"

Sally Blue laughed. "We've been in their system for an hour, honey. We have the budget for this mission. Trust me: We're bleeding 'em dry!"

WHEN IT BECAME CLEAR that Finnigan and Fiero were losing access to their allies—their banker, Ways and Means, and the military mercenary, Brodie McTavish—the partners reached out to the Black Harts, a gang of professional thieves who'd had a long-standing relationship with St. Nicholas Salvage & Wrecking. Their deal: They would help the partners hunt down bad guys, in exchange for which the Harts could steal anything they laid eyes on, up to and including the gold fillings in the teeth of the people St. Nicholas brought to justice.

While the partners were in Paris, Sally Blue—a *nom de felony*, but the only name they knew her by—had begun the process of infiltrating Sooner, Slye, and Rydell's operation. It had been her idea to use the *Rumpus* identity to gain access to the company's computers in Madrid, and the *Captain Kinney* identity to gain access to Cole Sanger's passwords and security protocol. She brought along Mercer, the redheaded man, and Zafirah Nasr, her driver, to make up the core of the faux Suicide Ride staff in Barcelona. Once they did, they separated Sanger from everyone else at the company, without his knowledge, much the way cheetahs will separate out the slowest calf from a herd of impalas. He was, after all, running an off-book operation in Barcelona to track down Finnigan and Fiero.

She dispatched Mercer to gather Finnigan and to play-act the punch in the stomach, in case anyone was watching.

She dispatched Zaf to drive around the city and to distract the mercenaries, the so-called Uber that was supposed to draw

CPO Swensen's men away from Finnigan and Fiero. That hadn't worked out, but they still weren't sure why.

Sooner, Slye, and Rydell had given Sanger access to any operatives he needed in all of Europe. But more importantly (from the perspective of the Black Harts) a budget well over three million dollars to track down the Khamsin Sayef.

In about twenty minutes, Sooner, Slye, and Rydell would realize that the money had vanished into thin air.

C51

The Black Harts were hell on roller skates when it came to theft and the con game, but no member of Sally Blue's crew had ever thrown a punch. Let alone hefted a firearm. The brassy American had made that clear from jump.

Once they'd rendezvoused with Fiero, Zaf pulled up in a stolen TV channel news truck—plenty of those all over the city today. Sally and Mercer hugged Fiero.

"Finnigan?"

Mercer spat in the grass. "One of those guys shot a cop. Our boy was pretty hacked off about it. Went all Hulk Smash on 'em. Mikey ain't the biggest guy in the world, but damn . . ." He shook his head in wonder.

Fiero nodded. "Yes. That would do it."

With that, Sally Blue gave her a photocopied map of the corporate office building, an all-access magnetic key, and details of Finnigan's whereabouts and that of Colonel Sanger and his bravos, to use a St. Nicholas Salvage & Wrecking term. Then the three thieves climbed into the microwave truck and zoomed out. About three million dollars richer.

Fiero studied the layout of the building and entered. Sally had selected a fake backup headquarters for Colonel Sanger—the Beta Site, she'd called it in her faux Welsh accent—on the fourth floor, because the corporate office complex wasn't doing too well and that entire floor was empty. Sally had wanted to minimize civilians in the line of fire.

Fiero climbed the stairs to the third floor.

She stepped out into the empty corridor. The building was depressingly generic, with industrial carpet, water stains on the ceiling tiles and walls of a color that possessed no known name. Fiero glanced at her map (Sally had left a cherry-red lipstick print in a corner, over a row of Xs and Os). She was on the far end of the building from Sanger's three-office suite. She drew the butterfly knife from her boot but kept the five-inch blade tucked into the handle for now; the tango fan deployment of the butterfly knife made for a fine distraction in a fight.

She turned a corner. No one in the corridor. Sanger's offices were dead ahead. According to the Harts, the office closest to Fiero was where they'd dumped Finnigan.

She turned the knob and stepped in.

A beefy man with a neck tattoo and a shoulder-holstered SIG turned, expecting a cohort.

Fiero kicked him in the center of his chest and heard the tell-tale *clack* of his sternum snapping.

The man's boots left the ground and he landed on his back and shoulders, head bouncing once.

Finnigan lay on his side, arms pinioned behind him, wrists secured with a white plastic tie. He appeared to be unconscious but as soon as the mercenary landed, he spun on his shoulder, reared back, and kicked the guy in the teeth.

Fiero knelt, deployed the knife, and sliced through his wrist tie. "Was that absolutely necessary?" she whispered. "My kick probably stopped his heart."

"Why should you have all the fun?" Finnigan rubbed his wrists for a moment and grinned at her. His left cheek was inflamed and a line of mostly dried blood decorated his chin and neck, and the collar of his shirt.

He gathered the man's SIG and handed it to Fiero; she was a much better shot. He searched the guy's pockets, took his phone, took his money.

"I wanna go turn Sanger and his goons into mincemeat."

Fiero said, "No. Sally cleared out their accounts. Sooner, Slye, and Rydell will think that Sanger went rogue and ripped them off. He's out of this. Keep our eyes on the mission."

Finnigan stood. "Said I wanted to. Didn't say it made sense."

He moved to the door and opened it an inch, peered out. He checked the direction of the other two offices.

Sanger's voice boomed from behind a closed door. "What the hell do you mean, *missing*? I'm right the hell here! . . . What . . . ? No, *you* wait . . . !"

Finnigan whispered, "Let's vamoose."

They headed down the corridor, back toward the stairs. Fiero led the way. As they got to the stairwell door, she whispered. "What's *vamoose*?"

"Spanish," he whispered. "For *Let's go*."

She suppressed a laugh. "It's really not."

THE BLACK HARTS HAD LEFT THEM a stolen car—property of Sooner, Slye, and Rydell. The partners wiped down Fiero's used motorbike and left it. Fiero drove.

"I spoke to Hugo. If Annie Pryor survives, he's going to get her out of the hospital so we can talk to her."

Finnigan gently manipulated his jaw, hearing it click a little in his ear. "Sally bought us time, is all. It's like knocking over a McDonald's in Passaic. The corporation won't notice. Suicide Ride's still gonna be all over our asses once they regroup."

"Hugo also believes your theory that this is about the Paris CIA station three years ago. He fears that Pryor could be the last target. If he's right . . ."

"Shit. Hit her, and whoever's behind this won't need the Khamsin Sayef cover any more. They'll disappear."

"Yes." She drove carefully but quickly, checking text messages on her phone from time to time.

C52

DeMarcus Washington had secured them a safe house, a shack on a little-used dock south of downtown, under the landing pattern of nearby Barcelona-El Prat. They'd had the space for weeks now, had used it when Frau Gunsen planned the restaurant bombing of Pete Newsom. Washington had set up lipstick cameras and motion detectors in the gravel lot, surrounded by cyclone fencing. The area stank of brackish seawater and oil and dead fish, reducing the likelihood of passersby.

Ron Perry sat at a wooden table with uneven legs and cleaned his rifle. It's what he did when he was upset.

"That was stone cold, man. Stone cold."

Washington checked the array of black-and-white monitors he'd stacked up on a fly-tying workbench. "Shit you talking about? You didn't even like Ritter."

Perry slumped over his disassembled long gun. "Don't matter. He was our crew, man. Just saying."

"Ritter was a fucking junkie." A flicker of motion on one of the monitors caught his eye. "She's coming."

He watched the grainy image of Gunsen kneel and slide through the vertical slit in the cyclone fence. She wore a hooded jacket, hood up, although the temperature hadn't dropped much when the sun did.

Both men turned toward the door as she entered. Washington made eye contact and raised his brows.

"The agency doesn't know where Annie is," Gunsen said. "Doesn't know if she's alive or dead. Just that she's missing."

The big man gestured toward the police scanner he'd set up near the monitors. He spoke fluent Spanish and had been able to keep tabs on the police. "That fight on Las Ramblas?"

"Blond woman, fifties, no ID." Gunsen brushed back the hood and shook out her limp, graying hair. She'd been sweating, and the burn scars along the right side of her neck and her cheek were shiny under the string of harsh, vice-grip work lights. "It was her. She's alive."

"The Spanish have her?"

"Likely." She went to her haunches and lifted the lid of the Styrofoam cooler they'd bought. She fished out a bottle of water, wiped chipped ice off with her palm, used that same palm to touch her burn scars, the cold quelling—a little—the near-constant ache.

Perry said, "You sure about the agency?"

Gunsen cracked open the bottle, rose to her full height, five five. "Pryor hired bounty hunters on Cyprus. She and a guy from Spanish Intelligence, Hugo Llorente. I didn't give it much thought, figured the bounty hunters were supposed to find the cleric."

DeMarcus Washington said, "But . . ." and drew the word out.

"*But* I think they're onto her. I think the bounty hunters, this St. Nicholas Salvage & Wrecking, were at the hotel where

Pryor got shot. Two hours later, CIA realized she was missing and started canvassing the hospitals for her. By the time they did, the unidentified blond woman had been treated and moved. That's this St. Nicholas outfit. Maybe."

"Or maybe Llorente?" Washington said.

Gunsen sipped her water. "Or maybe both."

"We gotta get her," Perry said, eyes turning from his disassembled gun.

Gunsen spoke softly. "Yes."

"She don't die, we got us big-ass troubles. Simple as that."

"Yes."

Perry sounded petulant. "Just saying. That bitch don't die, we do."

Behind his back, Frau Gunsen and DeMarcus Washington exchanged glances.

"Yes."

THE TEXTS LED FIERO through the night streets, out of Barcelona, to an isolated house behind a stone wall, with a long, serpentine driveway and dead lawns and two stone lions, one decapitated, the other moss-covered. The great house looked like it had fallen on hard times a generation ago and never climbed out.

Three cars had parked haphazardly out front of the brick monstrosity. Fiero pulled in among them. A small, nondescript man stood in front of the twelve-foot-tall front door of the mansion, hands in his pockets, watching them.

The partners climbed out. Finnigan studied the facade. "What's Spanish for *mausoleum*?"

Fiero said, "Mausoleum."

"Oh good. Then we're here."

The nondescript man led them in. The inside of the old house was twenty degrees cooler than the night air. The floor was a complicated geometric pattern of parquet tiles, the white faded to light gray and the black faded to dark gray. The high wooden walls had darkened badly over the years. Finnigan said, "You ever read *The Shining*?"

The nondescript man spoke English over his shoulder. "The movie was better."

"The movie was different."

The man shrugged.

He led them to a dining room that had been turned into a post-op. Annie Pryor lay on a gurney with an adjustable surface, her torso raised and lying on a pile of thin pillows with no pillow covers. An IV drip clung to her arm like a leech. A doctor—that is, a sallow man with a widow's peak and a long doctor's coat—was feeding her oxygen directly through her nostrils. Her skin was gray and she wore no makeup. She'd aged twenty years in eight hours.

Hugo Llorente smoked. The doctor cast accusatory eyes at the pall of smoke rising over his head. A beefy man in an orderly's teal smock watched the monitors that beeped on a rolling tray behind Pryor's bed. A tightly built woman with a butch haircut and a Heckler & Koch G36KE assault rifle stood at the window, watching the world and ignoring the partners. Someone else had let them into the old house. She was a sentinel: once they were inside, they were none of her concern.

Llorente said, "You are well, Mr. Finnigan?" His eyes strayed to the blood stain on Finnigan's collar and his swollen cheek.

Finnigan said, "You should see the other guy."

Fiero said, "The other guy looked fine."

Llorente let his poker face slip. The Fiero of old had had no sense of humor whatsoever, and the joke caught the spymaster off guard. He peered at Finnigan, sensing that he'd been the catalyst for Fiero's changes.

Fiero studied everyone in the room. "We had friends watching Sooner, Slye, and Rydell. Our friends threw a spanner in the works. You should be able to operate without those bastards for a few days at least."

Again, Llorente reacted with a hint of surprise. "That is impressive. Thank you."

Finnigan jutted his jaw toward the hospital bed. "Pryor?"

"Alive, obviously. The good doctor and I were just debating the best way to revive her."

"We were not," the sallow man said. "I will revive her, against my better judgment. But we will do it slowly, and we will do it my way."

Llorente shrugged. "But not too slowly. Yes?"

THE NONDESCRIPT MAN SHOWED FINNIGAN to a bathroom, where he washed the blood off his face and tried to rinse the brown stain out of his shirt. After, he wandered into a kitchen where he found coffee, and Fiero leaning against a counter, cup held in both hands.

The nondescript man poured a cup and handed it to Finnigan. "I like Kubrick's vision," he said. "I like his imagery. And, of course, Nicholson."

He took the cup. "They shot that at a spooky old hotel in Oregon. I saw it once. It's a ski lodge."

"My God." The man poured himself a cup and shook his head. "That, I'd pay to see."

The orderly stepped into the kitchen. "She's awake."

In the dining room, Hugo Llorente approached the hospital bed but Fiero put a hand on his arm and held him back. She nodded to Finnigan.

Finnigan asked for a facecloth. Annie Pryor was awake and

was crying. She'd been shot in the torso. Finnigan dragged a high stool over and sat next to her. He wiped tears from her cheeks. He showed her a sealed cup with a bendy straw. She nodded, and he helped her sip water.

She kept crying. Finnigan didn't ask any questions. The old house creaked. Llorente tried to step forward but Fiero touched his arm again.

"We never knew whose idea it was," Annie Pryor said, her voice like sandpaper on new wood. "May I have a little more?"

Finnigan held the cup. She sipped water.

He didn't say a word.

"Dinah brought it to us. Just us. Me and Pete. She said *higher ups* wanted to support moderates in Alsharq. In the city of Baharos. She . . ."

Finnigan wiped more tears from her cheeks.

"If we could have a bomb go off . . . blame the Islamists . . . the far-right in Alsharq would cheer. The moderates would revolt. They could announce a bid for independence. The sixth fleet was in position in the Med to support them."

Finnigan spoke for the first time. "Joan Caldwell had a website . . ."

Pryor nodded. "She filmed the confession. Scrubbed the video of any markers. Got it to Al Jazeera."

"The cleric?"

"A legend. He's . . . Major Saad Barakat created him. Barakat was Alsharqi Intelligence. But he favored independence. He . . . worked with Dinah."

Hugo Llorente looked aghast. He knew Barakat, apparently, or at least knew of him.

Finnigan kept the narrative going. "The Swiss banker, Cedric Brecher, handled the money."

Pryor nodded.

"This Barakat . . . ?"

"He was . . . intelligence agent. Opposed . . . the clerics. Supported the moderates. He invented Khamsin Sayef. Sword of the Storm . . . created . . ."

She winced, voice cracking. Finnigan let her sip more water.

". . . created a fake cleric. The tape . . . blamed the Islamists. Got the ball rolling for . . . for the moderates in Baharos."

Fiero was trying to keep it straight in her head: The boss of the CIA's Paris station had agreed to help bomb civilians, in France, and to blame Islamists, so that a cabal of moderates in Baharos could declare independence, just as the American Sixth Fleet was sailing through nearby waters. And thus was a coup born. Alsharq, a new friend of the West. Or, more importantly, friend of the West with natural gas reserves off its coast.

Finnigan said, "It went bad."

Pryor nodded and even coughed a hollow little laugh and more tears came. He gave her more water.

"Dinah found out."

Finnigan didn't understand. "I thought Dinah planned it all."

"No . . . Dinah found out . . ."

He gave her more water.

". . . about me and Teddy."

Finnigan turned in his stool and mouthed *Mariner's husband* over his shoulder to Fiero and Llorente.

He turned back. "You and Teddy."

"She . . . Dinah was my friend . . ." she choked out a sob. Finnigan waited. "I . . . we didn't plan it . . . it just . . ."

"I know. It just happened. Dinah found out about you and Teddy . . ."

"She planned the Khamsin Sayef bombing. But she changed the target. Changed it to . . ."

"Yeah?"

"To a hotel. My hotel. She tried . . . Dinah tried to kill me."

"You were meeting Teddy."

"I wanted . . . to break it off. He . . . tried to talk me out of it . . ."

Finnigan waited for her to cry through it.

"He brought . . . He had Bess."

"Their daughter."

"I think . . . I think Dinah found out. Found out Teddy and Bess were at the hotel. She went there. I'd just left . . . I don't know, two minutes maybe. She went there to stop it. It . . . they died."

Fiero hadn't realized she'd been gripping Hugo Llorente's sleeve. CIA Station Chief Dinah Mariner had died in her own fake bombing and had killed her husband and three-year-old daughter as well.

Finnigan sat and wiped Pryor's tears and waited.

The doctor made eye contact with Llorente and tapped the face of his wristwatch. Llorente waved him off.

Everyone stayed quiet for four, maybe five minutes. Everyone but Annie Pryor, who cried.

Finnigan eventually said, "The Khamsin Sayef . . . ?"

"They were a fake!" Pryor said, her voice pleading, cracking. "Dinah and Major Barakat invented them! *We* invented them."

He waited.

"Afterward . . . thought maybe . . . I don't know. Maybe it was worth it. Birth of a new moderate nation. But then . . . all hell broke loose in Alsharq. Citizens in Baharos rebelled. The new government cracked down. It turned into open rebellion. The new government . . . they bombed their own city . . . barrel bombs. White phosphorous . . ."

"And this Barakat reanimated his old legend and the fake Islamist group, the Khamsin Sayef."

"Kept . . . European Union from completely . . . rejecting

the Alsharqi government. Kept the Americans at the table. A new foe . . ."

"And the targets?"

She nodded. "Barakat killed . . . everyone who knew. Dinah was long dead. He's killed Brecher and Joan Caldwell and Pete. And"—her voice broke—"me."

The doctor cleared his throat. Llorente glared at the man, who actually took two steps back and gulped.

Finnigan said, "The bombers aren't Arabic. I saw them . . ."

"Don't know . . . don't . . ."

"Three. A woman. Two men. Black guy, white guy. Black guy's tall, shaved skull. White guy looks like a redneck; blond mullet."

Pryor had been staring at the ceiling, but she turned her bloodshot eyes on Finnigan now. "Freelancers. Washington and . . . Perry?"

"Okay. They were CIA?"

"No . . . ex-Rangers. Worked for . . . Dinah."

Finnigan blinked. "Wait. Those guys worked for Dinah Mariner?"

She nodded. "She had . . . her own private . . . thugs. She'd run . . . operations off books for . . . years."

"So this Barakat guy reanimates the fake terrorist group, and he brings in Mariner's old crew. Okay. How about the woman they were with . . ."

Pryor shook her head.

"White. Five-foot-five. Maybe forty, forty-five-ish. Burn scars all over her right cheek, the right side of her neck. Badly broken nose; it hooks to the left. She—"

Pryor cut in. "No."

"I think so. She—"

"No." Pryor started shaking her head. Her breathing turned even more ragged, and her eyes grew wide. For a second, Finnigan flashed on the eyes of a horse he'd seen in a demonstration in Central Park. The animal had panicked, had stomped a fellow officer. Its eyes had been the same.

"No. No. No, that's . . . no . . ."

"Annie? Shhh. Hey. No, what? Who is she . . . ?"

"No no no no no no no . . ." Her voice didn't raise, didn't fall, didn't speed up or slow down. She shook her head in perfect rhythm, like a metronome. "No no no."

"Annie? Hey. Who is she?"

But it was Hugo Llorente who spoke. Softly, his smoker's tenor carrying, "You're describing Dinah Mariner."

The partners spun on him, eyes wide.

"If she was caught in the explosion in Paris, she might have the burn scars you describe. But the rest is her."

Pryor was babbling: "Jesus God, no not Dinah can't be Dinah's dead Dinah killed Teddy killed Bess tried to kill me no, Jesus please Jesus not her can't be her . . ."

The doctor shouldered Finnigan out of the way and reached for the IV drip, reactivating the feed. Finnigan had no idea what was in the tube, but he saw the near instantaneous effect on Annie Pryor. Her head listed to the left and her eyes fluttered closed.

". . . not Dinah . . ." she gasped. ". . . not Dinah . . ."

Finnigan stood and turned to Fiero. Both of them blinked, too stunned to speak.

C53

THE PAST

In espionage jargon, Dinah Mariner had been an *Arab hand*.

As an operations officer, she spent two decades in Egypt, Libya, Iraq, and the Gaza Strip. She'd even served briefly in the dysfunctional little country of Alsharq, between Egypt and Libya.

When the Paris station chief job opened up, Mariner had been thrilled. It was a plum assignment in one of Europe's most beautiful cities. Plus, during a two-year stint stateside in Virginia, she'd given birth to a daughter, Bess. Dinah Mariner looked forward to finding out what kind of woman Bess would become if she grew up in Paris.

The move also marked an end to her husband's many dalliances with graduate students. Dinah knew about Teddy's propensities. She'd had her share of affairs too, so she couldn't very well complain. But with the birth of Bess, plus Teddy's long-delayed biography of Oscar Wilde to write, Paris kept him busy.

Her new field office was a good mix. She had a director of operations and a director of intelligence. The former, Pete Newsom, worked hard enough and netted enough wins, although he did it for all the wrong reasons: to serve his time and get a big payout at GE or Boeing or one of those private military contractors popping up all over.

The latter, Annie Pryor, was a godsend. Mariner and Pryor were the same age and had gone to the same law school; they'd been one year apart but knew of each other. They'd joined the agency within five months of each other. Pryor was a Europe hand, and she understood the politics of that continent the way Mariner knew the Arabic world.

Within weeks of Mariner's arrival, her shop began generating some noteworthy intelligence.

Mariner also built her own private shop, using ex-soldiers and others who were loyal to her first and to the CIA second. That let her chalk up some quick wins that Langley noted with pleasure. The agency never looked too carefully at successes, but it cast a laser-like eye on failures. As long as Mariner kept racking up the victories, the agency would ask few questions.

Bess struggled through her terrible twos; Teddy struggled to find the narrative in the life of Wilde; Dinah thrived.

A YEAR INTO THE JOB, DINAH MARINER received a call from her old mentor and a former station chief for Cairo. He reached out through Mariner's private communications system, letting her know that the topic was for her ears only. Mariner left Annie Pryor in charge of Paris and traveled on her own dime with one of her own secret stash of cover identities.

She met her former boss in a town square in Evian-les-Bains, France, directly across Lac Léman from Lausanne, Switzerland. They met at a little sidewalk kebab place, under the tinny cacophony of the bells of Eglise Notre Dame de l'Assomption.

The topic was the possibility of a pro-Western coup in

Alsharq. A separatist fringe element in the capitol city of Baharos had preliminary evidence of a natural gas discovery off the coast. This group knew which side of its bread was buttered, and they'd reached out to a few friends in the west, like a retired Cairo Station chief, Mariner's mentor.

Independence for the small country was possible, just barely, as long as it looked like a second Arab Spring. If the Europeans and the Americans could come on board, fast enough, the Alsharqi government wouldn't have time to crush the independence movement. Egypt would stay out of the fight, too . . . maybe.

What the conspirators needed was a way to get the European Union and the Americans to intervene on behalf of the revolution. The US Navy's Sixth Fleet was just sitting there in Naples. If they could deploy a little to the southwest, still inside the Mediterranean, as a show of force, it might make the Alsharqi government hesitate.

That's where the reports of natural gas off the coast came in. How do you motivate the Americans and Europeans to support democracy? As everyone in the Middle East knew, it's not the squeaky wheel that gets attention, it's the wheel with plenty of petroleum lubrication.

The moderates in the city of Baharos could take the TV station, police station, and a bevy of government buildings in Eastern Baharos, so long as the Sixth Fleet dropped anchor just offshore. By the time the government responded, the revolution would be well underway and the people would flock to their side.

But the mission needed something else: a way to really jump-start the support of the European Union.

The idea had been brought to Mariner by her mentor, and had been brought to him by Major Saad Barakat, a disloyal intelligence officer in Mukhābarāt Alsharqi, the Alsharqi Intelligence Service, who wanted the insurgents to succeed.

What was needed was something to inspire anger and even fear in the Europeans, before the revolution began.

At first, Mariner hadn't wanted to trust Major Barakat, who had also come to Evian-les-Bains. They scheduled a series of clandestine meetings to hash out a plan, finding each other in Chinese or Thai restaurants, in American Subway sandwich shops or Starbucks, places where it was guaranteed that no one would pay them any attention.

Barakat was five eight and slim, dressed in a European style, narrow-cut jeans and trim wool coats with the collars turned up. He sometimes sported suede ankle boots or pristine white sneakers. He looked like any other European lawyer or software developer. He had a fox-like face with a neat beard, an aquiline nose, and an easy, Western smile. He was roughly thirty-five, Mariner thought, twelve years her junior.

Mariner took the train out of Gare de Lyon twice per week for four weeks, leaving Paris Station in the more-than-capable hands of Annie Pryor and Pete Newsom. She also hired a competent and very male au pair for Bess, who was just sailing clear of the squalls of her terrible twos. Teddy apparently hadn't picked up his old habit of sleeping with students; either that, or he was hiding it better these days.

In the cities and towns around Lake Geneva, Saad Barakat rented hotel rooms and conducted countersurveillance legwork before Mariner's arrivals. They met in restaurants and pubs. Barakat might have been a Muslim, but he had no problem sharing a bottle of wine with a woman. Throughout the month, they painstakingly came up with a way to make sure the Europeans and the Americans would have skin in the game when it came to Alsharq.

It had to be a bombing, they decided. It had to have the fingerprints of the Islamist government of Alsharq. It had to be a civilian target with a sufficient body count. It was the only way to make sure Europe would intervene on behalf of the revolutionaries.

It would be a horrible, horrible job. Mariner and Barakat were realists; they knew they would have innocent blood on their hands. But the West also could gain a reliable ally in Northern Africa, and a wedge between the Islamists of Egypt and the failed state of Libya. Wasn't that worth it?

Saad Barakat agreed to be the liaison to the reformers in the city of Baharos.

Mariner agreed to provide the "terrorists." She had guys she'd used on other extracurricular missions over the years, two ex-Rangers named DeMarcus Washington and Ron Perry, who were good, reliable, and lethal. Perry was a wizard with explosives. She also had an excellent wheelman, a German named Julian Ritter.

The target, they agreed, would be Paris. The casualties: Europeans and Americans. There is no European city, save London, that Americans love more than Paris (plus Mariner had never been stationed in London and didn't know the city at all). The goal: maximum grieving, maximum anger. They needed a blow that would sever any ties between the West and the Alsharqi government.

Mariner quickly got over any qualms about working with Barakat. He was soft-spoken, calm, well-read in European literature, capable of quoting the Quran and *Time* magazine in the same conversation. He liked—surprisingly—Mountain Dew, clothes shopping, and the 1960s pop tunes of Burt Bacharach. He later admitted, sheepishly, that he'd first started listening to the music because their names were similar.

After the third week of meetings, they found themselves having a second glass of wine and just chatting, long after the time for planning was over.

Mariner was no neophyte; she electronically scanned Barakat for wires at every meeting. He did the same for her, although by that third week, he'd started scanning her only every other time.

"I trust you, Dinah. I have to. We hang together or surely we hang separately."

Mariner had almost snorted white wine across her plate. "Benjamin Franklin?"

Barakat had blushed. "He's one of my heroes."

She took the high-speed train back to Paris after every meeting, feeling more and more sure that their plan would work and would usher in a new era of Western influence in the Maghreb, that embattled region of North Africa.

At home, Teddy seemed absorbed in his research into Oscar Wilde, floating in a cloud of literary minutia. Bess gurgled happily at seeing her, which always managed to surprise and please Mariner. At the CIA Paris Station, Pete Newsom ran his joes well, paid them enough bribe money. He was siphoning some off the top, Mariner knew, but didn't call him on it. It happened.

Annie Pryor ran her Intelligence division smartly, her daily reports short and unadorned and always useful. Her information streams ran deep into the Paris embassies and delegations of the Russians, Georgians, Ukrainians, North Koreans, and Syrians. Her joes reaped a soft, subtle and substantial drip, drip, drip of information.

And while those two ran the station, Mariner's secret plan came together.

WHEN THE TIME WAS RIGHT, Mariner brought Pryor and Newsom into the tent.

Pete got on board first. This was the kind of thing he'd imagined doing when he joined the CIA. This bold move could rearrange the chessboard of Northern Africa, maybe forever.

Annie took some convincing. The plan included killing civilians, after all. But the goals? Those she got.

When Pryor got with the program, she provided two important elements: a computer expert to create the videos they would need to frame the Alsharqi hardliners and a banker to launder the money.

Meanwhile, Barakat provided a "cleric." Which is to say, an actor from Cairo who could dress up as the part and deliver the lines needed to convince the world that the Alsharqi government was behind this new threat, this Khamsin Sayef, this Sword of the Storm.

MARINER AND BARAKAT DIDN'T SLEEP with each other until the last scheduled meeting in Montreux, Switzerland. Everything had come together. They were *left of Boom*, to use a military phrase. The bomb itself would be *Boom*. All that came after that would be *right of Boom*. The Democratic People of Alsharq would denounce the Sword of the Storm and the Paris bombing and would rise up against the dictatorial, Islamist government.

Pete Newsom used back channels to make sure the Sixth Fleet would be on maneuvers just off the Alsharqi coast.

Annie Pryor's tech expert, Joan Caldwell, made the video of the cleric reciting his lines. She stripped the video of any metadata, making it impossible to trace.

Meanwhile, their banker, Cedric Brecher, arranged for payoffs for officials in Eastern Baharos, at the police station, the TV station, and elsewhere.

Mariner and Barakat met in Montreux to go over it all one last time. Mariner took the train to Geneva then another to Montreux, looping around the top of picturesque Lac Léman with the blue Alps hovering in the near background. She was reading Robert Caro's biography of Lyndon Baines Johnson on her e-reader. In Montreux, she bought a coffee and took a long stroll around the lake toward the castle, stopping to smile at the statue of Queen front man Freddie Mercury, an odd little cultural touchstone for this century and this country.

Barakat met her in a musty, slightly shabby pile of old masonry with a view of the lake and the Alps. He'd rented a room. He wore a turtleneck under a camel-hair jacket with a thin plaid scarf. Mariner suppressed a laugh: from Arafat's checkered kaffiyeh to cashmere Burberry in a generation. That was progress of some sort.

They had coffee and croissants and chatted for thirty minutes, ensuring neither had been followed. They talked about politics and literature. Later, they went to find a tiny restaurant off the beaten path. In an alley, Mariner used a monitor to scan Barakat for wires; he declined to do the same to her.

After dinner, they walked back to Barakat's hotel without ever acknowledging out loud what was about to happen. Mariner again swept the room for bugs. Barakat produced a bottle of Sancerre with two small glasses.

They toasted to success and walked through the plan for seemingly the thousandth time.

Thinking back, Mariner was never able to remember who kissed whom first. Or who started undressing first. It probably didn't matter.

What they were doing could—would—change the face of the Arabic world. It definitely would change Arabic relations with Europe. It most definitely would change their own lives forever.

Afterward, Barakat threw on a lumpy old sweater—avocado green—with his jeans, and stepped out onto the balcony to smoke. Mariner piled pillows behind her back, threw on her own sweater, and waited to find out what he wanted to say. Men always want to talk after sex.

Barakat returned to the room and sat on her side of the bed, smiling sheepishly at her. She waited.

"I probably am supposed to tell you you're my first Western

woman, or first American woman, or something, but I'm a spy, so . . ."

She laughed. "Thank you for avoiding the cliché."

He held out his hand, palm up. After a hesitation, Mariner took his hand in hers.

"This is it," he said. "Are we sure?"

"I think so. I am. My people are. You?"

He didn't answer.

"The moderates in Baharos want this," she said softly. "They're waiting for us."

"I know."

"Our terrorist cell will be seen as villains. They have to be. We're all trained to hate villains, but they're essential. They're the key to changing the world. If you want it done fast and efficiently, sometimes you have to be the villain."

"I know." He spoke softly. He squeezed her hand. "And the innocents we kill in Paris?"

"The innocents we save in Alsharq will outnumber them ten thousand to one," she said. "With pro-Democracy support on Egypt's western border, in Alsharq, and on its eastern border in Israel, we can begin bringing about some real change in Egypt too."

"I know."

Now it was her turn to squeeze his hand. "Do you? *Know?*"

"Yes," Saad Barakat said, and leaned over to kiss her. "I know."

IT WAS AGREED THAT PETE NEWSOM would spend that week in Brussels and Annie Pryor would spend it in London (her house outside Paris was being fumigated, so she had an excuse for a small vacation). They'd both rush back after the bombing.

Their computer expert, Joan Caldwell, and her husband,

Rick, an engineer, were in Greece. The banker, Cedric Brecher, was back in his office in Geneva.

Right around noon that Tuesday, Mariner received a text from one of her private soldiers, DeMarcus Washington. The matter, he indicated, was urgent. They met at a little café on Rue Dante, surrounded by nerds: a comic book shop to the east; a gamer shop to the west; an anime shop across the street. Mariner had a pinot gris, and Washington ordered a French beer.

"Now would be a bad time for distractions," he said, speaking sotto voce—not easy for a natural baritone.

"What's up?"

He poured a little beer into his glass. "You asked me to let you know if your husband was, you know . . ."

Oh. That.

Mariner watched the sidewalk traffic. So Teddy was back to his old tricks. She couldn't very well burst into tears and beat her chest; she'd just had sex with Saad Barakat the night before.

"You're right," she spoke softly. "This isn't the time for distractions. It'll have to wait."

Washington said, "Don't think so."

She turned fully toward her soldier now. He watched the passersby, especially the long-legged Parisian girls in tight denim.

"What is it?"

Washington reached into his leather jacket and withdrew a smartphone. He brought up the phone's photo gallery and handed it over.

Mariner scrolled through seven of the photos. Then set the phone down, rummaged in her purse, found cigarettes and a lighter. Her first inhale consumed half the cigarette.

Washington sipped his beer and waited.

She picked up the phone and swiped through the rest of the photos. She paused at each.

When she'd asked Washington to follow her husband, she had expected to find him with yet another little postgrad, blond, bland, and oh-so-earnest.

What she hadn't expected was Annie Pryor.

Mariner paid for the drinks, tucked the smartphone into her purse, and walked away without a word.

BEING A STATION CHIEF is a bit like being a priest in a confessional: You know what you know because someone comes by periodically and tells you things.

Then you judge those things and pronounce remedies.

Pray the rosary. Get a microrecorder in the automobile of the wife of an ambassador.

If you're a station chief, the person who tells you the things you need to know is your chief of intelligence.

The person who carries out your remedies is your chief of operations.

You trust them both. You have to.

To Mariner, the photos of Annie fucking Teddy—or Teddy fucking Annie, which didn't make it any better—seemed like an unbelievable level of betrayal.

At this, the most important moment of her career.

After a night of smoking and drinking scotch, her throat gritty from the tobacco, Mariner had picked up one of her own throwaway phones and called her soldiers. "Eighteen hundred hours tomorrow."

Ron Perry had replied simply, "Confirmed."

"New location."

"Say what?"

Mariner stubbed out another butt in the overflowing ashtray. "New location. Hotel Saint Guillaume."

She listened to the long pause over the burner phone. The voice that came back was that of Washington, not Perry. "Please repeat."

"Hotel Saint Guillaume. The bar on the ground floor. West side."

Washington said, "Understood," and hung up.

He didn't have to ask about the change of venue.

He knew that while her house was being fumigated, Annie Pryor had been staying on the second floor of the Hotel Saint Guillaume in a little flat directly over the bar on the west side.

IN LONDON, ANNIE PRYOR received an encrypted text from her station chief, using a CIA-designed app that allows for one reading then erases texts forever.

Switch. Come back. Lilac.

Pryor sat in a tearoom near Barbican Centre, frowning. *Switch* meant a change in plan. *Come back* was self-explanatory. *Lilac* was the rotating day code for Dinah Mariner.

Pryor booked a seat on the next train to Paris.

AS HER TRAIN EMERGED on the continental end of the Channel Tunnel, Pryor's phone vibrated.

Head to Gamma. Wait. Meringue.

The Gamma Site was Pryor's little flat on the Hotel Saint Guillaume. *Meringue* was Dinah's next rotating day code after *Lilac*. Pryor prepared to head to her flat.

AT FIVE P.M., DINAH MARINER PARKED a Nissan she'd hot-wired outside a Monoprix store, half a block from the Hotel Saint Guillaume. Like so many places in Paris, the business on the corner was both a café and a tavern. She chain-smoked—the equivalent of leaving DNA evidence in a stolen vehicle, but fuck it. She watched as DeMarcus Washington did a pass-through of the ground-floor café, re-emerging with a newspaper under his left arm: the go sign.

Ron Perry entered with a backpack thirty seconds after Washington left.

Mariner sat and smoked and watched the window directly above the café. A light was on. Annie must have cracked the window a bit, the ventilation inhaling and exhaling the lace curtains.

Perry had a coffee and left without the backpack.

The explosion would be set near a load-bearing wall. Annie's flat would collapse into the café, for sure. No question. Perry was a virtuoso with explosives.

Mariner lit one cigarette after another. She watched people arrive and leave the little café, with the black-and-white banner out front and the round, white-iron tables and chairs with heart-shaped backs. The window nearest her advertised "Happy Hour" and "Wi-Fi" in English, to attract American tourists.

She inhaled smoke and thought about the value of a pro-Western country on Egypt's western flank.

She thought about the career-defining mission. Even though no one would ever officially know what she'd done, the right people would. The right people would remember.

She thought about Teddy fucking Annie. And Annie fucking Teddy.

She waited.

She watched laughing tourists exit the restaurant, laughing tourists enter. One of them bumped into another, and they ricocheted apart, smiling, and for a split second, in the space where the tourists had been, she saw Professor Teddy Mariner enter the café.

With their daughter.

Mariner wrenched open the car door, smacking into the thigh of a pedestrian on the sidewalk, who cried out. She leaped from the car, around it, into the street, heard the screech of brakes and caught a glimmer of metal to her left. She leaped up onto the hood of a car, avoided falling under its wheels, landed hard on her left elbow, pain radiating down her arm, slid off to the other side, heard horns blaring to her right now, dashing, screaming, reaching the sidewalk and a priest in a cassock, shoving him aside, yelling, eyes turning her way now, tourists and passersby and waiters but not Teddy, not Teddy, as she shoved a man into the tables under the awning, saw him flying, coffee splashing away as the table collapsed, and she hit the door, into the café, every eye turning her way now, heard her name shouted in a deep rumbling baritone from behind her, ignored it, surged forward, saw a waiter turn toward the madwoman; the waiter showing Teddy and Bess to a table for three against the far wall, the load-bearing wall, Teddy holding Bess's hand, Bess in her blue cardigan with white daisies and a bow in her hair, always a bow in her hair these days, she insisted on it. Saw Teddy's eyes widen and Bess begin to smile/frown, surprised, happy, and wary, heard her name again, and now an arm the size of a tree trunk was around Mariner's waist, lifting her feet clear off the ground. Heard herself scream, *"NOOOOOOO!"* as DeMarcus Washington barreled back out, carrying her like a football under his arm, stiff-arming waiters out of the way. She reached for the doorjamb, grabbed on, felt herself slip from Washington's grip, land on her knees, as she reached toward Bess and—the light. The white light. It was everywhere. Filling her eyes, her ears, her brain, her soul. Searing, monstrous pain ripped through her face and neck, but faded, faded, until there was nothing but the white light.

And the memory of the little blue cardigan with daisies. And the hair bow.

And then blackness.

RON PERRY KNEW A DOCTOR IN BRUSSELS who would sign the paperwork getting Mariner installed in a clinic in Salzburg, Austria, where they treated the third-degree burns across her cheek and neck, plus a smashed elbow and four broken ribs. They couldn't do anything about her catatonic state, but Washington and Perry and Ritter had access to Mariner's own dirty-tricks slush fund, so they kept feeding money to the doctor, who housed Mariner in a unit for heroin addicts and asked no questions.

She pulled out of it eventually, although it took better than a month.

The soldiers couldn't very well abandon her; she'd always been loyal to them, and besides, she'd kept their presence a secret from US intelligence agencies. They found a place in Salzburg, far from the tourist crowds. Mariner went along with them willingly, doing as they said, speaking rarely.

Mariner's slush fund was fat; the four of them lived well enough for more than a year.

THEY WERE THERE WHEN THE SECOND ANNIVERSARY of the Paris bombing came and went, and none of them said a word.

THE SITUATION IN ALSHARQ STARTED WELL. Moderates took over the media and government buildings on the eastern side of the city. The Americans and Europeans were waging heated debates at the UN and the World Court about how to punish the Islamist government and its neophyte terrorist cell, the Khamsin Sayef, which had taken credit for the bombing in Paris. The Sixth Fleet just happened to be in position off the coast of Baharos when the revolution began, further hamstringing the Islamists.

The Alsharqi government denied any knowledge of the bombing. But of course they would.

Within a week, the Western-leaning moderates had taken the capitol building in Baharos. The people cheered in the Square of the Prophet. Al Jazeera and Western media covered the events. Tanks didn't roll—not with the world watching. A new parliament was sworn in nine weeks after the bombing.

Some of the citizens of the new, free Alsharq attempted to start their own newspapers and internet media sites. But it was too early for that; the new government asked them to please wait. Then asked them again. Then cracked down.

The Square of the Prophet saw more crowds as the months passed, but now they were protesting the new government, the moderate government.

Which responded by sending in police in full battle armor, clubs swinging.

The new government had taken its lessons from the old government.

The crackdowns continued.

But at least the Khamsin Sayef had disappeared, after its one and only bomb.

MARINER, WASHINGTON, PERRY, AND RITTER were in Salzburg when Major Saad Barakat of the Alsharqi Mukhābarāt tracked them down. Perry spotted him first, sitting at a table in the restaurant across the street from their safe house, reading a paperback and drinking coffee and smoking.

Washington and Perry walked a five-block perimeter but spotted no backup.

Ritter prepared their getaway vehicle.

Still, Barakat sat and read and sipped his coffee, never looking up or across the street.

They waited an hour, then Mariner stepped out of the apartment building and crossed the street to join him. As she approached, Barakat used an emptied sleeve of sugar as a bookmark and set it aside. He made a gesture to the waiter and ordered two more coffees, and Mariner pulled out a chair and sat opposite him.

While they waited for their coffee, Barakat made eye contact with her. His chocolate eyes studied the shiny, plastic-looking burn scars on her neck and cheek.

"They're bad." He spoke softly. "Worse than I'd heard."

Mariner watched him.

Their coffees came.

"I never yet met a bomber who didn't carry some self-made scars," Barakat said, and ripped open a new packet of sugar.

"What do you want?"

He doctored his coffee. Mariner sat like a person with extreme back pain. She hadn't bothered bringing a weapon.

"Your actions that day helped us to create a new, free Alsharq," he said. "You changed the map of the world. How many people can say that?"

"I hear you've started carpet-bombing the insurgents on the western side of the city."

"Fake news," he said, borrowing the cliché from across the Atlantic. "We have been attempting to root terrorists out of their spider holes amid civilian populations."

"If that gets you through the night . . ."

He sipped his coffee. "Our so-called allies in the West are feckless."

"Your so-called allies were sold a bill of goods."

"We need to keep the Europeans at the table. Also the Americans."

"You won't."

"The Khamsin Sayef might."

Mariner almost smiled. "There never was a Khamsin Sayef."

"Of course there was, Dinah. Those monsters blew up a café and a hotel in Paris, remember? They killed sixty-eight people. They outraged Brussels and Washington, DC. I'm sorry to say, their next bombs will do the same."

Mariner thought about his words, played them back, tried to make sense of them.

She said, "Fuck you."

"I'm sorry to insist, Dinah. A few well-placed bombs will keep our alliances in place long enough to destroy the opposition forces in Baharos."

"I'm dead," she said, and indeed, her toneless, gray voice sounded dead. "You have your own army, your own police state. You don't need me, and there's nothing you can offer me. There's solace in being dead."

He shook his head calmly. "You underestimate your value. I need you now more than ever."

She almost laughed, and would have, if that depth of emotion were still within her.

"It's been more than two years, Dinah, and, so far, your confederates have kept their secrets. The banker, the computer expert, your lieutenant, Pete Newsom."

"Why shouldn't they? Their secrets are keeping them out of an international criminal court."

Barakat leaned over in his chair and dug a device out of his trouser pocket. He set it on the table. It was a palm-sized digital recorder. He casually checked the café,. made sure the staff was well away from their table, and hit Play.

"The moderates in Baharos want this. They're waiting for us."

"I know."

"Our terrorist cell will be seen as villains. They have to be. We're all trained to hate villains, but they're essential. They're the key to changing the world. If you want it done fast and efficiently, sometimes you have to be the villain."

"I know. And the innocents we kill in Paris?"

"The innocents we save in Alsharq will outnumber them ten thousand to one. With pro-Democracy support on Egypt's western border, in Alsharq, and on its eastern border in Israel, we can—"

Mariner moved for the first time since sitting down, reaching for the recorder and stopping the playback.

He studied her eyes and guessed what she was thinking. "That night in the hotel in Montreux. You scanned my jacket and shirt and trousers for recording devices. But not the sweater I put on after we made love."

She remembered the avocado sweater. "So you were wired. So what?"

"So when this tape leaks to the CIA, when they discover that you and Messrs. Washington, Perry, and Ritter are alive and well, you will become the most hunted people on earth. Will Joan Caldwell and Cedric Brecher go to prison for you? I hardly think so. Then, of course, there's your own Pete Newsom."

Mariner didn't respond.

"So you see, I still have need of your bombs. And you." He smiled. "I am not one to shower praises on others, but your organizational skills, your connections, your planning . . . You are nonpareil, Dinah. Honestly."

She waited, dead eyes locked on him.

"We don't need your internet expert; we know now how to make the videos with no metadata. We don't need your banker; we have the Alsharqi treasury now. Newsom has left the CIA; did you know this? He has accepted a position at one of those private military contractors, the ones who have acted as gang lords in Afghanistan and Iran."

"You don't need me," she insisted softly.

"I do. A few bombs to keep the childlike Americans and Europeans focused on the atrocities of the old hardliners who are attempting to claw back power. And, if you could eliminate those people who know about our original operation, so much the better."

"I won't."

"There is one last incentive. I'm sure your men have failed to tell you the worst part."

She waited.

"Annie Pryor didn't die in the explosion."

Mariner literally gasped. Her hand went to her chest as if she'd been stabbed.

"Ah. They didn't tell you. I suspected. The bomb destroyed her apartment, yes. But she was no longer in her apartment. She left, possibly ninety seconds before the explosion. We don't know why. Perhaps she saw you sitting outside the hotel? Perhaps she spotted Mr. Washington or Mr. Perry? Or perhaps she saw your own beloved Teddy and your daughter, Bess? There's no way of knowing."

"Shut up."

He frowned a little. "A question for you: Teddy brought your daughter to the café. Do you think she knew about her father and Annie Pryor?"

"Shut up."

"Perhaps—and I don't know, I am merely speculating here—but perhaps Professor Mariner was truly in love with Annie Pryor. Maybe he had plans for their future together."

"Shut up."

"Why bring his daughter to meet his mistress? Curious. I'm sure you've asked yourself as well."

"Shut up." She pressed her fingertips against her sternum.

"Annie and Teddy and Bess . . ."

"Shut up."

"Did Teddy want a divorce?"

"Shut up."

"Or . . . I don't know . . ."

"Shut up."

He stirred his coffee. "Did Annie Pryor intend to do to you what you intended to do to her?"

"She . . ."

Her voice dried up and blew away.

"You need to finish what you started, Dinah." He drained his coffee, leaned sideways to retrieve his kid leather wallet. "Finish it. Buy my country the time to put down these terrorists. Keep our allies at the table. Clean up the mess you created."

Tears glittered but refused to fall. She pressed her fingers against her chest. She'd stopped breathing.

Saad Barakat threw down several bills, patted his lips with his napkin, and stood. He squared his chair back up against the table.

"It's good to see you again, Dinah. We will be in touch."

C54

It was going on midnight. Fiero showered first, then Finnigan. The nondescript agent—turns out, his name was Rodriguez—had their clothes washed and dried and returned to them. Hugo Llorente made phone calls. They gathered in the kitchen at the now-refilled coffeepot.

"Sooner, Slye, and Rydell," Llorente said, entering the kitchen and accepting a cup. Rodriguez dug half-and-half out of the fridge for his boss. "Their Colonel Sanger has been recalled to the United States. His superior officers believe he might have stolen three million from the company. His career is over and, as you predicted, I can maneuver without those bastards hovering over my shoulder. At least for a while. Thank you."

Fiero sipped her coffee and turned to Finnigan. "Go over it."

Her partner liked to think out loud when poring over complicated problems. It helped him but, equally important, it helped her sort through the pieces.

Finnigan sat on the counter, rubbing his sore jaw. "So, it's three years ago. A group of moderates in Alsharq come up with a way to free their country from a hard-line Islamist government. They dangle natural gas reserves to get Western support. And they decide to stage a fake bombing to alienate their government. The guy behind it all is this Major Saad Barakat."

Llorente said, "We know very little about him. He's a specter."

"This Barakat dude comes up with a plan. He reaches out to Dinah Mariner, CIA station chief in Paris, who apparently had her own crew of hitters and runs off-book projects."

Fiero stood with one boot on the floor, sole of the other against the wall. Llorente pulled out a chair from the kitchen table, as did Rodriguez.

"Together, Mariner and Barakat create a fake Islamist group, the Khamsin Sayef. Here's the plan: They'll blow up something in Paris, in the name of the Islamists. The folks in Baharos rebel, declare independence. The American Sixth Fleet sails into the port of Baharos, and a new petro-government is born."

The others listened.

"Mariner uses a corrupt banker to fund it all. She uses a web expert to create untraceable videos. They create a fake cleric. They lie about Islam and the infidels and all that shit. Mariner uses her own hitters, ah—"

Llorente said, "Former Army Rangers. DeMarcus Washington and Ron Perry. I made some phone calls."

"Okay. But—and here's where it gets complicated . . ."

Fiero said, "*Gets* complicated?"

"Stay with me. Mariner's chief of intelligence, Annie Pryor, is screwing her husband. Mariner loses it. She decides to kill Pryor in the bombing. But just before it all happens, she finds out her husband has taken their daughter to rendezvous with Annie. Annie herself has already left the scene. Mariner races to the bomb, tries to stop it. Boom. Husband dies, kid dies, Dinah Mariner dies. Only, not really."

"Washington and Perry," the old man spoke into his coffee cup.

"Probably, yeah. They were nearby to detonate the bomb. See their boss get blown ass over teakettle. She's still alive. They get her out of there."

Llorente crossed his legs. "I just had the files sent to me. The authorities positively ID'd Teddy Mariner and Bess Mariner. But the ID on Dinah Mariner was never confirmed. The father and daughter died, and another body was found in the ruins. Also Dinah Mariner's purse and ID, her transponders, her gun . . . It was assumed she died too."

Finnigan said, "Washington and Perry likely planted that stuff, sure."

Fiero said, "Then the Khamsin Sayef goes quiet for three years."

Finnigan gulped down his cold coffee. "'Course. 'Cause Mariner was recovering from her injuries. Meanwhile, the government of Alsharq is formed and quickly goes to hell on a luge sled. People revolt. The *friendly* new government proves just as nasty as the guys before them. Meet the new boss, same as the old boss. Shots are fired, there's a crackdown. There's a couple roadside bombs, and boom, like that, the *moderates* are waging full-scale war on the city of Baharos."

Fiero cut in. "Saad Barakat is still an intelligence operative. His side is losing. He needs the Khamsin Sayef again."

"Yeah, needs the boogeyman to keep the West from abandoning this new government. Dinah Mariner's not so dead after all. She and Barakat and her old crew revive the Khamsin Sayef gag. More bombs, more blame for the Islamists. More videos of the cleric. It keeps the EU and the Americans from backing out."

"Plus," Llorente added softly, reaching for his cigarettes, "Mariner kills everyone who knew about the fake Islamist threat.

And tries to kill the woman she likely blames for the death of her husband and daughter."

Fiero said, "Don't smoke."

He slid a cigarette back into the pack.

Finnigan said, "Mariner and her crew set up the bombs. Saad Barakat dusts off his cleric, tapes more confessions, blames the Islamists. The Alsharqi government continues to bomb the ever-loving fuck out of Baharos. The Europeans and the American dither."

Fiero said, "We won't be able to prove any of this."

"We will if Annie testifies," Finnigan said, and hopped down off the counter. He poured another cup. He made eye contact with Rodriquez, waggled the pot in midair. The man nodded, and Finnigan refilled his cup.

Llorente winced. "I'm afraid I have bad news. While you were showering, Annie Pryor began to bleed internally. The doctor went back in to stop it. She's still alive, but the doctor isn't sanguine she'll recover. She might. It's too early to tell."

Finnigan froze.

"Not your fault," the old man whispered. "Damage from the bullet."

"Fuck."

Llorente nodded his agreement.

"If Annie dies—"

Fiero cut in, "—her men will disappear. The Khamsin Sayef will disappear. Saad Barakat will pack away that alias, bury it. No one will ever know."

"No," Llorente said. "I'm afraid we won't be that lucky."

The others turned to him.

"The civil war in Alsharq is at a stalemate. The government has bombed entire neighborhoods of the capital, the citizens are in open revolt. Major Barakat and his masters need to keep the

Europeans from bolting. He has to keep the Khamsin Sayef alive. He has to bomb more targets."

"Whether or not Dinah Mariner and her crew take part," Finnigan added. "The bombings will continue, either way. The West won't move to stop the destruction of Baharos. Not while everyone's scared shitless of the Khamsin Sayef."

They silently pondered the situation.

Finnigan climbed back up on the counter, feet dangling. "Saad Barakat?"

Llorente nodded. "From what I've been able to dig up, he appears to be a very good intelligence agent."

"Where is he?"

"At the Ministry of Defense in Baharos, usually. Their Mukhābarāt—their intelligence service—works out of the basement there."

Llorente stared into his coffee cup as if hoping to see tea leaves. "He's out of our reach."

It was late, and Llorente told the partners they could stay the night in the spooky old house. Llorente arranged to get their bags from the hotel near Las Ramblas. He also provided a decanter of good whiskey and stood them both to a drink.

Finnigan accepted the drink but without a smile. "You paid us to find and bring in this cleric guy. We failed."

Llorente quirked his lips in a flash-smile. "Our nameless cleric, the boogeyman terrorizing Europe, is a fraud. We wouldn't have known that, had it not been for you. I'd say you more than did your job."

Finnigan and Fiero exchanged glances over the rims of their glasses.

"Some part of me admires the brass of it," Llorente said. "This

Barakat is a clever man. And he has the guts of a cat burglar. I admire his audacity."

They finished their drinks, and Llorente bade them good night.

RODRIGUEZ SHOWED THEM TWO GUEST ROOMS on the second floor. Finnigan took another long shower, feeling the aftereffects of the beating he'd taken at the hands of Sooner, Slye, and Rydell. He climbed into bed in his boxers and fell instantly asleep.

He woke up around three when Fiero crept into his room. She wore panties and a black camisole. She sat on the edge of the bed.

Finnigan propped two pillows behind his head. "Hey."

She sat quietly for a while.

She'd removed the stretch bandage around her flank. Finnigan put one of his arms behind his head and waited.

She brushed hair behind her shoulders and watched Michael's eyes. "This man. Major Saad Barakat."

"One of the greatest con jobs of all time. A fake terrorist cell, a fake cleric. Llorente's right: gotta hand it to him."

She sat, one thigh and knee up on the bed, her other bare foot on the floor.

"Barakat almost killed my father. They would have succeeded, if not for us. They started the panic in Barcelona that led to my mother's concussion."

Finnigan's eyes flicked toward a long knife scar over her kidney. She'd had that for as long as he'd known her. He waited.

"I think we should go get him."

Finnigan didn't respond.

Fiero ran a splayed-finger palm through her hair. "I'm serious."

"I know."

"You think it's stupid?"

"I think it's suicidal."

She smiled. The smile held the same glint as the knife that had caused that scar on her back.

Finnigan said, "He's in Baharos."

"Probably."

"Baharos is in the middle of a fucking civil war."

"Well, not the side of the city where the Ministry of Defense is. That's where we'll find Barakat."

Finnigan sat up in bed and rubbed his eyes with the heels of his hands. He realized she was serious and not just speculating.

"Holy shit."

Fiero moved to sit beside him on the bed, leaning against other pillows, her long legs beside his.

"We can't invade an African country, a capital city that's under siege, and kidnap the head of their intelligence service."

She said, "It's called the Mukhābarāt."

"They can call it the Indigo Girls. We still can't do it."

"With McTavish's help, we could."

"McTavish took money from Suicide Ride not to help us. Remember?"

She shrugged, her shoulder rubbing against his. "I might have an idea to make that go away. And you know McTavish has run military ops in other African countries. He could find the right people to do this."

"Even if we could get him, he'd charge a million bucks for this kind of op."

"Sally Blue and her people just stole three million from Sooner, Slye, and Rydell," Fiero countered. "I contacted her. I explained what we're up against. She's willing to bankroll the mission."

"Why?"

"Because Barakat tried to kill my father."

That made an insane sort of sense. Neither Finnigan nor Fiero knew that much about the brassy American who ran the Black Harts, but they knew how she felt about family.

"So the Black Harts are our bank. We hire McTavish, who, not for nothing, we can't hire because he took money not to take our calls. So with the military mercenaries we don't have, we invade the city of Baharos, which is in the middle of a civil war. We invade the Ministry of Defense. We kidnap Major Barakat and smuggle him back to Spain. This is your plan?"

Fiero looked at him in the dark and said simply, "Yes."

"It's nuts."

"We've done *nuts* before."

"Not like this we haven't."

She waited. They sat like that, shoulder to shoulder. They listened to the wind, the African sirocco, whistling past the old house. They heard the house settle.

Finnigan said, "Really?"

Fiero nodded.

Finnigan said, "Well . . . okay, then."

Fiero barked a little laugh. She almost never laughed.

He nudged her with his shoulder.

"Go get some sleep, crazy lady. We're gonna need it."

C55

In the morning, Hugo Llorente returned to the old mansion. Rodriguez made café con leche, sweet rolls called *bolos*, pots of jam and plates of cheese, and a cast-iron skillet of tortilla Españole with jamón, chorizo, serrano, and piquillo peppers. Finnigan looked at it all, then at the spy in an apron and a wooden spoon. "You made all this?"

Rodriguez shrugged. "I'm Spanish, man."

Finnigan turned and batted his eyes at Fiero. She used her fingers to break off a bit of crispy potato from the tortilla and said, without heat, "Shut up."

She sat and told Llorente about her proposal.

The old man said, "That's insane."

Finnigan heaped food onto a plate. "And we have two votes for insane."

Rodriguez removed an oven mitt and held up three fingers.

"Barakat is the author of this whole, murderous thing. More

so than Dinah Mariner, even if she's the one planting the bombs. How many deaths are on his head?"

Llorente made to answer but Fiero rode over him. "And don't just count the people who've been killed by their bombs. The bombs have kept the West from abandoning the government of Alsharq. That government has killed thousands of civilians and forced thousands more to flee. We bring Barakat in, maybe we put an end to that civil war."

The older man doctored his coffee and studied them. Fiero stared at him. Finnigan wolfed down his food.

When finally the spymaster spoke, it was to Finnigan. "Katalin was never one for the beau geste, Mr. Finnigan. Things have changed considerably since the advent of St. Nicholas Salvage & Wrecking."

Finnigan worked through his food like he was in training for an Olympic event. "You took a kid who knew how to fight and taught her how to hate. Or, at any rate, how not to give a shit. I find it kinda hilarious that you think you ever knew her at all."

Fiero reached for her coffee. Finnigan scarfed his food. Rodriguez got the next pot of coffee going and turned to them. He said, "We're never going to find Dinah Mariner, sir. She's one of the finest field agents in the history of the CIA. She kept us hopping, kept us blind until these two *idiotas* came along. Fiero's scheme may be harebrained, but it's also the first scheme anyone has come up with. Yourself included. Sir."

It was more words than the nondescript man had spoken since the partners arrived. From the look on Llorente's face, no one was more surprised than him.

Fiero sat with one boot heel up on her chair, her knee up by her shoulder, one arm draped over it. She said, "You find out where Major Saad Barakat is. We'll go get him. We have the manpower figured out. We have the funding figured out."

Finnigan didn't contradict her.

"We slip into Baharos, grab him, slip out. We hand him over to you. If we get caught, you, the prime minister, the crown, all have deniability."

The old man leaned forward. "There are other complications. You two managed to knock Sooner, Slye, and Rydell for a loop. I'm grateful. You removed their Colonel Sanger from the board. But I have my spies in their camp, too. I'm informed that Sanger has not reported back to his masters. He's at large. The same is true for Syarhey Valazko."

The partners glanced at each other.

"Sanger doubtless blames you for his stunning loss of face. And Valazko seems to hate you specifically, Katalin. The private military contractor is no longer making my life miserable, perhaps, but that doesn't mean they won't focus on you now."

Fiero said, "You believe they are coming for us?"

Llorente nodded. "I do."

Fiero said, "Then where better to hide than a war zone?"

They talked for another ninety minutes. Hugo Llorente never said he agreed with the plan.

But he stopped talking about it in the abstract.

C56

Syarhey Valazko found a safe house outside of the hill village north of Barcelona. The single-story house hadn't seen a fresh coat of paint since Francisco Franco's reign. The For Sale sign outside was a testament to positive thinking.

Cole Sanger sat on the couch, legs wide apart, leaning forward, elbows on his knees, fists clasped together. He might have been praying or attempting not to throw up. Valazko had stored a bottle of vodka in the safe house. He found it now, along with two mismatched glasses. He poured, and Sanger accepted.

Valazko's phone vibrated. Sanger looked up, startled. "Who knows where you are?"

Valazko retrieved the phone. He listened to the call. He sipped his vodka and smiled.

The very pale man turned and handed the phone to Sanger. "It's for you."

Sanger hesitated. Then took it and put it on speakerphone.

"Colonel? This is Hugo Llorente."

Sanger bolted up off the couch, vodka sloshing to the carpet.

"I'm here with an old colleague. Katalin Fiero Dahar. She wishes to speak to you."

Sanger's knuckles turned white around the phone. "What the hell is this?"

But the voice that answered was female, low, lyrical, and smoky. "Colonel? We have your missing three million dollars. And we'd like to make a deal."

Valazko shook his head and chuckled silently. He sipped his vodka.

Sanger forced himself to sound calm. "I'm listening."

"We know who the Khamsin Sayef is. We know who their leader is. We're bounty hunters; we believe we can bring him in."

"What's this have to do with the money you and that arrogant bastard partner of yours stole?"

"The man we want to bring in is hiding. In Baharos, Alsharq."

Sanger and Valazko both blinked in surprise. Sanger said, "Go on."

"We need a good team. The best. It will take resources. We intend to bring a small army. We intend to pay them with the money we stole from you."

"I see."

"You . . . that is, Sooner, Slye, and Rydell, paid a mercenary named Brodie McTavish not to help us. We want you to release him from that agreement. In exchange, when we get the man behind all this, we will turn him over to you. You'll get the credit for capturing him. We tell Sooner, Slye, and Rydell that you're the hero of the hour. You, in turn, give the man up to Hugo Llorente for trial. Spain gets what it wants. You get what you want. Sooner, Slye, and Rydell gets what it wants. And we get paid."

Sanger put her on mute and turned to the Belorussian. "You know her. Is she telling the truth?"

Valazko shrugged. He looked a little bored. "I hate her, but I can't say I know her. On the other hand, who would make up such a story?"

They heard Fiero's voice. "Colonel?"

Sanger ignored the voice, staring at Valazko. "Do you trust me?"

Valazko sipped vodka. "You've never lied to me."

Sanger nodded and thumbed off the mute control. "Katalin. May I call you Katalin?"

"If you must."

"Is Michael there with you?"

"No. Michael doesn't trust you. He thinks it was stupid to reach out to you."

Valazko laughed softly.

"That's fine. I can deal with you, and I can deal with Mr. Llorente. I agree to your terms. I'll let you have your mercenaries. You go to Baharos and find this guy. You use the company money. And I get the credit for masterminding the operation, *if* it's successful. Right?"

Fiero said, "Yes."

"Then I have a condition of my own. Your Michael doesn't trust me. I don't trust him. I don't trust you. This team you're putting together with Brodie McTavish? You take Syarhey Valazko along."

Valazko didn't react; he just kept smiling.

Fiero said, "No way."

"Katalin, you need the best possible team if you're mounting an operation in a war zone. Valazko has operated in more war zones than you have. Moreover, he's my guarantee that you guys don't screw me in the end."

"Valazko attempted to kill me. Twice."

"On my orders," Sanger confirmed. "Now you have my word

of honor as an officer and as a Marine. Valazko won't harm you, and he won't interfere with your operation. But he will make sure the guy you're going after ends up in my hands. Otherwise, no deal. No Valazko, no McTavish, and I let Sooner, Slye, and Rydell know where you're going. Then you'll have to deal with them *and* with a civil war."

He waited. The phone line hissed. He heard a soft change in the tone and knew this time it was they who'd been muted.

It took almost sixty seconds until the tone changed again.

Hugo Llorente said, "We have your word of honor, Colonel?"

"You do."

Fiero cut in. "Then we have a deal. Valazko is almost as good as I am. Tell him, Welcome aboard."

They arranged for a meeting, and Sanger hung up.

Valazko poured them both more vodka, smiling throughout. "Almost as good . . ."

"I know what I'm doing," the colonel said.

"I like you. I do. And I've made good money killing for you. But I am not going into that godforsaken city under siege."

"Of course not." Sanger drained his glass. "I still have contacts in the American military and intelligence communities. We'll meet with these morons. We'll find out what we can, then take it to the CIA."

"And Fiero's mission to Baharos?"

Sanger poured more for both of them. "She doesn't come back alive. Finnigan, the same."

"You gave them your word."

"I gave my words to thieves and liars. I want them both dead. You have a problem with that?"

Valazko smiled and touched his glass to Sanger's.

C57

Fiero arranged to meet the mercenary crew at a shabby hotel on the outskirts of Barcelona. She set a time and date, and Syarhey Valazko arrived three hours earlier.

He bribed a clerk to confirm that Fiero had rented a room for three days but had not yet arrived. The hotel apparently had a reputation of catering to both the Spanish intelligence community and the criminal element of the town. Valazko found that those two elements often blended together the world over.

He sweetened the bribe and got a passkey. The room, on the fifth floor, seemed ideal for a criminal enterprise. It was at the end of an ill-lit corridor, past both the cleaning crew's storage room and a room housing steam pipes. It was a suite, sporting a largish living room with a threadbare corduroy couch, two humpbacked chairs on plastic coasters, and a throw rug so old the miasmic pattern had been worn into invisibility except around the far edges. He drew his SIG-Sauer and checked the bedroom, the double bed made. He checked the bathroom with its old-fashioned footed tub, chipped sink, and floor tiles turned the yellow of old teeth.

Valazko could wait for the bounty hunters to arrive and surprise them here in the room, but he had no way of knowing who would arrive first, them or the mercenaries they were hiring.

No, better to take the meeting and wait for the opportunity to kill them.

Fiero first. She clearly was the more dangerous of the two.

He relieved himself in the bathroom then headed back downstairs, slipping more euros and the passkey to the clerk.

He found a discreet parking space a half block from the hotel and waited.

The first to arrive, thirty minutes early, was the American ex-cop, Finnigan, with his unkempt hair and two-days growth of beard. He wore an untucked work shirt, jeans, and boots. No shoulder bag, although he carried a grease-stained paper bag that could have included food or groceries. Finnigan wasn't carrying any weapon larger than a pistol. Well, that and the lead-filled sap that Valazko remembered well, rubbing his ear.

He spotted a man ten minutes later and bells went off in his head. He snapped a photo before the man disappeared into the hotel. He had a lumpy, bullet-shaped head, hair shaved close enough to show scars on his skull, a Cro-Magnon chin, and sunken eyes. Valazko sent the photo via direct message to an old friend in the killing business. It took seven minutes to get an answer.

Christophe Grenier. French merc. Good.

Grenier. Yes. Valazko recognized him now and another memory popped into place. Grenier had done mercenary work in North Africa, in Libya, for sure, and possibly in Alsharq. The Frenchman would be a good addition to this team.

Brodie McTavish arrived next. He was a bear of a man with wild, red hair and a massive beard. He looked like a Viking. Fought like one too, if his reputation was to be believed.

Katalin Fiero Dahar arrived within four minutes of the meeting time, and by now the sun had set. She wore all black: matchstick jeans, a tank under a weathered biker jacket that was too heavy for the hot weather, boots with chunky Spanish heels.

Years ago, in Oslo, Norway, that woman had rescued a Ukrainian journalist who Valazko had been tasked with assassinating. She also killed two of Valazko's men. She'd made him look like an amateur. He'd given the money back to the men who wanted the journalist dead, of course, but he also paid with a portion of his reputation.

Valazko wasn't so much of a sociopath as to be unaware that he was a sociopath. He knew his shortcomings. He neither loved nor hated, not like normal people allegedly do.

But he did understand the retail value of reputation. And he understood the need for revenge.

He was going to enjoy this job.

Fiero was far too skilled to rape and kill. He'd have to settle for just killing her.

Finnigan. Him Valazko could rape first.

AT THE TOP OF THE HOUR, Valazko climbed out of his car, unwrapped a stick of gum, and sauntered into the hotel lobby. He'd barely crossed the threshold when his phone lit up. Fiero.

Room 512. Don't be late.

He took the elevator up to the fifth floor for the second time that day, hands jammed in the side pockets of his sapper jacket, one fist around his SIG. He strolled past the janitors' supply room and the steam-pipe room. He rapped on the door to 512 with the second knuckle of his middle finger.

Fiero answered. She cracked the door a couple of inches and turned to look back over her shoulder. She said, "It's Valazko."

He could have killed her right there, while she was talking to the others. Then powered past her body, stormed the room, and taken out the others.

The American cop might get caught napping. Might. But with veteran warriors like Christophe Grenier and Brodie McTavish? No way. He might get one of them. Might get two. Likely wouldn't get all three.

Fiero turned back to him and studied him with jet-black irises. She maintained a perfect poker face.

The very pale man chewed his gum and flashed a lazy, lopsided smile. He jutted his chin at the space over her shoulder, a mute version of *May I come in?*

Fiero opened the door fully and half-stepped into the room's coat closet to clear space for him to pass in the short, narrow corridor to the living room. Their shoulders brushed. He thought again about killing her and again did his sums. The math was all wrong.

Valazko sauntered in, taking in the ugly corduroy couch and the two humpbacked chairs.

No one was there.

The old, faded rug was missing.

He said, "Oh."

Fiero came out of the coat closet with a .22 caliber automatic and a military-grade sound suppressor. She put a bullet in Valazko's back. The subsonic round tore out a chunk of his left lung but stayed inside his body.

He fell to his knees. His SIG clattered to the hardwood.

"I needed Sanger to offer your services," she said. "If I'd suggested it, you'd have known it was a trap."

She put the second bullet in his skull, and he tumbled forward.

Fiero disassembled the .22 and silencer and walked to the door.

Rodriguez, the nondescript agent of Hugo Llorente, stood by the steam-pipe room, wearing overalls and elastic-rimmed plastic slips over his boots. Two men stood with him, dressed the same, including the clerk whom Valazko had bribed. Between them sat a rolling laundry cart.

Fiero disassembled the gun and threw the component parts in the cart. Rodriguez and his guys rolled the cart into the room to clean up.

Fiero took the stairs to the third floor, to the other hotel room they'd rented. McTavish greeted her with a rib-bending bear hug. Grenier, the French merc, just nodded.

Finnigan said, "Where you been?"

"Sorry." Fiero closed the door behind her. "Traffic."

C58

"This," said Brodie McTavish, around a mouthful of sandwich, "is beautiful downtown Baharos, Alsharq."

He placed a photocopy of a Google map on the card table that they'd set up in Room 310 of the dowdy hotel outside Barcelona. Finnigan sat opposite the giant Scotsman. Fiero, as was her style, stood well away from the others, her back to the living room wall. But she stood behind Finnigan, which was odd; they usually liked to sit such that they could make eye contact with each other.

To Finnigan's left sat the laconic French mercenary, Christophe Grenier, a raw-boned, leather-skinned soldier with an oblong skull and a road map of visible small fractures under his buzz-cut hair. He drank coffee and ate one of the ham sandwiches that Finnigan had brought. He hadn't spoken since introducing himself.

To Finnigan's right sat a petite woman in her late twenties. Moran Silver, an American-born Israeli, had been the last to arrive. She stood a tad over five feet, seemed quite thin, and wore her brunette hair in a long braid. She also wore large, round, wire-rimmed glasses that made her look like a hipster barista. Finnigan didn't know much about her, other than that Hugo Llorente had recommended her for this job. Finnigan hadn't figured out why yet; she looked as if a mean thought would knock her over.

The map showed a blotch of urban development on the south coast of the Mediterranean, with large and active shipyards and commercial docks. The city itself was bisected by a thin river that ran south-to-north.

Silver leaned forward and pointed to the river with one small finger. "The Wadi Alsharq. It used to be dry three-quarters of the year, but it was dredged out in the 1980s and runs all year long now."

Which explained why she was in the room, Finnigan thought.

She pointed to the western side of Baharos. "This sector is where all the government buildings are. Also the banking district and a modern-looking retail sector. The east side . . ."

She tapped the map with a short fingernail. "That's where the rebellion began."

Grenier grunted. He might have agreed with her or disagreed or choked on the ham.

McTavish said, "Government's pounded the fook out of them eastern neighborhoods. Carpet-bombed them into dust. Entire neighborhoods've been flattened."

Finnigan shook his head. "And now those guys are our allies."

Fiero spoke from behind him. "Only because the opposition includes the Khamsin Sayef and its European bombs. We prove them to be false-flag operation for the Alsharqi government, and that *allies* nonsense ends quickly."

"Here." McTavish leaned forward and drew a rough red circle around a cluster of buildings to the west of the Wadi Alsharq. "This is the Alsharqi Parliament and government buildings. Including the Ministry of Defense. And that's where your Major Saad Barakat's likely holed up."

Finnigan shrugged. "Llorente is trying to locate Barakat for sure. So far: no luck."

The slight Israeli looked around the room and up at Fiero, as if eyeing up the competition at a poker table.

"And you're serious about all this?" She had a sheen of a Midwestern American accent under her Israeli tones. "You mean to invade Alsharq, go to the heart of the military and intelligence operation and kidnap a high-ranking official in their Mukhābarāt."

Finnigan said, "And now we have *four* votes for this plan being crazy-pants."

McTavish guffawed. "It's not half ambitious, that. And the bastards won't see it coming."

Moran Silver smiled up at Fiero, possibly to rob her comment of any vinegar. "It's ambitious if *ambitious* is Latin for *suicide*."

The Spaniard said, "Are you out, Sergeant?"

Silver kept smiling at the taller woman. "I've operated inside Baharos for weeks at a time. I have contacts you'll never match. And I speak Arabic with a Baharos accent."

"That doesn't answer my question."

Silver sized up the three men in the room to see where they were leaning.

Christophe Grenier powered through his sandwich, seemingly ignoring everyone.

Finnigan had caught that word, *Sergeant*. He turned to Silver. "You used to be Israel Defense Forces?"

Without replying, Silver turned to Fiero and raised one eyebrow. Fiero nodded.

Silver turned back to him. "Not *used to be*. I am IDF and I'm Mossad."

"What. Wait. Really?"

She smiled behind the vaguely hippieish eyeglasses. "For the official record, I'm an independent contractor. But my boss owes

Fiero's boss a couple dozen favors. Llorente called in those favors, and here I am."

"You're a soldier," Finnigan said. "What do you weigh, a buck-ten?"

She smiled. "Are you flirting with me, Michael?"

McTavish wiped his lips with the back of his hand. "Did someone say something about whiskey, then?"

Finnigan had brought a bottle and plastic glasses. Fiero used her shoulders to shove away from the wall and retrieved them.

Finnigan turned to the Frenchman. "How about you? You been awful quiet about this plan."

Grenier splashed whiskey in one of the glasses and passed the bottle on. "Doable."

Finnigan blinked. "You're kidding me. You buy this idea?"

Grenier shrugged and bolted down his drink.

"You've been there?"

Grenier nodded.

"And you think this is doable?"

Again he shrugged. "Come in through the east, yeah? Hit the ministry from across the wadi. Get the bastard and take him out the same way we came in. Doable."

McTavish boomed a laugh that shook the windows.

Finnigan shook his head. "Come in from the east. The side with the civil war." He looked around the room. "You know the worst part about crossing the city where the carpet-bombing is? It's the carpet-bombing."

The bottle made its way around to Fiero, who still stood. She poured herself a splash. "I like it. Element of surprise."

Finnigan said, "Yes. We'll be very surprised by the element of the bombs hitting us on the head."

Silver poured for herself and passed the bottle to Finnigan. "Well, to be honest, the bombing is predictable. A lot of the streets are impassable, and the military doesn't even bother patrolling them. If you don't mind climbing over buildings that have pancaked on themselves, you could walk right up to the Bridge of the Martyrs. Here." She pointed to the map. "The Ministry of Defense is directly across the bridge."

McTavish reached for another sandwich. "You'd need a small unit. I could get a dozen good fighters for the money you two are throwing about. But this approach? Skeleton crew."

Finnigan gulped his whiskey. "God, I hope you meant that figuratively."

C59

Hugo Llorente couldn't prove that the Khamsin Sayef was an Alsharqi false-flag operation. But his reputation was such that his opposite number in the Israeli Mossad agreed to provide Moran Silver, along with human and signal intelligence, to assist the raid. If the mission proved to be a fool's errand or became a diplomatic debacle, it was Spain that would take the heat.

In the meantime, Spanish and Israeli sources began trying to pinpoint the exact location of Major Saad Barakat.

BRODIE MCTAVISH, TRUE TO HIS WORD, put together a team of a dozen experienced mercenaries. But not to launch a raid on the Alsharqi Ministry of Defense. He and Fiero had come up with a plan to use most of the men and a bit of brute force to distract the defense forces, while a smaller team made a stealth run on the ministry building.

Christophe Grenier, it turned out, had been in the French

Foreign Legion and knew Baharos well. "I thought there were no Frenchmen in the French Foreign Legion," Finnigan had said. McTavish set him straight: Frenchmen make up a small but consistent percent of the Legion.

Grenier had good contacts all over the Med and suggested the team stage on Cyprus. "Can't," Finnigan told him. "We've got our office there. Sooner, Slye, and Rydell's still looking for us. Last we heard, they had guys on Cyprus."

Israel had already done its part for the mission. So St. Nicholas staged on the Greek island of Crete until all of the hired mercs could come together. That took four days. Once everyone was accounted for, Grenier whistled up the *Northern Promise*, a 120-foot clam vessel built in the 1970s that could make the coast of Egypt in under forty-eight hours. They would head straight to Egypt because Alsharq, a narrow country shaped more or less like a Doric column, had no nonurban coastline.

They used rubber dinghies to get the team of seventeen soldiers ashore an hour before dawn. That part of the Egyptian coast was sandy and lifeless, a vast expanse of weedy grass and sand dunes without any natural potable water within a day's ride.

Using a portion of St. Nicholas' stolen three million dollars, McTavish had two dilapidated farm trucks waiting for them, with stacks of Egyptian pounds and Alsharqi dinars stuffed into envelopes, ready for border bribes.

Moran Silver also packed a small square of aluminum foil containing a hefty serving of black tar heroin. She didn't explain why and the partners didn't ask.

Fiero used a satellite phone to check in with Hugo Llorente. The location of Major Barakat remained a mystery.

Finnigan—fair-skinned and thoroughly Irish—noted that the temperature as they crossed the border hit a hundred and four. They sat in the back of the badly bouncing thirty-year-old Russian

Kamas truck that had given up its shock absorbers a decade ago.

"You could have stayed in Spain," Fiero said sullenly.

"And a bright and sunny fuck you to you too."

The partners had been arguing nonstop. Fiero had been a soldier and a spy, and it was a given that she'd lead the mercenaries into Baharos. Finnigan had been a cop and a deputy US Marshal. He had no experience in war zones.

Fiero told him to stay safe in Spain.

Finnigan had refused.

The argument had been more heated and longer-lasting than most. As they made their preparations for the raid, Fiero had begun to fold in on herself, growing quieter, losing her recently gained sense of humor, welding her poker face in place day and night. In short, she became more like the Katalin Fiero Dahar he'd first met three years earlier.

La Oscura Asesina.

The Dark Assassin.

He'd confronted her on it, standing on the beach on the southern side of Crete, the night before the last of the mercenaries arrived, both standing on a high dune and holding long-neck beers bouncing against their thighs. "What's eating you? Worried that asshole Valazko's still looking for us?"

Fiero had stared out at the Med for close to a minute, before lifting her beer bottle to her lips. "It's nothing, Michael. We should go over the plan again."

C60

They drove the Bondo-splotched Russian trucks through a coastal neighborhood and saw a few damaged walls, a braille of machine-gun bullets on whitewashed cement, a few cratered sidewalks.

In the late afternoon they staged in a rusty Quonset hut near one of the commercial port docks that had been badly damaged the year before. The building had been a marine repair shop, the decaying husks of fishing boats propped up on cinder blocks awaiting repairs that would never come. Finnigan found a sixty-horsepower engine lying on its side, covered in oil that had turned almost solid, the consistency of tree sap in winter. Rats scurried as seventeen humans took over their domain, at least temporarily.

The rats could afford to be patient. Humanity had given up this outlying area of Baharos before and they would again.

Finnigan peered out of a glassless window and saw much greater devastation farther south, a cityscape of buildings with no roofs, no upper floors that looked like the broken-toothed grin of a cadaver's jaw.

He made the sign of the cross.

Moran Silver said, "It gets worse. When we go south, toward the heart of the city. It gets worse."

He hadn't heard her approach.

A blue-gray hijab was wrapped clockwise around her narrow shoulders. She unwound it, revealing her long, nutmeg-brown braid. She wore a simple white shirt, khaki trousers, thick socks, and sturdy hiking boots. She looked like a college student.

"Is the whole city ruined?"

She pulled her round glasses out of a shirt pocket and gingerly slid the curved stems behind her delicate ears. "The city's fine. Only the people have been killed."

"That supposed to be funny?"

She smiled kindly. "This is Baharos, Michael. It was razed by Amenemhat around 1870 BC. It was destroyed by Darius the Second in 410 BC. Someone else destroyed it around 160 BC. I don't remember who. Baharos was razed by Roman rulers a couple of times. By the Ottomans. By the Germans in World War I."

Finnigan studied her then studied the scene outside again. The sun was near setting. "I thought you just *looked* like a college student."

"I'm in an archeology doctoral program. The program's real, but it's also a cover," she said. "A cover identity isn't any good if it's just gloss."

"So that's just it? Baharos exists mainly to get pulverized by the next asshole who comes along? Now and forever, amen?"

Moran Silver studied him for a while before answering. "I'm a soldier, Michael. I *am* the next asshole who comes along."

"You're not bringing war," he said. "We do this right, you're bringing peace. We all are."

Silver reached behind her back, under her untucked shirt, and drew her SIG P-226 with an e2 grip for her small hand. She showed it to him.

"That's what Amenemhat's soldiers said to themselves, too."

THAT NIGHT THEY DINED ON MREs and room-temperature water. The guys talked about girlfriends and wives and cars and guns. A few told war stories. One of the mercenaries, a Canadian, showed off with tales of his wife-to-be. He'd only met her twice, both times in a strip club, but she was the one, for sure. "Flaxen hair. The longest goddamn legs you ever saw. Eyes like cornmeal. She plays the flute—did I mention that? The goddamn flute." He shook his head in wonder.

Fiero said. "She sounds absolutely perfect. Cornflower."

The Canadian lit a cigarette. "What?"

"Cornflower. Your fiancé has eyes like corn*flower*. If she has eyes like cornmeal, you're dating a fucking werewolf."

Finnigan did a spit take across the soldier in front of him.

THE KIT FOR THIS OPERATION WAS STRICTLY CIVILIAN. Jeans or cargo trousers, hiker's boots rather than soldier's boots. Everyone had ballistic vests but lightweight ones they could wear beneath shirts.

The mercenaries carried SIG handguns or MAC *pistolets semi-automatiques*, a favored weapon of the French Foreign Legion. Two thirds of the men carried short, robust FAMAS assault rifles from Saint-Étienne; at only about thirty inches long, they were easy to conceal even without coats.

The men wore kaffiyehs, mostly checkered, mostly in black-and-white or faded red. Silver showed Finnigan how to wear his so he didn't look like a doofus. She and Fiero wore hijabs.

Brodie McTavish brought military-grade maps made of waterproof, waxed paper. They spread one over the keel of an over-turned fishing boat and weighted it down with bolts the size of croquet balls. Silver used her finger to draw an imaginary, upside down T on the map.

"The Mediterranean. The Wadi Alsharq."

She used her other hand to point twice, to the south and to the north of the Quonset hut, fingers straight, palm open and flattened like a spade. "We're a quarter kilometer east of the wadi. The neighborhood here, nearest the wadi, is an old marketplace. A *souk*. It's a maze of tight alleys. Easy to get lost in. It's avoided the worst of the shelling. If you know your way around, you can travel south, paralleling the wadi, and get about halfway to the Grand Mosque."

Christophe Grenier stepped forward and tapped the map with a gnarled finger the color and size of a tycoon's cigar. He pointed to the southern end of the mazelike *souk*. "Gone."

Silver looked surprised. "Not as of two months ago, it wasn't."

He shrugged. "White phosphorus. Dropped by helo. Fucked up the whole block."

Fiero said, "You've been here that recently?"

The bullet-headed Frenchman shrugged, stepped back.

Silver bit her lower lip and studied the map. "Okay. The *souk* is still the best way to move south without drawing too much attention. Too many small tanks in the big boulevards to the east. The government's using surveillance drones too. We'll just have to move out . . . here." She tapped the map.

Grenier shrugged. By now, the others had begun to interpret his vast array of shrugs. This one meant *yes*.

"Then we climb through here, the Al Aziza neighborhood. It's mostly uninhabitable. It should get us right to the Bridge of the Martyrs. We cross the wadi. And we find the ministry buildings."

McTavish scratched his thick red beard. "Sounds like a plan. We bed down for now, wait for the brainy fellas to do their job. Yeah?"

Translation: the mission was on hold until Hugo Llorente located Major Saad Barakat.

THE TWELVE MERCENARIES were from everywhere: Europe, Africa, the Middle East, the Americas. McTavish explained to them— once—that Katalin Fiero Dahar had operational control of the mission. Professionals, none of them had to be warned about sexism. Fiero was the shot-caller, and that was that.

Their stolen money had provided plenty of meals-ready-to-eat and high-quality, US Army surplus sleeping bags. The crew ate surprisingly tasty but room-temperature food and slept through the night in the Quonset hut. Grenier and Silver explained that moving through Baharos at night would be way more conspicuous than trying to blend in during the day.

Everyone slept, taking turns on watch. Everyone but Finnigan. He couldn't get over the smell of the place or the brick dust in his nose and on his tongue. It was hot in the tin building. Fear gnawed at him. He'd been a cop and a marshal. He'd been in fights. He'd been shot at, had been shot, had shot others. But this was his first true war zone.

Around two in the morning, he got up quietly and walked to the north end of the hut, to the former marine garage office they'd turned into a makeshift latrine. He relieved himself and sneaked back to the far side of the building, to the glass windows and the ruined cityscape that now was a black silhouette against a deep gray sky.

Christophe Grenier spoke from the dark. The end of a cigarette glowed red and bathed his stubbly chin. His structure of his jaw looked more like a wrench than bone.

He said, "Scared?"

Finnigan studied his silhouette for a while. "Shit, yes. Scared as hell."

The cigarette glowed a little brighter.

"Good answer," Grenier said. "You okay."

THE SAT PHONE BLINKED TO LIFE AROUND 4 a.m. Fiero had been lying on her back, legs straight, hands clasped over her clavicle, sarcophagus-like. The green light of the phone blinked on, and half a second later the phone vibrated. But Fiero's arm darted out between the light and the vibration and plucked it from its charger before the vibrations began.

Finnigan had been lying on his back, too. He leaned up on one elbow and ran a hand through his unruly hair.

Fiero studied the silent readout on the sat phone screen then looked toward Finnigan.

She whispered. "Hugo. He has it."

"Barakat?"

Fiero allowed herself a brief gallow's smile. She shook her head. "Better."

C61

BAHAROS, THE SOUK AND AL AZIZA NEIGHBORHOODS

At dawn, McTavish took six guys and headed west along the coast. He sent six others east, also along the coast. Both teams carried explosives. They would split up into four teams of three or four guys each. The plan was to blow up a whole bunch of unimportant government assets and draw the military in their direction.

Fiero led Finnigan, Christophe Grenier, and Sergeant Moran Silver south toward the labyrinthine souk. All four carried large backpacks stuffed with supplies.

The alleyways of the old marketplace were narrow and winding, and at dawn, too dark to easily navigate. Silver took point; Grenier rode drag. Metal shutters had been pulled down over shop doors and awnings had been rolled up by hand crank, so Finnigan and Fiero had no idea what each market sold. They also had no idea how the slight Israeli threaded her way so easily through it all. The partners quickly lost any sense of direction: the alleys were narrow, the walls high, and the sun didn't penetrate deep enough to help.

Grenier trudged along quietly, his skull covered by a sun-faded red kaffiyeh, his sunken eyes everywhere.

Finnigan nodded to a long, curved alley of closed shops. "On the way back, we could put a dent in our Christmas shopping."

Silver and Grenier glanced at each other, probably trying to figure out the seemingly frivolous American and his stoic partner. And their relationship to each other. A lot of people spent time doing that.

Twenty minutes in, Grenier said, "White phosphorous."

Silver nodded, and took the next right.

Finnigan glanced at his partner.

"Vicious weapon," she whispered. "Burns to the bone."

"No," Grenier shook his head. "Melts bone."

They emerged from the souk, and Finnigan whispered, "Holy God."

The neighborhood had been a quadrant of apartment buildings with retail on the ground floor, but none of the windows in any direction still held glass. The pavement was covered in a fine white chalk. Each wall had been sandblasted raw, wooden studs exposed.

They saw their first civilians, scurrying along, ignoring them. One family carried what appeared to be all of their belongings in three plastic laundry tubs.

They saw the tread marks of small, urban tanks and knew the Alsharqi troops were nearby.

Silver turned to the dour Frenchman. "I want to cross over-land. This way."

He shrugged in the positive.

She turned to the partners. "We're going to literally climb over destroyed buildings," she said. "We can make good time and we're less likely to run into soldiers. The only problem: my route takes us to—and through—the Grand Mosque. We'd do well to avoid the locals."

Finnigan said, "ISIS?"

"ISIS, al-Qaeda, Muslim Brotherhood. Hardly matters their affiliation, Michael. They don't like foreigners."

As they marched south, the destruction got worse. At first, it was cracked white walls with no glass. Soon it was buildings with no roofs. Then two- and three-story buildings that had clearly been four or more, but the top floors were missing or pancaked into the ones below. The rubble grew larger, making it tougher to move. Soon they were climbing instead of marching from one crumbling bit of concrete to the next. Their boots and trouser cuffs became white, caked in powdered masonry. In the distance, Finnigan saw strange red trees standing crookedly out of the piles of rubble, but as his team approached, he realized they were patches of red brick still mortared together into free-form shapes, like crosses and waving stickmen.

They began to see bodies. Skeletons, mostly.

They saw a few civilians. The younger ones—all male—watched them with blank faces. A few carried knockoff Kalashnikovs, likely cheap South African replicas, which had an equal chance of firing true, jamming, or blowing up.

The team kept hands away from weapons, and the locals just watched them.

They came upon a half-demolished building that might have been a department store; Finnigan saw naked mannequins in one of the open ground-floor windows. The southern half of the building was four stories tall. The northern half had been smashed, its floors mashed together, the second floor flattened into the first; the third floor laying atop the second, and fourth and the roof atop them, like a four-story sandwich of concrete and steel and rebar. A few old satellite dishes lay on the street, aiming nowhere. The skeletal remains of cars and SUVs sat randomly. The building's roof sloped like a ski ramp.

Grenier shrugged off his backpack and produced leather gloves, rope, and pitons. Fiero did the same. Finnigan kept watch, but the teenagers with the cheap machine guns kept their distance.

Silver proved to be a determined and agile climber. Donning leather gloves, she scampered up the side of the department store, using the many handholds created by blast craters and bullet holes. The sandwich of floors proved advantageous to her, and within three minutes, she stood on what remained of the roof—albeit a roof barely thirty feet off the ground, the floors beneath it a squashed pile of destruction.

Grenier spun a rope buckaroo style and let loose. The rope arced through the air and Silver caught it, tying it off to something on the roof. Within two minutes the other three joined her on the roof.

Fiero noted a fine series of footprints in the chalky dust, size fives. "Yours?"

Silver nodded. "I've been doing recon for weeks."

"Not for us."

"No," Silver said, smiling. "Not for you." She offered nothing more.

The going wasn't easy, and every one of them slipped and fell a few times, but the foursome walked up the slope of the ski ramp roof toward the undamaged southern end. Take five steps, land on your ass and slide back three. Their clothes and gloves and faces soon were covered in the fine white masonry dust.

When they made it to the southern end, Finnigan finally spotted the minaret. Or what remained of it. The actual dome had been destroyed, leaving only the circular wall of the tower and a wide, 360-degree debris field.

"The Grand Mosque?"

Grenier shrugged *yes*.

"The government bombed a mosque. That's fucked up."

"Rebels were hiding in it," Silver said, her breathing labored. She took one knee and sipped from a canteen that Fiero handed her. "And by rebels, I mean women and children, grandparents and cripples. Helicopters hovered overhead and soldiers dropped barrel bombs on the place. No one knows what the death toll was. It was one of the first major offenses of the new government, when the rebellion had just gotten started. Come on."

They affixed rope to a thick metal pipes on the roof and tossed the loop off the end. Grenier went first, abseiling down the building, his boots against the bullet-pocket wall, easing himself down in a series of vertical hops.

Finnigan and Fiero followed.

Silver dislodged the rope and freestyled down the side of the building like Spider-Man.

The grounds of the Grand Mosque were a plaza that once had been floored in elaborate tiles of greens and pinks and whites, forming lovely and Byzantine mosaics. Some remained; not many. For no reason he could name, Finnigan pocketed a loose, undamaged pink tile. The plaza had been surrounded by four walls, and each featured recessed, curved arches like the Roman aqueducts Fiero had shown him throughout France and Spain. The remnants of the minaret stood in the middle of the plaza, now only ten to twenty feet tall and sheered off jaggedly by the explosions.

The foursome crossed the plaza at the perpendicular. At the end, a larger building had been constructed atop the aqueduct-like wall, but it, too, had been demolished, and an avalanche of smashed concrete had poured into the plaza like solid lava flow. Finnigan realized the plan was to climb out of the plaza over that slanted pile of destruction.

The sun exposed the western flanks of the plaza and the deep arched entryways.

From the eastern side, the still-shadowed side, fourteen men and boys with machine guns began stepping out into the open. Each wore kaffiyehs. Some wore military trousers and army boots and mismatched ballistic vests. Some wore board shorts and sneakers. Some had straggly new beards and others wore long, full ones. Some men held their rifles with their fingers safely indexed along the side; some were already applying pressure to the triggers.

Silver held up a fist and the other three froze.

A man of maybe fifty stepped forward. A puckered scar ran from his temple to his jawline and continued down his neck and into his khaki shirt. The beard wouldn't regrow on that side, so he'd shaved the other cheek as well.

He barked a question in Arabic.

Grenier answered in the same rapid-fire Arabic. *The most words the dude's said since we met and I don't understand a damn thing*, Finnigan thought.

He squinted at the scar-faced man and an absurd thought hit him. *I know that guy.*

Not *know* know him. They'd never met. But he was familiar.

The staccato question-and-answer volley didn't appear to appease the locals. Men glowered. Boys looked nervous. One stepped forward. The leader—and the scarred man was clearly the leader—shot him a look. The kid took two steps back.

Got him, Finnigan thought.

The leader and Grenier snapped responses to each other. It sounded more like growling dogs than a dialogue.

Silver spoke sotto voce for the other two. "This is his neighborhood. He figures we're government. Or we're looters. Or we're simply intruders."

The leader and Grenier shot unfriendly words back and forth. Their voices rose. The fourteen men and boys had formed a half circle around the team now, out in the open on the smashed face of the once-elegant mosaics.

Finnigan took a step forward, toward the leader. "You a cop?"

The man turned his way. Grenier held up a hand to get Finnigan to shut up. Several of the gunmen turned their weapons toward him.

The leader studied him. Then nodded.

"You've lived in the West. Maybe in America. Am I right?"

After a moment, the man nodded again.

"I'm Michael. This is Katalin. Uh, Sally and Dick." He knew *Moran* was a Hebrew name and didn't bandy it about.

The leader spoke in heavily accented English. "You are the cop as well, maybe, I think."

Silver said, "Michael, step back. Let—"

Fiero touched her arm, and she stopped.

Finnigan said, "Yeah."

He waited. The plaza remained quiet.

"A cop." The leader sneered.

"You bet. We came to get someone. Over there." He pointed toward the pile of rubble that sloped up twenty feet and, beyond that, the Bridge of Martyrs and the undamaged western half of the city.

"Over there?"

"Yeah."

"Who?"

Grenier was watching Finnigan now too.

"A criminal. A guy committed a bunch of crimes, and me and my people are gonna get him and take him back to Europe and put him in a courtroom. He's gonna get his trial and then he's going to prison. That's the plan."

Everyone stood a moment.

The leader spat into a pile of green and pink tiles. He studied the tops of the walls around the plaza, one eye squinted closed. Everyone waited.

"You are the police officer. You are the beat cop. Yes."

"Yeah. The beat cop."

"You have come for a criminal." The man sounded incredulous and almost, just the tiniest bit, amused.

"Yup."

"What did this man do? This criminal."

"He used bombs to kill innocent people. Men and women and kids. Christians and Jews and Muslims. Whoever."

Silence held reign for several long, agonizing seconds.

"You are the beat cop and you have come for a bomb maker."

"Yeah, and I gotta tell you, it's personal."

"What is this, is personal?"

Finnigan pointed backward, toward Fiero. "This is my best friend in all the world. The guy we want, he tried to kill her dad. And I can't have that, man. Can't just let that go."

The leader kept his dark and hooded eyes on Finnigan for the longest time then let them drift toward Fiero, who stood stock-still, no emotion on her face.

"This is true?"

She responded in her Algerian Arabic. "My father and others, yes."

"He is dead, your father?"

"No. Michael figured it out. Michael saved him. This was in Barcelona."

The scarred man nodded, understanding.

"We evacuated the building. The bomb blew up. My father is alive, by the grace of the Prophet. Peace be upon him. And by the grace of Michael."

Michael was the only word Finnigan caught in all that.

The leader watched the four of them for a while. His civilian militia seemed unsure of their footing now.

The leader nodded to the snowdrift of piled rubble at the western corner of the plaza. "That way is the government."

Finnigan said, "It sure is."

"Your criminal is there?"

"He sure is."

"Everyone there is a criminal."

"I'm not after everyone. I only want the guy who tried to kill my best friend's dad."

The leader spoke again, in Arabic. Not to the team, but to his own people.

Slowly, in groups of two or three, his people slung their weapons over their shoulders. A few stepped back away from the newcomers.

The leader turned to Michael and again hocked a gob of phlegm into the tiles. "You are the idiot."

"Probably, yeah."

"I was military police." The leader peered around, squinting at the destruction of the great mosque and its grounds. "A captain. Imagine. In the most corrupt regime on earth, trying to arrest those who stole truck tires, or beat up whores, or abandoned their post. I am the idiot, too."

"It's a fucked-up job." Finnigan wiped sweat off his brow and shrugged. "Somebody's gotta do it."

The leader thrust his chin to the west.

"You come back this way?"

Fiero cut in. "Yes," she lied.

"If you get this far, you have safe passage."

The foursome exchanged glances. Silver, Grenier, and Fiero all said *thank you* in Arabic, more or less together.

But the leader only nodded to Finnigan. "Good arrest now. Keep the chain of evidence. Get your conviction, beat cop."

Finnigan stepped forward to shake the man's hand, only then noticing his two missing fingers.

"Thanks, Captain. Will do."

The foursome turned and marched toward the pile of rock and rebar, steel and masonry. Fiero made eye contact with Finnigan and smiled, just briefly.

For a second there, she looked like her new self. Not the *Oscura Asesina*.

They began the arduous job of climbing up the slipping, crumbling slope of masonry, over the arched walls of the plaza, toward the Wadi Alsharq and the Bridge of the Martyrs and the Ministry of Defense. The sun rose higher and the heat spiked.

Grenier waited until they were three-quarters of the way up the shifting pile of rubble, moving with their gloved hands as much as their feet. "How did you know he was a cop?"

Finnigan gasped. Sweat soaked his shirt. "My dad's a cop. My uncles. My grandpa. I was a cop. Cops move different from other people. You just see it."

Grenier stopped climbing a second to catch his breath. Before pushing on, he slapped Finnigan on the shoulder. "Fucking guy . . ."

C62

The snatch team had to climb over one more destroyed building before the Bridge of the Martyrs came into view. Finnigan felt his gorge rise as he realized the building had been a school. The climb onto the roof revealed a playground beyond: broken teeter-totter with both ends nestled in the dust, a slide on its side, a cracked-in-half merry-go-round. He barely avoided throwing up, wondering if they were standing atop a tomb of children.

The wadi beyond wasn't much to look at. It wasn't a river, in the strictest sense, but a paved canal, not unlike the Los Angeles River. It ran straight as an engineer's ruler, north toward the Mediterranean. It was maybe seventy feet wide and deep enough that they spotted two military boats on parade. They were shallow water interceptors, the kind Finnigan had seen on the Rio Grande during his days with the Marshal Service. Both featured mounted machine guns on pivots.

The bridge itself had been a lovely, humpbacked affair, although now it was in sad shape. It was wide enough for two lanes heading east and two lanes heading west. Today, they saw no traffic whatsoever on the bridge, only an armed checkpoint, well staffed, halfway across.

The foursome knelt behind an HVAC construct on the roof of the school. "You have a way around that?" Fiero asked Silver.

"I do."

Beyond the bridge, West Baharos thrived. No bombings over there. The windows they could see all held glass panes, and beyond the glass the electric grid was up and running.

Silver sat against the HVAC housing and mopped sweat from her clavicle and shoulders. "I can get us to the other side. And I like your plan for getting back to McTavish and the rendezvous point. But this is the final rest stop. We can still back out. You *do* intend to raid the Ministry of Defense building and kidnap a major, right?"

Fiero peered through palm-sized field glasses. "Yes and no."

The Frenchman and the Israeli turned to her as one.

"Hugo Llorente radioed in, this morning. We know where Barakat will be today. In an office building, five blocks west of the ministry."

Silver sighed. "Well, that's something anyway. Should make it easier."

"Maybe," Fiero said. "But it gets a . . . little more complicated too."

Grenier growled. "How much more complicated?"

Fiero made eye contact with Finnigan, who nodded.

"By a factor of two."

THE NEW ALSHARQI GOVERNMENT hadn't bombed the Bridge of the Martyrs. But they had, foolishly, bombed the only street on the east side that led up to the bridge.

The bridge itself stood. It just didn't have any purpose now. It led only to rubble and ruin.

The Hadary family, though, was doing quite well for itself. The three Hadary brothers owned the franchise to operate a pull-rope ferry beneath the bridge. Their wooden rectangle of an affair slogged back and forth, back and forth, beneath the shadow of the ornate but now mostly ornamental Bridge of the Martyrs. They crossed four times per hour, east to west and west to east, carrying businesspeople, freight, sheep, automobile parts, wine, olives, frozen goods, prostitutes, soldiers, and vendors. The brothers charged a decent rate; American dollars, please, or pounds sterling. Euros, maybe. No dinars for them.

If you had the cash, the Hadary brothers would take you aboard the simple raft.

No questions asked.

STILL ON THE EAST SIDE OF THE WATER, the snatch team found an isolated space beneath the bridge with no line of sight for nearby buildings. The men stood guard as Silver stripped and washed her face, chest, back, and arms in river water. She dug a clean T-shirt out of one of the bags. Next came a long, dull brown burka, long enough to hide her dusty boots. It covered all but her eyes and fingers from the second knuckle down.

She and Grenier stood watch as the St. Nicholas partners cleaned up next. They knelt side by side, both naked from the belt up. The water before them turned milky from the chalky dust off their bodies. The French mercenary and the Israeli solder noted the lack of sexual chemistry between the partners. Silver raised her eyebrows, and Grenier shrugged in shared curiosity.

Once Grenier was cleaned up as well, and Fiero was tucked away inside a much-longer burka, they headed for the pull-rope ferry. Finnigan and Grenier carried large but empty crates. Just four people going about their business.

Grenier handed the ferry operator American dollars, and the man welcomed them aboard without making eye contact. If asked by soldiers, he would be unable to say who'd been aboard for which trip.

The quartet sat against crates of live chickens and sipped warm water as the trip across the wadi began. Fiero kept her eye on the closest military gunship, with its machine-gun turret and a second soldier on the prow. It was cooler down on the water and within the shadow of the bridge.

The trip across the Wadi Alsharq took six minutes.

They debarked on the far side and drew no attention. When the government watches everyone, nobody else does.

"There's an old television studio, five blocks up this way." Finnigan spoke quietly, eyes on the passing pedestrians and occasional soldiers, relaying what they'd learned that morning from Hugo Llorente. "It used to be a bureau for Sky News. The old Alsharqi government confiscated it but ignored it. The new Alsharqi government didn't know what the hell to do with it either. They didn't have much need for a free press, so they just mothballed it. Then Major Saad Barakat came long."

Silver glanced around, holding the edges of the burka away from her eyes. "He's using it today?"

Fiero nodded. "If Hugo's intel is good, yes."

"AGAIN, THE EVIL AND THE VIOLENCE of the West have come back to haunt the perpetrators," spoke the cleric. "Those who commit crimes against the Arab, against the Muslim, against the believers of the Prophet—peace be upon his name—have suffered that which they have sown. They use Arabic words for their Arabic buildings, hiding in them after killing the innocent Arab."

As always, the room behind him had been scoured of any clues regarding his location. The man himself remained an enigma: young, maybe in his thirties. His robe was colorless and cheap, his accent academic and urban.

"Once again, the Lions of the true faith have shown the aggressor that they are not safe, not ever, from the righteousness of the people. So long as the criminal government of Alsharq stands, the true followers of the Prophet will bring holy justice upon them and their loved ones. In the name of Allah—"

Finnigan cocked his auto. "Aaaaaand . . . cut!"

Major Saad Barakat reacted at the sound of the cocked weapon, not waiting for the taunting words. He'd been seated just outside the production studio set—cliché though it may be—on a folding chair, between the cameraman and the man holding the filtered microphone by a boom over the head of the actor who played the role of "the cleric."

Barakat rose, hand brushing aside his linen jacket, reaching for the fast-draw holster on his belt.

Fiero clocked him with the butt of her SIG, and he splashed forward into the well-lit cave set, his gun skittering away.

Silver used her P-226 to cover the actor and the audio and video technicians. The actor screeched, "Wait wait wait!" Gone was his slow, low, academic accent.

The team had found seven other people working in the mostly unused Sky News bureau, including two soldiers. Everyone had been gathered, disarmed of guns and phones, and locked in the basement by Grenier.

Fiero spoke in her Algerian-accented Arabic. "Moving results in death. Not moving means you get to live." The actor, cameraman, and audio man glanced at each other, then went to their knees, fingers laced behind their heads.

Finnigan checked the equipment and confirmed that the

scene was being shot to video and wasn't going out live anywhere. Unless there were surveillance cams they'd missed, they had the joint to themselves.

Saad Barakat rose to his feet. When he touched the back of his head, his fingertips came away damp with blood.

He was younger than the partners anticipated. Thirty-five, maybe. His clothes looked like they came from any Zara shop in Europe; cheap but okay, Western in style. He'd trimmed his beard neatly.

He stared at each of the intruders for three seconds, one by one, taking their measure, locking their faces into his memory.

Fiero kicked his gun to the far corner of the TV studio and patted him down. He glared daggers at her.

Across the studio, Finnigan stuffed tapes and scripts into one of the backpacks. "Shouldn't've tried to kill her old man, asshole."

Barakat kept his eyes on Fiero but bobbed his head toward Finnigan. "I don't speak English. What did—"

Finnigan caught the gist of the lie. "Oh, yeah. Dinah Mariner says hi."

Barakat spun on him, clearly shocked.

That was all the distraction Fiero needed to jab an EpiPen-style hypodermic into the man's neck. The narcotic worked quickly. Barakat's knees sagged and his eyes rolled up in his skull. Fiero likely should have caught him. Instead, she stepped back and let the major land, leading with his face.

Silver said, "He's of no use to you with a broken neck."

Finnigan kept stuffing documents into his pack. "Fun fact: most broken necks aren't fatal. We good here?"

Silver used an identical set of hypodermics to inject the actor, who keeled over.

Grenier stooped over a pile of thick, rubberized plastic bags with thick zippers. He undid one and spilled out a pick-up-stick pile of tripods and light hoods and synch cords. Empty, he held the bag up before his own shoulders. It hung to the floor, the size of a body bag.

He shrugged: *Should do.*

THE SNATCH TEAM WALKED back to the river, exactly the way they'd come. Instead of empty crates, this time the men pushed a wide wooden hand cart with wobbly wheels, piled high with video equipment and two thick, zipped, and bulky plastic bags. Whenever they passed near to soldiers, Grenier and Silver would begin to bicker loudly. Soldiers everywhere try to avoid squabbling couples. Who needs the hassle?

They veered away from the Bridge of the Martyrs and paralleled the river for a couple of blocks. They reached a high cyclone fence with a military plaque near the gate and an armed soldier in a tight, sun-faded wooden booth. The others stood back and kept quiet as Silver approached the solder and whispered to him.

Finnigan saw the aluminum foil packet of heroin change hands. She'd bribed this particular guard before, he realized. The soldier took a cigarette break, and Silver waved them forward.

Inside the compound, the foursome pushed their heavy cart into a military warehouse. The place was almost completely empty; McTavish's diversionary explosives, closer to the coast, appeared to be doing their job. They found an office and a locker room—Silver knew exactly where everything was—and Fiero picked locks until they had sufficient olive drab trousers and shirts for three of them to look the part of Alsharqi soldiers. A couple of guards appeared, but Fiero and Grenier quickly dispatched them.

In an office, Fiero found ancient Selectric typewriters, dot matrix printers with boxes of pin-feed paper, and piles of triplicate forms in white, green, and goldenrod, some of which had been pierced by an old-fashioned spindle.

Silver remained in her burka as they rolled the handcart out the far side of the building and found a small dock with one of the army patrol boats tied up. "My source made sure one boat stayed back," Silver whispered.

An armed guard stood near the boat, watching them, looking a little bored. That was, until they turned the corner and rolled the cart down the dock toward the boat.

He stepped forward and barked a question.

Finnigan touched Silver on the arm and gave her a quick shake of the head.

Fiero strode forward, brandishing the triplicate forms, her backpack hanging by one strap over her shoulder.

As the soldier reached for the forms, Fiero grabbed his wrist and dragged him forward, driving her knee into his groin. As he crumbled, she planted an elbow behind his ear and the others could see the consciousness seep out of his body before he hit the warped wood of the dock. Finnigan and Grenier carried the guard into a storage bin. They carried the two thick, makeshift body bags onto the boat. Finnigan unzipped each one and checked the pulse of the person within.

Major Saad Barakat was fine.

So, too, was the artist formerly known as "the cleric." He was still in makeup and costume, although beneath his thin robe he wore a mint-green Ralph Lauren polo shirt and his beard smelled of stage glue.

They carried the drugged men belowdecks. Silver stayed below to keep watch over them. Finnigan, dressed as a soldier, took a seat behind the topside machine-gun turret, his light skin and hair masked by his kaffiyeh and aviator sunglasses. Grenier stood at the bow with his machine gun across his chest. Fiero, who'd crewed racing yachts in college, took the helm. She switched to a soldier's tunic and a man's kaffiyeh and aviators. With her height, and behind the sun glare on the windshield of the pilot's bridge, she looked like one of the boys.

No other military boats were in the wadi. They were all to the north, looking for the culprits who'd blown up a half-dozen useless targets all across the coast.

The snatch team sailed clear of the city.

C63

They sailed back to Crete, where McTavish's twelve mercenaries—all twelve had escaped unscathed—received the second half of their pay, plus extra for operating in a war zone.

Hugo Llorente had whistled up a Hercules C-130 for the trip to Spain.

Christophe Grenier took his leave rather than accept a ride closer to his home in Marseille. He didn't say why but left them both with a handshake and a shrug.

Moran Silver also said her goodbyes. She was still working undercover in Israel and Egypt as an archeology doctoral student. She provided Finnigan with a website address for a fake company that sold vegan food supplies. "Contact me there if you need me."

He took the slip of paper with her spidery handwriting. "We don't wade into war zones all that often, but thanks."

Silver rose up on the toes of her combat boots and kissed him on the cheek. "All the better."

THE HERCULES WAS A STRIPPED-DOWN military warhorse, with no civilian accommodations inside, the floors and walls studded with tie-down rings, both long fuselage walls featuring unforgiving metal benches rather than the usual web-and-plastic belt seats Fiero had seen on troop transports before. Before they climbed aboard, Fiero touched the serial numbers on the flank and her fingertips came away tacky with paint.

Four Spanish agents, including the Stanley Kubrick fan, Rodriguez, flew back with Finnigan, Fiero, Major Saad Barakat, and Lieutenant Ramy Hamed, the Alsharqi Army officer who had worked as a stage actor in Cairo, and who'd so ably brought to life the character of "the Cleric." His captors hadn't given him the opportunity to remove his stage makeup or the fake beard, and his skin was blotchy and chafed from the facial adhesive.

Once airborne, Finnigan planted himself on one of the torturous iron benches next to Fiero. Both wore Mickey Mouse ears with their radios tuned to noise dampeners. Finnigan held up three fingers, and Fiero switched frequencies so they could talk.

"Anything?"

She'd been reading the papers Finnigan had confiscated from the sound stage in Baharos. They knew the videos had to be prerecorded before each bombing in order to get delivered to Al Jazeera television in Qatar in a timely manner. The last recording to air had erroneously celebrated the successful assassination of the Spanish foreign minister because Finnigan and Fiero had evacuated the Galician Trust building at the eleventh hour, too late to stop the tape from being handed off.

"I've read this thing three times." Fiero waved the script in the air. Her voice echoed through the headphones. "The target could be anything. Anyone."

"Read it to me."

She nodded. "*Again, the evil and the violence of the West have* come back to haunt the perpetrators. *Those who commit crimes against the Arab, against the Muslim, against the believers of the Prophet— peace be upon His name—have suffered that which they have sown. They use Arabic words for their Arabic buildings, hiding in them after killing the innocent Arab. Once again, the Lions of the true faith . . .* and I see we're capitalizing Lions now . . . *Lions of the true faith have shown the aggressor that they are not safe, not ever, from the righteousness of the people. So long as the criminal government of Alsharq stands, the true followers of the Prophet will bring holy justice upon them and their loved ones. In the name of Allah and in the name of the true people, the aggressor must learn to quake. And to suffer.*"

"And they all lived happily ever after."

She nodded. "It's nonsense. It's bile and rage but no specifics."

"We could ask our buddy Barakat."

They both looked across the stripped-down freight hauler to the Alsharqi Intelligence officer who sat, hands cuffed in front of him, on an identical metal bench. Barakat had been staring at both of them.

"He's a professional. He won't talk."

They sat and thought. The howl of the four mighty Allison T56 engines felt like a jackhammer in their chests. Finnigan nodded to the other prisoner, who looked frail and pathetic in his stage makeup, bathed in the harsh yellow grip-lights of the Hercules. "That dude is paid to read from a script. He's our evidence of a false-flag operation. He's gotta know more than—"

Fiero said, "No, 'fraid not. There's no reason Barakat would tell him anything about any of the bombings. My guess: he'd just read his lines or face a firing squad."

They rode in the cacophony of their shared frequency and the foam headphones. Turbulence jostled them, their shoulders bouncing off each other.

"You afraid of what I'm afraid of?"

Fiero nodded, dark eyes locked on Barakat. "Correct for a past mistake. Save face. Go after the one target who got away."

"Bingo."

"I warned Hugo," she said. "He's put Foreign Minister de Cordoba in protective custody."

More turbulence rumbled the plane. Lieutenant Ramy Hamed looked like he was about to pee his cheap robe. Barakat stared at the partners across the vast empty expanse of the fuselage.

Finnigan adjusted his voice wand closer to his lips. "The minister's safe?"

Fiero nodded.

"If Barakat wanted to save face by killing de Cordoba . . . and if he couldn't get to de Cordoba because he's in hiding . . ."

They rode for another ten seconds before Fiero's eyes shot wide and she turned to him. "My father!"

"Maybe. Alexandro had nothing to do with the original cover-up, but then again, neither did de Cordoba. Dinah Mariner is done killing her coconspirators. From here on out, it's just about sowing the seeds of terror. Your dad's a high-profile target. He's a friend of the minister. He's a friend of the *prime minister.* He's, like, a distant cousin of the king, for crissake. He's part of the Galician Trust, which initially backed Alsharqi independence. So . . . yeah. Maybe."

Fiero unbuckled her web belt and let the buckles clang against the steel bench as she rose. "I have to alert Hugo."

She fought turbulence, hands against the fuselage wall, and made her way to the flight deck.

As FIERO MOVED FORWARD, Finnigan undid his safety harness and knelt, removing his belt holster and Glock and stuffing them into in his duffel, piled with the others in the middle of the cargo.

Unarmed, he rose unsteadily—nothing to hold onto—and crossed the deck toward Barakat.

Rodriguez gave a little shake of his head that Finnigan ignored. He made a *gimme* gesture to one of the Spanish soldiers who—after glancing at Rodriquez for permission—passed Finnigan an extra headset.

Barakat sat with his wrists cuffed, the cuffs attached to a locked prisoner belt. He wore leg irons with a ten-inch hobble.

Finnigan adjusted the headset to *three* and, behind his back, held up three fingers. Rodriguez subtly adjusted his own frequency.

Finnigan fit the headset on the prisoner, adjusted the voice wand over the man's lips. "Can you hear me?"

"Yes. Thank you. It's awfully noisy in these things." Barakat's voice was warm and carefully enunciated. It carried a bit of a London accent. "I've figured out most of the players. These fellows are Spanish soldiers. They could play chauffeur once you got me to . . . where were we? Cyprus, I suspect."

It had been Crete. Finnigan didn't confirm or deny.

"As I say, they could play chauffeur, but they couldn't invade a sovereign country such as Alsharq."

"Ain't diplomacy a bitch?"

"The troops you had on the ground were mercenaries, I suppose. I believe I recognize the red-haired giant. Scotsman? Can't think of his name. He's done mercenary work in the Middle East and Africa for ages."

"If you say so. Me, I wanna know if there's another bomb in the works."

Barakat's smile could almost be described as sheepish. "Oh, sir. There is always another bomb in the works."

"But you got no stake in it anymore. You help us stop it, that plays in your favor. If you don't . . ."

"The tall woman." Barakat ignored the thread of the

conversation. And the threat. "I think I've finally figured out who she is. In my studio, you said I shouldn't have tried to kill her father. *Tried* being the operative word there. Suggesting the failed bombing of the offices of the Galician Trust."

"Speaking of which, Annie Pryor is still alive. And talking like an auctioneer."

"Pity. But back to the tall woman. At the studio, she spoke Arabic with an Algerian accent. She's stunning, by the way. Although the two of you don't move like lovers. Almost . . . almost like siblings? But no, not that, either. Partners?"

"If another bomb goes off—"

"I think her father must be Alexandro Fiero. He survived that last bomb. He's tall, quite handsome. My research says he married an Algerian woman. Who also is quite tall and quite lovely. Yes. Your friend there is Fiero's daughter, I think."

Finnigan had spent many an hour playing poker, and he'd sat on the right side of the table in too many interrogation rooms to count. He knew how to keep the quick spike of fear out of his face. In his peripheral vision, past Barakat, he could see Rodriguez shift uncomfortably on the metal pew.

"Next bomb, buddy. It's not gonna help you now."

"Which leaves you," Barakat said, smiling. "American, obviously. The least comfortable man in your raiding party, so not a mercenary, not a soldier, per se."

"If another bomb goes off, and you coulda stopped it . . . oh, brother! That is not gonna sit well with any judges in Spain."

Barakat looked up and to the left. "A detective, I think. An investigator of sorts. Yes, I think that's it. I think you're the one who peeked behind the curtain of the Khamsin Sayef and saw it for a fraud."

"I am a cop. That's good. Impressive. As a cop, I can tell you there are cops in Switzerland and France and Spain who can't wait to put together a case against you. They're drooling for it, man. I've never seen any guy piss off so many cops as you."

Barakat looked up and to the left. "You and the young Miss Fiero. I suspect you're the motor that drove this whole exercise. Independent contractors. Private military contractors, p'raps. Or private intelligence contractors. Either way, it explains how I didn't see you coming. Remarkable. Well played, Mister . . . ?"

Finnigan reached up abruptly and removed the man's Mickey Mouse ears. For Barakat, the roar of the engines grew to uncomfortable levels again, and he winced.

Finnigan tossed the headset back to the soldier who'd had it. He stood, holding a cargo net adhered to one fuselage wall, and began moving forward.

From his own headset, he heard Rodriguez. "He didn't tell you shit."

"The fuck he didn't."

FINNIGAN REACHED THE DOOR to the flight deck just as Fiero emerged.

He whisked off his headset. After a beat, she did the same. Nobody could overhear them on any frequency now. He grabbed her, held her tight, and spoke into her ear in a loud whisper.

"Barakat has a tell. When he bluffs, he looks up and to the left. I mentioned judges and cops in Spain, and he did it both times."

"He owns police and judges," she spoke a bit above her normal voice too. "We should have expected that."

"There's more. I been thinking: Barakat is a master spook. Barakat runs Dinah Mariner. Dinah Mariner was a CIA station chief, a spy's spy."

He waited, still holding her, both of them holding the hatchway to the flight deck as the turbulence washed over the Hercules.

Fiero spoke into his ear. "We cannot hand him over to police. We cannot trust the Spanish judiciary. And you assume we can't win playing the spooks' own game."

"I figure, yeah."

"Have a better idea?"

He pulled back from her and looked amidships.

Saad Barakat sat watching them, no emotion on his drawn face.

Finnigan put his lips near her ear. "If we can't win at their game, let's play ours."

C64

The Hercules C-130 was scheduled to land in less than thirty minutes.

Colonel Cole Sanger had not heard from his assassin, Syarhey Valazko, since he'd been sent to rendezvous with those bastards from St. Nicholas Salvage & Wrecking. Either Valazko had been bought, which seemed unlikely, or he'd been bested, which seemed unthinkable.

Either way, Sanger had come to realize he needed a new plan.

Sooner, Slye, and Rydell had been slow to tell the world that Sanger had failed to apprehend the mastermind behind the Khamsin Sayef; or indeed, that Sanger had been "caught" stealing from the firm. Admitting such a failure would reflect badly on the company. So before word could spread thoroughly, Sanger had bribed everyone he could still bribe, everyone who'd still take his phone call and his rapidly diminishing supply of his own money. He had previously spent weeks burrowing deeply into Spanish Intelligence circles and now he plundered those contacts one last time.

He found out that Hugo Llorente had arranged for a C-130 to pick up a prisoner or prisoners on the island of Crete. Sanger knew where Crete was, relative to Alsharq. It would be the ideal base camp for a raid on that country.

The prisoner or prisoners meant St. Nicholas Salvage & Wrecking had succeeded. They had captured the monster behind the bombings.

That man, or men, had to arrive in the European court-rooms at the hands of Colonel Cole Sanger. It was his last possible power play. It was that or return to the States. Maybe take up the auto insurance business, like his brothers. Maybe join a Rotary Club. Maybe eat his own gun.

Sanger still had connections to mercenaries. And now he had the inside information on the return flight of the Alsharq raiding party. They were scheduled to land in—Sanger shoved back his sleeve and checked his watch—twenty-three minutes. Here, at this isolated military airfield outside the hill village of Toledo.

Sanger lifted his walkie-talkie. "Count off."

One by one, the five freelance snipers he'd hired with his last cache of money called out. They waited in a semicircle around the airbase.

HUGO LLORENTE HIMSELF ARRIVED for the prisoner handoff, complete with several good agents, an armored prison transport truck and an assortment of Jeeps and motorcycles for the motorcade to Madrid.

It had been clear for the last ninety minutes that something had gone horribly awry. The Hercules was in the air, according to air traffic control for Torrejón Air Base, north of this isolated field. But since reaching European airspace, the aircraft had erected a wall of radio silence.

No messages in. No messages out.

Sitting in the back of his armored Escalade, Llorente fumed and chain-smoked. When the Hercules became a visible dot in the eastern sky, he tapped the shoulder of his driver.

"Get a helicopter in the air. Here. This whole field is starting to feel like a trap."

THE C-130 LANDED GRACEFULLY for so ungainly a beast and took the totality of the runway to bleed off momentum. The pilot finally turned and the massive plane began rolling back toward the hangar and Llorente's motorcade.

As all four Allison engines sputtered and died, the port-side aircraft door cracked open, even before the motorized stairs could be aligned.

Llorente's Escalade roared out of the shade of the hangar and screeched to a halt as the stairs slid into place beneath the fuselage door. Llorente's man, Rodriguez, stepped out of the airplane, his eyes blazing with anger.

Llorente was halfway up the stairs as his walkie-talkie chirped. He recognized the synchronized whooshing sound as the blades of a helicopter. He toggled the switch and shouted, "Go!"

"*Snipers!*" came the voice from the helo. "*Several of them!*"

Rodriguez grabbed his boss by the shoulders of his suit coat and hauled him into the Hercules.

"Where are the prisoners?"

Rodriguez handed his mentor the torn-out and useless radio from the cockpit. He drew a weapon and turned to his men. "We've got snipers out there!"

Llorente dropped the radio at his feet. He glanced around the empty cargo hold, spotting only Rodriguez's men.

"How? Where?"

"Finnigan and Fiero," his agent spat. "We landed outside Rome to refuel. I spotted that De Havilland Otter of theirs. Before I could react, they took over the cockpit, held us at gunpoint, and walked out with our prisoners!"

Llorente felt the blood rush from his face. He flinched as a bullet panged off the aluminum hull of the Hercules. The next thing they heard was an exchange of gunfire to and from the now-arriving helicopter.

Llorente ground his teeth. "Why in God's grace would they do this?"

Rodriguez grabbed the smaller man and roughly maneuvered him into the hatchway between the flight deck and the cargo hold—the most secure spot to avoid the incoming, heavy-caliber gunfire that could penetrate the skin of the aircraft as easily as the skin of the men.

"This is why!" Rodriguez shouted. "They took Barakat and the actor because they saw this trap coming!"

"Leaving you and your men in the crosshairs?"

Rodriguez shrugged. "It's what I would have done."

FIRST ONE EJÉRCITO DEL AIRE GUNSHIP, then three, arrived at the rural airbase, and whatever advantage Cole Sanger assumed his snipers gave him, it evaporated like tissue in the rain.

He'd parked a stolen car—courtesy of the still-missing Syarhey Valazko—outside the security fence and behind the hangar. As Spanish soldiers from within the Hercules joined their airborne counterparts in pushing back against the snipers, Sanger made a dash for his car.

He'd just gotten through the slit in the security fence when a van screeched to a halt, dust flying. The driver wore a droopy, 1970s mustache and a dirty blond mullet. A big black man slammed open the side door and a woman emerged. She had burn marks over half her face, and her nose had been badly broken in her youth.

The woman and the men all pointed weapons at Sanger.

"Get in!" the woman spat.

C65

"*Good evening from The Hague. Europe was rocked today by the arrest of two high-ranking officials in the Alsharqi intelligence community. Major Saad Barakat and Lieutenant Ramy Hamed appeared today in the courtroom of senior judge Heléne Betancourt, charged with being the masterminds behind a series of bombings throughout Europe that had been blamed on terrorists opposed to the Alsharqi government.*

Judge Betancourt, through a spokesman, said Lieutenant Hamed is an actor who portrayed the unnamed cleric who appeared in a series of videos, taking blame for the bombings on what is now believed to be a fictional terrorist cell, the Khamsin Sayef. The cell, we are told, is actually the creation of Major Barakat, a top intelligence operative of the Alsharqi government.

Both men have been handed over to the International Criminal Court . . ."

Finnigan and Fiero stood outside the criminal court in The Hague, bracketing their friend Thomas Shannon Greyson. He sat in a wheelchair, a thick blanket over his lap, his ruined hands in tight latex gloves that helped hold the bones together as they knit.

Greyson, the éminence grise and aide-de-camp of Judge Betancourt, smiled for the first time in many months.

"The Khamsin Sayef. Boogeyman of Europe. A false-flag operation by Alsharq to keep a quivering Europe from abandoning the failed state." He coughed, his frail body shuddering. "Michael? Katalin? Even by your standards, this one was spectacular."

"Thanks to you," Finnigan said. "We couldn't take these shitheads directly to Spanish Intelligence. Sooner, Slye, and Rydell would have been on them in seconds."

"You're right, you know. I checked. Hugo Llorente's aircraft was hit by snipers as soon as they landed on Spanish soil. The gunmen were all killed in the exchange. Two of Llorente's people were wounded, one killed."

Fiero looked down at him, surprised. "Not that many people know Hugo's name."

"I was the judge's fixer long before the advent of St. Nicholas Salvage & Wrecking." He spoke softly; his jaw was still recovering from surgery. "Hugo is a . . . complicated fellow but a good man."

They watched as the court's spokesman took question after question from the media, all standing on the steps of the International Criminal Court headquarters. The trio couldn't hear the questions. They had stayed well back to avoid the media.

"What now?"

Fiero touched Shan's shoulder. "Now we get you back to the rehab center in Grenoble. You've done more than enough."

"And as for the rest?"

Finnigan and Fiero exchanged glances over Shan's head.

Finnigan said, "We need to stop Dinah Mariner."

Shan frowned. "Dinah Mariner? I knew her, or *of* her. She died in . . ." He paused, shook his head, and another cough rattled his ribs like a xylophone. "Oh god. This just gets better and better."

C66

Ron Perry, wearing a Sweet Home Alabama T-shirt and smoothing down his 1970s mustache, hocked a gob of chewing tobacco into the workroom sink. He'd found a good-enough safe house outside the historic town of Toledo, where he and Dinah Mariner could work Cole Sanger over at their leisure. They'd figured out that the former marine had inside information into the hunt for the Khamsin Sayef. And they were, after all, the Khamsin Sayef.

Sanger had hired mercs to attack a military airfield, but both Perry and DeMarcus Washington had excellent connections in the merc community. It hadn't taken much sleuthing to figure out where they could pick up Sanger.

It was time to know what he knew.

That turned out to be quite a bit.

Sanger knew, for instance, that the quiet and rarely exposed Spanish kill shop run by Hugo Llorente had gone outside government circles and had hired a team of bounty hunters from Cyprus to hunt down Mariner and her team. At first Mariner misunderstood, thinking they were Cypriots, but Sanger—breathing poorly through a broken nose and split lip while tied to a chair in a bankrupt metal fabrication shack outside the town—had explained that St. Nicholas Salvage & Wrecking used Cyprus merely as a storefront. The actual bounty hunters consisted of only an American ex-cop and a Spanish ex-soldier/ex-spy/ex-assassin.

Michael Patrick Finnigan and Katalin Fiero Dahar.

Something about the latter party, this Dahar woman, made bells clang in Mariner's head.

Sanger also let them know that Annie Pryor had last been seen in the custody of St. Nicholas Salvage & Wrecking. It was believed the bounty hunters, or perhaps Hugo Llorente, had rescued Pryor after she'd been gutshot on Las Ramblas.

While Perry worked over the former marine colonel tied to a chair, Washington had headed out to connect to his sources, to see what they could find out about the situation on the ground.

With Cole Sanger unconscious from the beating, the three of them gathered in a kitchen attached to the old building. Washington's eyes were wide as he held out his phone for the others to see. "You are not going to believe this shit."

The first thing they saw was a photo of Saad Barakat and a fuzzy, pixelated image of the so-called cleric.

"Jesus," Mariner breathed, and kept reading. "They . . . they're under arrest. They got 'em."

"Just happened," Washington said, his voice thick with emotion. This, from a man who almost never showed emotion. "They're at The Hague. From what I'm hearing, some bounty hunters were hired by Spanish Intel to—"

Perry said, "Bounty hunters? Man and woman, American and Spanish?" He showed Washington the notes he'd been taking while Sanger bled on the poured cement floor of the shop.

Washington nodded. "So I heard. Explains how it happened.

Dinah, you got your claws deep in Spanish Intel. No fucking way they could pull this off, and we don't know about it. Had to be freelancers."

Perry filled in the bigger man on what they'd learned about St. Nicholas Salvage & Wrecking.

Mariner retrieved a room-temperature bottle of water from a plastic *supermercado* bag. She cracked it and drank about a third, thinking.

"These bounty hunters are all over this thing. I never even heard of them before this. Finnigan and Dahar? They're ghosts."

Washington glanced through Perry's notes. "Name's not Dahar."

Perry said, "You know her?"

"Nah, I'm saying, she Spanish. Patronym first, then matronym. Opposite of what we do. Katalin Fiero Dahar, she goes by Fiero."

Mariner damn near spat water across the kitchen. She couldn't believe she'd missed it!

"Fiero!"

Washington shrugged.

"Same as the man whose office we blew up. Alexandro Fiero."

Perry wedged a wad of chew into his cheek. He nodded toward the machine shop and their prisoner. "Jarhead said the woman was tall and skinny. Thirty, maybe, give or take. Could be the old man's daughter."

Mariner worked the angles, mindlessly tapping the spout of her water bottle against her lower lip.

Washington waggled his smartphone in midair. "So we done? Barakat's gone. No reason we can't be gone too."

Mariner turned to him. Then she turned to Perry, held his vision, and turned back to Washington.

"Annie. Annie's the reason we're not gone. Annie's still out there."

Washington said, "Maybe. Got herself shot."

"She's out there," Mariner said. "These two? Fiero and her partner? We go after a target close to them, we get them. We get them, we get Annie."

The two men kept quiet.

Mariner repeated softly, "We get Annie."

C67

To see Alexandro Fiero and Khadija Dahar safely on their way, the Centro Nacional de Inteligencia sent Hugo Llorente and a politically connected deputy assistant director, Guilherme Armentano. Armentano wore suits as fine as Alexandro and had married a woman as politically and culturally connected as Khadija. Armentano also was another distant cousin of the royal family. He was the one CNI often sent to interact with Spain's rich and famous.

Armentano was accompanied by a smallish, sour man with nicotine-stained fingers, Hugo Llorente, who stood well behind the deputy assistant director, left-flank rear, and peered into the nether distance.

The CNI officials met the well-heeled *madrileños* in the parking lot of a nondescript building owned by the Spanish Defense Department. The couple had agreed to travel by caravan in one of three heavily armored Cadillacs to the airport and from there to be ferried by helicopter to the Alcázar Real d'Aragon. The intelligence agency was rounding up everyone who might be a target of Dinah Mariner's fake terrorist cell and moving them to the so-called Fontainebleau of Spain until the threat had passed.

"This woman," Khadija Dahar said. "This CIA operative. She managed to get inside my husband's Barcelona office and plant a bomb. You're positive she hasn't done the same thing at the Alcázar?"

Guilherme Armentano nodded his appreciation of the question. "Using the cover of this *Frau Gunsen*, she and her coconspirators were able to slip into almost any important building in Europe, under the cover of hunting for bombs. But I misspeak: They didn't *slip in*. They were invited in! It was genius. As for the Alcázar, they did plant explosives there. And our agents have found them. We have arranged for four teams with bomb-sniffing dogs to inspect the castle. That includes agencies with which Dinah Mariner never worked, including a Chinese intelligence unit that I, myself, had brought in as a personal favor. As of right now, the Alcázar Real d'Aragon is the safest building in all of Europe."

He clicked his heels with a slight bow.

Alexandro checked the contents of his Louis Vuitton carry-on for the umpteenth time. He said, "And what of Ms. Mariner?"

"Every agency on earth is looking for her, and her two American compatriots. We'll find them."

Khadija laid a long-fingered hand on Armentano's forearm. "Thank you."

"Of course, madam."

She smiled, and it was the smile that preceded the Barcelona riot and the concussion. A smile, the young deputy assistant director thought, that could illuminate a coalmine.

Two of his aides helped carry her bags to one of the waiting cars. Alexandro said, "Guilherme? A moment?"

"Of course, sir." He stepped back. The silent Llorente with him did the same.

When they were alone, Alexandro pitched his voice low.

"My daughter joined the army when she turned seventeen."

Armentano said, "Spain is blessed to have such young people."

"She is the most competitive person I have ever met, second only to myself. She competed in the Olympic biathlon for Spain. She crewed racing yachts."

"You must be proud."

Alexandro stepped closer to him, his voice taking on a razor's edge. "That is, until she left the military to become a *clerk* for the European Union. She files *paperwork*. She collects *data*."

Armentano stopped interrupting. Something had changed in the conversation, but he couldn't decide what it was.

"The day that Dinah Mariner attempted to kill de Cordoba—attempted to kill me and the staff of our Barcelona branch—someone broke into the building, warned the guards, shattered all the windows to create an egress. Someone used the lobby guard's walkie-talkie to warn us. To get the evacuation going."

Llorente fiddled with a crumbled cigarette pack and a cheap lighter, staring into the middle distance.

"I spoke to this person over the walkie-talkie."

"Praise be to God that—"

"Do you know anything about who that might have been, Guilherme?"

"Been, sir?"

"Our rescuers."

The deputy assistant director frowned. "Virtually every agent within the CNI has been doggedly chasing this so-called Khamsin Sayef for weeks, sir. I do not know which agents got there first, but if you wish, I shall be glad to seek them out."

Alexandro stared into the young man's eyes.

Armentano said, "Ah . . . was there . . ."

"No, that will do, Guillermo, my friend." Alexandro Fiero offered his hand. The men shook. "Thank you."

From the back seat of the middle Cadillac, Khadija Dahar watched the interplay with growing unease. Her husband picked up his overnight bag and headed toward the vehicle.

Guilherme Armentano removed an embroidered hand-kerchief and blotted his brow. Llorente lit a cigarette, left hand cupping the flame.

"What the hell do you suppose that was all about?"

Llorente shrugged. "You know the rich. Unfathomable types."

"My dear Hugo. I *am* rich."

Llorente blew smoke into the air.

C68

Ron Perry and DeMarcus Washington spent a day asking around about Khadija Dahar. They did so at the university where she was a guest lecturer and at the TV station where she often appeared as a guest commentator. They did so at the various civic organizations to which she belonged.

They asked around using English and the accents they were born with.

They had a five-dollar bet on how quickly the word would get back to Katalin Fiero Dahar.

It got back to her pretty damn quickly.

C69

Stanley Berger had retired a couple of years back as an assistant director for the Central Intelligence Agency. But rather than raise a couple of sheepdogs and a couple of grandchildren in Connecticut, Berger had become something of a minister without portfolio for the CIA. Whenever a situation arose in which the agency needed plausible deniability, Stanley Berger would pack an overnight bag and a John Grisham novel and head to the airport.

In all his sojourns, Berger mused, he'd never been called to a place quite like the Alcázar Real d'Aragon.

The great castle hunched over a river, with clusters of bulbous trees along both banks. The central hulk of the castle, all one hundred and forty rooms of it, stood six stories tall, all honey-colored stone with tile roofs and rows upon rows of mismatched chimneys. The facade had a definite Moorish quality to it, but Berger didn't know enough about architecture to say how. Two long arms, both two stories tall, stretched out from the northeast and northwest corners of the building. The arms had contained dozens of government offices once upon a time, back when it had been the bureaucratic hub of the entire region. Today, the long, concourse-like structures were almost completely empty, the floors unsafe for human passage.

A checkerboard parade ground was tucked in between the empty wings; the grounds were about twice the length of an American football field, with alternating green squares of grass and white squares of crushed oyster shells. The far northern end of the parade grounds had been transformed into a helipad for incoming flights and armored vehicles for the security detail.

When his helicopter touched down, Berger was met by a Spanish intelligence agent who took his bag and escorted him up the long walk to the Omega-shaped stairs leading to the second floor and to the Great Hall. Berger was winded by the time they arrived. The hall was decidedly cooler than the outdoors.

He was greeted by Hugo Llorente. The two men nodded to each other.

"How is retirement?"

Berger said, "Ulcer's better. Blood pressure's better. No nightmares." He spoke without an ounce of irony.

Llorente took his elbow, the way no American man would ever do. "Come, please. I need to read you in on this situation with Saad Barakat and Alsharq."

He led the American through the vast maze of lesser halls and mind-boggling rooms with frescoed, thirty-foot-tall ceilings and peeling paint on the door and window frames. Berger spotted a couple dozen domestic staff and Spanish soldiers in fatigues and Kevlar, packing Rheinmetall MG3 machine guns with standard 7.62 mm NATO rounds.

Berger said, "I have to tell you, I checked with my old teammates at Langley. This Barakat was on nobody's radar. I mean, we'd heard of him. We knew his job description in Baharos. But this meshugas? This whole Khamsin Sayef thing?" Berger shook his balding head. "This guy is punching way above his weight."

"It was genius," Llorente conceded. "He fooled us completely. Fooled everyone."

He led Berger down an ill-lit staircase, the treads so narrow that Berger had to walk slightly sideways to get his whole shoe on each step.

"This guy ran a billion-dollar op on a buck-fifty budget. Langley would love to know how he did it."

Hugo Llorente looked back over his shoulder. "Yes . . ."

He opened a final door. Stanley Berger stepped forward to find two people in hospital scrubs and sneakers, a fairly well-supplied ER, and Annie Pryor, CIA Madrid station chief, presumed dead, sitting up in a hospital bed, eyes glittering with tears.

Llorente said, "I'm sure you would."

FORTY-FIVE MINUTES LATER, Rodriguez wandered through roughly fifteen rooms of the old castle until he finally found his boss. He considered leaving breadcrumbs behind to find his way back out again. He handed Llorente a sat phone.

"Fiero."

Llorente nodded and returned the call. He motioned for Rodriguez to stay.

"Hallo."

The other end of the call was on speaker mode. He heard Fiero first. "People matching the description of DeMarcus Washington and Ron Perry have been all over Madrid, asking about my mother."

Llorente pinched the bridge of his nose. "I had hoped this was all over now. I'd hoped Dinah Mariner and her cell would go to ground."

Finnigan spoke next. "Have you told the CIA the truth?"

"Yes, Mr. Finnigan. Within the past hour. An emissary from Langley just met Annie Pryor. She still faces more surgery, but I'm told she may be out of the woods. Langley knows about Mariner and the Khamsin Sayef. They, of course, want this whole thing to go away quietly. They will dig holes throughout the earth to find her."

"They don't gotta. She's heading your way, and you know it."

Llorente and Rodriguez nodded to each other. "The Alcázar is a fortress, Mr. Finnigan. I've an army here protecting Katalin's parents and the defense minister and Annie Pryor and a dozen other high-profile targets. They are safe."

Finnigan said, "Why there?"

"A worst-case scenario study conducted years ago said that this is the one building in all of Spain that would make the best fortress, in the event that we needed to protect specific targets from terrorists. Trust me, Mr. Finnigan. We're quite good."

Fiero said, "Hugo? Mariner is better than you."

Llorente bristled but . . . God's honest truth? That had certainly proven true.

Fiero said, "We're on our way."

"No. This is a military matter now. And besides, you stole our prisoners. We haven't forgotten that, you know.

"We got your prisoners to the International Criminal Court."

That also was true. "I appreciate your helping my agency. But this is a different matter. Stay away."

Neither of the partners responded.

Llorente said, "There's something else. Katalin, when you and Mr. Finnigan saved the day at the Galician Trust building, did you speak on a walkie-talkie?"

He listened to the silence on the other end of the line. Finnigan and Fiero, always quick on the uptake, likely knew where this was heading. He confirmed it anyway.

"Your father heard your voice, Katalin. I'm sorry. He knows."

IN THE PRIVACY OF HIS HELICOPTER, with the pilot smoking a cigarette forty feet away, Stanley Berger ignored the hundred-thousand-dollar, triple-password-protected CIA communications array, and instead drew a cell phone he'd picked up at a mall in Danbury, Connecticut. He scribbled in the margins of the paperback novel he'd brought, unpacking a mnemonic locked away in his brain, until he'd recalled a telephone number. He dialed it and waited.

It rang seventeen times. It was picked up without any words of greeting.

Berger said, "Annie Pryor is alive. The Spanish have her. She's being held at the Alcázar Real d'Aragon."

He listened to the long hissing emptiness over the line. It went on for almost a minute.

Finally, Dinah Mariner said, "When we met in Evian, when you brought Barakat into all this, did you ever imagine it would go so badly?"

Berger said, "Clean up your shit."

He hung up and disassembled the phone.

C70

Simultaneously, another call began in Houston, Texas, skittered off a satellite and reached a sat phone perched on a speaker/charger in the center of a bolted-down table, amidship in the de Havilland Otter of St. Nicholas Salvage & Wrecking. The call originated in the C-Suite of Sooner, Slye, and Rydell.

A voice dusty with the grit of Oklahoma oil fields boomed across the line. "I want to talk to the motherfucking shitbird who implicated my company in this fucking crap-storm at The Hague! I want to talk to the dickless, cow-fucking sumbitch right now!"

Finnigan said, "May I ask who's calling?"

"This Finnigan? Son, you are fucked up beyond all recognition!" The man on the other end, the CEO of the private military contractor, pronounced it as three separate words: Ree. Cog. Nition.

Finnigan sat in one of the four chairs around the table and leaned forward. "You think?"

"You told the International Criminal Court that my

company—my *company*, you East Coast elitist prick!—was running interference for these Khamsin Sayef fuckers!"

Fiero poured a Chianti from her father's winery into a glass and passed it across the table to Finnigan.

"Well, gosh. Okay, first, we're nowhere near that thing in The Hague," Finnigan said, as their pontoon plane bobbed on the coast just outside of The Hague. "Second, as I understand it, there are cops in Geneva and Annecy and Barcelona who've lodged complaints against Suicide Ride."

"Don't you use that goddamn tone with me, you piece of—"

"Mister—I'm sorry, can I call you Bob?"

They knew they were talking to Robert Slye, chairman of the military contractor. Fiero, meanwhile, poured two more glasses of red wine.

"Bob, the sitch is a bit less complicated than you maybe realize. We're not the enemy here. We respect you guys."

"Respect?" Slye's voice shot up an octave.

"Hell yeah. See, thing is, Bob, your people on the ground got in the way of local law enforcement and the CIA and the CNI and just about everyone else. And in doing so, you aided and abetted a terrorist organization."

"How dare—"

"Look, Bob. It's not your fault that you didn't see this coming. You run this shit-hot paramilitary organization, but you never served in the military yourself. You dodged the draft during the Vietnam war with . . . what was it? Flat feet? You've got three sons, all of whom went to Yale, and they never served. You stand for Truth, Justice, and the American Shock and Awe, and I get that. I do. But, hand to God, Bob? You're the fucking amateur hour."

Fiero handed one of the glasses across the table to Sally Blue, leader of the Black Harts, who had joined them at The Hague only hours earlier. She'd brought along her pet hacker, a man named Dave, who took the fourth chair, clacking away madly at his keyboard and ignoring his glass. He'd hooked his computer up to the partners' sat phone and was using the direct line into the office of the Sooner, Slye, and Rydell chief executive officer to burrow into the company's computers. From time to time, he made a spinning motion with his fingers, telling Finnigan to keep it going.

Dave turned his computer clockwise on his knee so Finnigan could see the screen.

"You smug sumbitch! I'm gonna—"

"Bob? I see here that you've recently squirreled away seven-point-nine million dollars from the elite Iranian Republican Guard. Man, the State Department's gonna shit a brick over that!"

Robert Slye stopped shouting.

"So let me lay this out, Bob. The CIA's gunning for you. The Pentagon and State are gunning for you. Every agency in Europe wants your head on a platter. And all that would be really, really bad news. But"—he paused, sipped the wine—"your actions also led to a bomb that damn near killed the father of Katalin Fiero Dahar. And by now, you know who that is, right?"

"Finnigan, how the fuck did—"

"Clam up, Bob. Listen, Katalin should be landing at George Bush Intercontinental right about, oh, now. Traffic in Houston being what it is, you got an hour, tops, before she knocks on your door."

He winked across the table at Fiero.

"Jesus. Finnigan, ah . . ."

"Bob? Check your personal bank accounts. The ones in Switzerland, the Caymans, and, uh—"

Dave said, "Chile."

"—Chile, Bob. You'll find that, while we've been chitchatting, we've cleaned you out. You got a couple grand left. And, Bob? Your

DC lobbyists aren't gonna take your call for a lousy couple grand. Your Manhattan law firm won't take your call. Your congressman won't take your call. Fact is, you might—just might—have enough to get you and your wife on the next flight to Cambodia. Ahead of the media, the CIA, the Pentagon, and the cops."

They listened to the phone. They could almost hear the man sweat.

"Just not," Finnigan added, "ahead of Fiero."

Robert Slye hung up.

Finnigan did too, then held up his glass. The others toasted.

"That," said Sally, raising her glass, "was a master class."

"You think?"

She laughed. "Poor fella brought a knife to an aerial dogfight."

C71

AIRBORNE

The mission statement of the Black Harts—if a group of career criminals had a mission statement—would have read: Steal as much as you can from the types of people who most deserve to get ripped off.

A group like the Harts doesn't willingly give up a three-million-dollar payday. But Sally Blue had made a choice: give St. Nicholas Salvage & Wrecking the three million plundered from Sooner, Slye, and Rydell's Spanish operation, with the promise of a bigger plunder from the military contractor's world headquarters.

It was a win-win situation. St. Nicholas got to fund its paramilitary raid on the city of Baharos; the Harts walked away with nearly eight million dollars, free and clear. Everyone was happy.

Okay, not Robert Slye. But everyone agreed that he was an asshole, so . . .

Satisfied with an honest day's thieving, Sally and her hacker said their goodbyes in the Netherlands.

As they left, Fiero said, "Hugo is hiding all of the potential victims at the Alcázar Real d'Aragon. If we want to catch Mariner, we should go there."

"What is it?"

"Castle," she said. "It's near the French border. I know of it, but I've never been there. Should be defensible enough."

"If Mariner attacks there, she'll be going up against an army garrison. Inside a castle. That doesn't sound like smart soldiering."

"No," she conceded. "It doesn't."

With the help of Lachlan Sumner, they got the seaplane ready to fly back to Spain. Lachlan did his walk-around.

Finnigan said, "Alcázar?"

She nodded.

"Is that Spanish?"

"It's an Arabic word. It means palace or fortress. It . . ."

Her voice trailed off.

Finnigan said, "Holy shit."

Fiero scrambled for her messenger bag, eventually digging up the script they'd stolen from the TV studio in Baharos. Her eyes darted over the script.

"*They use Arabic words for their Arabic buildings, hiding in them after killing the innocent Arab . . .*"

"Major Barakat knew where the next bomb would go off," Finnigan said. "He wrote it in the script. Arabic words for Arabic buildings."

"Mariner is definitely attacking the Alcázar."

THEY ALERTED HUGO LLORENTE to the upgraded threat. Lachlan flew the partners to a Spanish seaport near Valencia that was outfitted to accept pontoon planes.

Once airborne, Fiero settled down in the main cabin to clean and prepare her firearms. Finnigan propped open his laptop and began making notes about the Alcázar Real d'Aragon in his weird, asymmetrical scrawl. With his left hand, he fidgeted subconsciously with the pink tile he'd picked up from the piles of rubble at the Grand Mosque in Baharos.

The silence between them screamed.

Finally, Fiero said, "Michael? What is it?"

He closed the laptop and rubbed his eyelids vigorously with the heels of his hands.

He said, "You've stopped worrying about Valazko."

She knew, even before she asked, that he'd figured it out. She wiped her hands with a clean rag, sat back in her chair, staring into his eyes.

"Yes."

"Is he dead?"

"Yes."

"You kill him?"

"Yes."

Finnigan reached for a capped bottle of water, just to have something to do with his hands.

"When?"

"The day we met McTavish, Grenier, and Silver in Barcelona."

He nodded. "You were late to the meeting."

"Yes."

"Was it a fair fight?"

She said, "No. I lured Valazko into a hotel room and I shot him in the back. Then twice in the head. Hugo had a cleanup team standing by to sterilize the room. It was an assassination."

The de Havilland shuddered a little.

Finnigan sipped water he didn't want.

"Okay," he said.

She waited, knowing that *Okay* meant anything but.

He rubbed his face again. "Jesus. Don't remember the last time we slept in our own beds."

She waited.

"This is what I feared. Right here. Fucking Hugo Llorente. This is what I was afraid of."

She waited.

He unscrewed the cap on the water. Put it back on and said, "How come?"

"Valazko. In Oslo, years ago, I saved a journalist he'd targeted, and I killed two of his team doing so. I know him. The only way to even the score would be to kill you first, then me."

Finnigan took that all in.

"He wasn't an employee of Suicide Ride. They couldn't call him off. Win or lose with them, he'd still come for us. For the last couple of years, he didn't know where I was, or even if I was still alive. But then he did. He could wait a month, or several months, but he was coming for us. This way . . ."

She shrugged.

Finnigan said, "Yeah. Okay. I mean, we've killed people. I'm not naive. I know what we've done."

She waited.

After a while, Finnigan reopened the laptop and went back to jotting indecipherable notes on a legal pad.

Fiero finished cleaning her guns.

"I know why you didn't tell me in advance," Finnigan said, his back to her. "You were right. I woulda stopped you."

Fiero sounded sad. "You would have tried."

C72

ALCÁZAR REAL D'ARAGON

Finnigan and Fiero took a rental car from Valencia, north to the mountainous region near the border with France. They got a car with plenty of storage space, room enough for an arsenal.

They used Google Earth to find a switchback gravel road leading up the mountains toward a private hunting lodge. From there, they found a turnoff about two hundred feet above the high-elevation valley in which nestled the great castle and the river the castle straddled.

They used field glasses to study the castle, the two long administrative arms of offices and the green-and-white checkerboard parade grounds. The place was bustling.

"Four helos," Finnigan said. "I see . . . six military vehicles. Nope. Seven. The joint is, like, Hulkbuster Base."

"That's not one of those cultural references I'm supposed to get, is it?"

"Nope." He handed over the field glasses.

"My parents are in there. Minister de Cordoba. Annie Pryor. Hugo said he had about a dozen high-profile targets as well."

"Yeah, but Mariner won't want any of them. Target Number One is Pryor. Cause she's the one who was screwing her husband and who Mariner indirectly blames for the death of her daughter."

"Or directly blames."

"Yeah. Psychosis is the new black."

Fiero gave him a quick smile. They were back to their bantering selves, but she didn't mention it. Just went with it.

"Target One is Pryor. Target Two is, who? Your dad? Minister de Cordoba?"

"If Mariner is still acting on behalf of the Alsharqi intelligence agency, yes. And we have to assume she is."

"That means, far as we're concerned, your parents got a bull's-eye on 'em."

"I agree."

"And Mariner has proven she can run rings around Llorente. Him and the whole goddamn European intelligence community."

"Yes."

"So we gotta do this on our own. Get down there. Sneak in. Wait for her to make Llorente's guys look like the Three Stooges, then get her before she gets to her targets."

Fiero said, "Yes."

"Piece of cake."

They traded the glasses two more times, memorizing everything they could.

Fiero said, "P'raps we got lucky. P'raps Mariner isn't as psychotic as we assume. She could be halfway to Antarctica as we speak."

"Nah. She's down there."

Fiero lowered the glasses. "How can you tell?"

"This." He gestured to the turnoff from the gravel road to the hunting lodge, and the cliff before them. "You saw the map. This is pretty much the only place to get a birds-eye view of the castle."

"So?"

"So we're standing on a bunch of cigarette butts. American-made. Fresh."

Fiero glanced down at her boots and the butts in the gravel around them.

"Say," she said. "You really are a detective."

Finnigan circled the rental. "Bet your ass."

C73

ALCÁZAR REAL D'ARAGON

For Christmas one year, Finnigan got Fiero a coffee mug that read *World's Greatest Ninja.*

That's because, when she wanted to, Fiero made less noise than fog.

They decided the best way into the Alcázar would be through one of the long, dilapidated, seventeenth-century administrative wings. If Dinah Mariner and her guys were trying to enter—and they were—that's how they'd do it.

Finnigan and Fiero walked along the edge of the river, beneath holly oak and Portuguese oak, until they reached the first low stone walls of the Alcázar. Not yet 9 a.m., the heat already was rising. They could still taste the Saharan sands of the sirocco. Arid heat bathed the region. They'd raided the storage of the de Havilland for black T-shirts, combat trousers, and boots, as well as light ballistic vests and small, sturdy backpacks. Finnigan's scalp itched beneath a black watch cap. Fiero wore her hair in a tight French braid.

Fiero carried her favorite handguns, two full-sized P226

Tactical Ops SIGs—she had the upper-body strength and grip to use the full-sized weapon—with four twenty-round mags. A kickboxer, she wore both guns in holsters strapped tight to her thighs, so they wouldn't get in the way of close-in fighting.

Finnigan favored the Glock 17, the 9 mm, and still used the Gen4, not the newer version. He carried only one gun on him since he was about as accurate shooting with his left hand as he would be shooting with his teeth. He also brought along his beloved Halligan bar, a tool found in the trunk of most American police cars. It was a door-breaching device that looked like a Frankensteined hatchet, pry bar, tire iron, and mountain climber's ice pick.

It took them the better part of ninety minutes to sneak around the sentinels, heading away from the bulk of the castle. Fiero stopped them at one point, motioning toward a boarded-over ground-floor window that looked flimsy. Finnigan used the pry bar to get it loose enough to squirrel their way in, then returned the board to its original position.

The room had been elegant once, but Spain had seen two *fins de siècle* since then. The ceilings were twenty-five-feet tall, with decorative cornice moldings at all four corners. The ceiling could have had a fresco at some point, but it was too soot stained to tell. The wooden floor had rotted through in places, and the room smelled of ancient stone and rat droppings.

For decades, Spanish bureaucrats had labored here. They'd organized taxes or landholdings, bartered over matters of commerce, watched the French or Portuguese borders, rooted out the Jews or the Ottomans, planned for war or hoped for peace. Now the rats ruled the place. The castle itself was still grand. But the two long concourses jutted out from either end of the castle like dead limbs.

Finnigan bounced on the balls of his feet and felt the mushy floor give a little too much. "You think there's a basement?"

"Not this close to a river and built in the sixteenth century, no," she said. "If the floor caves in under us, it should only cave in a few inches."

He nodded.

"Okay. We reverse course. Head closer to the center of the castle. Go slow and watch for rotting floorboards."

"Mariner and Washington and . . . ah . . ."

He said, "Perry."

"Yes. They likely entered the same way we did—in which case, rotting floors ahead of us are the least of our worries. Or they used the northwest concourse."

He shook his head. "That side's too close to the village. Harder to get there unseen. No, they're ahead of us."

She checked both of her guns. "Three to two are about the best odds we've ever gotten."

"I know, right? Our luck is turning."

THE NORTHWEST CONCOURSE OF OFFICES stood four stories tall. Rather than being served by a single corridor, most of the offices were accessible by moving from one to the next to the next.

The wing included fourteen consecutive offices, then a reception hall with double doors leading out to the parade grounds, followed by fourteen more consecutive offices. As seen from the bulk of the castle, the abandoned offices could be considered as numbering one through twenty-eight, with office Number One at the center and Number 28 at the far northeast tip of the long concourse.

Finnigan and Fiero entered the concourse at Room 25.

Dinah Mariner knelt in Room 19, checking her backpack. Standing around her were DeMarcus Washington and Ron Perry.

And the six Alsharqi soldiers who'd been called up to avenge the kidnapping of Major Saad Barakat.

C74

Ron Perry sat on a plastic dustcover over a Victorian chair and hauled out his tablet computer. "We good to wait here a minute?" He spoke around a wad of chew. "Gonna whistle up the Roombas."

Dinah Mariner nodded. She issued an order to the head of the six-man Alsharqi unit. All of the soldiers spoke English, to one degree or another. Everyone settled in. The men began unwrapping granola bars and passing water canteens around. They'd paused at Room 19 of the northwestern wing of offices. Perry tapped his computer screen to deactivate the cell blocker that covered most of the castle and grounds. Instantly, his own phone lit up with three bars. They were in electronic reach of the surprises he'd left in the castle.

Mariner and DeMarcus Washington both moved to the door leading to the next old and unused room, peering out. They spotted the rotting corpse of an ancient chandelier, lying on the floor, keeled over like a beached whale, almost all it's crystal elements broken.

Washington glanced around to make sure the Alsharqi agents were out of hearing. "How we doing?"

Mariner nodded.

Washington waited.

When it was clear he wasn't about to let it go, she sighed. "You're not the only covert soldiers working for me, you know."

The big man nodded. "Figured you had others."

"I have people in The Hague right now. They're going to try to get Saad Barakat out of custody."

"Why? Fucker can die there, for all I care."

Mariner smiled up at him. "Isn't it obvious?"

"Not to me it ain't."

She again peered out at the room ahead of them. "The deal is this: If I remove the last coconspirator and if we get Barakat back from the International Criminal Court, you and Ron will be set for life. The payoff runs into nine figures. All you've done, all the good works, all the risks . . . you'll be able to go anywhere. Be anyone. That's the payoff."

He mumbled, "Me and Perry."

"Yes."

"And you?"

She almost laughed. She reached up and gripped his forearm, like gripping an oak branch. "I kill Annie. Nothing after that counts for a bucket of spit."

"We all get out alive."

She said, "I had two options in Paris: Die with my daughter or get us both out alive. That was it, DeMarcus. Two and only two. Bess and I both lived, or we both died. Then you saved me. I've been essentially dead ever since. In every way but the decomposition. This is it for me. This is the last mission. After Annie dies, you can remember me as a psychotic or remember me fondly." She smiled up at him again. "I only ask that you remember me."

Behind them, Ron Perry said, "We're online. And the crowd

goes wild." He looked up from his laptop and grinned, his teeth gray with chew.

Mariner said, "Roombas?"

The blond man hit a knuckle-buster combination of keys then reactivated the signal blockers he'd installed throughout the castle. "Roombas."

THEY WEREN'T, TECHNICALLY SPEAKING, Roombas. They were generic robotic vacuum-cleaning units, purchased online. Their vacuuming components had been removed and packed with C4 explosives. Also Bluetooth-capable cameras. Like the real robotic vacuum cleaners, they moved of their own volition like little flying saucers.

Half a year earlier, Dinah Mariner's unit, under the pretense of Frau Gunsen and her bomb-sweeping team, had entered the Alcázar Real d'Aragon and planted two explosive packages. They'd placed one in a heating vent and the other beneath an antique sideboard.

Both units had been found, eventually. They'd been placed in such a way that they would definitely be found.

Ron Perry also had set up four black-box traps. Each had been superbly well hidden on the main floor of the Alcázar. Each was a small metal box, the size of a portable typewriter, from which no electronic signals emitted, nor any aromas. Neither technology nor dogs would be able to find these boxes. They were, in a true sense, cloaked. Until Perry got within range to activate them.

When he did, the boxes opened, and four robotic vacuum cleaner bodies with explosives and electronic eyes awoke and whisked silently out of their black boxes.

Dinah Mariner's team hadn't simply brought bombs to the Alcázar Real d'Aragon. They'd brought fast, silent, hunter/killers.

Guilherme Armentano, the sharply dressed deputy assistant

director of Spanish Intelligence, had said that a years-old report had been commissioned showing the Alcázar to be the best possible fortress in the event of a terrorist threat.

That "years-old" report had actually been written only months earlier then inserted into the computer files of Spanish Intelligence by the one person who'd had access from the very beginning: Dinah Mariner.

Annie Pryor and the others, including Alexandro Fiero, Khadija Dahar, and Hugo Llorente, weren't safe within a redoubt. They were trapped in a slaughterhouse.

C75

ALCÁZAR REAL D'ARAGON

"That," said Finnigan, "is a shitload of boot prints."

They'd made it to Room 19, only to find a bit of plywood that had been pried off a window and reattached, plus a dizzying array of overlapping prints in the dust.

Fiero sighed. "I'd hoped Mariner only had two men."

"Yeah, well, now she's got the Rockettes."

Fiero danced ahead to peer into the next salon, Room 18. She spotted more prints in the dust.

Finnigan dug out his phone and thumbed it on. "No reception."

Fiero did the same, with the same results. "We're within a jamming field."

"Llorente's? Or Mariner's?"

"Does it matter?"

He shrugged and pocketed the phone. "Warning Llorente wouldn't help anyway. His unit's comms have been compromised since this whole shitshow started."

Fiero peered up at the soot-stained ceiling. "We have to flank them. Box them between us."

"How? We step outside, the Spanish Army will arrest us. Or shoot us. By the time your buddy Hugo steps in, Mariner will have reached her targets. We can't cut around them without going outside, because this is just one long chain of rooms. And not for nothing, but didn't anyone ever teach the Spanish about the concept of corridors? You know, one long hall, each room gets its own door. This moving from room to room is bullshit."

"You should let them know. I'm sure there's a suggestion box near the gift shop." Fiero checked her diver's watch. "It's a two-story wing. I'll head up to the next floor, sprint ahead, come back down, and we'll catch them in a pincer."

He shook his head. "No way. We damn near stepped through rotting floorboards about five times as is. The second floor will be worse."

She smiled and took a moment to retighten her French braid. "I'm spry."

"Can you also levitate?"

"Yes, but I'm not s'posed to talk about it." She glanced ahead again. "There should be a gallery between the fourteenth and fifteenth salons, with a stairway. I'll get above them, then get ahead of them and come back down. Give me ten minutes. Move up on their trailing men. Wait until you hear me fire."

"I hate this plan."

"You said you hated gazpacho until I made you try some. Remember?"

She turned and blinked away.

Finnigan knelt and checked the extra ammunition rounds in his backpack. He grumbled, to nobody in particular, "Gazpacho still sucks."

THE NORTHWEST CONCOURSE of abandoned offices was laid out as fourteen consecutive salons, a gallery with an entrance onto the parade grounds and a spiral staircase to the second floor, then fourteen more salons.

The Alsharqi agent riding drag checked the gallery one last time, then noted that the rest of the raiding party had moved from Room 14 to Room 13. He tucked in behind them.

Fiero watched, then emerged from the other side of the gallery and moved silently to the spiral stairs. *They're not a spiral,* she remembered her mother saying to her, in another ornate old manor house, when Fiero had been . . . what? Six years old? Seven? The two of them had stood at the base of a similar grand staircase and her mother, speaking Arabic, had said, "Spiral stairs aren't spiral, Little Mouse."

"Why?" Katalin had asked.

"You must figure that out for yourself," her mother had said. She was always, always testing her daughter's brain, teaching her to examine everything with skepticism.

Now all these years later, her mother was the target of a strike team consisting of a former CIA station chief, two former American soldiers, and who knew how many other Alsharqi soldiers—the follow-guard Fiero had spotted appeared to be Alsharqi. Which, of course, would make sense. She wished she had radio contact with Finnigan to warn him.

She placed a boot on the first riser of the spiral stairs, right at the very edge of the stairs, nearest the right-hand balustrade. She applied her full weight. It creaked but held.

The second and third risers however looked rotted through. The long-legged Spaniard stepped over them to riser number four. Again, it held.

She made her way in a spiral up the stairs, slowly, a little louder than she would have liked, to the second floor.

She had been away in college, taking math classes, when the answer to her mother's riddle had finally come to her. She'd called her mother that night. "Spiral stairs aren't spiral because spirals are two-dimensional shapes. A spiral staircase could only take you from the first floor to the first floor."

She remembered her mother's musical laugher over the phone. "My God, I can't believe you still remember me asking you that!"

"Spiral stairs are a helix," Katalin had said.

"That's right, darling. A helix is a three-dimensional representation of a spiral."

"I love you, Mum. Good night."

FINNIGAN HAD BEEN RIGHT: the ground floor had been a mess, but the upper floor was far worse.

Fiero stayed close to the outer load-bearing walls, rather than simply dash from doorway to doorway. The shortest distance between any two points in a rotted-out building was most definitely not a straight line. But Fiero was athletic and graceful. She also kept an eye on the floorboards. At several places, they were so worn through that she could see the salon beneath her. She paused at each, SIG in her fist, and peered down. Catching the assault force from above would be about as good as catching them from in front; in either case, they'd been in a crossfire.

She never spotted them.

She knew she was making good time. She also knew, silent as she was, that she was still making too much noise.

By the time she got to Room 3, two rooms away from the main body of the castle, she was fairly certain that Mariner's crew must have heard her.

SHE WAS RIGHT.

Mariner, Washington, and Perry watched as soot and dust drifted down from the ceiling of Room 4, just three doors from the center of the castle. They heard the creaking of old boards overhead.

"Soldiers?" Perry whispered.

"Risky," Mariner said, covering her nose and mouth with a hijab she'd brought along to appease the Alsharqi soldiers. "I wouldn't put a roaming patrol up there. Too great a chance of falling."

"So then who?"

Mariner shrugged. "There's a stairway outside Room 1. That's the beginning of the royal part of the castle. My guess is, we'll find out there."

Washington said, "If someone's trying to get ahead of us . . ."

"Yes. Then someone else might be behind us. Setting up a pincer." Mariner motioned everyone ahead, but nodded at Washington to head back the way they'd come.

She suddenly wished that she knew more about these bounty hunters she'd been hearing about. This St. Nicholas Salvage & Wrecking.

C76

Guilherme Armentano, deputy assistant director of Spanish Intelligence, made the rounds of the great castle in the company of three soldiers in full combat gear, plus Foreign Minister José Ramón de Cordoba. "How long do you imagine we shall be here?" the minister asked.

Armentano waved the question away as if it were a trifling. "Every agency in Europe is looking for this Dinah Mariner. Nobody wants to find her more than the CIA. It shouldn't be long now. I realize it is inconvenient, sir. If I could ask you to return to the chancellery . . . ?"

The tall, angular minister peered down at him, then shrugged and spun on his heels, returning to the great room and his dozen "guests."

Armentano turned to one of the soldiers and rolled his eyes. "Bureaucrats."

The soldier nodded then noticed a metal disc, the size of a Frisbee, hover into the room. It ran on wheels, very low to the parquetry. The motorized, automatic vacuum cleaner angled into the salon, then changed direction toward them.

Guilherme Armentano smiled. "My wife has those things."

The soldier, who'd been on security duty at Alcázar for a week, blanched. "This castle doesn't."

The robotic disc exploded.

FIERO WAS HALFWAY DOWN the spiral stairs, at the egress to the Northwest concourse, when an explosion rocked the building.

She stumbled down the last two stairs, going awkwardly to one knee. The banister broke off against her hip.

The explosion had come from behind her.

In front of her, a gunman stepped into the doorframe to the concourse, leading with a Czech-made CZ-805 BREN machine gun.

The natural reaction of anyone stumbling down the stairs is to halt your fall. Fiero reacted against instinct, going *with* her fall, turning it into a tumble, letting the helix of the stairs carry her away from the man in the doorway.

The soldier stitched a pattern of holes in the decorative structure of the stairs.

Fiero let her momentum carry her to the wooden floor, emerging on her right shoulder and right hip, SIG rising and sighting. She fired once.

The gunman ducked back into the Room 1 of the concourse. Back and to the left.

Fiero aimed one meter to the left of the door and fired three more bullets through the wall.

The .39 mm BREN clattered to the floor.

Fiero rose and tucked herself back behind the low, curved wall of the stairs, eyes on the door and the blood spatter on the doorframe.

The explosion had been bad news. It had been on this floor, she thought, and behind her.

In the main rooms of the castle.

Where her mother and father were in hiding.

FINNIGAN HEARD THE RUMBLE of an explosion, felt it under his boots. He'd been crouched behind one of many wooden crates scattered like huge chess pieces throughout the salon. The nearest crate held a downed but essentially intact chandelier, more or less the size and inverted shape of one of his mom's Christmas trees, maybe six feet tall, four feet in diameter. It had been removed gingerly from the ceiling, now standing upside down in a three-sided crate, the fourth side and the lid leaning against a wooden construction horse.

Before he could rise, he heard the tattoo of a machine gun, followed by the distinctive pop-pop-pop of Fiero's SIG.

He'd been crouching in Room 3 of the concourse, just slightly behind the assault force in Room 2. As soon as the gunfire erupted, he rose and moved toward the door.

A black man built like an NFL first-round draft pick stepped into the doorway with a .50 caliber handgun. The enormous gun, a Desert Eagle, looked perfectly normal in the man's huge hand.

Finnigan slid-ducked behind the downed chandelier and heard it explode. A geyser of glass, brass, and copper mushroomed into the air. Finnigan threw his arms over his head, head down near his knees, and felt the sharp bits begin raining down on him.

FIERO KNEW THERE WAS LITTLE or no chance that the gunman she'd shot would be acting alone. Another—or several others—would appear in the doorway within seconds.

The plan had been to catch Mariner and her assault team in a crossfire, with Finnigan tackling them from behind.

But that was before Fiero heard and felt the explosion coming from deeper within the castle, the area she suspected she'd find her parents.

She heard the basso profundo boom of a hand-cannon coming from the concourse of office salons. A Desert Eagle? she thought. You don't see—or hear—those every day.

With cell phone reception blocked, there was no way to tell Finnigan that she was about to abandon the plan, leaving him to his own devices. She was (to use Michael's term) calling an audible. She didn't know where the term came from, but she trusted that Finnigan would understand.

Before the gunmen in the concourse regrouped, Fiero leaped to her feet and dashed in the other direction, into the center of the Alcázar Real d'Aragon.

FINNIGAN USED THE DISTRACTION of the mushroom cloud of glass to slide free from behind the wooden crate, heading toward more crates, these loaded with old Victorian furniture. The guy in the doorway didn't fire again.

To his surprise, the big man spoke. His accent was American. "You Finnigan?"

Finnigan moved again, deeper into Room 2, toward even larger crates. He felt a glass shard in his back, felt warm blood trickle down his side.

"I'm honored! You Washington?"

The big man laughed.

"Ask you a question?"

Washington said, "Go ahead."

Finnigan doffed the backpack, shrugging out of the shoulder

straps was misery. He reached behind himself, his fingers blindly searching for a shard of glass the size and shape of a credit card, sticking out of his shirt just over his kidney. He pulled it loose. He dropped it, not bothering to turn to see that it was bloody. The backpack had protected a large section of his back and his entire spine, at least. "It's kinda personal!"

"Fine," Washington said. He sounded as if he hadn't moved from the doorway to Room 1.

"What're you, six five, six seven? Clock in a little north of two fifty?"

Washington said, "'Bout right."

"The fuck does a freight train like you need a Desert Eagle for? Seems like overkill."

Washington chuckled, low and guttural and menacing. "Never understood that term. Overkill. *Kill* should be like *unique*. Don't need no modifier."

Finnigan had thought he was stalling the big man. Turns out, the big man was stalling him. Likely Mariner had sent men up and over, getting behind him, using the second floor just as Fiero had. *Who's got whom in a pincer?* he wondered.

He didn't have time to question why the assault party had stopped shooting at Fiero, and Fiero had stopped shooting back. Only two answers. One: she was dead, wounded, or captured. Or two: she'd called an audible, heading toward the explosion and her mom and dad.

Finnigan couldn't allow himself to assume it was the first. And he was fine with the second; he'd have done the same.

He turned now, facing the other door, the one through which he'd come, leading back to Room 3. A shadow flitted across the doorway. Finnigan brought up one knee, planted the sole of his boot, rested his elbow on the knee and sighted up.

"Hey, Washington?"

The voice behind him said, "Yeah?"

A Middle Eastern man with a wire-brush beard crept into the doorway to Room 3. Finnigan assumed the assault team wore ballistic vests. He fired a single shot, catching the man in the hip. He could see the pelvis shatter, saw the man fall, his BREN gun clattering away.

Behind Finnigan, the Desert Eagle roared again. Bits of a Chippendale loveseat turned kindling scattering across the parquetry floor as one of the crates exploded.

But not, Finnigan noted with some satisfaction, the crate behind which he hid.

C77

ALCÁZAR REAL D'ARAGON

The great old castle shook as a second wheeled bomb slid into one of the grand ballrooms and detonated, taking out four more soldiers, plus an oil tycoon from Seville who'd been identified as a possible target of the Khamsin Sayef. Ron Perry's robots were silent and mobile, and their cameras fed images onto Perry's tablet computer. Their bombs spread shrapnel three hundred sixty degrees, but low to the ground. This second bomb sheared off the legs of every man in the ballroom. All five bled out in under a minute.

It was the same basic strategy Perry had used for the explosives under the porch of the cabin in rural France. No thickness of ballistic vest will help you if your femoral artery is slashed open.

AN ALSHARQI SOLDIER in Room 1 slid a flash-bang into the grand corridor with the spiral stairway, hockey-puck style. He ducked back, crook of his elbow over his eyes. The little device boomed and a harsh white light flared. The soldier stormed forward and to the left; a fellow soldier dashed in, forward and to the right. Dinah Mariner came next, straight on, holding a SIG-Sauer in a two-hand grip.

They studied the empty room that stank of sulfur and gunpowder.

She turned to the Alsharqi lieutenant. "You're sure it was a woman?"

He nodded. "I saw only a glimpse, but yes. Before she shot Amir. Tall. Black hair. Maybe Arabic."

Could be a Spanish soldier, Mariner thought. Could be this Katalin Fiero Dahar she'd heard so much about.

The question remained: Where the hell was she now?

"Spread out. Find the guests," she said. "Don't kill any civilians. Don't kill the woman whose photo I showed you."

The lieutenant said, "Pryor. Yes, we know."

Mariner nodded. "Go."

FIERO CAUGHT SIGHT OF ONE of the roving robot bombs as it skittered down a corridor lined with seventeenth century portraits so soot-blackened as to be indistinguishable. The little mechanical disc was the size a bathroom scale. It raced down the corridor away from her, its camera mounted on a flexible metal stalk.

No one else was in the corridor.

Fiero took a gamble, raised her P226 and fired a single round into the robot.

The explosion destroyed the western end of the corridor and sent Fiero landing on her ass. Her ears rang. She wiped hair away from her eyes, coughed, and scrambled to her feet.

One of the walls had caught fire. The flames spread quickly. She assumed the building had been converted to gas heat at some point during the twentieth century. Had she clipped a gas line?

Smoke began filling the corridor. This was not what Fiero had intended. But then again, as distractions go, a fire wasn't a bad one.

She headed away from the explosion as quickly as she could.

Two minutes later, she rounded a corner and found a dead woman, dressed as a working professional. Probably one of the staffers of the foreign minister, she thought.

Fiero spotted the woman's purse. She knelt and rummaged through it, finding a lipstick.

DUST AND SOOT RAINED DOWN on the raiding party as a quake rocked the castle. Ron Perry frowned at his tablet. He looked up at Mariner.

"Who'd you get?"

"Nobody. She went off by herself," he grumbled. "We've only got one more left."

It annoyed Mariner that he assigned a gender to his bombs, but she kept it to herself. She switched her walkie to Frequency 2. She tapped the Send button twice, waiting for DeMarcus Washington to respond.

WASHINGTON IGNORED THE TWIN vibrations from the walkie snapped to his belt. Holding the Desert Eagle in a two-hand combat grip, he edged into Room 2. The room looked like a massive checkerboard, with crates arranged randomly, filled with old furniture and more chandeliers. Some had wooden tops nailed on; most didn't. Some had four wooden sides in place; some had three. Most were large enough to lurk behind.

For a big man, Washington could move with absolute silence. He'd learned the trick in the cities of Iraq and Afghanistan. He was too goddamn big to hide in the desert, but he'd learned to make the most of natural camouflage in urban settings.

He rounded one of the crates. No Finnigan. But he spotted a modern backpack made of tough material. The guy had been here. Washington toed it gently with his boot and saw extra mags in the bag. Finnigan was down to the bullets still in his gun.

He edged around another waist-high crate. Nothing.

He whipped to his right, sighted up behind a third crate. Nothing.

The little Irish prick could move quietly too, he thought. Good. Another pro.

He heard something small clatter in a corner. It sounded like wood-on-wood. Washington froze.

The sound didn't repeat.

He turned on his vertical axis, as if he had become a gun turret, the forward sights on his big, Israeli-made gun taking in a sweeping arc of the room.

Walking on the balls of his feet, he moved back the way he'd come. Away from the noise.

Which had been something thrown to distract him. No question. Finnigan was a pro. Bad news for Finnigan: Washington was, too.

Washington slow-walked toward the nearest crate. Saw nothing.

He edged around it, toward the next one, which had three wooden sides; the fourth side and the lid lying on the ground. He spotted a twinkle of light on crystal from inside the crate.

He stepped softly, drew nearer.

He was right over the last crate, peering past it, when Finnigan fired.

The 9 mm slug dug deep into the remains of the chandelier in the crate.

Like last time, this chandelier erupted like a volcano, driving bits of copper and crystal shards upward in a glittering mushroom cloud of destruction.

Right into Washington's face.

The man fell, the room vibrating with the impact of his frame.

FINNIGAN ROSE FROM BEHIND another crate, the Halligan bar in his hand. He raced across the room and drove the bar down as hard as he could on Washington's right forearm. Bones cracked like dry wood. His hand twitching, the Desert Eagle spun free and skittered across the room.

Finnigan dropped the pry bar and raised his Glock, aiming at the door to Room 1, then turned toward the door to Room 3.

He reversed, did the double-check again.

Nobody else entered.

He looked down at the man, who lay on his chest, struggling with his one unbroken arm to turn over.

He did.

Finnigan took a shocked half step back.

Shards of glass stuck out of Washington's face and neck.

Both eye sockets were blood-filled craters. The eyes themselves were gone.

Washington gasped in unimaginable pain. "F . . . fuck . . . you . . ."

Finnigan whisked the walkie-talkie off the man's belt. He stutter-stepped away as Washington kicked out blindly.

Finnigan retrieved the Halligan bar from the floor, then went to find his backpack. He knelt, slid free the mag in his Glock, checked the rounds, and swapped out for a fresh mag. He checked both doorways again. The cut on his back bled but not badly.

"Fucker . . . fucking . . . kill . . ." He heard Washington swing away with his one good arm, saw the blind man punch one of the crates.

Finnigan walked back the way he'd first arrived. The Alsharqi soldier in the door had bled out from the wound in his hip. He retrieved the man's BREN machine gun. He hated using a weapon he'd never taken to a firing range, but beggars can't be choosers.

Finnigan rose and moved on to the next room.

Washington moaned. "Kill . . . you . . . fucking . . ." His words were slurred by a ragged hole in his left cheek that exposed teeth and gums. He swung a massive fist at nothing at all.

Finnigan knew that the bits of crystal glittering in Washington's pulpy eye sockets would haunt his sleep the rest of his days.

C78

Alexandro Fiero took his wife in his arms as the two Spanish soldiers on guard duty fell. They'd been shot, simultaneously, from two separate doors in the grand Chancellery de Trastámara.

The dozen civilians now found themselves without protection.

A woman with a handgun and two soldiers entered from both doors. Alexandro positioned himself to stand between the attackers and his wife, but also in front of the foreign minister, José Ramón de Cordoba.

The woman was familiar; burn scars decorated one cheek, and her nose had been broken and badly healed.

"Frau Gunsen?"

"My name is Dinah Mariner, Señor. I apologize for this inconvenience."

"Incon—"

She rode over his outrage. "Where is Annie Pryor?"

One of the civilians stepped forward. "I don't know who that is. But my company is prepared to pay well over one million euros for my safe—"

Dinah Mariner shot him in the head.

Civilians screamed and danced in place. One man puked.

Alexandro Fiero and Khadija Dahar held each other close.

"Again: Where is Annie Pryor?"

Behind the Fiero couple, de Cordoba cleared his throat. "They took her to the kitchens. Lower floor, on the east side. Please, she is very weak. She is on a gurney. She might die anyway."

Mariner pointed her gun at the deputy minister, and at Alexandro Fiero, who stood in the way.

"Who took her?"

"Seven soldiers," de Cordoba said. "The woman isn't even Spanish. She's of no importance to us. Just take her and go."

Mariner holstered her weapon. She drew a walkie-talkie from her belt. She went to Frequency 1 and toggled the button twice.

Perry said, "Go, boss."

"A team of seven soldiers is taking Pryor to the kitchens. Ground floor, east side. She's on a gurney. Go."

She switched to Frequency 2 and toggled the button twice. She waited.

A low, rumbling and ragged voice said, "Washington."

Mariner frowned. "Are you all right?"

"Shot. I'm good."

She looked murderously angry for a second then literally shook the emotions off her face.

"Perry is moving toward the east side, ground floor, to find Pryor. There's a big Spanish team there. Head his way."

The voice said, "Okay," and clicked off.

Pryor moved away and spoke to one of her Middle Eastern soldiers.

Khadija Dahar leaned back and whispered without turning her head. "Do you smell smoke?"

Alexandro nodded. "Yes."

Khadija turned to de Cordoba and offered a brief but heartfelt smile. "A team of seven? Taking her to the kitchens? You lie convincingly, José."

The minister whispered as well. "I am a politician, my dear."

FINNIGAN DISCONNECTED THE WALKIE and clipped it to his backpack. He thought his impression of Washington had been pretty good.

He'd been smelling smoke for the last minute or so, and now he could see it hovering like fog around the ceiling. Something on this floor definitely was aflame.

He skip-stepped over to a window and checked the sun. Okay, east was thataway. He began moving thataway.

HUGO LLORENTE SWEATED and grunted as he half-carried Annie Pryor to the third floor of the Alcázar, peering out a window at the west-facing windows and the scattered cluster of helicopters way the hell out at the end of the parade grounds.

Pryor, on her feet—barely—managed a dusty smile through cracked lips. "Those birds would be handy right about now."

"They might as well be on the moon," Llorente said. He could see no Spanish soldiers, although three were supposed to be on duty. He spotted only one of their corpses from his vantage point. "Ms. Mariner brought a sniper, I assume."

"DeMarcus," Pryor said, wincing. Blood from the wound that had reopened began painting her shirt as well as Llorente's jacket. He'd thrown one of her arms over his shoulder and had physically dragged her up to the third floor. She stank of sweat and blood—but she was lucid. That was something. Llorente had given her a gun from a dead soldier and had taken one for himself.

"I don't usually pry into the private lives of others, but your affair with Teddy Mariner was ill-advised."

"Shut up," she said through clenched teeth. "I loved Teddy. He was going to divorce Dinah."

"And, ah, Bess, was it?"

Pryor hiccoughed a sob. "Shut up. Just shut up."

Katalin Fiero Dahar stepped into the room, P226 sweeping strategically for all the corners. "Sir."

Llorente allowed himself a true smile. "Thank you for disobeying orders, Katalin."

She nodded.

DINAH MARINER GLARED at the hostages and her mind skipped nimbly over the last walkie-talkie conversation.

Something about DeMarcus Washington's voice was bugging her.

The guard said, "I think the castle is on fire."

"We don't have time to check. Head to the kitchen, lower floor east. Washington might be dead. If he is, the American, Finnigan, is heading that way. Kill him."

The lieutenant nodded and turned to head out. He spotted a fire extinguisher mounted near the door and took it.

Leaving Mariner with only one Alsharqi soldier and a dozen hostages.

Khadija Dahar gripped her husband's forearm, her nutmeg eyes blinking wide.

"Finnigan?" she whispered.

Alexandro leveled an emotionless gaze at his wife. He refused to blink.

"Could she mean Michael? My . . . my God. Then . . . ?"

Alexandro looked away.

THE ALSHARQI SOLDER with the fire extinguisher tumbled to the floor as Finnigan stepped out from behind a medieval suit of armor and clocked him upside the head with the Halligan bar. Blood began pouring from the man's scalp wound.

Finnigan rounded a corner and found yet another cadaver. This was a young woman in a black skirt and white blouse, one of the various political aides who'd been brought along, he assumed. He made the sign of the cross then noticed that her purse was open by her shin. Open, and a lipstick stood upright near her leg.

What the hell?

Finnigan shifted position and only then saw the lipstick writing on the corridor wall. He recognized Fiero's handwriting.

Small discs on wheels w/ bombs

Finnigan understood. In fact, he'd seen something like that ten minutes earlier, a Frisbee-shaped thing that had spun past an open door in front of him.

He turned, heading back the way he'd come, looking for the little robot. More smoke rolled into the room. He yanked hard on the collar of his T-shirt, drew it out from beneath the ballistic vest, and covered his mouth and nose with it.

RON PERRY CHECKED in on Frequency 1. "We're in the ground-floor kitchen. Nada."

Mariner's voice came back over the line. "Who do you have with you?"

"Two of the ragheads."

"Only two?"

"Confirm."

He waited. Mariner said, "Annie?"

"That's a big negative. Nobody here."

He waited again. When she spoke next, he could almost hear her teeth grinding. "I think DeMarcus may be taken. I think we're down to just three of the soldiers; I have one with me, but I sent another to back you up. He should have arrived by now."

"Jesus fuckin' A. Did you know the second floor's on fire?"

"Yes. But concentrate on the forces still loose in the building. It's the bounty hunters. The American and the Spaniard. Finnigan and . . ." Her voice faltered. "Get back up here. Watch your six."

"Affirm."

MARINER DEACTIVATED THE WALKIE-TALKIE. She glared glaciers at José Ramón de Cordoba. The tall diplomat gulped, his pronounced Adam's apple bobbing. He still stood in a trio with the handsome couple in their fifties. She nodded to the Alsharqi guard to keep watch over the others, then moved closer to them.

"You might have lied to me, Minister."

De Cordoba said, "I believe my home is on fire."

She ignored him, shifting her gaze to the other two. "Señor Fiero. I assume this is your wife."

"You are a monster," Alexandro spat.

"Yes. That's true. Señora . . . Dahar, is it?"

Khadija stood up straighter.

"And your daughter is—wait, I almost had it . . ."

"My daughter works in Cyprus. She has nothing to do with—"

Mariner turned to Alexandro and smiled; the burn scars made

her smile jerk slightly, one side of her face a fraction slower than the other side. "Does she not know?"

Alexandro glowered at her.

"Katalin. That's it. Katalin and . . . Michael Finnigan? Yes? I understand he's a simple cop." She sneered at the word. "Hard to believe your daughter couldn't do better than that. Times must be hard."

Khadija fought to maintain eye contact with Mariner. "We have no idea what you're talking about. You are insane."

Mariner turned to de Cordoba. "Is there a PA system in the building?"

"A . . . ?"

"A public address system. I notice speakers on the walls. Is there a building-wide communication system?"

"Yes. Of course. In the event of—"

Mariner turned to the Alsharqi soldier. "I'm taking these three with me. You watch the rest. If someone requires killing, kill them all. Understand? Nobody dies, or everyone dies."

He nodded. "I understand."

She waved her gun at de Cordoba, Alexandro and Khadija. "Come with me. Show me how it works."

RON PERRY POCKETED HIS WALKIE-TALKIE and checked his tablet computer. He only had one robot left. He peered at the screen as yet another ancient corridor zipped by.

"Where is it?" One of the soldiers peered over his shoulder.

"Dunno."

"You are bomb maker. Yes? How is it, you don't know—"

"They rove, man." Perry glared at the man. "They rove, freestyle. Until they see a human being. And yes, dumbass, I programmed 'em to know what a human being looks like. Then they ping me. Until then, this li'l guy's a rolling stone, dude. Gathering no moss. He's . . ."

His voice trailed off. He squinted at the screen.

The soldier said, "What?"

"Dunno, man. The image. It's . . . wrong . . ."

FINNIGAN HELD THE ROBOT in both hands. He scrunched over, holding the thing about a foot off the ground. The camera was facing forward and hadn't seen him whisk it up from behind. Walking bent over had reopened the slice in his back, and it bled freely, but he didn't have time to deal with it yet.

He hoped whoever was on the other end of that camera hadn't noticed that the damn thing was about twelve inches off the ground, not three.

He heard voices coming from a doorway in front of him. Speaking English.

"Dunno, man. The image. It's . . . wrong . . ."

Finnigan got to the door and tossed the robot inside.

INSIDE THE KITCHEN, Ron Perry glanced up to see a shadow in the doorway, then one of his robots flew through the door from about ten inches off the ground. The thing landed right-side up, noted human beings in front of it and pinged Perry's tablet.

Perry said, "Shee-it."

Finnigan appeared in the doorway long enough to hit the robot with five rounds from the stolen machine gun, then ducked back quick before the little roving disc exploded.

Which it did.

C79

Fiero's cell phone vibrated. She'd been leading Hugo Llorente and Annie Pryor up to the fourth floor of the castle. Surprised, she drew the phone. "Michael?"

"I just killed one of the Americans. Perry, I think. He had some high-tech gizmos with him. Figured I should try the phones. He was the source of the jamming signal."

She couldn't repress a smile and caught the surprise on Llorente's face. The Katalin Fiero Dahar he'd trained had rarely, if ever, shown much emotion.

Llorente drew a small phone of his own and hit the number *1* five times. "The, ah, cavalry, as you'd say, is on the way."

Fiero said, "Good. Michael, I have Pryor and Llorente. We're on the top floor."

"I'm in the kitchen, ground floor. The other hostages?"

The phone was on speaker and Llorente said, "Mariner's men were herding people toward the chancellery. It's on what you'd call the second floor, Mr. Finnigan."

"Bastards set the second floor on fire."

Fiero said, "Well, actually, I set the second floor on fire."

"That seem like a good idea at the time?"

"It seemed like *an* idea at the time. You saw my note about the robot bombs?"

"Yeah. I used one to take out Perry."

"The other American? Washington?"

"I got him, too. Mariner's just down to her Alsharqi dickheads."

"That's a start. We—"

They were interrupted by a burst of static that seemed to come from all around them.

Pryor, breathing shallow and sweating, said, "The PA system?"

Over the phone, Finnigan said, "Here too."

An American voice, female, tinny and static-laden, erupted from the old speakers. "*Ms. Fiero. I need to see you and Mr. Finnigan walk out onto the parade grounds, immediately. Or I will kill your parents.*"

Pryor's voice cracked. "Dinah."

Llorente nodded to Fiero. "They are here. But I don't know how Mariner identified you and Michael."

"*I repeat: Both of you, out on the field. Where I can see you. Oh, and of course, I need Annie, please. Have her come, alone, to the chancellery. It's the very large room with the huge chandelier, second floor, west side.*"

They heard Finnigan groan. "Ah, crap."

"Michael, my parents . . ."

"I know. Dammit. Hey, Pryor, you hear me?"

Pryor leaned against a wall, leaving an almost perfect palm print of blood. "Yes."

"If you had a gun in your hand, could you shoot this bitch?"

"I do have a gun in my hand, Finnigan. But if I go in there, I'm dead."

"Not all that concerned about your ass getting popped, just this minute. I'm half inclined to do it myself. Llorente?"

"Yes?"

"Give us five minutes to get out on the big lawn. Then take Pryor to this chance-whatever room. Take two guns. Kill Mariner. I don't know how many guys she's got left, but if she's dead, they lose their reason for fighting."

"Dinah Mariner is a gifted tactician, Mr. Finnigan. The chances of her standing still while her archenemy and I walk up to her are nonexistent."

"You got a better idea?"

"Once the mobile phone blocker was down, I was able to alert the army. We should have teams arriving by helicopter."

Fiero said, "How quickly?"

His face gave away his answer.

Fiero spoke into the phone. "Not quickly enough."

From the PA system, Dinah Mariner spoke again. *"I'm certain you can hear me. Annie: Here, now. Fiero, you and Finnigan, out in the center of the parade grounds. Alexandro and Khadija might survive all this. Certainly, they've done nothing to me. And once I have Annie, I, my men, and the Khamsin Sayef we created will all go away. We will end our threats to Europe. You have nothing to lose by doing as I say. Now, before—"*

The PA system crackled again. And the next voice was that of Finnigan.

"Hi. Hello. This thing working?"

DINAH MARINER STOOD IN A SERVICE room across the grand corridor from the Chancellery de Trastámara, where her last remaining soldier held the other hostages. She'd forced Alexandro Fiero and Khadija Dahar to come with her. They stood ten feet away, her gun pointed at them.

The smell of smoke was growing stronger.

Mariner frowned as an American voice rode over hers.

"*This is Michael Finnigan. I'm in the kitchen. Got the PA system working here, too. How you doing?*"

Khadija recognized the voice and squeezed her husband's arm.

Mariner toggled the microphone in her hand. "Mr. Finnigan. You and your partner have done well. Honestly. I'm impressed. Now, there's an easy way for you to end this whole thing. No more Khamsin Sayef. No more bombs. It will be your biggest win yet."

"*Dunno,*" the American said over the PA system. "*Killing Ron Perry felt like a win. I blew him up with one of his own bombs.*"

Mariner coughed. The smoke was visible now.

"*And Washington? He's not quite dead, but I did manage to blind him. Ripped his eyes right outta his skull. That's gotta sting.*"

Mariner realized she was gripping the microphone, with its curly, pig's-tail cord, so tightly that her fist shook. Perry dead? Washington maimed?

They'd been with her from the start. They'd saved her, kept her alive after losing Bess.

"*You're just gonna let me walk out there? Really? Just let me stand in the yard and flip you the bird? Don't think so, sweetie-pie.*"

"I will kill your partner's parents."

"*Yeah, but you're gonna do that anyway, 'cause you're a fucking psycho,*" Finnigan replied. "*Alexandro? Khadija? Sorry, guys. Really. But this bitch is as crazy as a bag of cats. So here's how we do this: The Fieros walk out toward the helicopters. And once they're free and clear of this, then you get Annie. Deal?*"

"Finnigan, I have hostages. I have a dozen hostages. You are in no position to—"

That's when they heard the shots coming from the room across the corridor; from the Chancellery de Trastámara.

As soon as Finnigan began talking on the PA system, Fiero spun and hit the stairs, taking them four at a time, hopping down, arms akimbo for balance. She hit the third floor, then the second, seeing no more Alsharqi soldiers.

Her boots hit the parquetry of the second floor, and she threw an elbow over her nose and mouth. The smoke was much worse now. She spotted open flames down one corridor, a good distance from where she'd started the original fire.

Squinting, eyes tearing up, she moved quickly, kept low, headed straight for the chancellery.

She sprinted right in, spotted up on the only armed man in a room full of civilians, and shot him in the chest. He fell backward, gun flying.

Fiero put her boot sole flat on his chest and put the next round through his head.

Someone shrieked. The nine civilians cringed away from her, all but the tall, bony man with the expensive but ill-fitting suit. Fiero recognized Spain's foreign minister.

She did not see her parents. Or Mariner. Of course, she berated herself silently. The PA system wouldn't be in the chancellery. Mariner had separated her parents from the others.

She picked up the Alsharqi's Czech-made machine gun and marched past the hostages, who parted like the Red Sea.

She fired a round from the BREN gun into the nearest window, which shattered. Outside, a covered walkway ran the entire width of the castle, with the omega-shaped double stairs in the middle.

"Out," she said. She held the gun sideways and used it to scrape glass shards out of the window frame. "Go."

The civilians began pouring out through the glassless window. De Cordoba held his ground.

"You too, Minister."

"This is my ancestral home. I will stay, thank you."

She pointed the BREN gun at him. "No. Go."

Realizing her resolve, de Cordoba gave her a short bow then awkwardly crawled through the window and out of the building.

Fiero coughed, an elbow over her mouth and throat. A lot more smoke wafted in, drawn by the shattered window.

She had no idea where Mariner was. Nor her parents.

She moved to a corner where she could watch the whole room. She drew the phone from her jeans, hit the speed dial.

Finnigan picked up immediately.

"Good distraction," Fiero said. "All the hostages are out. Except my parents. She has them. I don't know where."

"You gotta figure the PA system is to be used by servants, right? We're looking for a side room. No pomp."

"I realize that now. I'm in the chancellery."

"I'm hitting the second floor. It's still a hostage sitch. We do this by the numbers. Ready?"

She dropped the BREN gun, drew her own P226. "Ready."

C80

Several of the Spanish soldiers had handcuffs; they might have been military police, Mariner thought, picked as the best soldiers to guard the castle and the likely targets of the so-called terrorists. She used two sets of cuffs to secure Alexandro Fiero and Khadija Dahar, hands behind their backs and their left and right elbows linked to each other so they could only move in lockstep.

The couple coughed as she herded them ahead of her down the grand corridor of the old castle. Their eyes teared up as the smoke built. They spotted open flames down one side hallway.

But no smoke alarms screeched. They wondered how that was possible. Maybe the old building simply didn't have them.

Mariner had tied her hijab over her mouth and nose.

She held the SIG-Sauer against Khadija's spine, rightly guessing that the threat to his wife would be more effective than to actually threaten Alexandro himself.

They were moving toward the western entrance, the grand double doors that lead to the omega stairs and the checkerboard parade grounds. Last she checked, there was a small fleet of vehicles among the helicopters at the far end of the parade grounds. She was no pilot, but she could hot-wire a truck.

She spotted Finnigan and Fiero a second before they spotted her. They came at her from in front, between her and the exit.

Mariner yanked on Khadija's collar. The Fieros stumbled into each other as she hauled them to the side of the grand corridor, under the portrait of an eighteenth-century aristocrat.

Finnigan and Fiero raised their weapons but stopped approaching. Finnigan hacked a phlegmy cough.

"Close enough. Both of you, lose your guns."

Khadija let out a quick cough/sob. Her eyes glinted with tears, not just from the smoke.

"Mamá," Fiero said. She spoke quietly, emotion bled out of her tone. "Papá."

"Put your guns down!" Mariner barked.

"Okay, okay, okay." Finnigan moved slowly to his left, putting a little distance between himself and his partner. "Is there a scenario here in which this thing ends well for you? Me, I'm not seeing it."

"Stop moving," Mariner said, eyes now watering from the smoke. She yanked harshly on Khadija's collar.

Fiero stood her ground, face blank.

Finnigan took another step to his left. "Okay. All right. Be cool. Seriously, I'm asking here. Barakat's in custody. The whole scam with the Alsharqi government and the bombings is all over the news. The CIA wants your scalp. Your two soldiers are dead or bleeding out."

Mariner glanced at Fiero, who seemed to have slipped into a meditative state. She stood with her boots together, back ramrod straight, hands folded in front of her but still holding the SIG. She kept her eyes downcast, as if avoiding her parents' eyes. She wore twin holsters laced tight to her long thighs. Both were empty. She held the gun in front of her pelvis, left hand holding her right wrists. Almost like praying.

Mariner said, "Drop your weapons."

Fiero quickly and obediently bent at the knee, going to her haunches and setting the SIG lightly on the intricate, wood-tile floor. She stood again, hands folded and now empty in front of her ballistic vest and her trouser belt.

While she did all that, Finnigan took another step and a half to his left, opening the gap between them.

Mariner was at a point that she had to bob and weave between the heads of her hostages to see both Finnigan and Fiero.

She said, "You drop your gun, Finnigan, or I'm going to shoot Fiero's mother in the elbow. Do it right, and I guarantee the doctors will have to amputate to save it. Unless you want your partner hugged by her mom's stumps for the rest of her life, I suggest you put that fucking weapon down. Now."

Finnigan said, "Can I get a second opinion? Hugo?"

Behind Mariner, Hugo Llorente cleared his throat.

She spun on him. The fierce fireplug of a man held a white handkerchief over his mouth and nose, his eyes like shards of obsidian. He held a small, snub-nose revolver by his thigh.

Mariner had no choice but to back up into the doorway of the nearest salon, dragging Alexandro and Khadija with her. They stumbled off balance over each other's feet and nearly dragged all three of them to the ground.

Finnigan moved farther to his left—now almost exactly opposite the doorway to the salon. Fiero shifted slightly to her left as well. Hugo Llorente kept his distance, off to the right.

"You're still holding that goddamn weapon!" she barked at Finnigan, her voice rising an octave. "Do you doubt my seriousness? Do you doubt my resolve?"

"This old thing?" Finnigan tucked the Glock 17 into his belt. "This isn't a threat to you."

He drew the Halligan bar from the loops in his backpack. "Now, this fucker will do some damage."

"You think this is a joke?" Mariner took a moment to glance to her right. Llorente held his position. She blinked to her left. Fiero stood, hands clasped, eyes down, like a butler awaiting orders.

Before her, Finnigan smiled, held the Halligan bar in his left hand, tapped it menacingly into the palm of his right.

"Drop it, goddamn you!" She screwed her gun into the back of Khadija's skull. "I mean it! Now. Do it! Drop the—"

Behind her, in the salon, Annie Pryor said, simply, "Dinah?"

IT HAD BEEN FINNIGAN'S IDEA to use himself, Fiero, and Llorente as chess pieces, to push Mariner into that particular salon. He'd planted Pryor there and was sure that her voice would be just the distraction they needed.

But later, when asked, Finnigan would admit that what happened next came too damn fast for him to see.

The same was true for Llorente, though ego wouldn't let him admit it.

Annie Pryor spoke from inside the salon.

Dinah Mariner turned toward the sound of the woman she blamed for the death of her little girl. She spun to her right.

Her SIG pivoted away from Khadija Dahar.

Earlier, Fiero had set down a SIG she'd stolen from a dead soldier. Now she reached under her ballistic vest, fingers grasping her P226, which pressed against her belly, barrel facing upward. She drew the weapon in a two-hand grip, raised the sights. Right-hand draw, right-eye dominant, she barely moved her head as she squeezed the trigger and watched the bullet sail past the ear of her father and embed itself in the cheek of Dinah Mariner.

The bullet hit her on the left side, as she was spinning to her right, swinging her own gun around toward Pryor. The momentum of the bullet and the move made her keep spinning, almost a pirouette. Her free hand left Khadija's collar. She spun a full three hundred and sixty degrees, throwing out an arc of blood like a lawn sprinkler. Her gun sailed free of her hand. She completed the spin as her center of gravity tilted and she landed, hard, on her back, arms outstretched, legs twitching once, her boot heels rapping out a little tattoo on the hardwood floor.

Alexandro flinched as the bullet passed by his head (but this was many, many nanoseconds later. When Finnigan brought up the image in his mind later, it would seem like a minute had passed). He stumbled into his wife, to whom he'd been pinioned. Together, they fell against the doorframe then went to their knees out in the hall.

Finnigan was on them before they landed, grabbing them both by their collars, yanking them clear of the doorway.

He dragged them, their shins taking the punishment, past Llorente, who raised his gun and stepped between them and the doorway.

Just in case Fiero had missed.

Inside the salon, Pryor leaned against a wall that had been papered in a lovely lilac design somewhere around the start of the eighteenth century. As her legs gave out, she left a bloody smear down the wallpaper.

Fiero stepped forward, P226 aimed, and checked her target.

The bullet hadn't made more than a quarter-sized hole in Mariner's left temple.

The exit wound at the back of her skull was the size of a tea saucer.

Finnigan knelt behind Llorente, dropped the couple, drew his Glock again, and began checking both ends of the hallway.

Had they gotten all of the hostiles? Likely. But likely isn't for sure. Llorente had his back and Finnigan took no chances.

Alexandro and Khadija, arms locked together, struggled to turn over. They were sandwiched between their guardian angels, Finnigan and Llorente. They managed to sit up.

They turned back to their daughter.

Who stepped out of the salon and turned to them.

It was the icy coldness of her eyes that did it.

Khadija managed to keep her emotions in check.

Alexandro began sobbing.

C81

ALCÁZAR REAL D'ARAGON

Finnigan helped Hugo Llorente mop up the scene as army helicopters arrived and Special Forces solders fast-roped down onto
the roof and parade grounds of the Alcázar Real d'Aragon. They
found a dozen civilians huddled on the checkerboard lawn and
great clouds of smoke roiling from windows of the ancient castle.

A firefighting team began addressing the second-floor blaze.

With the help of Finnigan and Llorente, the bodies of Dinah
Mariner, three Alsharqi soldiers, more than a dozen Spanish soldiers,
and several government personnel were hauled out of the burning
building and laid out shoulder to shoulder on the parade grounds.

Several bodies had been too badly destroyed by bombs to
remove.

DeMarcus Washington remained alive and was air evac'ed to
a hospital in Madrid. There was no chance of saving his vision
however since there was nothing left of his eyes to salvage.

The military drove the civilian survivors, including Foreign
Minister de Cordoba, into the local village, where rooms were found.

As the bodies were being carried out, Finnigan received a text from Fiero asking him to come join her.

Her parents wanted to speak to him.

AT THE URGING OF THE FOREIGN MINISTER, a Spanish Army mobile command unit had been abandoned to let the Fiero family have their privacy. Finnigan found them there. Both wore windbreakers with Spanish Army lettering stenciled on the back and shoulders. They held mugs of coffee and sat around a low table that was designed for reconnaissance maps. Khadija had also managed to change into a different hijab, but the bandage on her forehead was still visible

Too much of Dinah Mariner's brain matter had hit their own clothes to salvage.

Katalin had undone her braid, her hair hanging straight. She'd doffed her holsters. She'd doffed her boots and was barefoot in the stirrup pants she always wore on missions.

Finnigan took them all in and said, "Hey."

The family stared at him glumly.

"I've told them everything." Fiero spoke softly. "How we met. What we do. Why."

Finnigan found the coffeepot and poured himself a cup, too. He stood, butt against a bolted-down computer table, and tried to rub the fatigue out of his eyes. It just made his eyes more irritated. "She tell you she stabbed me when we met?"

Fiero turned to her parents and held her thumb and index finger an inch apart: *Only a little.*

Her parents didn't smile.

Khadija's voice caught when she spoke. "I wanted my daughter to make a difference in the world, Michael. I wanted her to be a force for good."

"She does. She is." He sipped the coffee, scalded his tongue.

"Not like this."

"Yeah, like this."

Alexandro shot him a smoldering look. Nobody back talked Khadija in his presence. "What you both are doing is illegal," he said. "It is, essentially, criminal."

Finnigan said, "Yeah," and sipped coffee.

Fiero had been studying him. Now she turned to her parents again.

Khadija said, "If you no longer wished to be a soldier, Katalin, you could go into government work. Or . . . law. Or—"

"I was a soldier," she said. "Right after the Madrid train bombing in 2004."

"We know, darling. And we were so proud of—"

She said, "I was a soldier. And then I was a spy. And then I was an assassin."

Khadija blanched.

Alexandro sat up straight. "Many soldiers, after they serve, question the ethics of the work. I did, after my time in the army. I—"

Katalin looked directly into her father's eyes and leaned in a little. "I worked for a covert operation within the CNI, Father. Our office didn't have a code name or a number or anything like that. We were assassins. The government identified people who they needed dead. And we killed them. For king and country."

Alexandro looked like he might throw up. Khadija dabbed at her cheeks with a wadded-up handkerchief.

Finnigan pretended to look into his coffee cup.

"I couldn't do that any longer. But I wasn't . . ." Fiero paused, rubbing her neck. "I was lacking . . . something. Father, I think you might call it my soul. Thank God, I found it again. Or, at least I think I have. Working with Michael. What we do is illegal. Sometimes. It's dangerous. Often. And yes, we've killed people.

We killed some today. But it's not cold-blooded. We don't target and eliminate people. We track them down. We get them to the International Criminal Court."

Alexandro snorted. "Surely the court doesn't sanction such actions!"

Finnigan said, "You're right. The court doesn't acknowledge our existence. And because of that, our actions don't negate the prosecutions. It's the Golden Platter doctrine. We hand 'em over. Since we don't work for the court, the court is held blameless."

Alexandro said, "Legal double-talk."

Finnigan said, "Oh, hell yeah." He set the coffee down, turned and reached for the trailer door.

Alexandro stepped closer to him. "I blame you for this, Michael!"

Finnigan turned back. Alexandro glared at him, his hands curled into fists.

Finnigan smiled and shook his head.

"Your daughter and I uncovered the reality behind the Khamsin Sayef. We brought an Alsharqi warlord to The Hague. We saved the life of everyone in your Barcelona office. We saved the life of the hostages here in the castle. Some of that's on me. But a lot of it? A whole lot of it is on your daughter."

Alexander stood his ground, his face a rectus of pain.

Finnigan watched as behind the nobleman, Khadija stood and slowly crossed to Katalin, resting a hand on her daughter's shoulder. Finnigan watched, his mind drifting to all he'd lost when he'd alienated his own family.

Finnigan said, "You wanna know what? Some of this is on you too, you know."

Alexandro stiffened. "How dare—"

"You raised a hero. Get used to it."